The Paris Spy

Also by Sarah Sigal

The Socialite Spy
The Paris Spy

THE
PARIS
SPY

SARAH SIGAL

LUME BOOKS
A JOFFE BOOKS COMPANY

Lume Books, London
A Joffe Books Company
www.lumebooks.co.uk

First published in Great Britain in 2025 by Lume Books

Cover design by Cherie Chapman

ISBN: 978-1-83901-617-2

To Mom

Part 1

'In France that is the one rule, never make trouble.'

Nancy Mitford

October 1938

I

'Unity claims to be his new best friend,' said Diana Cooper, raising a carefully plucked eyebrow. 'Nancy's taken to calling her "that crazed Valkyrie", which I'm sure will make its way into one of her books.'

'"His new best friend"?' Pamela echoed. 'They sound like teenage girls.'

'Nancy says he does impressions for her. His favourite is Mussolini. Quite funny, apparently.'

'Funny isn't the first word that springs to mind when I think of Adolf Hitler.' Pamela opened a silver box on the side table and offered Diana a cigarette.

'And he's a great fan of Snow White. But thinks Mickey Mouse is a degenerate.'

'The Duke of Windsor, on the other hand, loves Mickey Mouse.'

'That's because he's a child.' Diana lit her cigarette. 'Speaking of which, I take it you're still getting regular reports from the Wicked Queen? Or the Wicked Duchess, as it were.'

'You know what she's like. Never satisfied,' Pamela replied.

And Diana *did* know, having gone on a cruise with Wallis and Edward the summer before the Abdication, suffering their ever-changing whims. Two years ago, Pamela had been approached by MI5 to gather intelligence on Wallis Simpson and then-King Edward VIII, using her role as a social columnist for *The Times* as a cover for her mission. But all Diana — or anyone else — knew was that Wallis had taken a shine to Pamela after she'd written an article on her wardrobe.

After the scandal of the Abdication, Wallis and Edward married and settled in France. The following autumn, they went to Germany as official guests of the Third Reich and were given a tour of the Nazis' great social and economic achievements. Not quite the low profile the Palace and Downing Street had hoped for — especially when political relations between the great European powers had been on shaky ground for the past couple of years, Anglo-German diplomacy was on a knife-edge and the Windsors were hardly known for their tact or discretion.

Wallis had continued to write to Pamela; her letters catalogued a litany of daily grievances and ongoing injustices.

The Royal Family has been downright cruel. Can you believe they refused me the HRH?

I've searched all over Paris and the South of France but it's been nearly impossible to find somewhere to live. Once one has been a king, one cannot live just anywhere.

All summer I was absolutely run ragged getting La Croë set up and now I have to make our Paris house liveable. Antiques dealers skin you alive once they know who you are.

She even found reasons to complain about their trip to Germany.

The British Embassy in Berlin was ordered to snub us. It's shocking how we've been treated.

Wallis was even more loathed and isolated now than when she was Mrs Ernest Simpson of Bryanston Court. The friends the Windsors had managed to retain were few and far between, especially since the Royal Family were threatening to excommunicate anyone who continued to receive them, which, Pamela assumed, was why Wallis persisted in writing to her, even though her replies were lacklustre at best.

Pamela and her husband, Francis, were hosting a dinner party that evening, and everyone was now retiring to the drawing room for digestifs. Francis was one of the more politically engaged peers in the House of Lords; he felt it was his duty to attend Parliament as often as possible, read up on the various bills that were proposed and foster political allegiances. The Mores' dinner parties were popular, as people knew that the conversations were more candid than they might otherwise be within the corridors of Westminster or Whitehall. Pamela had a talent for compiling the guest lists of politicians and fashionable socialites and arranging the seating — who would get along, who wasn't to be seated next to whom. Francis — though not naturally inclined to be social — had a calm and measured air that put others at ease, encouraging them to speak openly.

Since her mission, Pamela had struggled to return to playing the happy hostess, making polite chatter and muting her own political opinions, while Francis and his friends debated domestic affairs and foreign policy. If only these MPs, civil servants and diplomats knew that she, Pamela More, had provided MI5 with enough information to engineer the previous monarch's abdication. The reason why the more reliable, stable King George VI was now on the throne was because of her hard work, achieved without any training or knowledge of espionage whatsoever — even if no one would ever know, thanks to the Official Secrets Act.

Tonight the mood was mixed, as everyone was mulling over the Munich Agreement that Chamberlain had signed the previous week. Pamela looked over at Diana's husband Duff Cooper, who was deep in conversation with Francis. Usually a bluff, good-natured man with a round, beaming face, he was leaning dejectedly against the fireplace, looking grim-faced. He had resigned from his role in the Cabinet in protest of Chamberlain's appeasement of Germany only a few days before. The papers had quoted him as saying that he could live with 'war with honour or peace with dishonour', but not 'war with dishonour'.

Pamela rose and crossed the room to refresh her drink, lingering momentarily to see if she could overhear their conversation.

'It's been utterly manipulated by the press, much to Chamberlain's advantage,' Duff was saying. 'We wouldn't go to war with Germany over Czechoslovakia any more than we went to war with them the last time over Serbia. It's about preventing their brutish domination of Europe.'

'The poor Czechs,' Francis replied wearily.

Much of Britain had breathed a sigh of relief after Chamberlain and Daladier strong-armed Czechoslovakia into giving the Sudetenland to Germany and Silesia to Poland. The sacrifice of a few slices of land in a far-off country seemed a small price to pay to shelve their gas masks and evacuation plans. And to some, it seemed as if the Germans had been treated unfairly after their defeat in 1918.

The crisis created strange bedfellows in Parliament. Francis and other like-minded men felt that the appeasement of the Third Reich was a foolish waste of time that could have been better spent preparing for war. He was a member of a secret committee of MPs and Lords that had been meeting to discuss the issue and strategise in terms of tactical voting and allegiances. Normally on opposite sides of the House floor, they had all spent time in Germany before '33 and had watched helplessly as the country changed before their eyes. Like Francis, some had studied at German universities and others had enjoyed the Berlin nightclubs that sprang up in the '20s but had since been shut down by the Nazi regime. Most had fought the Kaiser's army in the previous war.

Chamberlain had accused the group of warmongering and labelled them a rebel faction. The pressure on the committee had grown over the past two years; their phones had been tapped, they had been followed and they had even been threatened with deselection. The Prime Minister's allies dubbed them the 'Glamour Boys' — insinuating that the group engaged in debauched practices with other men. The press had gleefully picked up on the moniker, associating anti-appeasement with homosexual acts.

As Pamela refilled her glass, the wife of an MP complimented her dress and asked where she'd had it made. But Pamela's mind was elsewhere — something that seemed to be happening more and more lately. She looked around the room, with its dark blue drapes and Turkish rugs, at the portrait of Francis's mother above the fireplace, done by Sargent, and at the shelves filled with books. And the people in their dinner jackets and elegant gowns. It was a well-appointed London house, as were its well-appointed Belgravia neighbours, probably also filled with smartly dressed people enjoying their postprandial drinks. She imagined what life in Prague — just across the border from the Sudetenland — was like this evening. If the Czechoslovakians, hundreds of miles away, were simply carrying on with their lives in a similar fashion. Or if they were already planning to flee. Pamela had been wondering if these political dinners were of any use at all or if, like her, everyone was just going through the motions.

'What a delightful evening, Lady Pamela.'

Snapping out of her reverie, Pamela looked up to see Donald Jenkins had come over to the bar cart to refresh his whisky. He was a Labour MP and a member of Francis's committee, but — unusually for the Westminster set — someone Pamela knew independently of her husband. She and Donald had first met through Percy Blakley, her editor at *The Times*, who hosted parties in his Bloomsbury flat after the Soho clubs had closed for the night or been raided by the police.

'It's always nice to attend one of your lovely dinners, especially considering the ghastly state of things these days. My compliments to your cook on yet another one of her excellent soufflés. And to whoever designed this gorgeous frock.'

Donald admired Pamela's bottle-green dress, draped in what designers were calling the Delphic style. Like many of Percy's friends (but unlike most other politicians), he had a sharp sense of humour and an easy charm.

'Why, thank you. That would be House of Worth.' Pamela inspected Donald's pale blond head and asked, 'Have you changed your hair?'

'Yes, I've done away with the parting. I'm hoping to distract people from the fact that I've put on a stone or two lately.' Donald patted his midsection and sighed.

'Don't be silly, darling. You look ravishing as ever.'.

Donald gestured to the man standing next to him. 'May I introduce Captain Arthur Macaulay?'

Macaulay shook Pamela's hand enthusiastically. He was about fifty-odd, sandy-haired with a trim, military-style moustache. He supported himself with a walking stick.

'The captain is on the Board of Trade.'

'My wife was a great follower of "Agent of Influence". She's always said you'd be an asset to the Board,' said the captain.

'That's very kind of her,' replied Pamela.

'The Board are looking for ambassadors to various countries, to represent different sectors of British industry. Champion the country's economic interests abroad.'

Was the man just making conversation or extending an overture? Pamela briefly tried to imagine herself selling a tractor or a Vauxhall sedan to a group of foreign businessmen.

'We think *you* are someone who could be quite useful in terms of liaising with French fashion, textiles, that sort of thing. We're looking for someone who knows both the British and the French fashion industries and has connections — industrial and social.' Macaulay gestured to the other people at the party. 'And has a certain amount of political savvy.'

'I rather think my husband is the one with the political savvy in this household, Captain,' Pamela protested.

Donald leaned in and whispered, 'Darling, we both know you have more savvy than most of the people in this room put together.'

Before she could reply, the captain took out his pocket watch and said, 'I'm afraid I'm needed across town. Thank you for the invitation, Lady Pamela.'

Which was strange.

Pamela hadn't invited him.

II

The next afternoon, Pamela was lingering in the hat section at Liberty's with Percy. When she worked for him at *The Times*, they would snoop around department stores for research and make notes about what women were buying. Even though Pamela was now at *Vogue*, they still did it — usually after lunch and a few afternoon cocktails — enjoying nothing more than judging other people's taste. Usually, it cheered her up, but she had been out of sorts since last night's dinner and felt she was dragging herself around the department store.

'The Board of Trade? What on earth was Donald thinking? It sounds tedious and dreary. Heaven knows who you'll be made to have dinner with,' sniffed Percy. 'Though I suppose it couldn't possibly be any worse than those political dinner parties you're obliged to organise.'

'It could be interesting. Something new, anyway.'

'Panda, you do have an air of melancholia about you these days,' said Percy as he peered at her.

'What on earth does that mean?'

He watched a young blonde at the counter. 'Someone needs to tell that woman she doesn't suit a turban. Looks like a Home Counties Scheherazade.'

'No need to be so judgemental, Percy.'

'I thought being judgemental was the basis for our friendship.' He paused, looking momentarily thoughtful. 'You seem sad, Panda. And I've no idea why. I would *love* to be at *Vogue*. And they sent you to Paris!'

'It was just the one time,' she sighed as she examined a navy wool beret.

'Just the one time, she says!'

Percy held a jaunty red felt tilt hat at arm's length, squinting at it. (He was too vain to wear his glasses in public.)

'You can't go around being so down in the mouth. It doesn't suit you.'

'I'm not *down in the mouth* ...'

But as soon as she said it, Pamela knew he was right. Percy always saw right through her. She had been feeling flat and generally disengaged from the world lately.

'I've said it before, and I'll say it again — you should have an affair.' Percy put on the hat at an angle, covering one eye and performing a kind of Marlene Dietrich-style seduction.

She smiled, rolled her eyes and tried on a small, slouchy fedora. She had been hoping for the Greta Garbo look but couldn't work out where exactly it was meant to sit on her head. She took it off and picked up one that looked somewhat like an ice-cream cone.

'What do you think of this style of pointy hats? I think it makes women look like gnomes.'

'Don't change the subject.' Percy rolled his eyes. 'You need to have affairs while you can. None of us is getting any younger, ducks.'

'Which is a bit rich, considering you're even older than I am ...' She replied with a raised eyebrow.

Pamela didn't know how old Percy really was; he dyed his hair and had claimed to be thirty-five for as long as she'd known him.

'Older than you? How very dare you?' he gasped in mock horror.

What would he say if she confessed that she'd already had an affair two years before — with her MI5 handler, Charlie? Pamela had convinced herself it was only because they had worked together so closely. She had been under quite a lot of stress. And had been three sheets to the wind that evening. A momentary lapse of judgement. Nothing more.

'And besides, I do *not* have an "air of melancholia", whatever that means,' Pamela retorted sharply.

'It's what Dr Freud would say, darling,' Percy replied in a patient manner that made her instantly regret her tone. 'And one would think he knows from whence he speaks.'

Later that afternoon, Pamela found herself at Hatchards, looking through their selection of Sigmund Freud's books. Having always seemed so quintessentially Viennese, it was strange to think that he had taken refuge in Hampstead last summer. Pamela flipped through a copy of *Mourning and Melancholia*:

> *In melancholia, a person grieves for a loss he is unable to fully comprehend or identify, and thus this process takes place in the unconscious mind.*

Pamela used to enjoy dinners and parties and nights out in clubs. She prided herself on knowing nearly everyone in London society — who they were with and what they were wearing. But it was maddening to think that MI5 hadn't been in touch with her since spring of the previous year, after Edward had stepped down off the throne and he and Wallis had been packed off to France. And no one could ever know what she'd done. She had signed the Official Secrets Act and was expected to return to her ordinary life. Which was feeling increasingly alien by the day.

November 1938

I

As Pamela walked into the *Vogue* building on New Bond Street on a chilly, drizzly morning, the girl behind the reception desk called out her name.

'There's a gentleman waiting to see you. He's in Mrs Penrose's office,' she said, hardly bothering to look up from her copy of *Film Weekly*. 'A Captain Macaulay. From the Board of Trade.'

Pamela was taken aback. Donald had rung her up after the dinner party and asked if she wanted to speak to Macaulay about the work. She told him that she hadn't made up her mind yet and would let him know. She didn't hear anything again but decided that she would decline his offer. Pamela's social calendar was as full as it had ever been: luncheons, cocktails and dinners with her friends and Francis's colleagues; trips up north to see Francis's brother and to the West Country to visit her parents; the occasional swooping-in of her sister Charlotte and brother-in-law Peter from Italy (and them dumping their children on Pamela and Francis). As *Vogue* was more exacting when it came to fashion and society than *The Times*, Pamela found herself working harder on her writing style, as well as the research and interviews she did for the pieces she wrote. And while she had been feeling restless lately, working for the Board of Trade wasn't likely to be the change she needed. Percy was probably right — it did seem a dull prospect, not to mention one she hardly had time for.

Macaulay leaned on his walking stick to stand when Pamela entered. He wore a dark suit with a regimental tie — likely either the Royal Hussars or the Light Dragoons. Strangely, Penrose was nowhere to be seen.

'Lady Pamela!' he exclaimed cheerfully, as if greeting a long-lost friend.

'Captain Macaulay. I'm flattered by your persistence, but I'm afraid I'm going to have to turn down the Board of Trade's offer.'

He seemed unsurprised by her reply.

'Are you sure?'

Pamela frowned. 'Yes, quite sure. I am awfully busy as it is.'

'No interest in taking on a role that might help your country?' His tone had turned strangely playful, almost teasing. 'Would you mind closing the door behind you?' he asked as he sat back down in his chair.

'You see, I'm with the Secret Intelligence Service. And do please have a seat.'

Slightly stunned, Pamela sank into the chair opposite him.

'I'm aware of your previous work dealing with Mrs Ernest Simpson, as was.'

All of a sudden, the discreet persistence made sense. Turning up unexpectedly — at her party and now in Elizabeth Penrose's office — to ensure privacy. Even being friends with Donald Jenkins, who seemed to have a habit of involving himself in intrigue.

'We have an assignment for you, should you choose to accept it.' He had a glint in his eye. 'Everyone thought that packing the Duke and Duchess of Windsor off to France would be like plunking them down in cow corner, but it's become a bit of a sticky wicket.'

'I'm afraid my knowledge of cricket lingo doesn't extend to "cow corner".'

'It's a fielding position between deep mid-wicket and wide long-on. Few batsmen hit the ball there. A corner of the field so remote, it would be safe for cows to graze. Everyone was hoping that once the dust settled, they would reconcile themselves with a quiet life. However, they continue to remain in the public eye and have been making certain *unfortunate* remarks about His Majesty's government, the palace and so forth.'

Pamela thought of the extensive complaints in Wallis's letters. The most recent one, received only two weeks before, was no different:

> *David's brother George continues to refuse to receive us at court. We can't set foot in England now. It would be too humiliating.*

'Combined with the embarrassment of their trip to Germany and the *delicate* political climate of late, now is an awkward time for the former King of England and his consort to be speaking their minds. Your name was mentioned, as someone who might be able to monitor the situation.' Macaulay smoothed his tie.

'May I ask who it was that mentioned me?'

The captain only smiled and raised his eyebrows theatrically. Pamela had forgotten how opaque these people could be.

'We're hoping you'll be our twelfth man. A substitute fielder who steps in for another player, to make up the twelfth man on a team. Or woman, as it were.'

'You mean go to France and spy on them.'

'Exactly. Find out about the Windsors' moods, how they seem, what they're saying and who they're speaking to. Build on the relationship you already have with the Duchess. Be someone in whom she can confide and look to for guidance. The Duke listens to his wife above all others. And if she listens to you …'

'I don't imagine Wallis listens to anyone.'

The unsubtle subtext of every letter was that she didn't think there could possibly be anyone in the world who knew better than she did.

'In your correspondence, she does seem to be rather appreciative of your sympathy.'

'So, you *have* been reading my letters … I haven't heard a peep out of you people since I was asked to keep writing to—' Pamela stopped herself; she had nearly said *that woman*. 'The Duchess.'

'Ah, no. That's Security Services. They're the ones who had you carry the bat for them the last time. I suspect that once the Windsors were out of the country, MI5 felt they were no longer their problem. You see, the Security Service — MI5 — is responsible for domestic intelligence and counterintelligence. While we — the Secret Intelligence Service, MI6 — are responsible for what goes on abroad.'

This was getting rather complicated. Pamela fished her cigarette case and lighter out of her handbag and lit a cigarette.

'Then I was referred to you by MI5 … ?'

'We don't collaborate with one another. There are a number of, shall we say, strong personalities in both camps.'

As she tapped her cigarette against an ashtray on the table, Pamela wondered if the captain was one of those personalities. Judging by the tie, walking stick and scar on his left cheek, it was clear he'd served in the last war. He had a solid, middle-aged appearance: not especially tall, stocky build, starting to grey slightly. He looked ordinary, like someone able to blend into a crowd or hide in plain sight. Which was the point of men like him. And Charlie. The MI5 agent with a librarian job, tartan rugs and unassuming nature. (Which was why he had appealed to the NKVD too, presumably.) At the party, Macaulay had said his wife was a great follower of 'Agent of Influence'. As she eyed his bare ring finger, Pamela doubted that he even had a wife.

'The Duke has a bodyguard from Scotland Yard who maintains general surveillance of the Windsor properties and reports back on their activities. We also have someone who has been monitoring the Duke since the Abdication. An old friend, privy to his personal life: Major Edward Metcalfe. He's become his equerry, though somewhat informally, as the Duke no longer enjoys an official position. The Duchess dislikes and mistrusts him. Seems to resent having him around, which appears to be compromising how much the Duke shares with him. Which is why it would be jolly good to have you fill that gap in our intelligence.'

Fruity Metcalfe — the husband of Baba and cuckold of Oswald Mosley — was on the MI6 payroll? He had been the Duke's aide-de-camp and one of his closest friends when the Duke was the Prince of Wales — he had even been the best man at his wedding. Francis had known Fruity in the war and had said that when Edward became King, Fruity had thought he would get a job working for the palace but was passed over. Pamela had only met him briefly and didn't know him particularly well, but it looked like Fruity bore enough of a grudge to have turned against his old friend. Which wouldn't be surprising, considering how many other people the Windsors had managed to alienate in such a short space of time.

'And how do you propose I go about doing all this?' asked Pamela as she leaned back in her chair.

'Your cover would be that you're based in Paris, representing the Board of Trade, promoting the interests of the garment industry and encouraging commerce between our two nations. And you could still file articles for *Vogue*. I've already spoken to your editor.'

He'd already spoken to her editor. MI6 seemed to take a more aggressive approach than MI5 had.

'Why would Mrs Penrose believe that I would have been plucked out of any number of people who could do the same job?'

'You're well connected. Not only are you a journalist for the most widely read women's magazine in the country, you're also the wife of a member of the House of Lords.'

Pamela looked at the table where the *Vogue* editors had laid out articles and photos for the next issue. To *Vogue*, fashion was culture, and culture was serious business. It showcased the work of people like Man Ray and Vita Sackville-West. To be chic was not just about which hairstyle was in fashion: it was also about knowing the latest play by Jean Cocteau. Pamela wrote a column called 'Out and About with Lady Pamela', which reported on what fashionable society was wearing, saying and doing. Although her connections were useful as *Vogue* sometimes had trouble convincing socialites to pose for them, Pamela also worried that her social position cast her in a negative light. The notorious Daisy Fellowes had been the *Harper's Bazaar* Paris correspondent for a couple of years until she'd grown bored and lost interest.

Pamela felt that the other staff writers saw her as just another fickle aristocrat dabbling in journalism. Which, in some ways, felt a bit unfair, as she had only married into a title; compared to Daisy Fellowes — the daughter of a duke and the Singer Sewing Machine heiress — Pamela's parents were merely minor gentry. But once a woman married into an old, established family like Francis's, her name and identity became synonymous with his. She sometimes wondered how Pamela Plumbley would have fared at *Vogue*. Would she have had a better chance of being taken seriously if she wasn't married to a peer? Or would she have struggled to break into that world without her impressive social connections? Would MI5 have approached her to trail around after Wallis two years ago? Would MI6 be speaking to her now? Highly unlikely.

'I suppose that makes sense,' Pamela began as she drew her shoulders back. 'Fashion is a valuable export, but of course our industry isn't nearly as strong or as influential as the Chambre Syndicale. The Paris fashions are the ones that are copied and showcased around the world. When people think of British designers, they think of tailoring, suits. Sports clothes, hunting jackets. Not haute couture. Some of the best British designers even work in Paris because that's where the best ateliers and seamstresses are. But of course, we don't want to make their designers feel threatened, as if we're ratcheting up the competition. Especially now, when France might very well be one of our few allies left in Europe. And fashion can be an effective way of strengthening diplomatic relations. I'd imagine Frogue is as influential to French women as Brogue is to the British.'

'Frogue?'

'French *Vogue*. They refer to us as "Brogue" — British *Vogue*. We're all published by Condé Nast, but we each have different editors and staff. Perhaps a bit like the relationship between MI5 and MI6 — not always cordial.' Pamela gestured to Macaulay and smiled wryly.

'But a mission to Paris might be useful for improving the relation-ship. Keep British readers up to date on French trends and persuade French readers that British fashion isn't all dowdy tweeds and sturdy walking shoes.'

Pamela felt rather pleased with herself. It was nice to have the expertise and the upper hand for once. To be the one explaining things to a man, rather than having things explained to her.

Macaulay considered her for a moment, rose from his chair and said, 'I won't take up any more of your morning, Lady Pamela. No need to make an immediate decision, of course. I'll give you some time to think it over.' He paused and, almost like an afterthought, added, 'There's a night train that goes direct from London to Paris now. Only takes eleven hours. Very convenient. And it's possible you won't have to be in France for too long. Might be able to bang it in.'

Pamela looked at the captain quizzically.

Using his stick, he mimicked a bowler with a bat. 'It's when one bowls on a shorter length, but with considerable force and speed.'

II

Entertaining the idea of dashing off to Paris to spy on deposed royals for MI6 was one thing; actually doing it was quite another. After all, it wasn't as if she would be carrying on with her everyday life in London, as she had last time. She needed to discuss Macaulay's proposition with someone before making a decision, and there was only one possible candidate. On the one hand, there was no guarantee Donald Jenkins knew anything more than the captain's Board of Trade cover story, and that Pamela was simply being offered the position of a trade envoy. He was always very enthusiastic about women taking proper jobs — typically Labour. He might be completely in the dark about MI6.

On the other, there were a number of dynamics at play. Too many to ignore. She had met Donald through Percy. Percy had also introduced her to a Russo-German journalist-turned-spy called Baron Jona von Ustinov. And Ustinov knew Baron Wolfgang Gans zu Putlitz, a German diplomat-turned-spy. Ostensibly the Labour MP for Kennington and Lambeth North, Donald had surprised Pamela by turning up at the German Embassy party she'd attended while following Wallis around London two years earlier. Putlitz had also been there. And both Donald and Putlitz had lived in Berlin during the Weimar years.

Working with Percy at *The Times* had been an education. No one in her circle spoke about such things openly, but she'd had inklings about friends' bachelor brothers and absent husbands, people's maiden aunts who had 'companions'. But Percy had introduced her to an entire *omi-palone demi-monde*. Pamela learned where the best clubs were, the passwords to get into them, the coded language used and even the gossip about who was involved with whom. She'd come to understand something of the risks and dangers — the illegality — of this kind of existence. And it made sense that people already practised at leading one kind of double life would be well equipped to lead another. After all, the first time she'd met Donald, he was wearing a Charles Creed gown and had introduced himself to her as 'Betty'.

When she got home that afternoon, Pamela rang up Donald, saying that Francis was at his club and she was at a loose end. Did he fancy meeting at the Savoy for a cocktail?

She looked at Donald over the rim of her *Death in the Afternoon*, a drink lately popularised by Ernest Hemingway. It was said he'd created it, but who knew if that were true or merely an invention of the Savoy, renowned for capitalising on the glamour of its guests. Having intended to ask for two gin martinis, Donald and Pamela had been persuaded to order the novelty cocktail by the American Bar's outrageously handsome waiter.

'This is dreadful!' cried Donald as he made a face. '*Death in the Evening*, more like.'

'I suppose this is what comes from allowing our judgement to be clouded by a pretty face.'

'Wouldn't be the first time …' Donald sighed.

Pamela adjusted the strap on her dress.

'Is that a Maggy Rouff … ?' he asked.

'Does everyone in the Labour Party have such an excellent eye for couture?'

'Just because I'm Labour doesn't mean I can't have good taste. And besides, it's not that I want to keep people from owning nice frocks; it's that I think everyone should be able to afford them.'

'That's what Debenhams is for.'

Pamela looked around. Fortunately, the American Bar was quiet that evening.

'Speaking of which,' she continued as she examined her nail varnish, feigning nonchalance, 'your friend Captain Macaulay … He dropped in to see me today.'

'Did he?' replied Donald, equally nonchalantly.

'And we had a chat about his Board of Trade offer.'

'What did you say?'

'It sounds like it could be quite a consuming role. Involving some rather difficult people.'

'Yes, but you're good at that.'

'I'm not sure I have the time for it. I am rather busy.'

Pamela sipped her cocktail, trying to appear nonplussed.

'I think it's probably a good deal more interesting than it sounds.'

'I don't know that I want to upend my entire life for what sounds rather like a public relations campaign.'

'All in the good cause of propping up the economy,' Donald chirped. 'Which needs all the help it can get.'

Maybe he wasn't in on MI6's machinations. Maybe he *did* think the captain was from the Board of Trade.

'It's just selling frocks and stockings, or what-have-you. Charming French government officials at cocktail parties. Having dinner with buyers for French department stores. And I'm not sure *anyone* could convince Le Bon Marché to be receptive to "le style Rosbif".'

'Darling, you're not just any Rosbif, you're "Agent of Influence".'

'I *was* "Agent of Influence".'

'Yes, and now you're "Out and About with Lady Pamela". At *Vogue*. Everyone knows you as a paragon of good taste. And we all know there aren't nearly enough people in the civil service who can pride themselves on that.'

Pamela ran a finger across the round, lacquered table between them. It was clear she wasn't getting anywhere, and she knew she was starting to sound contrary. She looked around the bar, which was beginning to empty out. Looking at her watch, she realised the other patrons probably had tickets for the play that was on in the theatre next door.

'Anyway, I don't know that I'm cut out for a civil service job. Especially if it means being away from London so often. Whatever would Francis do without me? Shall we have another drink?'

Donald frowned in concentration. He then peered into his *Death in the Afternoon* with scepticism, took a swig and made a face. He dabbed the corner of his mouth with a cocktail napkin, moved his chair closer to Pamela and lowered his voice.

'Alright, let's quit beating about the bush. I assume the captain explained to you why you're the girl for the job?'

She remembered something Ustinov had once said to her: 'There is no such thing as a true secret.'

'I believe we have a mutual friend. Baron Ustinov?'

Donald nodded.

'And he passed on my name?'

'Our very own Agatha Christie.' He leaned forward. 'The Baron says it's a bad business, with the Windsors.'

'I know they've been indiscreet, which is embarrassing. But *plus ça change*. And surely, they're irrelevant now.'

Donald leaned in a little further and gestured for Pamela to do the same.

'Putlitz was transferred to the German Embassy in The Hague. Ustinov moved to stay close to him and pass on his intelligence. The little bons mots coming out of the mouths of the Windsors are embarrassing for Britain, certainly. But in the current political context, we can't afford anything that might weaken our position in the world. And Putlitz has heard some worrying things about the people in their coterie. Therefore, he thinks it would be a good idea if we had someone in situ to cover our you-know-whats.'

Pamela realised that Donald himself wasn't just an MP with his ear to the ground; it seemed likely that he too was in the pay of MI5 or MI6. She glanced around the room. Everywhere she looked, there seemed to be a mirrored surface. On the walls, behind the bar, framing the entryway. It had a disconcerting effect, to see two or three versions of everything.

'Getting the Duchess's letters is bad enough. But having to be *friends* with them. Clean up their messes ...'

'You won't have to clean up anything. Just point out where the messes are and who made them.'

'What about my reputation? No one would be seen dead with the Windsors.'

She could only imagine what rumours getting back to London society might do to her social profile. Mixing with the former King and his wife, who were not only speaking openly, loudly and badly of the Royal Family, but had also been demonstrating their admiration for the Hitler government.

'Hence your cover with the Board of Trade. It can fall under the guise of your role. You can tell people you're *obliged* to see them. Think about what it could do for the greater good.'

'Very socialist of you.' Pamela sighed.

'Normally, I'd take that as a compliment. But these days, the Socialist Party seems to think that if the workers want Hitler and Mussolini, who are they to argue?'

'That's rather worrying, isn't it?'

'Oh, simply one of many rather worrying things playing out on our country's political stage.'

Donald said it lightly but Pamela could see the tension in his face.

'I've heard things have been rather difficult in Westminster,' she replied.

'I'm no stranger to mud-slinging and vicious insults. Always useful to know who one's enemies are. And we're not the only "Glamour Boys" knocking about, I can tell you. Those who live in glass handbags shouldn't throw stones ... But it's the same the world over. I remember, in Berlin, seeing Brownshirts in the bars, flirting with their *papenjungen*.'

'*Papenjungen*?'

'Their dilly boys. Trade.' Donald smiled. 'Why do you think they so adore the Hitler Youth? Little blonds in lederhosen.' He paused. 'Of course, that doesn't stop them from driving all the queers out of Germany or into internment camps. After beating them up in the streets, of course.'

Two years ago, Donald's friend Mary had told them a story at Percy's party about getting beaten up by Blackshirts in the Docklands when they cornered him with his boyfriend. They had sworn they would string up them and every other homosexual in the country when the British Union of Fascists got into power. Pamela couldn't imagine such a thing happening in Britain; the BUF was such a small minority. But then again, that's what the Nazi Party had been in Germany years ago. Donald wasn't someone who was prone to exaggeration or overreaction. Pamela knew she couldn't simply hide her head in the sand and hope for the best.

III

Pamela hadn't lived in Paris since her early twenties — a decade ago now. If she accepted, she would be living in a foreign country, away from her friends and family. And Francis. But finding things out, making connections, passing on intelligence — it made her feel alive in a way that little else did. And her last mission felt like she was doing something important for the first time in her life. Something that mattered in the grand scheme of things. Percy was right — she *had* been in the doldrums. Maybe this mission would give her the purpose that her life had seemed to be missing.

On the other hand, espionage was a dirty, deceitful business. It made you feel distant from everyone you knew and suspicious of everyone you didn't. You could never forget what you were meant to be doing, but at the same time, you could never tell anyone about it. And being in a foreign country, where Pamela knew hardly anyone at all, would be even more isolating.

To make matters more complicated, Pamela hadn't discussed it with Francis yet. Though perhaps he already knew — having been recruited by MI5 himself some years before, he had been told about her first mission. They had, essentially, asked his permission to recruit his wife. In the end, Pamela had exerted an enormous amount of energy sneaking around and keeping her secret from him, when in reality, he'd known about that secret all along. How much easier might the whole thing have been had he just told her he'd known from the very beginning? And if the roles had been reversed, if she'd been recruited before he had, no one would have asked her if she minded her husband taking on a covert operation for MI5. Then again, she probably wouldn't have been tapped on the shoulder in the first place if she hadn't been the wife of Sir Francis More. But maybe she was being irrational. After all, she didn't know many women who made any significant decisions without their husband's knowledge or consent.

It seemed likely that MI6 would have said something to him, or to their opposite number in MI5, who would then have had a word with Francis. Probably even before Macaulay approached her. (Which was an irksome thought.) Regardless, Pamela had to admit that speaking to Francis before making a decision was the right thing to do. Even if she was dreading it. Although Francis said he didn't want to put pressure on her, he kept dropping hints about adoption. He loved children and had come to terms with the fact that Pamela was unable to have any. Knowing she couldn't get pregnant from a young age had pushed the idea of motherhood completely to one side. And now she felt ambivalent about being a mother. In theory, having children added to one's life, gave one purpose, etcetera. But going to Paris would put such a decision on hold indefinitely.

A couple of days after she'd spoken to Donald, Pamela decided to raise the subject. She brought it up after a quiet midweek dinner at home, sitting by the fire in the library with their foxhound, Patricia, curled up in the corner. Francis looked up from his paper in shock.

'You've been approached by MI6? Why did no one tell me?' he asked incredulously as he gripped his pipe tightly in one hand and his copy of *The Times* in the other.

Pamela felt a sudden rush of exhilaration. No one thought it necessary to ask her husband for permission at all.

'Francis, *I* am telling you.'

'No, what I mean is … You know what I mean.'

What you meant was, why didn't someone more consequential than your wife tell you?

Pamela watched Francis fold up his paper and set his pipe down on the side table. She had rarely seen him look quite so troubled. Even Patricia had looked up from her pillow and was watching them, sensing unease.

'Surely, you're not considering it.'

Pamela bristled. 'Why wouldn't I?'

Francis ran a hand through his thinning hair and leaned back in the wing chair. The fire crackled and popped in the grate. She could tell from the tension in his jaw that he was grinding his teeth.

'Because you'd have to move to Paris. It wouldn't be like the last time, where you were able to operate your mission in London while carrying on with the rest of your life.'

'That's what spies do, isn't it? Go where they're needed?' Pamela replied testily as she rose to refill her sherry.

Patricia went over to her and nudged her head under Pamela's hand, seeking comfort. Pamela stroked her, realising that she had grown weary of Francis's moods, of him spending entire evenings in silence. Of his nightmares and how he resisted discussing anything to do with the war. She was starting to understand that there was so much about him that she might never know, because he wouldn't tell her. And so much about her that he would never know either because he didn't ask. And Pamela had begun to resent always having to be the cheerful one. Maintaining relationships with their friends, remembering all the dinners and parties on their social calendar, the birthdays and friends' children's birthdays. She could well imagine those tasks multiplying tenfold if they adopted a child.

Francis stood. 'Besides, what on earth would we tell people?' His voice sounded strained.

'You — we — would tell them my cover story. That I'm working as an envoy for the Board of Trade and writing pieces on French fashion houses for *Vogue*.'

To hell with sherry — Pamela decided what was needed now was whisky. She poured herself a large measure and then watched Francis pace around the room.

'Do you even know how long you'll be in Paris?'

'No.'

'So, you'd be moving abroad for an indefinite period of time.'

'Possibly.'

'Where are you going to live?'

'I don't know. A flat somewhere,' Pamela snapped. She knew she was starting to sound petulant. She took a cigarette out of a box on the mantle and lit it. She stared into the fire for a moment and then murmured, 'Francis, I assumed you of all people would understand.'

'Understand what? That MI6 wants you to play caretaker to the Duke and Duchess of Windsor?'

'That I have a duty to our country.'

Pamela knew Francis would never argue with the idea of duty. But she also knew that it was what she believed. They looked at each other. Patricia planted herself in between the two of them, looking back and forth anxiously, feeling the tension in the air.

Finally, he said quietly, 'I will respect whatever choice you make, Pamela.'

She felt a pang of guilt as Francis sat back down in his chair, looking bewildered. She tried to imagine how she would feel if he had presented her with a similar scenario. Would she feel just as wounded?

As Pamela lay in bed later that night, her busy mind wheeled and thoughts crowded into her head. With her last mission, MI5 had thrown her in at the deep end, totally unprepared; she'd had no choice but to rely on her instincts alone. Worse, her handlers had kept it from her that she had been sent in to replace Gertrude Leigh — the previous agent, who had worked with Pamela at *The Times* until she fell in front of a train one dark, rainy night. Likely pushed by the NKVD, after they'd suspected she was onto their London agents. Possibly by Charlie, Pamela's handler, who was most probably a double agent for the Soviets. MI5 had knowingly put Pamela in danger. What if MI6 was no different from its sister agency?

Going to Paris to insert herself into the lives of the insufferable Windsors was an unappealing prospect. But people like Putlitz and Ustinov wouldn't raise the alarm for no reason. After all, as a mole within the German Embassy, Putlitz was putting himself in grave danger. And he had decided to place his trust in her. In her letters to Pamela, Wallis did sound dissatisfied with her life and was surprisingly candid about this dissatisfaction. And if the Windsors were as socially isolated as people said, Wallis — and perhaps the Duke too — might let their guard down in the presence of a friendly face: one fresh from London and seemingly unbothered by the scandal of the Abdication.

And with that, she knew she'd made her decision.

December 1938

I

54 Broadway sat in an especially unlovely but quiet corner of St James'. A stone's throw from the park, the tall building with the vertiginous mansard roof seemed as if it was lurking, casting a shadow over the tube station opposite. It gave Pamela a sense of foreboding, which was only heightened by the fact that the plate next to the entryway read, *Minimax Fire Extinguisher Company*. She double-checked the address Captain Macaulay had given her. It was a dreary Monday morning and there was hardly anyone around. Pamela looked to see if anyone was watching and then rang the buzzer. A porter let her in and took her name. The interior of the building was dark and dingy, with frosted glass windows that cut off the outside world. Even the air felt stagnant.

The elderly lift creaked its way up to the top floor. She knocked on the door at the end of the corridor and was welcomed in by a dark-haired woman who looked to be around Pamela's age. She introduced herself as Miss Joan Ashburn and efficiently went through various papers with Pamela. She had a calm and capable air about her, amplified by her sensible navy suit, brogues, tidy hair and spectacles. She inspected a piece of paper.

'Your code name will be …' She paused. '"Show Boat".'

'"Show Boat" … ?'

'Captain Macaulay thought you looked a bit like Irene Dunne.' Pamela looked at her blankly. 'Who starred in the film *Show Boat*.'

'I suppose it's better than being called "Frankenstein" because he thought I looked a bit like Boris Karloff.'

Ashburn raised an eyebrow and gave the faintest hint of a smile. 'He can be a bit eccentric, as you've probably discovered by now. All his code names are derived from some kind of joke or pun relating to the agent's identity.'

'Doesn't that rather defeat the purpose of having a code name?'

Ashburn shrugged, and after looking through Pamela's file for another minute, said, 'You've come to us from the Security Service.'

'Yes.' Pamela paused. 'I'm hoping I'll be more prepared than I was the last time. I assume there will be some sort of training?'

Ashburn leaned her elbows on her desk and entwined her fingers. 'They don't really go in for that sort of thing. They expect you to learn — whatever it is you need to learn — in the field.'

'How do they expect me to do that? Just toddle off to Paris and sort of skulk around for weeks on end?'

'There's no school for what you do, as such. There are a number of agents who have experience, but of course, they're not allowed to speak about what they've done.'

The secretary reached across her desk for an envelope. Pamela caught a glimpse of her watch. Small and practical, yet elegant, it had a black alligator strap and a square, gold face.

'What a lovely watch. Looks like an Omega.'

'Well spotted,' said Ashburn. 'A present from my parents when I graduated from Oxford.'

'You went to Oxford?'

'Lady Margaret Hall. I read Modern Languages.'

Pamela had never met a woman who'd gone to Oxford before. It felt as if she'd encountered someone who'd been to the moon. She had a feeling that keeping the books and filing paperwork wasn't what Ashburn had intended to do with her hard-won education, even if it was for MI6.

'I would have given a good deal to have been allowed to go to university.' Pamela smiled slightly at the thought of such an impossibility.

'I try not to bandy it about here. C isn't overly fond of "university men". Thinks they're a lot of "effete intellectuals".'

'C?'

'Our director. Captain Cumming.'

Pamela opened her cigarette case and offered one to Ashburn. The two women smoked in a pleasant kind of silence for a moment. Ashburn looked in the direction of the frosted window, then turned back to Pamela.

'Charles Buchanan was your case officer?'

Pamela nodded slowly and then took a deep drag on her cigarette. It had been a long time since she'd heard Charlie's name, and it had a curious effect on her.

'I worked for MI5 before they transferred me here,' Ashburn explained. 'How did you find him?'

Pamela felt strangely unmoored. Was it a test? Were MI6 assessing her to see if she was indiscreet enough to share her views on her previous case officer? Ashburn was watching Pamela carefully. Could it be that she knew somehow that Pamela had gone to bed with Charlie? Was she going to have to endure some kind of awkward questioning about — or worse, a lecture on — relationships with case handlers? Her toes curled in embarrassment at the very idea of it. But Ashburn's face was inscrutable.

Pamela chose her words carefully. 'Funny chap. Bookish, unassuming Cambridge librarian on the surface …'

'But difficult to tell who he really was?'

Was it possible that she knew? It was said in an offhand way, but could it be that, like Pamela and David Stern, Ashburn also suspected that Charlie Buchanan was a Soviet double agent? Was this an open secret in MI5?

Pamela took another drag on her cigarette, trying to buy time while she considered her reply. 'Yes … a very good description of him.'

There was a silence. It felt almost like a standoff, as if each woman were waiting for the other to open up first. It was quiet in the building and the only sound Pamela could hear was that of footsteps down the hallway. Maybe she was just being paranoid. Surely, all spies made it their business to make it difficult for anyone to know who they were? Ashburn might have just been making conversation.

'We'll be in touch shortly about the details of your assignment, Lady Pamela.'

'Do I need to make arrangements for Paris? Travel, lodging and all that?'

'Oh no,' Ashburn replied. 'We'll take care of everything.'

II

After weeks of waiting, MI6 had finally let Pamela know that she would be required in Paris on January 1st, giving her precious little time to pack and say her goodbyes. She wondered if everyone got so little notice before being expected to overthrow their regular, everyday lives for the service. The pressure of having to be ready so quickly only added to the tense atmosphere that had developed between her and Francis since their quarrel a month before. Pamela could tell that he had taken her decision personally and was holding it against her, even if he wouldn't admit it and was pretending everything was completely normal. They never rowed openly; they had terse disagreements which would usually result in periods of detached civility and avoidance. Sometimes Pamela wished they could just have it out with each other, get everything on the table and then sort it out, rather than letting their resentment atomise and linger in the air — like the remnants of a burnt dinner.

It was bitingly cold and snowing by the time Christmas Eve came around. She and Francis were spending Christmas with her family in their rambling country house in Gloucestershire. Normally, Pamela dreaded family holiday gatherings, with the squabbling between her and her mother, Alma, between her and her younger sister, Charlotte, and between Charlotte and their mother; with Charlotte's husband Peter braying about his various work achievements and airing his endless opinions on things; and her father Duncan receding into his own little world. But this Christmas, Pamela was somewhat relieved to have the distraction — however maddening — from the froideur that had descended on her marriage. And while Pamela had been content to have left her horsey, country childhood behind her — hunting prints, wellies in the mudroom, dead birds brought in by her father from a shoot — she was finding the rustic, slightly shabby atmosphere comforting.

As usual, Francis was listening to the BBC's annual broadcast of the King's College Choir. Pamela had never been enthusiastic about

Christmas carols, especially those sung in a cherubic falsetto, but this year she found them more grating than usual. Alma was next door in the kitchen, overseeing the cook's preparation of the Christmas goose. Duncan was talking to Peter — or rather, listening patiently while Peter droned on. And Pamela was listening — somewhat less patiently — while Charlotte droned on at her. Their nine-year-old daughter, Alexandra, was sitting quietly in the corner drawing, while her ten-year-old brother Christopher was building a model airplane with Francis.

Charlotte and Peter's children were often left with Pamela and Francis during school holidays, and Francis had grown quite fond of them. Watching him with Christopher made Pamela feel even more guilty; she knew nothing would make him happier than to become a father. But she didn't know if it would make her happy and was wary of the potential consequences — of how it would change their life. How it would change *her* life. She had seen her friends' lives irrevocably altered by having children, the considerations and arrangements that had to be made — organising nannies and governesses and schools and holidays and clothes and shoes and trips to the doctor — while their husbands carried on as before.

'We're going to see Peter's family in Hampshire for Boxing Day.' Charlotte paused and added (somewhat gratuitously, Pamela thought), 'And then we're going to a party at the Italian Embassy for New Year.'

Pamela's sister and brother-in-law lived in Rome and sent their children to school in England. The only reason why they were in the freezing West Country instead of in a milder, sunnier climate was because Peter had business in London.

'If they know what's good for them, they'll accept the deal. It's a damned good one too.'

Pamela watched her father wince at Peter's vulgarity. Alma and Duncan had been less enthusiastic about the marriage than Charlotte, who had been dazzled by Peter's familial wealth. Her mother had initially found the Hugheses to be new money and gauche (they owned a factory), but over time, she became impressed by the jet-set lifestyle her younger daughter and son-in-law led. Frequent trips abroad. Ocean liners to America. Rubbing elbows with diplomats and film stars. Whereas Pamela's father found their approach to life completely baffling and would often mutter under his breath, 'Why do they insist on living amongst foreigners?'

'Government orders these days are trifling. Diversifying by seeking other branches of business is going to place us in a strong financial position. And Haraway and Sons get to be a part of an international operation. It's a coup, if you ask me.' Duncan let out a small sigh while Peter continued, 'I've met an American chap who's an expert in those sorts of things. I've brought him in to maximise the factory's efficiency. The Italians haven't the foggiest about productivity, so they've been falling all over themselves to grease the wheels for us. The old Commando Supremo hasn't yet built up the industry he needs, but there's scope. And the will. Not like Britain. And the army thinks it's a good idea to buy horses rather than guns. They're giving one to every tank commander. What a tank corps is meant to do with a horse is anyone's guess. Military manufacturing in this country is completely inadequate.'

Francis turned away from Christopher and his model aeroplane. 'By whose standards?'

'You know as well as I do that this government is content to twiddle its thumbs while other countries join the twentieth century. The least they can do is take their foot off the neck of the free market and let the rest of us get on with it.'

Peter and Francis had never got along. Francis thought Peter was superficial and greedy. Peter thought Francis was a boring old snob. Pamela was just glad that even though Peter had originally made a pass at her during her debutante days, it was Charlotte who ended up falling for his charms. (Whatever they were.)

'Government policy has done rather the opposite, actually. They've let armaments companies go completely unchecked, selling to whomever they like. I'm sure you're aware that there was an official enquiry into the arms trade,' replied Francis in a steely voice. 'It concluded that we need state control.'

'What, like the French? Nationalise everything?' Peter laughed.

'We cannot officially back one country and then allow British arms dealers to sell to their enemy.'

Peter waved his hand dismissively. 'You spend too much time in Westminster, old boy. You should see what the real world is like.'

'You mean from the perspective of war profiteers?'

Everyone had grown quiet. Alma had come in from the kitchen and was standing in the doorway looking uneasy. Peter and Francis hardly agreed on anything, but for the first time, Pamela thought it might actually come to blows.

'The enquiry,' continued Francis, 'proved that the government needs to have a firmer grip on the private arms trade. Because it's corrupt, inside and out.'

Peter pursed his lips together in a tight little frown. 'Are you calling my business *corrupt*?'

'I don't know, Peter. You're the one who has Mussolini greasing the wheels for you.'

They stared each other down.

Then Peter smiled in a cat-like way. 'It's just business, old boy.

I daresay, if you opened your eyes, you'd find things have changed since the days of fixed bayonets and cavalry charges.' He finished his drink and then turned away.

'And if you'd fought in the last war, you would have seen what unchecked, industrial-scale, *twentieth-century* weaponry looks like. In the flesh.'

Peter turned back around. Francis took a step closer. Peter curled his hand into a fist.

Charlotte gasped. 'Peter!'

'I'm moving to Paris!' Pamela blurted out.

Everyone turned to look at her.

'What?' cried her mother.

'You're what?' echoed Charlotte.

'What do you mean, "moving"?' said her father.

Pamela stood. 'I'm going to Paris. Next week, in fact. I've been asked to represent the Board of Trade.'

'In the Bleak Midwinter' played softly from the wireless.

'The Board of Trade?' exclaimed Peter, astonished. 'What on earth would they want with *you*?'

'To give a helping hand to the *free market*,' Pamela replied. She had been practising her cover story with various friends in London, but as she stood there in the middle of the room, she realised that her family — who had never understood her lifestyle or interests to begin with — might be a more sceptical audience. 'They've asked me to go to Paris to speak about the British fashion industry. With my work at *Vogue* and my connections, I'm going to be very important to the delegation.'

'Going to Paris? To sell British clothing?' Charlotte was incredulous.

'Working for the Board of Trade? Sounds pretty rum to me,' grunted her father.

'You're going *alone*? Without your *husband*?' demanded her mother.

'It's not fair,' pouted Charlotte, sounding every inch the disaffected younger sister. 'Pamela always gets to go to Paris.'

'Charlotte, you've been to Paris,' said Peter.

'Yes, but I never got to *live* there. She went to Paris and you' — she pointed at her parents — 'sent me to Switzerland for finishing school because she' — pointing at Pamela — 'couldn't behave herself.'

'I've always thought the French were a bad influence,' grumbled Alma.

'Do you know how utterly tedious Switzerland is?' Charlotte protested.

'I thought you said the skiing was good,' replied her father, looking confused.

'I hate skiing! It's Pamela who likes to ski.'

Pamela rolled her eyes. It was like being teenagers all over again.

'I wouldn't allow *my* wife to go gallivanting across Europe,' Peter sniffed.

'See! This is exactly what I mean!' cried Charlotte.

'Oh, Charlotte, calm yourself,' huffed Alma.

'I don't understand,' muttered Duncan.

'Whatever will people say?' asked Alma, sounding decidedly shrill.

'They'll say she's doing her duty to King and country,' replied Francis as he looked coolly at Pamela's family.

Charlotte glowered at Peter and folded her arms. 'At least *some* husbands support the things their wives want to do …'

'Pamela, you're not serious about this. You can't go to Paris and live *alone*,' cried Alma, wringing her hands. 'Francis, you can't possibly allow it.'

'She's her own woman. She can make her own decisions,' he said firmly.

Pamela was surprised and touched. It was comforting to know that she didn't have to face her family alone, and whatever his reservations, Francis was willing to back her publicly. Which was far more than most husbands did. In fact, Pamela could hardly picture a single man she knew doing such a thing for his wife.

Later that night, when they were in bed, Pamela rolled over to Francis and murmured, 'It means a good deal to me, what you said.'

He closed the book he was reading. 'It's your right to make your own decision. If you feel that what they're asking you to do is important, I'm not going to stand in your way.'

'Francis, maybe we should—'

'I'm rather done in, I'm afraid,' he replied curtly. 'Shall I put out the light or were you planning on reading for a while longer?'

Pamela could tell by the look on his face that, as suddenly as he'd opened up, Francis had closed back down again. Like a door slamming shut. He looked at her with such blankness that it was as if he wasn't there at all, his pale blue eyes conveying nothing.

She shook her head. 'No, you can put out the light.'

Francis switched off the bedside lamp and turned away from her. Even though he was right there next to her in bed, Pamela suddenly felt completely alone.

If she'd had any doubts about whether she should go to Paris, they had just dissipated.

III

When Pamela wrote to Lettice to say she was coming to Paris for a time, her old friend was delighted. The two had been best friends at school, and when Lettice had moved to Paris at eighteen to be 'finished',

Pamela had begged her parents to be allowed to go too. Her father was disdainful ('Can't stand the bloody French'), but her mother was ultimately won over by Lettice's old-world, old-money French mother, who assured her that being finished in France was, *bien sûr, de rigueur* for well-bred young ladies. And so, Pamela and Lettice had lived in the heart of Paris during *les Années folles*, when the city was alive with jazz clubs and fashionable cafés, and populated by artists, writers and wealthy Americans eager to spend their money. It had been an education for both of them — a far cry from their cloistered lives in an English boarding school — and had drawn them even closer together.

Lettice's London society marriage to Ashley Wakefield had imploded two years before, when he caught her having an affair with Giles Langdon. Everyone knew Giles was a philanderer and about as loyal as a goldfish, but Lettice was so unhappy with Ashley that she convinced herself she was in love with him. Pamela thought it had been a subconscious act of sabotage, a means of escaping the loveless marriage that had been arranged by her father years before. A good many in their circle had affairs and most people did the decent thing and turned a blind eye. But Ashley insisted on naming Giles in the divorce and dragging his wife's name through the mud. And while infidelity was one thing, a high-profile, scandalous divorce was quite another; people behaved as if it were a contagious disease. Lettice's reputation was ruined, most of her friends grew decidedly distant, and, on top of that, Giles dropped her in the blink of an eye.

Lettice moved to France, deciding to swear off English men, English people and England itself forever. She moped around her family's Normandy chateau until a friend convinced her to come to Paris. Lettice had taken well to her friend's Bohemian crowd of artists and writers precisely because they were the exact opposite of the people she had known in London. She met the artist Mikhail Bloch at a party; captivated by her beauty, he asked her to model for him. And before they knew it, the two of them had fallen in love.

Pamela had only arrived at the Hôtel de Crillon the day before and was exhausted from her miserably cold, snowy journey from London, but Lettice had insisted she come to the New Year's party at Chez Bricktop. The stock market crash of '29 had left its mark on Paris, and while most of the wealthy Americans had left and the departure of their money had dampened the art scene, the city still boasted some of the best restaurants, bars and clubs in Europe. Chez Bricktop was in an area of Montmartre known as 'Harlem-sur-Seine', in honour of the American jazz clubs that had sprung up since the war. It was owned by Ada 'Bricktop' Smith, an American (so named for her red hair), who had come to Paris in the '20s as a singer and had become a prominent fixture of Paris nightlife and something of a celebrity. Cole Porter was a great friend of hers and they had opened Chez Bricktop together. Porter had known that putting her name on the building would attract a following; people were drawn to Bricktop not just for her singing, but for her beauty, charm and stage presence. She made everyone who came to her club feel as if they were her personal guest. She had mentored the great Josephine Baker (and had been more to her than a mentor, if rumours were to be believed). And having sung with the likes of Duke Ellington, Jellyroll Morton and Louis Armstrong, you never knew who might drop in to Chez Bricktop when they were in town.

A jazz band played the latest music out of New York and New Orleans, while couples spun each other around on the dance floor. Streamers hung from the ceiling, champagne bottles stood on every table and a banner reading 'Happy 1939!' adorned the wall behind the stage.

'Mikhail, this is my very dear, very old friend,' said Lettice as she introduced a serious-looking man with a mop of dark, curly hair to Pamela.

'Ah … the famous Pamela,' he said in a Russian accent as he kissed her hand.

Mikhail was in his late thirties, of medium height and had large hands and broad shoulders. And what Lettice had described (accurately, as it turned out) as 'smouldering eyes, like Valentino'.

'Pamela is the only one of my friends who stood by me when everyone else cut me dead,' said Lettice as she smiled and clasped Pamela's hand. Dressed in a dark green velvet gown that showed off her pale skin and black hair, she looked radiant.

Although Pamela had initially doubted that Lettice had found true love, as she claimed, and this new man was simply part of a post-divorce, rebellious phase, she had never seen her friend quite so happy. She was clearly smitten with the Russian sculptor, who was everything her ex-husband was not. Ashley had been cold, conceited and humourless, with a tendency to shout (mostly at Lettice). Mikhail struck Pamela as solemn but passionate and certainly devoted to her friend.

'Lettice tells me you're an artist, Monsieur Bloch. What sort are you?' Pamela asked.

'A sculptor. But only a poor and unsuccessful one.'

'It's a terrible exaggeration — typical Slavic dourness. He's very successful.'

'She is only saying this for my ego. Many months I haven't sold a piece,' Mikhail protested to Pamela.

'Darling, I do think you'd sell more work if you didn't insist on making such disturbed, monstrous things. Even Georges says so!' Lettice said to Pamela. 'He has such a fixation on the macabre.'

'It is the world that is disturbed. I reflect the world in my work.'

'Do you know, he collected animal bones from the butcher and kept them in his studio?'

'You would like I should keep them in my apartment instead?'

'You could have at least cleaned them first!'

'The blood gives texture,' he replied matter-of-factly.

Pamela tried to imagine what Lettice's stern cavalry officer father would say if he could see her now. They'd fallen out with each other over the divorce, and she suspected Lettice had told him nothing about her life in France.

'But the smell, chéri! People thought you'd murdered someone.'

'French journalists love nothing more than a good murder. Might be useful publicity for his next show.'

Pamela turned around. She was startled to find herself facing a strikingly handsome man. He was tall and had brown hair, hazel-green eyes, ruddy cheeks, a prominent cleft chin and what some might describe as a Roman nose. His thick, wavy hair looked as if it were trying to escape the pomade that had been forced on it. And whatever cologne he was wearing, it smelled divine.

'Meet our friend, Sid White,' said Lettice.

'How do you do, Mr White? Pamela More.'

She leaned in for the customary cheek kiss, but the man stuck out his hand and — in a pronounced American accent — said, 'Nice to meet you, Miss More. Call me Sid.'

Lettice laughed, exclaiming, '*Lady* More! She's an aristocrat, darling.'

Sid took another look at Pamela and smiled. 'Well, well, well …
I beg your pardon, *Lady More*.'

'She's one of my dearest friends in the world, and she's just moved
to Paris. And if you want to do it properly, it's the *Right Honourable*
Lady Pamela More,' said Lettice.

Pamela could feel herself flushing a deep scarlet. She could have
killed Lettice.

'At your service, Lady Right Honourable. Welcome to Paris.' Sid
gave a little bow with a flourish. Then he turned to the band and
said, 'Play that thing, jazz band! Play it for the lords and ladies' — he
winked at Pamela — 'for the dukes and counts, for the whores and
gigolos, for the American millionaires …'

'I'm sorry?'

'Langston Hughes. He's a poet in New York. Used to work as a
busboy at the Grand Duc around the corner.'

'And are you from New York, Mr … Sid? What's Sid short for,
anyway?'

'I'm from Chicago, which I only miss when the White Sox are
playing. Sid stands for Sidney. But no one calls me Sidney unless they're
sore at me. Do people ever call you Pam? Or is that too American?'

'As I recall, you have some friends in London who call you "Panda",'
said Lettice with a wink.

'Panda?'

Pamela once mentioned in a letter that Percy had a tendency to
refer to her as 'Panda' (usually while drunk). She had forgotten that
Lettice had an airtight memory and regretted having said anything.

'And what is it that you're doing here in Paris, Mr—?'

'Sid, please. I'm a journalist. I write for the *Herald Tribune*. Went
to Spain last year to cover the war. The way things are right now, it

seems like a good idea to stick around Europe for a while. Papers need idiots like me, willing to risk their necks for a story. And Paris is a good place to be based — the French don't censor journalists like they do in other countries.'

Sid ran a hand through his unruly hair. Pamela could see that his cuffs were slightly frayed and the elbows of the dinner jacket had become shiny with wear. The cut looked slightly outmoded, with a single button instead of double-breasted, as had become popular more recently. Either he didn't have the money to keep up with the fashion or didn't care about such things. After all, what use was a tuxedo if one was stuck in a Spanish trench?

'And they like Americans here.' Sid gestured to the band. 'Or at least they're used to putting up with us. And how about you, Lady Right Honourable? What are you doing in this fair city?'

'I'm working for the British Board of Trade. But as it happens, I'm also a journalist. I'll also be writing about French fashion for *Vogue*.'

Although Pamela had already given this story to numerous people, it suddenly sounded quite glamorous.

The four of them spent the next two hours chatting with people they knew and dancing to the band. Maurice Chevalier made a surprise appearance and sang to a delighted audience.

'How is it that you're such a good dancer?' she asked Sid.

'I have a little sister and when I lived in Chicago, my parents made me play chaperone when she went to dances with her friends. She said it was embarrassing enough having her older brother there. The least I could do was learn the dances.'

Pamela found this charming and somewhat refreshing. It made her think of all the embarrassed brothers of the debutantes who dutifully agreed to make up the numbers at various balls but usually spent the evening stepping on the toes of their dance partners.

'Isn't he a dish?' whispered Lettice, as she reapplied her lipstick in the mirror of the ladies' room.

Pamela took her compact out of her handbag and reapplied powder to her face. 'Who?'

Lettice gave her a look in the mirror. 'You and Sid were getting on like a house on fire.'

'Like a house on fire … You've been spending too much time with Americans,' Pamela sighed, in an effort to be nonchalant.

'Damnit!' a woman behind them exclaimed.

Pamela and Lettice turned around to discover Bricktop herself sitting on a pouffe in the corner of the powder room. The train of her dress had become caught in one of her high heels, and she was cursing under her breath. Pamela immediately recognised the gown from one of Elsa Schiaparelli's collections from the previous year. It was ivory with a halter neck and a train, and the lining was a rich salmon colour.

Pamela turned around and gestured to the train. 'May I, Miss Smith?'

'Be my guest!' she replied as she threw up her hands. 'These damn trains. Only brides should wear trains. And only if they have brides-maids to carry them.'

'It's exquisite. The surprise of the pink under the white … the line of it. Where it hits the waist. The ruching under the arms. And it suits you perfectly.'

'A friend gave it to me.'

'Your friend has excellent taste.'

'Well, she's married to the former King of England, so I'd hope so!'

Pamela froze.

'Oh!' exclaimed Lettice. 'The Duchess of Windsor?'

'The Windsors are regulars here. And I've known the Duke for years. I taught him the Charleston many moons ago.'

Pamela knew the Duke loved jazz, but she wouldn't have assumed that Wallis would be keen to hang around in small, crowded jazz clubs filled with ordinary Parisians. It made her wonder what else might surprise her about the Windsors, and she mentally filed it away.

'I remember dancing the Charleston when you were at Le Grand Duc,' Lettice said, starry-eyed.

'You Brits are ok,' Bricktop said with a half-smile. 'Once you like someone, you like someone, and you like them best if they don't try to be something they're not.' She looked at Pamela. 'Say, where'd you get your dress? It's not so bad either.'

Pamela ran a hand down the diagonal neckline of her blue silk crêpe de chine crinoline, edged with dark blue sequins.

'House of Lelong,' she replied as she carried on attending to the mangled train. 'And yours is Schiaparelli?'

'You've got a good eye ... You know, I didn't catch your name.'

Pamela reached out a hand. 'Pamela More. This is my friend Lettice Wakefield.' Pamela finally freed the heel from the train of the gown. 'There! It's going to need mending but I've done my best to limit the damage.'

The woman inspected the train of her dress, holding it up to the light. 'Thank you very much, Miss More. I probably would have destroyed the damn thing.'

'Please, call me Pamela.'

'Then you'll have to call me Bricktop.' She clapped her hands together. 'Ok. I'm fixing you ladies a drink. Everyone is my guest, but you are now my guests of honour.'

The crowd of raucous partygoers parted like the Red Sea for the club owner. Walking behind Bricktop was like being a lady-in-waiting to a queen. Table after table, people greeted her, toasted her, offered her a drink, asked her to sit with them. As they reached the table where Mikhail and Sid were sitting, Bricktop hailed one of her waiters and ordered a bottle of champagne.

Suddenly, the band played a drumroll, and the bandleader leaned into the microphone to mark the countdown. As the clock struck midnight, he wished everyone a Happy New Year. The band played 'Auld Lang Syne' as people cheered and kissed on the dance floor.

At the table, everyone toasted each other. Mikhail and Lettice kissed passionately. Bricktop got up to welcome in the New Year from the stage.

'Happy New Year,' Pamela said as she turned to Sid.

'Happy New Year.' Smiling, he leaned in slightly and said, 'May I … ?'

And before she could think twice about what she was doing, Pamela leaned in too, and they kissed. She felt a warm glow light up her entire body.

'Swell way to kick off the New Year,' he said with a smile. As if reading her mind, he asked, 'So, you here in Paris with anyone?'

Pamela was suddenly reminded that she was no longer, in fact, carefree and eighteen, but on an intelligence mission for her government. And she had allowed herself to get caught up in the boisterous New Year's spirit, avoiding the awkward fact that she had a husband in London. Maintaining a cover story didn't give her leave to kiss handsome strangers.

On the other hand, it was true that she wasn't in Paris with anyone. And an American journalist who likely had the inside scoop on international politics and current events might be a useful connection to nurture. Perhaps even an asset.

Pamela hesitated and then admitted, 'Not really, no.'

'I'm new to this town too.' Sid paused. 'Maybe we could get to know it together sometime?'

'I'd like that,' she replied.

It wasn't a lie, just an omission. And omissions weren't the same as lies.

January 1939

I

The next morning, Pamela dragged herself out of her large, comfortable bed at the Hôtel de Crillon and stumbled over to the sink to get a glass of water. Having woken up rather hungover, she chased down two aspirin, put on her dressing gown and went to the window. 1939 had begun grey and cold, but as she looked out over the Place de la Concorde, she sighed with happiness at the view. To her right was the Jardin des Champs-Élysées, and to her left was the Jardin des Tuileries. Straight ahead, she could see the Seine and the Assemblée nationale, which sat on its left bank. Her head throbbed, her mouth was dry and her feet hurt from dancing, but she felt strangely content.

When she and Lettice lived in Paris fourteen years earlier, Pamela took classes in conversational French and went to museums with a group of other well-bred young English girls. She lived in the flat of the genteelly impoverished Comtesse de Montagnac, who lived in faded splendour in the 16th arrondissement. Their once-great fortune had been eaten away by numerous wars, bad investments and miscellaneous gambling debts. It all began to go downhill when Napoleon was defeated at Waterloo, which, for such an old family, was considered relatively recent. The Comtesse was fond of the English and so was willing to overlook the shortcomings of Wellington. After all, the de Montagnacs found sanctuary in England 150 years before, when their friends were being guillotined. The family had once owned the entire building but had been obliged to sell most of it off over the years. They retained the flat on the *étage noble* — the floor in Haussmann buildings known for the highest ceilings and largest balconies.

Pamela considered the Comtesse a romantically tragic figure — like a character from a Balzac novel. She had lost two sons in the Great War and then a husband to the influenza epidemic. Her remaining son Laurent had been gassed in a trench at Ypres and blinded. If Pamela found the Comtesse romantic, she thought Laurent impossibly so. A talented pianist before the war, he spent his days teaching piano lessons and composing pieces of music, when his damaged lungs would allow him. Laurent had taught Pamela how to waltz, and he was so kind to her that she couldn't help but fall hopelessly in love with him.

'Oh Pam, look at your face — you're besotted!' Lettice had said to her. 'You *do* always go for the wounded ones. Though there is something positively devastating about a man like that.'

They had decided that all desirable men fell into one of two camps: confident and conceited, or romantic and tragic.

Pamela's first beau, whom she'd met as a deb during her first season 'out', had belonged to the first camp. Bunny Russell-Jones had pursued Pamela doggedly at parties and balls, alternating between teasing and complimenting her. After many walks, dances, moonlit drives in his father's Bugatti, and, eventually, a (in retrospect, lacklustre) proposal of marriage, Bunny succeeded in winning her over and leading her to believe he was in love. Soon after, Pamela discovered — to her horror — that she was pregnant. She had hoped that when she told him, Bunny would take her in his arms, reassure her and propose something like an elopement — ideally, as quickly as possible. People were always eloping in novels, weren't they? But when she tearfully revealed her condition, he retreated as quickly as a cavalry regiment facing a tank corps and called off the engagement. And Pamela was left to fend for herself and face the much-whispered-about, much-dreaded last resort of abortion, with only Lettice for help.

In her heart of hearts, it was precisely what she had feared would happen. She knew Bunny didn't give two figs about doing the honourable thing. If he had, she wouldn't have been in that predicament in the first place. She didn't even know if she loved him or only thought she did. She hadn't been naïve; she'd heard the rumours about Bunny being what other girls called NSIT (Not Safe in Taxis). But after a year of gazing longingly at Laurent, Pamela had been primed for love — however fraudulent and underhanded. Paris, she realised, had turned an English country girl into a hopeless romantic.

Ironically, in the end, the whole experience of throwing caution to the wind in the name of love — or what she thought had been love — made Pamela cautious, if not downright cynical. And had caused her to marry a man who belonged to the second camp. Francis was not unlike Laurent in that he was a casualty of the Great War, having spent three years after the Armistice in a psychiatric hospital being treated for shell shock. By the time he and Pamela were introduced, he had become a withdrawn, quiet soul whose first fiancée had left him for someone else. His friends and family hoped that an engagement to a younger woman might save him. Pamela's family had thought that giving her hand to an older man from a distinguished, aristocratic family would not only rescue her from spinsterhood and obscurity but also cement her place in high society. She did love Francis, in her own way. But she couldn't say whether she had ever been *in* love with him, or he with her.

But maybe it was for the best. After all, would Pamela have been able to be separated from someone she considered the love of her life for a mission like this, for an indefinite period of time? By the time she left, their froideur had eventually thawed, and she and Francis had parted on amicable terms.

Pamela shook her head. She needed to snap out of her Parisian reverie and pull herself together. It wouldn't do to moon around the city, indulging in navel-gazing. She was going to have to steel herself for a new life, watching the Windsors.

II

Later that afternoon, as per her briefing, Pamela made her way to a building in the 9th arrondissement. The MI6 safe house was hidden in a side street of Pigalle, a neighbourhood known for cabarets, dance halls and brothels. Two women — one quite young, one middle-aged — had been lingering in the doorway of the building as Pamela came in, smoking cigarettes in their kimonos and lingerie. The flat was freezing cold, dingy and, at first glance, completely ordinary.

Fruity Metcalfe — whom Captain Macaulay introduced to Pamela as 'codename Black Sheep' — was bringing Pamela up to speed. She had met Fruity briefly at various social occasions with Francis. The last time she saw his wife, Baba (hence 'Black Sheep', presumably), was two years earlier; she had been canoodling with Oswald Mosley in the drawing room during a party at Cliveden House. A tall cavalry officer from Dublin, known for his charming, buoyant personality,

Fruity now looked uncharacteristically subdued. Tired. Sallow skinned. Much like Tommy Lascelles, his predecessor.

'He's foolish, arrogant and has a tendency to interfere,' Fruity complained. 'It was bad enough when he was King and it's even worse now that he's got bugger all to do. When everything went to hell over the Rhineland, he threatened to abdicate if Baldwin made war with Germany. Last year, he dined with the American ambassador to Austria, who told him that a train going from Germany to Italy had crashed and that the naval shells it had been carrying were discovered. Fruity shook his head angrily. 'He then stupidly passed this information on to his Italian friends. I think he thinks he's trying to "help" prevent war. He likes to say there's no one in the whole of Europe who cares more about peace than him.

'And now that he's no longer the Palace's problem, he surrounds himself with any sycophant and charlatan who tells him what he wants to hear. Charles Bedaux, for instance. A French "management consultant", whatever that is. Every time business owners try to impose his so-called system on their workers, they go on strike. Seems to have a finger in every pie. Knows everyone. Finagled the Windsors' trip to Germany. Complete crook. Acts like a bloody gangster.'

The Windsors had been married at the Bedaux chateau in the Loire Valley.

'And then there's *her*,' Fruity continued to fume. 'Never know what she's up to. Seems even more miserable than before they were married. She uses her ex-husband's solicitor — a nasty little chap called Armand Grégoire. He has a number of high-ranking Nazi clients. Used him to sue her cousin's husband for writing a piece on her for an American paper. Vicious woman. All she does is go shopping, get her hair made up and whinge.'

Pamela would have to be a very good actress indeed if she was going to pretend to be a friend to the American divorcée and maintain that pretence for who knew how long.

'You will liaise with Black Sheep when it comes to tracking the Duchess's movements and moods,' explained Macaulay as he handed her a thick file. 'Which, of course, is where you come in, Show Boat. This file contains information about the Board of Trade and your role in it. And reports on the textile and garment industries, British and French. It's absolutely imperative that you know everything in here, inside and out, in order to maintain your cover.'

The captain then unpacked a shopping bag from Galeries Lafayette that had been sitting on the floor next to the sofa. He picked out two handbags. One was brown; the other, black. Both crocodile, made by Asprey of London, and looked surprisingly smart.

'These come fitted with a recording device. If you find yourself having — or overhearing — an interesting conversation, you press this button here.' He indicated the snap on the side. 'And it starts recording. Each one has a false bottom where the device is hidden. You can remove it to retrieve the tape or take the device out entirely. Our secretary Miss Ashburn picked the handbags out herself.' (Pamela made a mental note to thank Joan Ashburn for her good taste.) Macaulay then produced a pack of Lucky Strikes from the suitcase. 'It's a camera. The lens is on the side. To take a photo, push down the cigarette sticking out of the top.'

Pamela looked over at Fruity, but he was sitting in an armchair by the window, looking blankly out over the zinc rooftops of Paris. He reminded Pamela of Francis; so many men of that generation who had seen action in the war seemed to retreat into that void of detachment when they were troubled.

'You're going to employ a cipher system to communicate with us. Using this.' Macaulay handed Pamela an English translation of Émile Zola's *Nana*. 'Each word has a number. And that number is the position where that word occurs in the book. For instance, if you were to write, "We have news", you'd use numbers instead of letters. Let's say "we" is the fourth word in the book, "have" is the 12th and "news" is the 57th. You would write 4, 12, 57.'

If MI6 wanted their agents to be proficient in so many tricks of the trade, whyever didn't they train them? Did they just have an enormous amount of confidence in their choice of recruits? Pamela started to feel overwhelmed and found herself missing the more whimsical version of the captain she'd met in London.

'If, for any reason, you're writing under duress ... that is, someone is *making* you write something, you will tack extra letters onto the end. Like, "SSSS". Then we'll know not to trust the contents of the missive.'

'Why would I be writing under duress?' asked Pamela.

'It's always a good idea to plan for contingencies,' said Macaulay carefully. 'Speaking of which, if this safe house ends up becoming brûlé—'

'Burned?'

'Yes. If anyone's found it. Someone will try to warn you.'

Try.

Pamela felt her skin prickle.

'If — or rather when you lie, mix grains of truth in with the lie. It will come across as more natural and be easier for you to remember. If you think you're being followed, look into a reflective surface — a mirror or a window. Never look behind you. It's unnatural. Gives the game away. Ditto running. Never run. I assume you can drive?'

Despite the fact that she rarely drove and wasn't very good at it to begin with, Pamela nodded.

'Do you know how to complete a brush-past?'

Pamela had heard of this: when an agent gives something — a letter or a package — to another agent in public. She had never done it herself but nodded anyway, not wanting to give the captain the impression that she wasn't up to the task at this late stage. But she could feel a sense of unease growing. Considering this mission from the comfort and safety of her London home was one thing. Facing down the reality of it in a safe house in Paris, realising all the things she would have to teach herself, was quite another. It was just as well she was now alone in Paris, away from the distractions and obligations of London.

'If you need to draw attention away from yourself, cover up a slip, avoid answering a question, create a diversion,' Macaulay continued. 'There's a decommissioned post box just behind the Odéon — the theatre on the edge of the Jardin du Luxembourg. You'll use that as your dead drop. If you think you've been followed, you can pass by it and duck into the theatre. Or the gardens, if it isn't open. It should be a convenient location for you, as you won't be living far from there. On the Left Bank.'

He handed her a piece of paper with an address in the 6th arrondissement. Pamela was surprised. She had assumed she would be living somewhere more well heeled, like the gilded 16th, not the Bohemian quarter near the Sorbonne, surrounded by students. Though standing around in the seedy, frigid little flat above a brothel, she realised it could have been worse.

'Madame Garrote is the concierge. She's a fearsome old thing, but she works for us. Keeps an eye on the building and knows whenever anyone is coming in or out.'

Pamela wondered if Garrote was her real name or a codename made up by Macaulay to make her sound terrifying.

'I appreciate this is rather a lot of information at once,' he added in a somewhat conciliatory tone.

'Better too much than nothing at all,' Pamela replied. 'I was somewhat ... unprepared for my last mission.'

'Well, that's MI5 for you ...'

'They hadn't even told me I was replacing an agent who'd been eliminated. It came as quite a shock when I found out.'

Macaulay and Fruity exchanged a glance. Pamela suddenly remembered what he had said to her back in London. Her blood ran cold.

'I'm your twelfth man, aren't I? The substitute player who steps in for someone else.'

Fruity crossed the room and approached her. 'There was someone working in the Windsor household staff who had been on our payroll. They became quite ill all of a sudden. We can't say for certain what happened or who was responsible, but there's some suspicion that it was poison.'

Pamela noticed that Fruity didn't specify whether this person had recovered or not. She thought about Gertrude Leigh, never waking up from her coma.

'And who would want to poison a member of the Windsor staff on the MI6 payroll ... ?' She tried to mask her creeping worry.

Again, Macaulay and Fruity exchanged a glance. The captain gave a small nod.

'This is all speculation, of course,' Fruity began. 'But it's possible that there is someone in the Windsor household or connected to their social circle who is working for ... well, it's hard to say. The

Germans, the Italians, French fascists … perhaps even a group of British fifth columnists.'

'Like Oswald Mosley?'

Fruity stiffened. Had Baba's affair with the leader of the British Union of Fascists ended, or was it still carrying on?

'We don't know. As Fruity said, it remains pure speculation for now.' Macaulay produced a small pistol from the suitcase. 'This will be here, behind the toilet cistern, if you need it. It's doubtful you'll ever use it, but it's better to be prepared.'

Pamela nodded, even though she would have been more likely to believe that statement at the beginning of the conversation rather than now, when she was getting a sense of the potential risks involved in her mission.

Macaulay then felt around in a pocket in the inside of his jacket and produced a small, brown envelope. He handed it to Pamela.

'What is this?'

'It's a cyanide capsule,' Fruity explained grimly. 'In case anything should happen.'

Pamela stared at him in disbelief.

'As I said, planning for contingencies,' said Macaulay quickly. 'Our agents generally keep it on them at all times.'

Pamela started to feel faint. She sat down in the nearest chair.

'I'll get you a glass of water,' said Fruity, and went into the kitchen.

Looking at Macaulay, Pamela could tell that he was worried. And suddenly, the fear of being taken off the mission, of being sent back to London in disgrace as a frightened little woman, was greater than anything that the gun, cyanide capsule or mention of her murdered predecessor had aroused in her. She couldn't return home now. What would she tell everyone? That she had proven a failure at the Board of Trade? And what would she tell Francis? That she turned tail at the first sign of danger? She had to pull herself together and focus on the task at hand, not work herself into a lather. Maybe pistols and cyanide capsules were pro forma for MI6, required for all missions. Nothing to worry about.

'I'm afraid I was out 'til all hours, ringing in the new year with some friends. I have a terrible head today from all the champagne.' She smiled brightly. 'Silly of me, really. But I'm sure I'll be quite all right in a moment.'

Pamela returned to the hotel to retrieve her things with the shopping bag Macaulay had given her (from a French department store, to make it seem as if she'd spent the day shopping), and by the time she was in a taxi on her way to the 6th arrondissement, it was dark, cold and sleeting.

She stepped through the door to the courtyard, dragging her suitcases behind her. She got her heel caught in the cobblestones and fell over trying to pull it out. She swore under her breath and then spotted the lodge to her right, which was dark except for a candle in the window. As soon as she knocked on the door, Pamela heard barking. A woman answered. She was petite, wizened and wore a severe grey bun and a pair of spectacles on the end of her nose. The barking was emanating from a terrier at her feet.

'Tulipe! Shush!' she hissed at the dog. 'Oui, madame?'

When Pamela introduced herself, Madame Garrote looked at her watch and replied sternly that she had been expecting her at five and that she was late. She took a ring of keys and an old-fashioned hurricane lamp from her lodge. She pulled a key off the ring and handed it to Pamela.

The concierge then gestured to the lamp and said curtly, 'The electricity is out.'

Four flights, three suitcases and one blackout later, Pamela flopped onto the small floral sofa in what appeared to constitute a sitting room. When she got her breath back, she inspected the flat with the lamp that Madame Garrote had given her. It wasn't quite as grim as the safe house in Pigalle, but it was certainly a far cry from the opulence of Hôtel de Crillon. Of course, it wouldn't do for an intelligence agent to be living in the lap of luxury, but at least they could have put her somewhere with fewer flights of stairs. Warily, she went to the bathroom and tried the taps. She was relieved to find that she had hot water. She would have put her foot down at a cold-water flat.

Pamela saw that there was already coal in the grate and lit a fire. After she unpacked, she sat down at her kitchen table and looked at the copy of Émile Zola's *Nana* that they had given her. A novel about a courtesan living in Paris. (A comment on the Duchess of Windsor and perhaps another example of Macaulay's humour.) Pamela took out the file on the Board of Trade and started rifling through the notes. She was tired but she knew her time to prepare was limited, and she needed to make sure her cover was airtight.

As she reached into her handbag to get her cigarettes, her fingers brushed against the small envelope. She took it out and examined it in the firelight.

February 1939

I

In addition to reading up on British trade policy, Pamela spent her first few weeks in the depths of a damp and gloomy Paris winter spying on the Windsor household as much as she could, watching the house, observing the couple's comings and goings, their servants and any visitors. The Windsors had recently moved from a nine-room suite at the Meurice (a favourite of deposed royals) into an elegant four-storey house on the Boulevard Souchet, across from the Bois de Boulogne. Tall and upright, with pillars and a Louis XIV façade, it was surrounded by iron fencing and high hedges. The striped awnings over the windows had the disconcerting effect of making the house look as if it were watching passers-by under hooded eyelids. Meeting in a small park nearby on a biting Wednesday afternoon in early February, Fruity had filled her in on the rest.

1) The Duke and Duchess spent much of their time in their private apartments on the second floor. They rarely entertained, preferring to go out instead.

2) His bedroom was on one side of the house and hers was on the other.

3) He used his bedroom as an office; he liked to sit in a low chair with papers spread out on the floor in front of him, which irritated her. She complained to the servants immediately if anything was left untidy.

4) They had sixteen servants of various nationalities in total, running both the Paris house and La Croë in the South of France. Hale was English and had been recommended by the Bedauxs. There was a caretaker who lived at La Croë with his wife and disabled son.

5) The Duke and Duchess each had a secretary who dealt with most of the bookkeeping, correspondence and organisation of their social life.

6) Their Carin terriers were with them at all times and accompanied the Duke when he went golfing. Which was every day.

7) The Duchess's time was taken up with shopping and decorating. She was superstitious and had a woman come in to read her horoscope each week.

8) They kept two cars in Paris and one in the South of France. Neither of them drove, so they each had a chauffeur. Whether travelling by car or by train, they were always accompanied by an enormous amount of luggage.

9) In addition to Philip, the bodyguard from the London Met, there was also Monsieur Magin from the Sûreté, providing security for the Windsors everywhere they went.

After meeting with Fruity, Pamela went to the Meurice, claiming that Wallis had lost a bracelet in one of the rooms. The concierge sent her upstairs with one of the maids who had cleaned the Windsors' suite. A few acidic, well-placed remarks about the couple endeared her to the young chambermaid, who enthusiastically complained about how demanding and difficult they were.

Over the following days, she went into various antique shops, pretending to be a buyer, mentioning the Windsors in passing. They had developed a reputation for being indecisive, nitpicky, snobbish and quick to haggle but slow to pay their bills. Everyone had been anxious to compete for the couple's custom until they realised that it involved sending every rug, table and lamp for a trial period.

And once she was satisfied that she'd done a sufficient amount of initial background research, Pamela wrote to Wallis, saying she would be living in Paris for a time, writing for *Vogue* and working for the Board of Trade. It was clear she was lonely and isolated; Wallis's response was quick and even more enthusiastic than Pamela had hoped. She gushed about how relieved she was to know that one of the few people still loyal to her and David would be in Paris and had invited Pamela for tea.

Everything in Boulevard Suchet struck Pamela as a feeble attempt to recreate palace life — grandiosity on a domestic scale: high ceilings, marble, pillars, a sweeping staircase, caryatids with crowns of candles in the entryway. Even the livery worn by the staff was scarlet and gold, a replica of that used at Buckingham Palace. Hale, the butler, led her into the morning room, where the decorator was supervising his assistants while Wallis supervised him, hanging curtains and moving furniture. The room was a mix of the English, the French and the Far East: Chippendale chairs, chintz upholstery, Louis XVI tables, jade ashtrays and a Japanese screen. Paint and fabric samples had been scattered across various surfaces. Pamela couldn't help but wrinkle her nose in distaste at the *WE* monogram prominently displayed on the sofa cushions.

Wallis was carefully inspecting a lacquered Chinese desk for damage. She was, as usual, immaculately dressed. Her dark brown hair was perfectly set, her nails manicured. According to the intelligence Pamela had gathered, Wallis had twice-weekly manicures and her stylist came each evening to do her hair. She wore a navy-blue dress, almost certainly a Mainbocher — one of her favourite designers — with a diamond and emerald brooch. Pamela noted the engagement ring the Duke had given her — an emerald, said to be an enormous twenty carats. As always, her posture was correct to the point of rigidity. Despite the freezing February weather and overcast sky, the windows were open. Although she had made the Duke install central heating in Boulevard Suchet and La Croë, Wallis was known to keep the windows open at all times, professing the health benefits of fresh air. Pamela shivered and could tell the staff were equally frozen, but Wallis seemed unaffected by the temperature.

The Duchess greeted Pamela surprisingly warmly and gestured for her to sit. Pamela carefully placed one of the crocodile handbags given to her by Macaulay between herself and Wallis, ready to subtly switch on the recording devise, should the American say anything worth capturing. After talking about the house and the demands of interior design, she launched into her complaints about how awful everyone had been to her — the Royal Family, Westminster, the British people. The Duke had to be banned from ringing his brother George because he had taken to calling him day and night with unsolicited advice. The French press referred to Wallis as 'la putain royale'. French society snubbed them in public places, sometimes even leaving the room when they entered. Neither of them had bargained on living in exile; they thought they would be allowed to carry on living under the nose of the new King, badgering him to reinstate the royal privileges they'd relinquished.

While the Duke did sound genuinely happy, having married the women he adored, Wallis was now married to a man who was far more demanding and dependent on her than Ernest Simpson had ever been.

'The morning after our wedding, I woke up and found him watching me. "What shall we do today?"' Wallis said in an uncanny imitation of the Duke. 'I realised that I would need to plan each and every one of our days from then on to keep him entertained. I suppose I should be grateful he spends so much time playing golf.' She shrugged her narrow shoulders, fell silent and stared morosely out the window.

Pamela couldn't imagine living with someone who had been the centre of attention all his life and was now being ignored by his entire family and the majority of his friends. It was apparent that the flurry of decoration, shopping and primping was a distraction from the disappointing, lonely reality of Wallis's new existence. Pamela was about to take out a cigarette but thought better of it, remembering that the Duchess didn't smoke.

'I don't know what they expect us to do here. Flit from place to place, going to dinner with the same small group of people week after week?' Wallis bitterly demanded. 'Gratefully sign fan mail and respond to requests for autographs? Write thank-you cards for unwanted gifts? We get dozens of letters every week from people asking when we'll come back to England.' She paused. 'And if the rumours are true …'

'Rumours?'

'That David is going to return to the throne.'

Pamela already knew from Fruity that the Windsors received an enormous number of letters of appreciation and support; people around the world cheered on the man who gave up the throne for the woman he loved and the woman who supported him unconditionally. What Pamela and Fruity hadn't realised was that these same people were also anxiously awaiting the return of the King and Queen of Hearts to Windsor Castle. Pamela remembered something Francis had said to her: 'If there ever was a lightning rod for disgruntled fifth columnists, cranks and fascist appeasers …'

'And what do you tell them?' Pamela tried to mask her apprehension. She could just imagine the couple writing to their besotted fans ginning up excitement over the delusion of a grand homecoming.

'We say we're living happily in France and making a simple life here for ourselves. As private citizens. Even though it's very difficult to maintain appearances in such straitened circumstances. And in a house too small for entertaining,' she grumbled.

Fruity told Pamela that Wallis ran both houses like a business, keeping an eagle eye on the accounts each week and bringing up any petty expenses she deemed unnecessary. A bottle of mineral water for their chauffeur on a hot summer's day, for instance. And making minute changes to the household budget. Pamela spotted the notebook she recognised as Wallis's 'Grumble Book', where she noted her criticisms of the food ('too hot', 'too cold'), the housekeeping ('peonies where hydrangeas should be') and the behaviour of her staff ('cigars handed out at the wrong time').

There was a knock at the door. A neatly dressed woman, wearing spectacles and an outmoded hairstyle, who looked to be in her late thirties, entered the room carrying a notebook.

'The Duke telephoned to say that he would lunch at the club,' she said in a clipped English accent.

'Of course he will …' Wallis rolled her eyes.

'Will Madam be having lunch today?'

Not wanting to overstay her welcome, Pamela took her handbag, rose from her chair and said, 'It has been such a pleasure to see you, Wallis. I'll leave you to your afternoon.'

But Wallis put a hand on her arm and said, 'Pamela, it would be such a pleasure if you could stay and lunch with me. We have one of the best chefs in Paris. We so rarely get to share him with anyone.'

Pamela could almost hear a note of pleading in her voice. It was clear that Wallis was lonely in her gilded cage. Maybe even lonelier than Pamela had anticipated.

'I would like nothing more,' Pamela replied.

Wallis smiled. 'Miss Blythewood, we'll take lunch in the dining room please.'

II

Pamela felt even more reassured that things seemed to be going according to plan when Wallis extended an invitation to dinner for the following night. She had played up the fact that she was more or less alone in the French capital, insinuating that she would be ever so grateful for Wallis and the Duke's company.

'It will just be a few friends of ours. And the American Ambassador,' Wallis added with a hint of smugness.

Fortunately, Lettice was a terrible gossip and a font of knowledge of Parisian society chatter. When they took a walk in the Jardin du Luxembourg the next morning, Pamela mentioned she was having dinner with Ambassador William Bullitt and asked what her friend knew about him. Lettice explained Bullitt was known across the city as a bon vivant with exquisite taste in racehorses who threw extravagant parties. He came from an old Philadelphia family and was enormously wealthy, which was part of the reason he had been posted to Paris in the first place. The fact that money was no object when it came to his diplomatic soirées had won over the notoriously hard-to-please French. Bullitt had been divorced twice —from some American socialite and from a suffragette-turned-journalist-turned-communist. The second wife had left him for a French lesbian sculptor and then died of an obscure disease several years later. He was rumoured to have been impotent and had gone to Vienna to be analysed by Freud. Who must have been able to cure him, as Bullitt was also rumoured to be a tremendous womaniser. Lettice warned Pamela that the ambassador was a great Francophile but disliked the British for reasons unknown even to her.

Restaurant Larue was an old-fashioned but popular establishment in Place de la Madeleine, with an interior that had remained unchanged since the Belle Époque, staffed by cold-eyed White Russians. While Wallis seemed to be in her element, holding court with her fellow countrymen, it was strange for Pamela to see the former King of England sitting there like an ordinary person in an ordinary restaurant, chatting away with a group of Americans. Wallis embraced Pamela warmly, but the Duke didn't seem to remember her at all, despite them having met several times. It seemed to Pamela that his face had a pinched-ness to it, and he looked physically smaller than when she had seen him last. Perhaps this was what happened when one relinquished the throne — one shrivelled, like a cursed fairy.

Bullitt was a solid, bullish-looking man in his late forties who was balding, with an expressive face and a wide mouth.

'You taught the Reds to play polo!' exclaimed the Duke in delighted, childlike surprise.

'They couldn't hit the ball to save their lives, but they could certainly charge down the field and frighten the other team away from the goal,' Bullitt smirked.

'I can well imagine the Soviet cavalry would ride like a lot of Cossacks,' mused the Duke.

'Have you seen them play at Meadow Brook? So do plenty of Americans. But I can't imagine that surprises you — you Brits think we're a bunch of savages anyway,' sniped Bullitt in a suddenly hostile fashion.

Everyone turned to look at him. The steeliness in the ambassador's voice caused the whole table to grow quiet for a moment. All the diplomats Pamela had known were calm, even-handed people, but it was clear that Bullitt was emotional and reactive — the kind of man who could single-handedly change the temperature in the room. His personality had a vigorous quality bordering on aggression that struck Pamela as particular to certain kinds of American. She couldn't help but wonder what Francis would have made of him. In that moment, she wished she could write to him after dinner and tell him all about it, but knew she would have to censor herself, making up titbits from a fictitious life working for the Board of Trade.

'Well, I think the British are the ones who are behaving like savages towards *us*,' Wallis interjected.

'Poor darling,' murmured the Duke from across the table. 'They have been simply beastly. One's own family. Can you imagine?'

'They don't know how lucky they could have been,' said Bullitt as he raised a glass to the Windsors. 'A toast! To the Duke and Duchess of Windsor. Britain's loss is France's gain.'

Everyone raised their glasses and echoed his toast. Pamela forced a smile, having forgotten how unnatural and uncomfortable it felt when she was in the Windsors' circle.

'I certainly know how lucky *I* am,' chirped the former king as he reached for Wallis's hand. Pamela noticed that she allowed him to hold it for only the briefest moment before pulling away.

Bullitt turned unexpectedly to Pamela. He leaned back in his chair and appraised her. 'I understand that you're one of the last friends of the Windsors to stick around.'

Did he seem suspicious? Or was she just being paranoid? Pamela was going to have to get used to feeling out of place and convince herself to act more naturally. Francis had been right; this wasn't like her last mission where she had been able to insert herself into various social engagements relatively easily. This was more complicated and entailed constructing an alternative persona. And sitting there in plain sight with the Windsors and their entourage, Pamela was starting to worry about what anyone who knew her would say.

Ironically, Wallis then interjected, 'Lady Pamela has been a rock. She doesn't care what people think of her.'

'Loyalty is an admirable quality.' Bullitt smiled. 'What brings you to Paris?'

'I'm representing the British Board of Trade,' Pamela replied smoothly. 'For textiles and fashion. I'm also writing for London *Vogue* about French couture.'

'I've got a teenage daughter. She's a big fan of your magazine. All she cares about are horses and clothes.' He added, 'I used to be a journalist myself.'

'How marvellous. And how do you find life in Paris, Ambassador?'

'Besides Philadelphia, it's my favourite city in the world. Though I sometimes wish I could spend more time enjoying it and less time trying to get France and Germany to be a little more well-disposed towards one another.'

'Very wise, very wise,' intoned the Duke, nodding. 'I've always said Germany isn't our enemy.'

Pamela subtly reached for her handbag and turned on the recording device. She hoped that the recorder was sensitive enough to pick up what the Ambassador and the Duke were saying from beneath the table.

'The immediate threat — in an existential sense — is the Soviets. They want to keep Europe divided and foster Marxist sympathies across the world, so that communists will act against their own governments as soon as the Kremlin gives the signal. I've always said that the United States needs to take a more active role in fostering European unity. Best way to thwart the Bolsheviks. Besides, poor diplomatic relations are bad for trade. But your ambassador seems a little …' — Bullitt paused and rubbed his chin — 'resistant to the idea of Franco-German reconciliation.'

'I don't care for Ambassador Phipps,' grumbled Wallis. 'He refuses to do a thing to try to get the Palace to reconcile with us. If I were you, I wouldn't rely on the British as any kind of allies, Ambassador.'

Pamela almost choked on her caviar but tried to cover it up as a small cough. She hoped the recorder had caught this glaring indiscretion.

'Now, now, darling,' interjected the Duke. 'It won't do to look like bad sports in front of your compatriot.'

'We need to get the Germans to the table, not push them away,' complained Bullitt. 'Czechoslovakia isn't worth the wholesale destruction of Western Europe.'

'I'm sure if anyone can do it, you can,' purred Wallis.

Pamela realised that Wallis's increasingly ingratiating attitude towards Bullitt bordered on flirtation.

'Have you spoken to the German government?' asked the Duke, as if inquiring after a mutual friend.

'I did meet Reichsmarschall Göring …' Bullett started.

'So did we!' the Duke chirped excitedly. 'On our trip to Germany.'

'Repulsive man, I thought. Mannered. Looked like the hind end of an elephant. Had the nerve to say I should consider the views of five million German-American voters.'

'Well, I suppose he does have—'

'I told him that there were enough trees in the United States to hang all five million if their loyalties to Uncle Sam should prove wanting. Just because I don't want Stalin meddling in American politics doesn't mean I'm inviting Germany to try their luck.'

Bullitt's steeliness had returned. Wallis and Edward exchanged glances. Perhaps they were learning that their bright ideas for world peace weren't as popular as they had expected. Pamela couldn't help but feel a sense of satisfaction as she watched the Duke being put in his place. She wished that she was at liberty to say something to support what Bullitt had said about putting Nazis in their place, but reminded herself that her mission was to feed the Windsors' imprudent bon mots back to MI6. So, Pamela did her best to look politely interested, playing the part of the charming, unobtrusive dinner guest.

'I do miss American candour.' Wallis sighed. 'I'm quite exhausted from years of having to interpret British smoke signals.'

Bullitt smiled at her. 'If only everyone was as appreciative as you.'

He seemed surprisingly easy to win over, though it was difficult to say who exactly was flattering whom. It would be useful to keep an eye on the relationship between the Windsors and the ambassador, and to find out if the friendship was social, instrumental or both. Clearly, the Windsors were disparaging the British government out of spite, like petulant children. But what were they hoping to gain? Perhaps they saw Bullitt, with his connections and parties, as a way back into the upper echelons of international society. Maybe they were simply trying to anticipate what he wanted to hear.

At the end of the evening, when she returned to her dingy flat on the Left Bank, Pamela checked to make sure the matchstick she'd inserted between the door and the doorframe was still in place. On her first mission, she hadn't known that she had been sent in to replace an agent who had been eliminated. This time, she would be better prepared and more careful.

How many of these sorts of dinners and parties was Pamela going to have to bear witness to in the coming weeks, if not months? How often would she need to bite her tongue when the Windsors said something careless or damaging? Although if they continued to be as forthcoming about their political opinions as they were tonight, perhaps this would be a relatively straightforward information-gathering exercise and she could indeed 'bang it in', as Macaulay had said. Maybe this was going to be easier than she thought.

III

A few nights later, Pamela told herself that she was going back to Bricktop's to see what she could discover about the owner's relationship with Wallis. And to ask an American journalist what he knew about his country's ambassador. The fact that she found Sid funny and attractive and that they had already met for lunch, a film, a chilly walk along the Seine and dinner (twice) was, she told herself, by the by. It was late and most of Bricktop's patrons had gone home. Musicians from other Montmartre clubs had come to play with the band. Many of them already knew each other and flitted from club to club, improvising in 'hot jazz' sessions late into the night. Pamela sat at a table with Sid, Lettice and Mikhail, watching a group of American, Martinican and Cuban musicians playing. Sometimes there would be two trumpets, sometimes two guitars, sometimes just a piano and a lone singer.

'I haven't met Bullitt personally. Journalists from Chicago who write for the *Herald Tribune* aren't exactly shoo-ins for Ambassador Bullitt's guest list,' Sid said.

'Doesn't he want publicity?'

'From the French press, sure. Making a good impression on the French is the whole point. He'd probably think I was just a two-bit hack from the South Side of Chicago. Bullitt's a Mainline blueblood — an American aristocrat. But at least he's a Roosevelt man.'

'What do you think of his politics?'

'He doesn't want war any more than any other American does, but I've heard he's a little more realistic than everyone else. He's loyal to FDR, who trusts him.'

'He seems a bit volatile for a diplomat,' Pamela said.

Sid looked surprised. 'You've met Ambassador Bullitt?'

Had she said too much? Pamela really needed to get the hang of the give and take of information — what to let people know and what to keep to herself. Or lie about.

'At a small engagement recently, yes.'

'More trade board talks?'

Pamela nodded. Of course, it would be impossible to say she didn't know the Windsors at all, but she was trying to avoid talking too much about when, where and how often she saw them.

'I only spoke to him briefly. He seems to be … a man of passion.'

'He used to be a journalist and well, we're all men of passion.' Sid smiled. Pamela felt a pleasurable tingle in her body, and then silently admonished her wandering mind. 'I've heard he can be easily influenced. And that he's susceptible to gossip and rumours.'

The idea that Bullitt was close to the Windsors, a confidante of the American president *and* easily influenced worried Pamela. What poison could Wallis and Edward be dripping in his ear that he was reporting back to Roosevelt?'

'You say Roosevelt trusts Bullitt?'

'They're part of the same club. Fellow American bluebloods. America is run by rich men.'

'But he doesn't seem to be like your Ambassador Kennedy in London,' Pamela mused aloud as she absent-mindedly swirled the ice cubes in her drink.

'You certainly know your American ambassadors. Even the Hitler-appeasers.' Sid looked at Pamela. 'Joe Kennedy isn't a blueblood. He's an FDR supporter too, but new money, Irish-Catholic. And he's a buddy of Father Coughlin — you ever heard of him?' Pamela shook her head. 'A right-wing priest with a popular radio programme. He uses it to rail against the 'Red Menace' and so-called 'Jewish cabal' taking over the world, running the banks, the press, Hollywood. My mother thinks Coughlin is the devil incarnate. Him and Lindburgh. She's worried that they're the kind of guys who could incite a pogrom.'

'You mean, in America?'

'Both my parents left Russia to escape marauding Cossacks, before me and my sister were born. It's the kind of fear that never leaves you, I guess.'

'Your parents are Russian?' Pamela asked in surprise.

'Russian Jews. Like Mikhail.' Sid gestured to the artist, who was sitting across from them on the banquette. 'He told me about what happened to his shtetl during the Civil War. They saw killing Jews as a sport. The Whites *and* the Reds.'

Pamela was at a loss for what to say.

'I used to think that was just what happened to Jews in Russia. And the rest of Europe was …'

'More civilised?' Pamela offered.

'Something like that.' Sid furrowed his brow. 'Since Kristallnacht and the Anschluss, France has had every Jew from Mitteleuropa beating down the door to get in. Which has only been playing right into the hands of the fascists. It's why Mikhail's having trouble selling his work. His dealer, Georges, will tell you it's the economy but … you can't pretend there's no connection between people turning their noses up at Jewish art and Jews getting beaten up in the streets.'

Pamela felt a chill go through her body. 'What, here in Paris?'

'The Parti Populaire has been taking inspiration from the Nazis. Everything is the fault of the Jews. Etcetera.'

Realising all these things she didn't know made Pamela feel blinkered and naïve. Unworldly, somehow.

'But you don't—' she corrected herself quickly. 'White doesn't sound like a Jewish name.'

'It was Warschauer. Pop thought White sounded more American. I used to be high-handed about it. I didn't think there was any reason to be ashamed of a Jewish name. But now … let's just say it's better not to have Warschauer on your identity papers if you're travelling around Europe, even as an American.'

Pamela's old *Times* colleague, David Stern, who had recruited Gertrude Leigh for MI5, had a cousin who had managed to leave Berlin three years before. What had become of the rest of their family?

'You didn't realise I was Jewish, did you?' Sid leaned back, watching Pamela.

'Well, no. But that doesn't make any difference, does it?'

'To guys like him, it does.' Sid pointed to a man in a dark grey suit, sitting across from them, flirting with a blond woman in a tight dress.

'Who's he?'

'A Nazi officer. He comes in all the time. At least he isn't dumb enough to wear the uniform.'

'He certainly can't listen to jazz back home in Germany anymore. The verboten fruit, one might say,' Pamela replied ruefully. 'How do you know who he is?'

'Bricktop told me. She reports them all to the Sûreté. They like to keep tabs on all the Nazis creeping around Paris.'

It seemed everyone had their spies. She looked over at Bricktop, who was sitting and chatting with the musicians.

'It can't be easy, can it? A woman running a club in a business like this. Lettice was saying clubs around here have been opening and closing all the time,' Pamela offered, curious to know what Sid knew about Bricktop.

He took out a packet of cigarettes, offered one to Pamela and then lit it, his hand gently touching hers.

'It's easier here than in the States. Even if you're playing somewhere like the Cotton Club — you ever heard of the Cotton Club?'

'Am I going to disappoint you if I say no?'

'I don't think a woman like you could ever disappoint me.'

Pamela found Sid's overt, unabashed manner both exciting and unnerving. It was more difficult to engage in flirtation with an Englishman; unless they were very drunk, their fear of rejection made them taciturn, causing them to communicate almost entirely through subtext. It meant they could claim ignorance if the other party rejected their advances. Francis had never spoken to her like that, even when they were courting. This was partly due to his Englishness, but also to his somewhat shy and retiring nature. And, of course, they had been introduced by mutual friends who had decided that the two of them needed to get married and would make a suitable match. Not exactly flirting in nightclubs.

She cleared her throat. 'So, the Cotton Club … ?'

'It's a club in Harlem. Well, *the* club in New York, really. Everyone's played there. Duke Ellington, Bessie Smith, Louis Armstrong … But, like everywhere else, it's segregated. Anyone who isn't lily-white enters that building through the back door, and only to perform, serve drinks or sweep the floor. Even if they just want a drink, they have to go to the bar next door. Can you imagine? Kicking Duke Ellington out into the street right after his set?'

'But I thought segregation was only in the South.'

'Oh, it's everywhere alright — in spirit, if not in law. Why do you think a woman like Bricktop is over here, on the other side of the ocean?' Sid looked back at the Nazi officer. 'Those bastards knew where to look for inspiration when they wrote the Nuremberg Laws. Jim Crow and Father Coughlin.'

'Do you know that Josephine Baker song, "Si J'étais Blanche?"'
Sid shook his head.

'*Mais je suis franche … Dites-moi, Messieurs: faut-il que je sois blanche … Pour vous plaire mieux?*'

Sid smiled. 'You've got a nice voice.'

Pamela realised that their knees were gently touching. Even though she knew she should have pulled back, away from Sid, she didn't.

'How about you? Doesn't your family miss you?'

'My parents weren't exactly thrilled. It's not the "done thing", a woman going off to Paris on her own.' She paused. 'Without her husband.'

Despite the fact that Pamela knew Sid must have seen her wedding band, they had never discussed her marriage.

Sid finished his drink. 'And how does your husband feel about it?'

A lone saxophone plaintively played something familiar.

'Francis was understanding. Most husbands wouldn't even countenance such a thing.'

Even though you've hardly written to him since you've been in Paris, a little voice said.

'He's a good guy then, huh?'

'Very decent.'

Pamela thought about how dutifully and regularly Francis had been writing to her, telling her about what was happening in the Lords, commenting on the state of politics and relaying messages from their friends (most of whom continued to be baffled by what she was doing in Paris). He never asked when Pamela was coming back to London; having worked for MI5, he knew better than to ask anything about her mission.

'You have kids?'

Pamela shook her head. She realised the band was playing 'A Foggy Day'.

A foggy day in London town
It had me low
And it had me down

She was married. And they both had lives to return to, sooner or later. Thousands of miles apart. As charming, flirtatious and complimentary as Sid was, entertaining the notion of anything happening between them was out of the question.

Later that night, Pamela ran into Bricktop with two of her bouncers, who were strong-arming a customer out of the club.

'You want to carry on like that?' she growled. 'Go on over to Le Jockey — they don't care how many geed-up dope fiends they have getting high in their bathrooms. They'll even sell it to you!'

The man — a dishevelled blond with bloodshot eyes, looking much the worse for wear — slurred a few angry words of protest, 'You'll be hearing from my lawyer!'

'Go ahead! Tell him to give me a call!' she shouted as the bouncers dragged him out the front door. With one fist on her hip, she puffed angrily on a cigar. She then turned to Pamela. 'I'm sorry you had to see that. The wildlife comes out in the wee small hours. Rich little American boys are the worst offenders. Think they can come here and act however they want. Think they can walk all over me.'

'That's outrageous … You shouldn't have to put up with that kind of behaviour.'

'In this business, you have to put up with all kinds of behaviour. The last thing I need is to be raided by the gendarmerie for having dope in my club. As if I don't have enough to worry about.'

'I think what you need is a little escape,' Pamela offered. 'I'll be covering the Schiaparelli show on Friday for *Vogue*. Wallis is going to be there as well. Perhaps you'd like to join us?'

Bricktop sighed and shook her head. 'Nice as it sounds, I'm too busy for that kind of thing.'

Wallis had mentioned she was going to the défilé de mode at the house of Schiaparelli, and having a friend of the Windsors with her certainly couldn't hurt Pamela's charm offensive. Besides, she wanted to know more about the mysterious woman who reported her Nazi patrons to the Sûreté.

She put a hand on Bricktop's arm and said, 'You must work incredibly hard, running this place on your own. You play hostess to half the city. Surely, one morning off won't hurt … ? And perhaps a spot of lunch across the way at the Ritz afterwards? My treat.'

Bricktop looked at her in surprise. Pamela momentarily worried that she had pushed the boundaries of their nascent acquaintance too far. But then Bricktop smiled.

'Hell. Why not? You only live once, right?'

IV

In her short time in Paris, the eccentric Italian Elsa Schiaparelli had become one of the most in-demand designers in the city and one of the few who could rival the heretofore unrivalled Coco Chanel. The Schiaparelli fall/winter show was guaranteed to be a gathering of the good and great of Paris society and its couture industry. Ever since Louis XIV decreed that his courtiers wear clothing made only in France, Paris couture had been one of the main engines driving the French economy. It was the envy of the world — elegant but bold, reinventing itself each season. England had been the centre of men's tailoring since the days of Beau Brummell (who, ironically, fled to France to escape his debtors), but designers and department stores from New York to Shanghai copied women's fashion from the Paris collections. An entire global industry relied on the creativity and hard work of the country's designers and seamstresses. Pamela would have liked to have worn her Schiaparelli suit but had to remind herself that she was meant to be a trade envoy, championing British designers, so chose a suit by the young and promising Hardy Amies instead.

Bricktop arrived in a taxi on a cold, misty Friday morning and stepped out smoking her habitual cigar, in a sumptuous fox fur coat.

'What a stunning fur!' Pamela exclaimed.

'A gift from Cole Porter. The man spoils me.'

The Schiaparelli store on the prestigious Place Vendôme was famed for its dramatic interiors, particularly the enormous birdcage made from gold-painted bamboo that framed the entryway.

'I guess it's one way to keep out the riffraff …' quipped Bricktop with a wry smile.

The ground floor shop was filled with exquisitely dressed socialites, fashion journalists, department store buyers, as well as the wives of industrialists and politicians. They headed up to the main salon, with its minimal, monochrome rooms and dramatically draped curtains. As people found their seats, the room buzzed with excitement. Pamela had always felt that the French approached couture like the British approached horseracing: with an eager anticipation bordering on obsession. Schiaparelli's creations had grown increasingly elaborate and had captured Paris society's imagination. The previous collection had a commedia dell'arte theme, with harlequin patterns, bright colours and masks; the one before embraced the zodiac, with lavish embroidery and intricate beading depicting planets and stars.

Schiaparelli was like a costume designer. Each collection had a distinct motif and each piece she designed — each cape, skirt and jacket — had character. Even her unusual and intricate buttons depicting parrots, acrobats and mermaids were renowned for their whimsical detail. And to wear a Schiaparelli ensemble was to become a character yourself. But not just any woman could wear her clothes; unless you had the chic and confidence to carry off a skeleton dress or a constellation jacket, you risked looking as if the clothes were wearing you.

Sure enough, as Pamela had predicted, Wallis made her appearance. Shortly before her wedding, Wallis had a photo shoot with Cecil Beaton for *Vogue*, aiming to humanise her after the debacle of the Abdication. The centrepiece of the shoot was a Schiaparelli dress featuring an enormous lobster designed by Salvador Dalí. The idea was that the gown would make Wallis look softer, more whimsical. And while even a dress like that couldn't evoke anything close to whimsy in a humourless woman like Wallis Simpson, the arrangement was mutually beneficial nonetheless as it associated her with the House of Schiaparelli and brought the Italian couturier a good deal of publicity as the surrealist designer par excellence.

As Pamela had hoped, Wallis seemed pleased to see both of them. And while they were chatting, in walked Ambassador Bullitt.

'My daughter has a birthday coming up and Wallis assures me there's nothing she would like more than a dress made by Madame Schiaparelli.'

Wallis sat down next to Bullitt, while Pamela and Bricktop found a place to sit a few seats away. Pamela strained to listen in on their conversation, but the show was filled with people chattering excitedly. The woman in the seat next to Bricktop gave her a dirty look. Bricktop just ignored her and continued puffing on her cigar. The woman got up with a huff and found a seat on the other side of the room.

'Do you know that woman?' asked Pamela.

'No, and I hope I never will. I'm sure she's American. French women don't treat me that way. White women come over here from the States and they think things should be like they are back home — that negroes should know their place. Well, except for Wallis. She's more sophisticated than women like that.'

Sometimes Pamela found Wallis to be an enigma. Before the Abdication, she had carried on an affair with Joachim von Ribbentrop, Hitler's ambassador to the Court of St James. And she and the Duke had seemed content — even eager — to befriend the Third Reich's high command on their trip to Germany, even smiling and nodding while visiting a work camp for political prisoners. Yet she had no issue with carrying on a public friendship with a Black woman.

'The first time I met the Duke, I threw him a birthday party just before we opened Bricktop's. He was like a giddy little boy when I let him play the drums with the band. I didn't know what she was going to be like, having heard all the rumours. That she was just a money-grubbing American and all she wanted was the throne and the power. But she's a generous woman. And the Windsors love coming to the club and they've been kind to me.'

It was strange, getting such a different, unexpected perspective on Wallis. It was as if her personality was refracted through a mirror.

The theme of the collection was 'Music in the Air', complete with embroidered musical notes, buttons in the shape of instruments and even a belt featuring a real music box. The audience was enchanted, emitting hushed murmurs of appreciation for each piece and applauding wildly at the end.

'It is no surprise that Madame Schiaparelli is so well received. People want fantasy, escape. Confection. No one in Paris wants to think about anything serious right now,' said Michel de Brunhoff, frowning pensively.

The *Vogue* Paris editor-in-chief was a short, balding man with bushy eyebrows and a pipe sticking out of the side of his mouth. Where American and British *Vogue* were run by elegant but steely fashion mavens, their French counterpart was a man who looked as if he would be more at home in a smoky newsroom than at a couture show.

De Brunhoff was right, and it wasn't just Paris. After all, the Republicans had lost the war in Spain and Spanish refugees had been streaming into France since the beginning of the year. The Home Office was discussing building air raid shelters in parts of Britain most likely to be bombed in the event of war. Thousands of American fascists had rallied at New York's Madison Square Garden and there had been fighting in the streets.

'And so? You are with your country's trade delegation here in Paris? To sell us British tweeds and raincoats?' de Brunhoff asked playfully.

'One hopes we would have more to offer than that. Think of it as an extension of the Entente Cordiale, Monsieur de Brunhoff. A strengthening of the relationship between France and Britain,' Pamela replied diplomatically.

'Yes,' the editor nodded, resigned, 'we cannot bury our heads in the sand.'

Out of the corner of her eye, Pamela spotted Wallis and Bullitt heading for the exit.

'Are they leaving together?' Pamela quietly asked Bricktop.

'Wallis certainly does seem to spend a lot of time with the ambassador, if you get my drift. I've seen all kinds of things in my life. I don't judge. If you live long enough, you play all the parts.' Bricktop shrugged. Then she paused, lowered her voice and said, 'Between you and me, if I was making a habit of seeing a man who wasn't my husband, I wouldn't do it here.'

'What do you mean?'

She looked around, leaned in and whispered, 'People say that Schiaparelli has her staff report back everything they see and hear to her.'

Since Bricktop was reporting undercover Nazis to the French equivalent of Special Branch, it seemed logical to Pamela that she would be a reliable authority on a) Schiaparelli's own spy ring and b) Wallis's extracurricular activities.

Because of von Ribbentrop, Pamela knew that Wallis had a penchant for dalliances with powerful men. But that was before her marriage to the Duke. Granted, Wallis seemed unsettled, bored and lonely in her Paris life and she had been flirting with Bullitt at dinner. And while affairs were commonplace in Paris — even more so than in London — would she risk getting caught in a betrayal of that magnitude? Having barely survived one scandal, she could hardly hazard another. There was no telling how the Duke might react.

Pamela didn't want to suggest to Macaulay that Wallis was having an affair with Bullitt and set MI6's alarm bells ringing until she had proof. The American ambassador was a susceptible man who had the ear of the American president and already harboured anti-British sentiments. If Wallis was fuelling them with her own anger towards the Palace and the government, who knew what damage it could do to Anglo-American relations?

V

When Wallis mentioned going to the Longchamp racetrack to watch one of Bullitt's horses run the next weekend, Pamela told her how she'd grown up with horses (true), how much she loved them (false) and how she loved horseracing (also false). Walking to the Windsors' box through the sodden grass the following Saturday morning in late February, with the wind and drizzle blowing into her face, Pamela was starting to regret having accepted the invitation.

'Lady Pamela?'

She turned around.

'Monsieur de Brunhoff! What a pleasant surprise.'

De Brunhoff was wearing a trench coat and looked as cold and miserable as Pamela, his habitual pipe clenched between his teeth. Standing next to him was a well-dressed man wearing a morning suit under his overcoat.

'Lady Pamela, may I present Pierre Wertheimer.'

Wertheimer courteously removed his top hat and then kissed Pamela's hand. The Wertheimer family had made their money in cosmetics — first Bourjois, then Helena Rubinstein and then Coco Chanel's famed No. 5.

'Lady Pamela writes for *Vogue* in London and is in Paris as a fashion diplomat, of sorts.'

'I'm with the British Board of Trade, Monsieur Wertheimer.'

Pamela had now given her cover story so many times, she was starting to feel as if it were true. How funny that she could slip into a new life and a new identity as easily as if she were trying on a new coat.

Wertheimer's eyes lit up. 'I love nothing more than combining business and horseracing. Especially with such an elegant woman. Would you care to join us in my box?'

Macaulay hadn't told her what to do when her cover story conflicted with her mission. Pamela didn't want to miss her chance to see Wallis interacting with Bullitt. She also didn't want a Board of Trade representative to be seen as snubbing an influential French businessman. But she was relieved at the prospect of a short reprieve from the Windsors. So, Pamela joined the two men and spent a charming hour discussing the fashion world and watching Wertheimer's horse run.

When she finally joined the Windsors and Fruity in their box, she said, 'I'm so sorry I'm late. I ran into the editor of Paris *Vogue*. My Board of Trade duties obliged me to join him in Pierre Wertheimer's box.'

'It is a pity that such a woman like you should have to spend a Saturday morning with a Jew businessman.'

Pamela turned to look at a short, stocky man with a receding hairline and a face like that of an ageing prize-fighter, leaning against the railing of the box.

'Pamela, this is our dear friend Charles Bedaux and his wife Fern,' said Wallis.

Fruity gave Pamela a brief look that told her that he wasn't pleased to see the Bedauxs. He and Pamela were careful not to be seen speaking together too often and only met to exchange intelligence away from Boulevard Suchet. Following Macaulay's advice to mix grains of truth with lies, Fruity and Pamela had led the Windsors to understand that Fruity had known Francis in the army, but that he and Pamela only knew each other slightly.

Pamela wanted to reply that she'd much rather spend a Saturday with the sophisticated, intelligent Wertheimer than with a man who got his start in life working for a pimp in the Pigalle — a rumour she'd heard from Fruity but one she could well believe.

'Lady Pamela is an absolute peach,' said Wallis as she took Pamela's hand. 'I'm sure she's very good at putting up with all kinds of disagreeable people.'

If only Wallis knew that was exactly how Pamela had ended up in Paris.

'I've heard what a good friend you've been to our Wallis here,' said Fern — a tall, slender woman with a long nose — in a flat American accent.

'Did Wertheimer mention that he and his brother are cheating Coco Chanel out of her money?' growled Bedaux. 'The Wertheimers only let her have ten percent of the profits from the perfume. *Her* perfume. She tried to take them to court but she lost the case. Everyone knows the trial was fixed. Men like the Wertheimers have their connections in the courts and the Assemblée. How else would a Jew like Blum have become the president of France?'

It was no coincidence that Charles Bedaux was the one who arranged the Windsors' trip to Germany to meet Adolf Hitler.

'Darling, the next race is about to start. Let's try to enjoy the day,' murmured Fern to her scowling husband.

Pamela spent the next hour trying to look politely interested (but not too interested) while taking mental notes as the Windsors and the Bedauxs engaged in a conversation that ranged from financial investments to fascist politics.

'Now that Catalonia has fallen, the nationalists are finally on the road to victory,' said Bedaux.

'We think Franco will bring stability to Spain, which is what Europe dearly needs right now,' replied the Duke. 'Don't you agree, Fruity?'

'I couldn't have put it better myself, Your Highness.' Fruity attempted a smile that seemed to Pamela to be more of a grimace.

The experience reminded Pamela of the ball she'd gone to at Cliveden over two years before, where she had to spend an evening listening to British aristocrats repeat Nazi talking points to Nazi officials. Bedaux was certainly an unpleasant character with dubious morals, but it would be useful to know where his allegiances lay. Was he like the Cliveden Set and looked at Hitler admiringly? Or was he more like Pamela's brother-in-law Peter — perfectly happy to make connections with whichever people and governments would 'grease the wheels' for him?

After the drinks were brought to the box, the horses in the next race paraded in front of the crowd.

'There he is,' exclaimed the Duke. 'There's Capricorn. Handsome animal. He's the bay with the white stockings.'

Everyone turned to inspect the thoroughbred on the course below. Pamela peered through her binoculars and saw Bullitt walking alongside his horse, groom and trainer. The horses lined up and took off around the course, taking one enormous hedge after another at breakneck speed. As soon as the race finished, Pamela turned around to find that Wallis was leaving the box. She waited a moment and then followed her from a distance. At first, it seemed as if Wallis was heading to the ladies' room, but then she bypassed it and walked in the direction of the stables. She stopped and waited under a tree in a quiet spot. Pamela hung back and watched her through binoculars.

Five minutes later, Bullitt appeared to meet Wallis underneath the tree. He took her hand, and Pamela took out the tiny camera disguised as a pack of Lucky Strikes. She tried to get as close as she could without drawing attention and took a picture, wishing she could get closer so she could hear what they were saying. They spoke for a moment, then Bullitt looked around and kissed Wallis. Pamela took a picture. She waited, hoping there would be more demonstrations of affection, but the two parted. Pamela turned and hurried back to the box, hoping nobody would mark her absence. Wallis returned shortly thereafter, and Bullitt followed a few minutes later.

Fern, who was watching Wallis, turned to Pamela and said quietly, 'She should be more careful …'

'Yes, it does seem risky,' Pamela replied carefully, wanting to encourage her, but not come across as a gossip, or worse, disloyal to Wallis.

'You know what she's like though — Wallis enjoys that kind of thing. *Danger*,' Fern intoned before taking a sip of champagne.

Pamela decided to try to gently draw her out. She reached into her handbag, trying to appear as if she were searching for her handkerchief while she turned on the recording device.

'Wallis does like excitement.' She paused, testing the waters. 'And it doesn't seem as if there's much of that in her life these days …'

'It's not what she bargained for, is it? I can't really blame her. She met Mr Bullitt when the Duke was staying with Kitty Rothschild after the Abdication.'

'Oh, really … ?'

'Can you imagine? A woman leaves her husband for you, upends her life, becomes persona non grata everywhere she goes and you run right into the arms of another woman? And a you-know-what at that.'

'I beg your pardon?'

'A *Jewess*. A rich Jewess, but a Jewess all the same. Turns my stomach just thinking about it,' Fern replied in her nasal American accent.

'Mmm … Quite.'

'There she was, alone in France, without a friend in the world, going through her divorce from Ernest without any kind of actual guarantee that the Duke would marry her in the end. You remember how long it was before they were allowed to see each other again.'

'So, it's been going on all this time?'

'Oh, yes. The ambassador adores her. It sounds like nothing can put him off. And honestly ...' Fern leaned in. 'I'm happy if Wallis finds someone who makes her smile. But of course, we must encourage her to be more discreet.'

'Yes, of course,' nodded Pamela. 'Absolutely.'

VI

Later that day, Pamela left a note for Captain Macaulay in the dead drop in the post box behind the Odéon. The next day, she received a reply instructing her to meet him the following morning in the Bois de Vincennes.

The two of them walked around the Bois as the cold February sun broke through the forest and dappled the ground.

'And this affair has been going on for the last two years?'

'That's what Fern Bedaux claims.'

'Does that mean Charles Bedaux knows too?'

'I'm not sure.'

'He must, if his wife knows all about it.'

'Wives don't always tell their husbands everything.' Pamela paused. 'But he might.'

Macaulay stopped and leaned against a chestnut tree. 'That's the problem with infidelity — it's fodder for blackmail. If someone like Bedaux had the ability to blackmail the American Ambassador to France ... God knows where that might lead and what he could use it for.'

'Fruity's right — he is a nasty sort. And a bully.'

'Did you get the impression political loyalties are genuine?'

'I don't know. He has fascist leanings, anyway.'

'Unfortunately, that describes half the continent of Europe right now,' Macaulay said with a grimace.

They both grew quiet as they heard hoofbeats approaching, and two women trotted by on a grey and a bay — out for a morning hack. Once the horses passed, they continued walking down the path.

'Speaking of blackmail ...' Pamela continued.

'Yes?'

'There's a rumour that Elsa Schiaparelli spies on her clients. That all her staff are trained to eavesdrop and pass along information. And the Duchess and Ambassador Bullitt have been meeting at Schiaparelli's.'

Macaulay stopped, leaned on his walking stick and closed his eyes for a moment, looking pained. 'So, what you're telling me is that not only is the Duchess having an affair with the American Ambassador, but the place where they meet is owned by a woman who gathers intelligence about her wealthy and powerful clients?'

Pamela nodded. A cloud passed in front of the sun, cloaking that part of the Bois in shade. The wind picked up and she drew her coat around her.

The captain swung his stick as if it was a cricket bat, looking pensive. 'Could you find a way to put a stop to it?'

'As in, convince the Duchess to stop seeing the ambassador?'

Macaulay nodded.

'She doesn't know that I know. As far as I'm aware, she thinks it's her little secret.'

'And if she took you into her confidences?'

'She confesses to me and then I tell her to stop seeing him?'

'You could give her some friendly advice.'

'Wallis doesn't like advice.'

'Then you could gently remind her of the scandal that will ensue if they get caught. And that all the blame would be on her side.'

'It usually *is* for women,' Pamela retorted, somewhat more sharply than she'd intended. She tried to soften her tone. 'Captain, Wallis has been through this twice already. I rather think she knows all of that.'

'Then what on earth is she doing?'

'I suppose, behaving in the disordered, unpredictable ways in which humans do. I'll see what I can manage, but I can't alienate her just as she is beginning to trust me. I'd risk falling out of her favour after building up all this goodwill.'

'Point taken.' He sighed. 'Let's do what we can to make sure that the Duke doesn't find out about this. It would be a disaster if he discovered that the woman for whom he gave up the throne was unfaithful. There's no telling what could happen. The last thing the Royal Family needs is another scandal.'

A policy of containment. Pamela had no idea how to ensure such a thing. She thought her mission would consist of reporting on the Windsors' idle, undiplomatic chatter. Now it involved the added complexity of keeping a woman who had already left two previous husbands from jeopardising her marriage to the third. How many other difficult — if not impossible — things would MI6 ask her to do?

March 1939

I

As glamorous as espionage might have sounded to those on the outside, the reality was far more tedious. It demanded not only secrecy but also discipline, attention to detail, and a high tolerance for boredom. Although Pamela spent part of her time joining Wallis for dinners and shopping excursions, as well as maintaining the façade of her Board of Trade role, the rest was spent staking out Boulevard Suchet, the Duke's golf course, and the shops and restaurants the couple frequented. And then watching and waiting, sometimes for hours. In addition to that, Pamela had to remember that she could be under surveillance at any time. She made sure to change her appearance and her routes to and from places, as well as to keep a lookout for anyone who might be following her.

After a month of tailing them around Paris, the thing that was beginning to concern Pamela was the Windsors' general dissatisfaction which was plain for all to see. She had hoped that the grumbling she'd heard from them the previous month would soon ebb away, or at least become more muted as springtime in Paris started to bloom and the sun emerged. Pamela was starting to worry that theirs wasn't a winter of discontent but rather an eternity. They remained obsessed with how the King and Queen had treated them and the Duke, in particular, was fixated on continuing to seem important in the eyes of the public. This, combined with his running political commentary about the state of European politics, seemed particularly worrisome. Chamberlain had announced in the Commons the month before that any German attack on France would be considered an attack on Britain. It was one thing for the Duke to talk about Nazi policies admiringly in private; it was another to do so in public, in front of diplomats and French government officials, especially at such a tense and difficult moment.

Wallis continued to hint at the possibility of an interview with Pamela for *Vogue* and Pamela fobbed her off with some excuse or other. MI6 and the Palace didn't want Wallis to have a platform for her ideas and political opinions. She had thought her hunger for publicity would finally be satisfied when *The Tatler* put her on their cover. But then one day, Fruity warned Pamela that he'd heard Wallis giving an interview to a reporter from *Life* magazine. He'd overheard her say things like, 'There were so many lies told at the time.' And: 'It is utterly untrue that the Duke didn't want the throne. Do you think he would have given it up after he'd worked so hard?'

Macaulay told Pamela that the Palace wanted the story killed. They couldn't have something so controversial and inflammatory going to press. They couldn't have the public thinking that she and the Duke were planning to stage some sort of comeback.

'Perhaps with your connections in the press, through *Vogue* or Condé Nast, you could have something arranged,' he suggested.

First, convince Wallis to end the affair with Ambassador Bullitt. Now kill the story being written for one of the most high-profile magazines in the United States. Pamela appreciated being thought of as capable, but she wasn't a magician. She couldn't picture going to de Brunhoff or Penrose with a strange request to help suppress a story in another publication.

Her mind whirred. *Focus*, she told herself. *What other connections do you have in the press?*

Sid.

While it seemed possible that he might know someone useful, Pamela felt ambivalent about asking him for help. She had been trying to keep Sid at arm's length; it wouldn't do to become distracted from her mission by indulging in a flirtation. But Sid had persisted in ringing her up and asking her to go for a walk or to the cinema or to dinner and it was hard to resist a handsome man who was excellent company and made her laugh. The truth was that Pamela was starting to feel a particular kind of loneliness that she had come to associate with espionage, with keeping secrets and maintaining a façade. She worried that if she continued to see Sid, this persistent feeling might lead her to commit another indiscretion, another lapse in judgement, like she had with Charlie.

Pamela would simply have to steel her resolve and focus on the task at hand. Sid seemed to know every journalist in the city, and besides, if he'd survived the trenches in Spain unscathed, he must be clever and resourceful.

II

A couple of days later, on a rainy Thursday afternoon, Pamela and Sid found themselves sitting on the banquette in the middle of one of the Louvre's famed Salles Rouges — the red-walled galleries that displayed the largest paintings in the museum.

'What's your maiden name?'

'Plumbly.'

'Pamela Plumbly, huh?'

'Don't laugh! I always hated the alliteration.'

'What were you like before you got married?'

'Oh, I don't know. Wilful, perhaps. I wasn't very good at doing what I was told.'

'My kind of girl.'

'I actually lived here for a bit, to be "finished".'

'Like when you glaze a pot or something?'

'Yes, something like that. But my finishing school was running around the city with my friends, staying out until all hours, drinking cocktails and going dancing. Not the kind of finishing my mother was hoping for.'

'Sounds like a pretty good education to me.'

Pamela had always been merciless about men's appearances, condemning someone for a poorly cut suit or a misjudged haircut, which she felt was only fair, given the high standards to which men held women. For instance, she once admonished Francis for buying what she had deemed an unflattering pair of shoes. But Sid had a smile so charming that it made his generally shaggy dog appearance — threadbare wool coat, fedora that looked as if it had been in a fight, five o'clock shadow — part of his appeal and the reason why, despite everything, Pamela found him so easy to be around.

'Maybe that's what *his* problem was.' Sid pointed at the massive painting by Jacques-Louis David of Napoleon's coronation. 'Talk about wilful tendencies.'

It was as good an excuse as any to turn the conversation.

'Speaking of coronations …'

'I don't know about your social circles but that's a change of topic I don't hear often.'

Pamela looked around. Fortunately, it was the end of the day, and the galleries were beginning to empty out. She realised that although she and Sid were developing a friendship of sorts, she didn't know him that well. And she suddenly felt uneasy, wondering if she was about to breach a newly formed, delicate sense of trust.

Pamela took a deep breath. 'Could I ask you for a favour? I need to kill a story. About the Duchess of Windsor.'

He gave a low whistle and glanced down at the hat in his hands. 'OK …'

'She did an interview for *Life* magazine and has said some rather indelicate things.'

'Well, you know what we Americans are like. Indelicate is our *raison d'être*.'

'She told the reporter that the Duke hadn't abdicated voluntarily. That he'd been forced off the throne.'

Sid raised an eyebrow.

Pamela had rehearsed her reasons for wanting to stop the publication of the story, once again following Macaulay's advice to mix lies with the truth.

'Working for the Board of Trade, I hear quite a bit of Westminster gossip. The government is nervous about things like this. Stirring up rumours and people's emotions about the Abdication all over again.'

'I can imagine, what with the kinds of things those two say in public about Hitler and Mussolini being just swell. And we all remember their little vacation to Germany. Though even if the hoi polloi of merry England think they're treyf—'

'Treyf … ?'

'In Yiddish, it means something that isn't kosher. Not allowed. But your average, ordinary American schmuck — you know what "schmuck" means, right?'

'I can guess.'

'—*loves* the Windsors. Well-dressed, jet-setting couple. Love conquering all. A girl from Baltimore winning over a king. Etcetera. They see them as celebrities, like Carole Lombard and Clark Gable or something.'

Pamela thought about the piles of fan mail that the Windsors received every week.

She had considered presenting the excuse that Wallis was a friend and that she was just trying to protect her from the ramifications of such a story coming out. But why would a Jewish journalist help protect a woman with fascist sympathies? And what might he think of Pamela for excusing them?

As if reading her mind, Sid asked, 'Say, isn't she your friend or something?'

Pamela glanced back at David's depiction of Napoleon crowning the Empress Joséphine. When Wallis first began her affair with Edward, she probably had a similar image in her mind.

'Well, *friend* is rather a strong word. We know each other socially and I suppose you could say I'm obliged to spend time in her and the Duke's company, for social reasons. But I wouldn't say she and I see eye to eye on politics.'

Truth and lies.

'And I bet those gossips in Westminster aren't too happy with her

104

right now, spouting off about how great the Nazi Party is.'

'Quite. It's making people nervous. Rather bad for trade with the French, you see,' Pamela added in a moment of inspiration.

'Not to mention diplomacy,' replied Sid with a melancholy half-smile. 'I guess if your prime minister is going to convince the French that his country is willing to leap to its defence, you can't have Carol Lombard getting too much airtime.'

'Yes, exactly.'

'Didn't know you were such a politico,' he teased her.

'Excuse me … I'm an envoy for the British Trade Board, don't forget. I'm not just a pretty face,' she replied playfully.

Sid held Pamela's gaze. 'No, you're not. And that's what I like about you.'

Pamela hadn't meant to back Sid into a corner using her 'feminine wiles' as some would call it. But she had. Or maybe he had charmed her with his masculine ones. At this point, it was impossible to tell.

Sid looked around the gallery for a moment, thinking. Then said, 'I'll see what I can do.'

Pamela felt a wave of relief course through her body.

'Thank you, thank you, thank you,' she murmured. 'I can't tell you how much I appreciate this.'

'Shouldn't be impossible. Stuff gets censored all the time.' Sid sighed. 'Either the country you're reporting from won't let you send it back to your editor, or the paper doesn't think it should be printed. And all you can do is observe and write stories. Interview people. But you're a bystander. To terrible things. The worst things. You're powerless to actually do anything, to save anyone.'

'But Sid, no one's *expecting* you to save anyone. You're a journalist,' Pamela protested.

'Well, that's where you're wrong. People hear you speaking English and they're so desperate that they beg you to help them get a visa to get the hell out. To France or England or America — wherever.' Sid looked angry. 'And how do you tell some Czech Socialist Party leader from the Sudetenland or a Jewish professor who's already done time in Dachau that you can't help them? How do you tell a woman in Barcelona who's taken off her wedding ring and dolled herself up like a streetwalker …'

He stopped himself. He was twisting the brim of his hat in his hands.

'… because she's desperate enough to try anything to get her family out of the country?' finished Pamela.

'Refugees are flooding into France. Franco is about to declare victory. Spain has been crawling with journalists from all over the world for the last two and a half years and what good has it done? Sometimes I think everyone is a hack and all hacks are wide-eyed idealists from *The Daily Worker*. Or thrill-seekers. Or cynical dipsomaniacs.'

'You're none of those things, Sid.'

'Sometimes I think I'm a little of all three,' he confessed.

'You're doing the best you can. And that's more than most people. Even the diplomats can't seem to be able to do anything right now. Besides,' — Pamela smiled — 'how can you be an alcoholic when you drink far less than most people I know?'

'Because most people you know are Brits and most Brits are alcoholics?'

Sid laughed and she gave him a playful shove. He grabbed her hand. If Pamela didn't know any better, if they'd been two other people in different circumstances, she thought they might have kissed in that moment.

But then Sid said, 'Pam, I'm leaving for Poland next week. Try to see what it's like in Czechoslovakia now that Hitler's made another land grab and sent troops into Prague. If they'll even let us over the border. Krauts aren't too wild about journalists.'

Pamela felt her heart leap. She didn't want him to go. She could tell herself that it was because he was a useful asset to her, but she knew that she just didn't want him to leave her. And she didn't want to have to worry about him on some potentially treacherous assignment.

'When are you back in Paris?' she asked, trying to sound casual.

He shrugged. 'Who knows?'

Sid and Pamela sat in silence, looking at the painting of Napoleon's coronation.

'What happened to British chutzpah? Audacity. To stand up to guys like that. Where's Lord Wellington when you need him?'

And to that, Pamela had no reply.

III

A few days later, Pamela came home from a shopping excursion with Wallis to a letter from Charlotte. She and her sister hadn't lived in the same country since Charlotte and Peter moved to Rome five years before, so the distance between the two of them was nothing new. When Pamela was in London, they maintained a habit of writing to each other every couple of weeks, but since she moved to Paris, Charlotte had been writing to Pamela more regularly, mostly asking about French fashion and Parisian society gossip.

At first it seemed much the same as any other letter her sister would send.

Hope you're getting as much beautiful springtime weather as we are in Rome — though I know Paris is often quite rainy this time of year.

Can you believe Mummy is still in a state that you've run off? All her friends seem to think 'Paris' is some kind of euphemism and your marriage is on the rocks.

The Lanvin collection you described in your last letter sounded absolutely delicious. Did you buy anything?

Peter is thinking of taking a house in the Tuscan countryside. I think it's a bit far from Rome, but he wants to be near his vineyard. Besides, it's far too big. And who would have to decorate it? Me, of course.

But there was something unusual towards the end.

He's been meeting with this American businessman who wants him to start another company in order to sell aeroplanes or something like that. You know Peter, he's usually so take-charge with people, but he seems awfully impressed with this man. I don't like him, personally. Seems a bit of a disreputable Johnny-come-lately. I'm going to ask my clairvoyant what to do.

Charlotte had always been superstitious; she had brought in two priests and a medium when she thought their Roman palazzo was haunted. But it was strange for her to even take an interest in Peter's business dealings. Charlotte hardly batted an eye when he'd set up a munitions factory in Abyssinia after Mussolini invaded. And Pamela couldn't understand why Peter was even considering setting up another company when he seemed to be making more than a healthy profit with the one he already had. Then again, Pamela had always thought Peter was greedy. He was probably just looking for ways to 'maximise his profits', as he would say.

June 1939

I

Pamela spent the spring and summer dutifully carrying on with her work. It was strange how used to her Paris life she had become. She attended events on behalf of the Board of Trade, meeting department store owners, designers and businesspeople, discussing the merits of British wool and the British need for French silk. What had begun as a cover was feeling almost like a real job and surprisingly satisfying. Macaulay and Donald had been right — she was a natural at it. In between, she filed articles for *Vogue* on French fashions, which turned out to be a hit with British readers. The fantastical, imaginative designs she had seen at Schiaparelli were becoming more and more of a trend and British women were enjoying the escapist romanticism of French designers — clothing that took inspiration from Spanish bullfighters, Russian peasants, Ancient Greece, the zodiac.

Lettice took Pamela to parties, jazz clubs and gallery openings, which made her feel like they were eighteen again. She met a series of eccentric people through Mikhail's circles, including his dealer

Georges, with whom he seemed to be close. It was as if she were rediscovering her old self, before she was married and relegated to stuffy dinner parties where MPs and other members of the ruling class spoke over her, explained things to her or ignored her altogether. It was a strange, alternative life she'd found for herself — not quite real but (apart from having to spend time with Wallis) all the more enjoyable for its surreality.

Sid was in and out of Paris, coming and going from his travels around Europe. But he never failed to send a postcard from each new place — funny and affectionate, with little doodles. He would call her at the last minute and say he was in town for two or three nights. Even if she had been busy earlier in the evening, she would meet him for a late supper or a nightcap. Sid once asked if he could kiss her but Pamela said no. He never asked again — even though she secretly wanted him to. In a way, Pamela was grateful that Sid wasn't in Paris more often and that her time was taken up with so many things. She didn't like to think what might happen if she was more idle and he more available.

Pamela felt like she was caught in a kind of limbo. As strange as it was being away from Francis in the beginning, Pamela had grown accustomed to it. Perhaps disconcertingly so. She tried to keep up with his letters but was aware that she sent fewer than he did. She did miss him sometimes, especially when the Windsors or one of their entourage said something ridiculous. And maybe she would have had more incentive to write to him more often if she could have been candid; but, due to the secrecy of her mission, she could hardly tell him anything about what was actually happening. Ultimately, the longer they were apart, the more disconnected she felt from Francis.

Pamela continued to monitor the lives of the Windsors, accepting invitations to anything Wallis invited her to. Or rather, the Windsor secretary Miss Blythewood invited her to, on her behalf. As the Duchess didn't have many real friends, Pamela was now in the routine of seeing her at least twice a week. And from what she could conclude from her stakeouts of Schiaparelli's, Wallis seemed to be continuing her liaisons with Ambassador Bullitt. The Duke had made a controversial broadcast for NBC from the battlefield of Verdun, calling on world powers to bring about a peace agreement, which, although the BBC had refused to air it, had further irked the Palace. And the Windsors had been delighted to be the guests of honour at a party at the German Embassy earlier in the month. There was nothing the Palace, MI6, the government, Fruity or Pamela could do to stop them, so they decided they might as well let them satiate their desire to be treated like royalty.

One evening towards the end of June, Fruity, Pamela, the Windsors and some of their friends went to celebrate the Duke's birthday at the restaurant in the Eiffel Tower. They were in the middle of the second course when a table of people across the room screamed in horror and a woman fainted. They had seen a man fall past their window. At first, everyone assumed it had been a suicide. But when the body was identified as a Czechoslovak government official, there were murmurs that it had been an assassination.

'Who would want to assassinate a Czechoslovak diplomat?' the Duke asked nervously.

Probably the same people who were occupying Czechoslovakia, Pamela nearly replied.

He tried to be nonchalant about the incident, but she could tell that even the Duke of Windsor — a man whose charmed life of golf and cocktails was largely unaffected by global politics — was unnerved. Pamela thought the incident might make him think twice about political meddling

II

The day following the incident on the Duke's birthday, Pamela received a letter from Francis that took her by surprise, asking if he might visit her in Paris for a week or two. It was exciting to live such a different, untethered life, but Pamela knew it would end and when it eventually did, returning to London would be strange after having been gone for so long. They hadn't seen each other in nearly six months and spending time with Francis might lend a semblance of normalcy to her life. Besides, he had always been a reassuring presence, and it would be a great relief to finally have someone other than Macaulay and Fruity to talk to about her mission. On the other hand, Pamela felt apprehensive about what it would be like when they saw each other again. This was by far the longest time they'd ever been apart and while their letters had been cordial, the way they had left things before Pamela boarded her train for the ferry at Dover had been uneasy.

And then, of course, there was the issue of the growing affection between her and Sid, which would likely continue to grow if Pamela didn't see Francis soon and be reminded that she was married. In some ways, it was a relief to be brought back down to earth and into the realm of good judgement before she got too carried away. And fortunately, Sid would be travelling around the Soviet Union with a group of journalists from the West for the next month, so there wouldn't be any danger of running into him while Francis was visiting.

At their next rendezvous, Pamela asked Macaulay for clearance for Francis to visit her. He looked so surprised that she thought he'd forgotten she was married.

'Ah, Lord Francis … yes …' He pondered this for a moment. 'Batting for the opposite team, isn't he? One of MI5's chaps.'

'Oh.' She paused. 'Yes. He is.'

'Rather convenient your husband is also an intelligence agent. Otherwise, I would have had to say no.'

Pamela wondered how long MI6 was able to hang on to their agents if they expected them to go without seeing their spouses after months in the field.

She met Francis at the station and as soon as she saw the smile on his face, felt a deep sense of relief knowing that he wasn't harbouring any resentments and was simply happy to see her.

He laughed when she showed him her flat. 'You've been living *here* all this time? MI6 must be on a tighter budget than I thought.'

But he was quieter than usual, distracted. When he suggested they go to Maxim's for dinner, he seemed to have purpose in his voice. And there was something about the way he said, 'We could use some time to talk,' that made Pamela uneasy. It suddenly occurred to her that perhaps it wasn't that Francis had missed her, but rather that he wanted a separation. Or a divorce. After all, what was stopping him from falling in love with someone else in all that time they'd been apart?

Francis had never been exciting. He could be stubborn and set in his ways; he liked quiet nights and going to bed early. But the thought of not having him around, even at a distance, was alarming. Had she been taking him for granted? Pamela thought about how many tepid, distracted letters she'd sent him, days if not weeks after he had written to her. How she had been relieved to go to Paris and leave him behind. About her affair with Charlie and her feelings for Sid. Pamela felt terribly guilty. She wouldn't blame Francis if he had met someone else and decided to leave her. If he had treated her the way she had treated him, she would have done the same thing.

In the taxi on the way to Maxim's, she felt almost sick with anxiety. Her mind reeled. She knew that even if they decided to divorce, Francis wouldn't put Pamela through the kind of humiliation that Lettice had endured at the hands of Ashley. He would do what most other, decent men did and arrange to be discovered by a private detective in a hotel with a tart. But even then, Pamela might not necessarily be much better off than Lettice. Women did get divorced, but one would need to have a very high social standing and nerves of steel to endure the resulting gossip and possible censure from society, not to mention their families. Pamela didn't even want to think about how her parents would react — not to mention Charlotte and Peter.

They had just sat down at their table when he said, 'Darling, are you alright? You look awfully peaky.'

'Yes, absolutely fine. Just a bit tired, is all.'

Pamela forced a smile, finding herself slipping into their usual routine of masking her feelings.

'Well, first things first,' he said as he reached a hand into the pocket of his dinner jacket. He pulled out a small, velvet box and laid it on the table. 'I feel sorry I missed your birthday. Better late than never though, eh?'

She looked at Francis in surprise. Her birthday? That's what all this was about?

'But my birthday was in May ... and it isn't your fault we couldn't spend it together.'

No, it's yours, said a voice in her head. She'd been the one to run off to Paris and had then done a terrible job of keeping in touch with him, of asking him how things were in London, how he was doing. And there he was, telling her he felt guilty that he'd missed her birthday.

115

She opened the box to find a beautiful pair of diamond clip earrings from Chaumet — one of the oldest jewellers in Paris — that looked a bit like a pair of geometric wings.

'Oh, Francis,' Pamela gasped.

'I know you're very particular about what you wear, so if you don't like them, we can go back to the shop and you can pick out something else.'

'No, no, they're absolutely beautiful. I love them.'

'And I wanted to say that I know I haven't been at my best this past year or so. I don't want you to think I'm making any excuses. But I've realised that I've been finding all this talk of war … Even just the *thought* of facing another one … I must admit, I was hurt at first by your decision to come here. But eventually, I realised that you might have been looking for a respite. An escape. I can't imagine I've been easy to live with.' They made eye contact over the candlelight. 'I know you've made certain compromises, marrying a man a decade your senior. Who lived a whole life before you met him.'

Alma had told Pamela that she was lucky to have the chance of an engagement to a Peer. Even if he was ten years older than her and had been engaged once before. After all, there had been rumours about her engagement to Bunny and how it had ended and, at twenty-four, she was considered long in the tooth in terms of the marriage market, so she couldn't be too particular. Pamela often speculated what her mother would have done if she'd found out about the abortion she'd had at eighteen, after Bunny had got her pregnant.

'I hadn't exactly been born into the world anew when you met me.'

'Yes, and that's what I admired about you. You weren't like all the other young ladies that people kept trying to introduce me to. I didn't think I'd ever be engaged again until I met you. You were so beautiful and funny and charming and interesting. And you've been patient with me whenever I've had an episode.' He paused. 'I can't imagine any youthful dreams of matrimonial bliss involved marrying a man who'd gone completely gaga in the trenches and then had to spend three years committed to a sanatorium …'

Pamela reached for Francis's hand across the table. Early on in their marriage, he told her that he didn't want to disturb her by talking about the gruesome reality of the Western Front. Her brother William had died at Amiens and Francis didn't want to remind her of that. And he didn't want to be seen as weak or complaining or ungrateful, because not only had he survived the war, but he was physically intact — he still had all his limbs, his lungs weren't damaged from gas, he hadn't been blinded or disfigured like so many men one often passed in the street. Pamela had protested and told him that she wanted to know, but he refused. She eventually realised it wasn't her Francis was protecting with his silence, but rather himself. How lonely it must be for him to be constantly visited by memories from the war, by nightmares that he couldn't share with anyone. She doubted there truly was a cure for shell shock and that it was something a person simply had to live with.

'I'm sorry I've been so rubbish at keeping in touch, Francis.' Pamela reached across the table for his hand. 'I know I need to make more of an effort than I have, really. It's been a strange time.'

'Yes, I can imagine.' He lowered his voice to a murmur, 'They're difficult people you're looking after, especially considering the circumstances. I'm sorry I doubted you, that I thought that this … assignment wasn't important.'

Pamela's relief that Francis wasn't planning their divorce, that he was forgiving about her failings as a wife and recognised the difficulty of her mission quickly gave way to a sense of guilt. She considered if she should come clean about her doubts about their marriage, and even her relationship with Sid.

Look how kind he's being, how open and generous. Are you really going to tell him all your little secrets now? said the voice. *Best to be grateful for what you have and not make a mess.*

July 1939

It was unseasonably chilly for early July with a chill in the air and gloomy skies — probably much too cold for the elephants shambling through Elsie de Wolfe's garden. All three refused to be ridden and looked balefully around at the jugglers, fire-eaters and acrobats spread out across the grounds of Villa Trianon, previously owned by Louis XV. Pamela was no stranger to elegant parties, but the extravagance of the circus-themed ball was beyond anything even she had ever seen. Enormous striped tents had been pitched around the property and a makeshift ring had been set up in the middle of the lawn, where the horses were performing. She knew it would be one of the most prominent social events of the season, with a glittering array of international socialites and diplomats — including the Windsors — so offered to cover it for *Vogue*. It would be useful to see the couple at such an occasion — who they spoke to, who spoke to them, who avoided them, what people were saying. And it wouldn't hurt to be seen in public with Francis after so many months of going to events by herself — to maintain her cover, as well as keep people from speculating about the state of her marriage.

A sea of fur wraps, tailcoats and diamonds filled the grounds of the estate, where guests chatted, smoked, drank and watched the festivities. One could hardly move for the enormous flower arrangements, champagne-carrying footmen or women wearing breathtakingly expensive necklaces. The ball marked the end of the Paris social season before the smart set headed off to Biarritz, Monaco or Cap d'Antibes.

Elsie's guest list was one of the most impressive and starriest of any ball in France: aristocrats, Hollywood stars, millionaires, politicians and diplomats. And there was also a significant presence from the couture industry: Jeanne Lanvin, Maggy Rouff, Lucien Lelong, Elsa Schiaparelli, Cristóbal Balenciaga, Coco Chanel.

'I didn't know circuses were *de rigueur* these days ...' Francis quipped. 'The French certainly know how to overdo it, don't they?'

'Elsie's American, actually. And her husband is British.'

Elsie wore a Cartier aquamarine and diamond tiara and had dyed her white hair a pale blue to match the gemstones. A successful American interior designer and former Broadway actress, she was in a *marriage blanc* to Sir Charles Mendl, the press attaché at the British Embassy. He had married her for her money and she for his title; she was rumoured to spend most of her time with her female companion — not unheard of in society marriages.

'I still blame the French,' retorted Francis, with a raised eyebrow as he watched a parade of trained dogs and ponies trot by them. 'I suppose this is what happens when one buys a house next to the Palace of Versailles.'

'It's been rather a decadent summer. All the couturiers are working overtime to meet the demand for new gowns for all these balls.'

'Are the gowns wildly extravagant too?'

'The latest trend has been a throwback to the eighteenth century — corseted waists, full skirts, embroidery, things like that. For the past few seasons, French designers have been turning to dresses from earlier historical periods for inspiration. And I suppose it makes a kind of sense. A retreat from the complexities and confusion of the twentieth century.'

Underneath the summer's feverish gaiety ran an undercurrent of paranoia. Rumours across Paris abounded regarding sightings of spies and German officers, clandestine diplomatic meetings, political slights and new allegiances. France seemed to be taking in more refugees by the day. People had been streaming over the border from Spain since the beginning of the year and southern coastal towns were filled with German and Austrian political dissidents, artists and Jews. There was a great deal of excitement over the Festival International du Film, which would have its first outing in Cannes at the end of August. The French had decided to start their own festival, as they had been furious with the judges at Venice for bowing to fascist pressure and awarding the grand prize to a film produced by Il Duce's son and to *Olympia*, a documentary produced by the Nazi Ministry of Propaganda.

Elsie had joked that instead of RSVP, she should have marked the invitations 'INW' (If No War).

'Ah,' said Francis. 'There's Marie Antoinette …'

Wallis was circulating around the garden with the Duke, wearing what Pamela recognised as a Lanvin silk gown in midnight blue, in the eighteenth-century style she'd only just described. As soon as she spotted Pamela, she waved. As Wallis wove through the other guests, past the waiters and the clowns and the strong men, the Duke trailed along behind her.

'Is it just me or does he look smaller now? Perhaps he's shrunk in stature as well as rank,' Francis whispered.

'Pamela!' said Wallis. 'What a pleasant surprise.'

'I'm here to cover Elsie's ball for *Vogue*. Have you met my husband, Francis?'

Francis bowed to the Windsors. It was a comfort to have him by her side for once, a reprieve from having to go to every dinner and party on her own. The two couples spoke briefly before the Windsors flitted off again to speak to Princess Karam of Kapurthala, who was recently touted as one of the most beautiful women in the world and the evening's guest of honour. The elegant Indian woman sported a Paquin gown and a dazzling diamond and ruby necklace (on which her husband had spent a fortune at Van Cleef).

Pamela took a bemused Francis around the party, where he looked on while she made notes in the small notebook she kept in her handbag for her article for *Vogue*. It gave her a useful cover while she monitored the Duke and Duchess out of the corner of her eye. Having Francis by her side was also useful, as he was able to act as a second pair of eyes for her.

As Pamela was admiring Coco Chanel's Spanish-style, ruffled lace gown, Francis put a hand on her shoulder, leaned in and whispered, 'The Duke has just interrupted a conversation between the German ambassador and the French foreign minister …'

Pamela got her cigarette case out of her handbag and opened it up. The inside of the lid was mirrored and allowed her to watch the trio without having to turn around. (A trick Charlie had taught her.) She held it up subtly, pretending to briefly check her lipstick. Francis glanced into the reflection at the three men.

France and Germany had been at daggers drawn for months over Danzig, and before that, Czechoslovakia. President Daladier was furious that the Germans bribed *Le Figaro* to print pro-Nazi propaganda, and Ribbentrop was furious that the French expelled the German diplomat who had bribed them. Ribbentrop ordered Ambassador von Welczeck to meet with Daladier to find a peaceful solution to the problem, but Daladier refused to see him.

'I was under the impression that no one was speaking to the German ambassador,' said Pamela quietly. 'Perhaps the fact that they're speaking is a good sign.'

'Trying to arrange a peace agreement with Hitler once he's taken Czechoslovakia and Danzig is like trying to satisfy a shark with a tin of cat food,' Francis muttered.

Pamela took one last glance into the mirror and saw that the Duke was laughing with von Welczeck. Bonnet, the French foreign minister, was standing apart from them and frowning.

Suddenly, the crowd was gasping and applauding. It was like a scene from a film: cued by a top-hatted ringmaster in the circus ring, a team of white Lipizzaner horses in jewelled harnesses reared up in perfect syncopation, the feathers in their bridles gently blowing in the breeze. Pamela tried to look back at the three men but people were moving towards the circus ring and she could no longer see them through the crowd.

'There's a Roman adage about bread and circuses distracting the people from politics,' said Francis as he took a cigarette out of the case.

Pamela took one as well and Francis lit it for her.

'Or, in this case, circuses and champagne.' Pamela frowned. 'I just wish I could have heard what they were saying.'

August 1939

Pamela had been sick as a dog for the last two days and was forced to stay in her room at La Croë — the Windsors' chateau in the south of France — while the other guests enjoyed themselves by the pool. The last time she was that ill, it had been food poisoning. But she had been eating exactly what everyone else had. She thought it might be flu — though again, no one else seemed to have it. And then there was a third possibility: poison. After all, that was exactly what had happened to her predecessor. Could it be that there was an enemy agent at La Croë and they were targeting Pamela?

The first morning she had woken up not feeling like death, she walked down to the sea to clear her head. It was the end of August, which meant she'd now been in Paris for nearly nine months, far longer than she'd imagined. Macaulay was concerned about the report of the Duke speaking to the German ambassador and the French foreign minister, but he knew it wasn't enough to go on, especially if they didn't know what had been said. Ultimately, MI6 didn't feel that anything had escalated enough over the past year to justify keeping Pamela in France.

In some ways, she was relieved at the thought of no longer having to be Wallis's keeper, worrying about who she was seeing or what she was saying. And she had spent a pleasant and surprisingly romantic two weeks with Francis; the change in setting and the feeling of forming a united front against the Windsors gave her a renewed sense of being in a marriage with Francis. But she couldn't help thinking what it would be like when she returned home. Whether that quality would endure or soon wear off, leaving things to return to normal. And worse, if her malaise from the previous autumn might resurface once the mission was finished.

Looking out over the turquoise waters of the Mediterranean, brilliant with the reflected sunshine, Pamela felt a sense of sadness as soon as she found herself thinking about Sid. Despite the stern talks she'd had with herself in her head, her heart leapt at the sight of one of his postcards, and she couldn't deny her excitement every time he returned to Paris. After Francis left, Sid returned from his tour of the Soviet Union and they fell back into their old pattern. Pamela tried to tell herself that she was maintaining the relationship because he might prove himself useful again as an asset, but she knew that her feelings for him had only continued to grow.

And as for the mission, Pamela knew that if she returned to London at this point, she would feel like a failure. Last time she was so successful that the intelligence she'd gathered had led to the Abdication. What had she accomplished this time? Pamela turned around to look back at La Croë, which resembled a wedding cake with its layers and ornamentation, a brilliant white under the sun's rays. She knew there was something she was missing but couldn't put her finger on what. Was she close to discovering something that the Windsors wanted kept secret? Was that why she'd been so ill for the past few days? Or was she imagining things?

Pamela thought about her childhood hero, Virginia Dalkeith, a character from a series of books written pseudonymously by Gertrude Leigh, the woman who had preceded her at MI5. Virginia would have been able to work out the truth of what was going on in the Windsors' circle by deftly piecing together a series of subtle and minute clues under the noses of everyone around her, only to reveal the culprit with a flourish at the end. Virginia was accompanied everywhere by a Scottish Terrier called Angus, who was helpful in ferreting out secrets — dragging bloody handkerchiefs out of handbags and barking at bodies hidden in closets. But Virginia was a fictional detective, not an intelligence agent, and she wasn't forced to operate in the shadows. And her creator, Gertrude Leigh, had been dead for three years.

When Pamela returned to the château and reached her door, she froze. The matchstick she habitually placed between the door and the doorjamb was lying on the ground. Someone had been in her room. When she opened the door, she found that her suitcase wasn't where she had left it and the things on her dressing table had been rearranged. Fortunately, she'd had the presence of mind to conceal her handbag, which held the recording device, under her bed. But then again, she couldn't be sure it hadn't been discovered. Pamela decided to remove the recorder from the bag and hide it in a secret compartment behind the lining of her suitcase.

The little voice in her head said, *If you're not careful, you'll end up like Gertrude Leigh.*

Pamela didn't know what to do. She thought about trying to contact Macaulay but there wasn't a secure way to reach him quickly. And Fruity was back in Paris for the week, taking care of something for the Duke and Duchess.

She heard a knock on the door. She took a deep breath and tried to compose herself before answering. It was the Windsors' secretary, Miss Blythewood. Despite the fact that it was a hot summer's day, she still dressed as if it were autumn in London in her neat little pleated skirt, cardigan and brogues.

'Lady Pamela, the Duchess wanted to inquire as to how you were feeling.'

'Better, thank you. I suspect it must have been something I ate.'

'How unpleasant! I'll have to have a word with the kitchen. The Duke and Duchess would be very displeased to hear that something from their kitchen has made you ill.'

'Oh, please don't worry.'

'You know how the Duchess likes everything to be absolutely perfect for her guests.'

Though well meaning, Miss Blythewood's insistence was exhausting. Wherever did she get the energy? Or the enthusiasm? The Windsors seemed to have her working constantly. Pamela had witnessed her taking dictation for the Duke, standing for hours at a time — he didn't like to see anyone who worked for him sitting in his presence. But there was a certain kind of person the Windsors attracted, both in their friends and staff: obsequious and sycophantic. And Miss Blythewood was particularly good at this.

Pamela went down to sit by the side of the pool and consider what to do. As the bright sun shone down on her, she dangled her feet in the water. She hoped to enjoy some peace and quiet but sighed when she spotted someone coming down the lawn to the pool, carrying a drink and a towel, wearing a pair of swimming trunks and a loose, short-sleeved shirt. Much to her surprise, it was Noël Coward. He must have arrived while she had been laid up in bed.

'How nice to see a friendly face, Lady Pamela,' he said as he kissed her on the cheek. He sat down on a sun lounger near her. He then removed his sunglasses and craned his neck to look towards the other weekend guests, who were talking and sitting in the sun on the lawn, further away. He scanned the immediate area around them and then lowered his voice. 'Or should I say … Show Boat?'

Pamela looked at him sharply. 'What?'

'Vortex', he replied in a mock-serious fashion, putting one hand on his chest. 'With names like these, I imagine Captain Macaulay must be a great fan of the theatre. Though being named after one of my own plays seems a bit much. I've been hoping to get a moment alone with you so we could talk and you could catch me up on …' He waved his hand towards the house.

Noël Coward, the author of *Hay Fever* and *Cavalcade*, was working for MI6? Maybe Pamela shouldn't have been surprised. After all, Noël was part of the same anti-appeasement circle in which Francis, Donald and Duff Cooper moved; the MP Robert Boothby (a fellow Glamour Boy) was his neighbour in the Kentish countryside. Pamela had met him briefly once before, at a party at Diana and Duff Cooper's. A sociable man with a sharp wit who maintained the public image of a successful West End playwright, Noël was known for passionately discussing politics until the wee hours of the morning.

He smiled and patted the spot next to him. Pamela swung her legs out of the pool and sat down on the sun lounger. He reached for his cigarette case and offered her a cigarette. He then lit it with a gold lighter engraved with his initials. Pamela felt a sense of relief, knowing she wasn't alone at La Croë.

She exhaled a puff of smoke and said, 'Were you sent here to help me?'

'*They*' — Noël looked at Pamela meaningfully — 'have sent me all around Europe this summer on lots of long, uncomfortable train journeys. Pretending to be some sort of cultural ambassador so I can wheedle the true allegiances out of neutral countries.' He paused, his cigarette smoke curling above his head in the slight breeze coming from the sea. 'The Windsors like to invite me to their parties to keep everyone entertained. They have a habit of saying whatever they like in front of me because they think I'm a fool. Which is rich, coming from them.' Noël narrowed his eyes as he looked over his shoulder towards the Windsors, standing on the lawn. (Pamela had heard that since he was the Prince of Wales, the Duke would invite Noël over to play the piano but would then snub him in public.)

They decided to take a stroll around the garden to remove themselves even further from the rest of the guests.

'I thought we could do a little double act. Nothing more than a bit of theatre, this sort of thing,' said Noël dismissively, with a wave of his hand. 'A series of performances.'

Pamela thought of the number of times she had been forced to nod along agreeably to Wallis and Edward's inanities.

'We'll wait until they've all had too much to drink, I'll do my little song and dance routine, and you can slink around.'

'*Slink around?*'

'Yes, you've very slinky,' he said with a smile. 'Fruity has been trying his best, but I think he's on his way out. It seems Wallis has been dripping poison in her beloved's ear so one would imagine that it's only a matter of time until he's replaced.'

'Wallis does seem a bit jealous of their friendship.'

'It was a bit more than a friendship at one point.' Noël raised an eyebrow suggestively. '*Entre nous* … there's a reason why he hates me. I'm queer, and he's queer, but unlike him, I don't pretend not to be.'

Pamela was so surprised she dropped her cigarette in a rose bush. 'But he's married!'

'So was Oscar Wilde.'

'He's had affairs with women all over the world.'

'Some people like apples *and* oranges.'

'Oh …'

'I hope I haven't shocked you, Lady Pamela,' he said in a tone that indicated he didn't care if he had as he bent down to smell a bunch of lilacs.

Had Fruity and the Duke been lovers? Pamela felt very unworldly, having never considered the prospect that there were people in the world who might choose to go to bed with both women and men. She debated saying something to Macaulay. But he might already know. And if he didn't, that would be a very awkward conversation indeed.

Pamela pushed her sunglasses to the top of her head and looked at Noël. 'I've been terribly ill the last few days. And I thought it was food poisoning or some kind of flu. I started to feel better this morning, so I took a walk to the sea. When I returned to my room, I could tell someone had gone through my things.'

'Did they take anything?'

'Not that I can tell. But it makes me think … Captain Macaulay told me that my predecessor had been poisoned.'

'You think someone is … ?'

'I don't know.'

'Who do you suspect?'

'I'd be rather surprised if it were Somerset Maugham or Maurice Chevalier,' quipped Pamela, as she kicked the gravel on the garden path with her sandalled toe.

'Even more extraordinary if it were Maxine Elliott. She was the Duke's grandfather's mistress.'

'And I somehow doubt that the Secretary of State for War searched my room and poisoned me. Besides, Leslie Hore-Belisha is Jewish.'

'Probably not a fascist agent, then.'

'I overheard Beaverbrook and Rothermere calling him a "Jewish warmonger" behind his back.'

'Well, they are in Chamberlain's appeasement camp.'

'But the one person I would most suspect …'

'Is … ?' Noël lowered his sunglasses. 'Go on — don't keep me in suspense.'

'Charles Bedaux.'

'Oh yes, the greasy Frenchman with the nasal American wife …'

'But he and Fern aren't here.'

'How anticlimactic.'

'They're at their chateau in the Loire Valley.'

'Where the Windsors had their sad, decidedly non-royal wedding.'

'They've supplanted all the Duke's London friends and made themselves indispensable. And from everything I've seen and heard, Bedaux certainly seems like a bit of a Nazi sympathiser.' She paused. 'However …'

'However?'

'Hale — the butler — worked for Charles and Fern before he came to the Windsors.'

'So, you think he's some sort of plant?'

'An enemy agent hiding in plain sight. Possibly. Or maybe I'm just grasping at straws.'

'Well, if this were a play, the character of a butler would be well placed for subterfuge. He can go anywhere he wants in the house.

The other servants do what he tells them to do. And he has easy access to the food.'

Pamela and Noël spent the next few days watching Hale, trying to discern whether he was doing or saying anything out of the ordinary. Pamela noticed that he would disappear for a period of time once dinner had been served and again as soon as the after-dinner port and brandies had been handed around. One night, Noël encouraged everyone to make requests of him while he sat at the piano, playing and singing their favourite songs. Pamela moved to the back of the group and slipped out to look around the house to see where Hale had gone. Was he meeting with someone? Making a phone call? Going through guests' rooms?

Pamela started upstairs, looking in all the rooms and even poking her head into the servants' quarters. Then she crept down into the kitchen where the cook and the scullery maid were cleaning up after the dinner preparations. Fortunately, there was a window into the butler's pantry, just off the kitchen — presumably so Hale and his predecessors could keep an eye on the comings and goings of the other servants. Pamela peeked through the window to see if Hale was in there. At first, she didn't see him. But when she looked again, she realised he was lying on the floor on a blanket, doing some sort of stretching and grimacing.

Pamela was in one way relieved and in another, disappointed. She would have felt a sense of achievement if she'd discovered something, anything suspicious to pass on to Macaulay. Instead, all the intelligence she could provide on Hale was that he suffered from back pain. Maybe they were right to send her back to London. Perhaps she had discovered all that she could.

Part 2

'Is it worse to be scared than to be bored, that is the question.'

Gertrude Stein

Part 2

September 1939

I

As successful as they had been socially, the flurry of elaborate political dinners and balls held over the last few months by government officials and diplomats now seemed to be nothing but a pantomime, a performance of mediation and peacekeeping. A staving-off of the inevitable.

Pretending to be Polish soldiers, SS officers attacked German towns on the Polish border in a false flag operation, giving Germany an excuse to invade Poland in the name of national defence. It was reported that Ribbentrop, Hitler's Reichsminister of Foreign Affairs, had advised Hitler to invade because — in contrast to the advice of the other ministers — he was certain that Britain wouldn't come to Poland's defence. When he had been Ambassador to the Court of St James, the British had thought Ribbentrop an unhinged bureaucrat and had dubbed him 'Brickendrop'. It turned out that he thought as little of them as they had of him; Ribbentrop had assumed that the cowardly British, along with the cowardly French, wouldn't lift a finger to help the Polish neighbours of the Czechoslovaks they'd sold down the river.

Pamela remembered how rude he had been when she met him briefly at the German Embassy. And his affair with Wallis, which she'd witnessed herself from the shadows of a corridor. She did wonder if the Duchess had somehow maintained the connection, though that seemed doubtful, considering that every waking hour not consumed by the management of the Duke, his houses and social schedule was taken up with her ongoing affair with Ambassador Bullitt.

The news at the end of August had been fraught and everyone knew war was coming. The Windsors insisted on staying at La Croë, but their guests left before the end of the month, including Pamela and Noël. She took a train back to Paris and he, concerned about his mother, returned to England. By the 1st of September, the Germans had declared war on Poland.

Because France had been preparing for war for the last week — and perhaps because the news had been slow and scant — Paris was strangely calm. Even Gare de l'Est, where all the soldiers were gathering to be shipped to the northern garrisons, seemed orderly. Or perhaps it was a collective resignation. Another war, another march to the front to defend the border. The most panic seemed to be emanating from hotels, where frightened American tourists tried to bribe the staff to help them get away as quickly as possible.

Pamela headed straight to the post box to see if Macaulay had left a message for her. She was relieved to discover that he was ordering her to return to England, before things escalated and returning became impossible. She said her goodbyes to Lettice and Mikhail, feeling uneasy about when she might see them again. She visited the *Vogue* Paris offices and asked de Brunhoff if there was anything she could do for the magazine upon her arrival in London, but he told her not to worry. Pamela packed her suitcases, booked her train and ferry passage and managed to take care of her affairs within a few days.

Pamela and Sid managed to cross paths briefly at Gare du Nord as she was heading north to catch a ferry from Calais to Dover, while Sid was returning from covering the escalation of hostilities on the Polish border. The general chaos at the station felt like a scene from a film, with all the people rushing around, the porters and the luggage, groups of children being sent to the countryside, women holding crying babies, women tearfully bidding farewell to their husbands, sons and sweethearts. Pamela had been trying to ignore her growing sense of unhappiness at being separated from Sid, as well as her mounting worry for his wellbeing. Like all the other foreign correspondents she knew, he put the prospect of a good story ahead of his safety.

'I bet your family will be happy to see you. And relieved you're back home,' said Sid with a melancholy smile.

'Yes, I'm sure they will be.' Pamela thought of Francis. 'Are you staying in Paris?' she asked politely, feeling like a true Englishwoman of her class, masking her feelings to avoid a scene.

'A lot of us are staying; it's close to the front. And I know a few people from Chicago and New York who are coming over here to cover the war.'

'You will be careful, won't you?'

Sid looked over at a soldier whose mother was fussing over him while trying not to cry. 'Look at it this way —I'm safer with a notepad and a guy with a camera behind the front lines than in an infantry unit or on a battleship.'

'I don't suppose America will be joining the war any time soon, anyway ...'

Sid nodded resignedly. 'We have even less appetite for a European war than we did last time.'

Her train's whistle blew, and a porter came to take her luggage to the baggage car. Pamela felt her heart tighten.

'I guess this is goodbye, Lady Right Honourable.' Sid turned his battered hat round and round in his hands.

'We don't know when we'll see each other again, do we?'

Pamela threw her arms around him, embracing him tightly. They stood there for a moment and as she began to pull away, he kissed her. It was the most delicious kiss Pamela had ever experienced, as if they fitted together perfectly. Like there was something tender yet electric between them. She wished they could have stayed like that for ever and ever. But the train whistle went again and she wrenched herself away. Sid grabbed her hand and kissed it. Pamela quickly turned away and boarded her train before she could have any second thoughts. She sat down in her seat and looked out the window to get one last glimpse of him. Sid gave her a little military salute as her the train pulled out of the station.

II

The passage over the English Channel had been calm, but the ferry itself had been packed to the gills with British people frantically trying to return home and the French fleeing France. The train from Dover was also full — of civilians, as well as soldiers and various military and medical personnel. People on the ferry and the train to London anxiously swapped bits of information they'd heard about the new wartime measures Britain had taken.

Gas masks were being distributed to every man, woman and child in the country, in case of a gas attack from the air.

Hospitals were adding beds, preparing to receive thousands of casualties a day.

A machine gunner had been stationed at the top of Broadcasting House, so that the BBC would be able to continue to broadcast up to the last minute in the event of an invasion. Goebbels had been running an English-language propaganda station to demoralise the British, in preparation for their inevitable defeat.

It was strange enough returning to London after nine months away, but Pamela's return to the city was made even stranger by the war preparations. Having been a child living in a large country house during the previous war, she had never experienced London in wartime.

Ever a beacon of streetlights, traffic lights, neon advertising and thousands of buildings lit from within, Pamela could see as she got off at Victoria Station that evening that the city had become a place of grey outlines and shadows. Cars were like ghosts, gliding slowly through the darkness, their headlights casting only a glimmer through cross slits. She was startled to see that the theatre across from the station had shut and, according to the notices she'd seen posted on walls, various sporting events had been cancelled. Windows were taped up and buildings sandbagged. Although Pamela had seen the same preparations made in Paris, they somehow seemed more real — and more frightening — in her own city. She was told by one of the stationmasters that the newly imposed curfew was fast approaching and that she ought to be getting home soon.

After the quick journey from Victoria to Belgravia, as her taxi reached the white-pillared house on the square, Pamela thought of everyone she'd left behind in France — Lettice, Sid, Mikhail, de

Brunhoff and the other Frogue staff, even Madame Garrote — and hoped they would be safe.

Francis had been waiting for her when she came in and hugged her tightly. Patricia greeted her excitedly, whimpering softly as she sniffed Pamela's jacket and suitcases.

'Thank god you're alright.' Francis looked tired and drawn, as if he hadn't been sleeping.

'I hope you haven't been worrying, darling.'

He took her by the shoulders and said, 'Of course I've been worrying! I hardly heard a thing from you and of course, *they* weren't much help.'

Pamela could only imagine what it must have been like for Francis, with his wife stuck on the other side of the Channel, a war breaking out, and MI6 being typically tight-lipped. After all, he was the one who had fought in the last war and had seen at first hand the chaos that conflict could unleash. She suddenly felt a pang of guilt for not having given Francis more thought. And for letting Sid kiss her.

She squeezed his hand. 'I'm here now.'

'Have you had supper?'

'No, just some ghastly little sandwiches on the ferry.'

Francis had Cook bring up the roast she'd been keeping warm for them and they sat down to dinner.

'Flossie's been ringing the house frantically to see if you'd been able to get out of France,' he said as he poured Pamela a glass of wine. 'Also, she wants you to know that she's begun a clothing drive for refugees and would like to know if you'll pitch in.'

Pamela felt grateful for the reminder that she had a whole life waiting for her in London, including one of her best friends. People who cared about her. She looked around their dining room and realised how she'd missed their house. It was strange to think that this was her actual home and the life she'd been living had been temporary. They chatted for a little while about what had been going on in Parliament and what Chamberlain was doing. And then Francis suddenly became quiet.

'What is it, darling?'

He got up and closed the door. He then sat back down, looking grave. Pamela felt a sense of foreboding wash over her.

'Pam, I need to tell you something … They're sending me to Washington.'

She looked at him blankly, startled into silence.

'Some people in government still think that we'll simply blockade the Germans until the Reichswehr batters itself to pieces against the Maginot Line and their people are half-starved. The cabinet is forever squabbling and seemingly everyone in government is having an affair. Things aren't …'

Francis stopped himself, but his face told Pamela exactly what things weren't. *Organised. Strategic. Going well.*

'Some people reckon it would be a good idea to send a charm offensive to Washington to persuade Roosevelt to enter the war. Duff Cooper's already been shipped over. He's trying to work out how powerful the pro-German lobby there is.'

Pamela remembered what Bullitt had said about Hermann Göring telling him to consider the views of five million German-American voters.

'How long will you be there?'

'If only we knew how long the war was going to last.'

'But surely, they don't expect you to spend the entire war in America.' Pamela paused. 'Do they?'

Francis shook his head. 'I have no idea, I'm afraid. I'm to leave in the next week.'

'A week? But … I've only just returned.'

He took her hand across the table and said, 'I'm sorry, Pam. There isn't much I can do about it.'

How strange that there they were, less than a year later, and now it was Francis telling Pamela he was going off to a foreign country. The thought that she might have to spend the entire war without him struck her like a sharp blow to the head. What was she going to do? In bed that night, Pamela struggled to get to sleep, her thoughts racing. About the war, about France, about England, about Francis. U-boats in the Atlantic. A funeral for her husband. And what about Sid? Should she simply forget about him? *Could* she forget about him?

Pamela tried deep breathing to calm herself down and wished she had a sleeping pill. She felt deeply disloyal, unpatriotic even, for missing Sid. He would stay in Paris and she would be in London. Doing what, she didn't yet know. Neither Macaulay nor anyone else had yet told her so she was left in limbo. Maybe her mission was over now that the war had begun. If MI6 had decided to ground her, perhaps she could volunteer for the Red Cross. Drive an ambulance. Encourage British *Vogue* readers to do their patriotic duty for king and country. If nothing else, she could sort and fold donated clothing in church halls with Flossie Brackenberry.

III

The Windsors had been at La Croë when France declared war on Germany and Fruity had been given the task of getting them back to Paris, packed up and on a plane to England. Not being allowed on any of the royal properties, the Windsors were staying with the Metcalfes while in England. Just after Francis left for Washington the following week, Pamela received an invitation — or perhaps a desperate plea — from Fruity to come for the weekend to Little Compton Manor, an ancient pile in the Cotswolds that he and his wife Baba had bought that summer. Pamela could already sense his exasperation.

She couldn't help but be somewhat amused by the competing versions of the events surrounding the departure from France that Fruity and Wallis each gave her.

'It was terrible,' complained Wallis. 'Everyone was in a panic on the Riviera and they'd turned Cap-Ferrat into a military zone because the French thought the Italians were going to invade. Do you know, we had an entire squad of Senegalese troops moved onto the grounds of La Croë? They didn't even ask us!'

It was typical of Wallis to complain about something like the French Army setting up defences on their property to protect the country from an invasion without their permission.

'Absolute bloody nightmare,' fumed a miserable Fruity, his faint tinge of an Irish accent showing through as he complained to Pamela. 'I had to get all the servants away — eight of them, plus a secretary. They wanted to *drive* back to Paris, even though I told them it was impossible with every road in France blocked by troops. I have no idea how their minds work.'

Pamela was grateful she left La Croë when she did, before the war started; she might have been the one who Macaulay charged with wrangling that situation — something she didn't dare imagine.

Wallis: 'We wanted to drive back to Paris but Fruity insisted we take the train, even though Cannes station was chaos.'

Fruity: 'And when Walter Monckton was sent with a plane, they wouldn't go because Wallis has a fear of flying and there wasn't enough room for all their luggage.'

Wallis: 'Can you believe Fruity expected us to get on an aeroplane? I refuse to fly — those things are dangerous.'

Pamela could only imagine how nerve-racking it must have been to have Chamberlain's Director General of the Press and Censorship sent to fetch the Windsors in the middle of a war, only to have Wallis refuse to board the plane. Not to mention awkward, as Monckton once had an affair with Fruity's wife Baba. When Baba greeted Pamela on arrival, she thought about how the last time she had seen her was three years ago at a ball at Cliveden House during her last assignment, when Baba had been *in flagrante* with Oswald Mosley.

'Then they sent Lord Mountbatten to fetch us in the HMS whatever it was. Who pretended to be some great friend, even though he's *never* come to see us in France,' Wallis sniped.

'And of course, before they agreed to leave, we had to go through all the rigmarole with the Paris house and what would happen to it,' groused Fruity. 'It was as if no one told them there was a war on! People are being bombed to pieces across Europe and all they can think of is who will take care of their house in Paris? And of course, they've done nothing but complain since they've been in England.'

'The band played the short version of "God Save the King" for David when we arrived in Portsmouth Harbour,' complained Wallis bitterly. 'Then they confiscated the terriers and put them into quarantine. And *then* we were told that we wouldn't be staying in a royal property. Some way for the King of England to treat his own family.'

'Like two spoilt children. God, it makes me sick,' spat Fruity. 'But I haven't told you the worst part yet … The Duke sent a telegram to Hitler, asking him not to go to war, if you please. And he signed off as "David"! He didn't tell me until he'd already done it, for God's sake.'

Pamela wondered what the British people would think if they knew that their former king had been sending personal telegrams to a man who was now hoping to bomb them to kingdom come. A man who was sending U-boats to hunt down British naval convoys. Like the one Francis was on as he crossed the Atlantic on his way to America.

IV

After she came back from the Cotswolds, Pamela found herself killing time while waiting to hear that Francis had landed safely on the eastern seaboard of the United States, and to receive her debrief from Captain Macaulay. So, when Percy rang her up, inviting her to the basement bar at the Ritz with him and Donald, she leapt at the chance to take her mind off everything. Since everyone's servants had either been called up or had marched off to work in factories or on farms, the great London society houses had been shut up and their owners had gone to the countryside or moved into hotels. As a result, hotel bars like those at the Ritz had become even more popular than they had before the war.

'Maybe Unity fancied herself a tragic heroine in a Wagner opera,' said Pamela, sipping a martini.

'I didn't know Brünnhilde botched a suicide in front of the Reichstag,' replied Percy tartly.

'She did immolate herself on a funeral pyre for Siegfried.'

'How do you know that?'

'Francis loves German opera.'

'Personally, I quite liked Wagner before Hitler went and ruined him. High drama and high camp,' said Donald.

'Speaking of high camp,' started Percy, looking at a group of men in uniform crowded into a corner. 'With the war on, the Ritz has become as shameless as some seedy little Soho joint.'

'You're lowering the tone, Percy,' Donald said as he rolled his eyes.

'"Lowering the tone", he says. La di da.'

'We're here to toast the marvellous Lady Pamela.'

'For what? Services to the Board of Trade?'

Pamela and Donald gave each other a look.

'I'm not buying you any more whisky and sodas,' Pamela said to Percy.

'He's just jealous.'

'Of course I'm jealous! I would love to be dashing about Paris.' Percy paused. 'Though perhaps not at this very moment ...'

'We're very glad you made it home safely.' Donald patted Pamela's arm.

'And speaking of lowering the tone ... is that Nancy?' Percy was looking across the room at a slim man with dark hair and a trim little moustache in an RAF uniform. The officer glanced over and gave him a sly wave. 'I'll be right back,' he said as he finished his cocktail, straightened his black tie and got to his feet.

'Good to see the war hasn't changed him.'

'On the contrary, lots of people are finding the blackouts rather fun,' Donald replied as they watched Percy flirt with the pilot. 'Harold Nicolson and Sibyl Colefax saw the Duke at lunch yesterday, looking "grotesquely young". After a week of his complaining, I think the King was reminded of why he banished his brother to France in the first place.'

'I imagine he wishes he wasn't the first monarch to have to manage a predecessor who's still alive.'

'The Duke has been given the post of inspecting French defence lines. Something to make him feel important. Appeal to his military instincts. And get him out of everyone's hair.'

'Really?'

Pamela had been spying on the Duke because the British government was suspicious of him and now, he had been sent to spy on the French Army. Didn't anyone else find that strange?

'I suppose it won't hurt to have someone out there to see how secure the French fortifications actually are. Apparently, they've been tight-lipped and unhelpful about it.'

'Are they worried that the Maginot Line won't hold?'

'I think I probably know as much as you do. It's all been a bit of a scramble. The French were begging us to hold off declaring war because they needed more time to complete mobilisation.' Pamela remembered watching hundreds of troop vehicles lining the roads as she headed to Le Havre on a crowded train to get an even more crowded boat back to England. 'We could have crushed Germany a year ago if we'd called their bluff before they'd fully mobilised. Our mutual friend has been sending reports all summer from The Hague, warning of Hitler's intentions in the East. At great personal risk.'

Putlitz.

'He's not still there, is he?'

'He and Willy made it safely to London, thank God. They've been far luckier than most. Unlike my friend who …'

Donald suddenly looked as if the colour had drained out of his face. Pamela reached over and put her hand on his.

'Are you quite alright?'

'I've been trying to get him out of Germany for some time. He should have left years ago, but he didn't want to leave his elderly mother. And, of course, communication is impossible now. Many of our other friends have already been arrested. Everyone I knew in Berlin in the '20s — they've either fled or disappeared.'

'I'm so sorry.'

'Do you know that some people are wearing swastikas — hidden under their lapels?' Donald looked despondent. 'They want the Nazis to be able to identify them as "True Believers" when they invade. The Right Club has a list of people they want executed by the provisional Nazi government.'

Pamela felt a shiver run down her spine. The thought of people in her own country drawing up a retaliatory list for the invading Wehrmacht filled her with horror. She realised now that it was for the best that Francis and Duff had been sent to America. But what would happen to people like Donald, Percy and even Noël if the worst should come to pass? What would they do? What would she do?

Donald sighed and finished his drink. 'I'm sorry my dear, I'm being a terrible wet blanket. Another round?'

V

'What if the Boche start dropping bombs on London? What will you do then?' Alma insisted as she vigorously mixed the batter for a Victoria sponge cake she was making for the garden club meeting that afternoon.

'If my house is bombed to smithereens, then I suppose I'll have to move in with you, Father and Charlotte ...'

'But what if you're killed??'

'Well, then I suppose there won't be anything more to discuss.'

'That isn't funny, Pamela.'

Pamela drank her tea while her mother frowned disapprovingly. She squinted into the sunshine coming through the kitchen window and looked out into the garden where Alexandra and Christopher were playing with the two evacuated children Alma had taken in. (She'd complained that the little girls were riddled with lice and inappropriately dressed for the countryside.) Her visit to Gloucestershire for the weekend was the first time she'd seen her family since she went to Paris. Pamela decided to wait until she'd got a telegram from Francis, saying his ship had docked safely in New York and that he was en route to Washington. She knew that if she'd gone while she was still anxiously waiting for news, Alma would have made the situation worse by wringing her hands and being generally aggravating.

Pamela took her copy of *The Times* and her tea and retreated to the morning room, where Charlotte was painting her nails. Charlotte and Peter had moved back to England in early August when war with Germany was starting to look inevitable. After six weeks with their parents, she looked like she was going stir-crazy. Her hair was frizzy, the dark roots underneath her platinum blond were beginning to show and she had an unhinged look in her eye.

'I heard Mummy pestering you to leave London.'

'It's nothing new — she's been doing that for years. Only now she can use the war as a cudgel to beat me with.'

'She's always hated London.' Charlotte rolled her eyes and then inspected a bright red thumbnail. 'Of course, she's absolutely thrilled that I'm here, if only so that she has someone other than Daddy to boss around.'

For once, Pamela felt a bit sorry for her sister. While she and Peter looked for a house in the Home Counties, Charlotte and the children were living with Alma and Duncan. Peter had taken a flat in London, ostensibly for work; just before the war began, he had reinvented himself as a great patriot, working with the War Department to increase armaments production. Considering how enthusiastic he once was about Mussolini, Pamela assumed his motivations were financial rather than moral. And from the amount of travelling he claimed was necessary for his business, and the way he behaved around women not his wife, Pamela suspected that Peter likely had motivations other than safety from German bombs for cloistering his family in the countryside.

'It's so dreadfully dull here,' sighed Charlotte. 'Mother wants me to go riding with her and help her with the garden. And I've somehow become responsible for those evacuees from London. At least Alexandra and Christopher are going back to their schools next month. I can barely handle two, let alone *four* children.'

'I imagine the poor things are missing their parents,' Pamela said pointedly.

'Yes, I suppose ...'

Knowing how easy it was for the two of them to descend into an argument, Pamela tried a more sympathetic tone.

'I'm sure the English countryside is rather a letdown after the excitement of Rome.'

Charlotte looked uncharacteristically pensive. 'I must admit, if it had been up to me, I would have left Italy sooner.'

'Oh, really?'

'But Peter insisted it would be alright. Italy was likely to remain neutral if war came. Like Switzerland. "Then why don't we move to

Switzerland?" I asked him. After all, Peter has money in a bank in Geneva.' (Knowing the kind of wheeler-dealer Peter was, he probably had many bank accounts stashed away in various corners of the world.) 'But he can be such a bully sometimes,' Charlotte continued darkly as she focused on painting the nails on her right hand. 'He's always right. He *has* to be right. Even when I told him I didn't like that man he wanted to do business with. The one I told you about. The American. Bit of a weasel, I thought. What was his name … ? Bedaux. That was it.'

Pamela folded her paper and laid it down on the coffee table.

'Charles Bedaux?'

'Yes, that's him.'

She looked at Charlotte, feeling a growing sense of alarm. How had that man got himself involved with her brother-in-law?

'The French businessman?'

'French? I thought he had a peculiar accent. Oh, perhaps he'd only lived in America. Anyway, Bedaux wanted Peter to form some other company with him through an intermediary that would allow them to continue to sell weapons to the Italians, even if Britain put restrictions on trade.'

Pamela took a deep breath and tried to think of how to alert her sister to the kind of man Bedaux was without giving anything about her mission away.

'But I put my foot down,' finished Charlotte, looking satisfied with herself.

'You did?'

Pamela was stunned. Charlotte rarely put her foot down about anything with Peter and generally deferred to him in the belief that he knew best.

'I let Peter have his way most of the time but this Bedaux sounded fishy, so I spoke to my friend Elizabeth, whose husband works at the British Embassy. She said it was a terrible idea and told me not to let Peter go through with it. That it was illegal and if Peter got caught, he'd probably go to prison. So, I read him the riot act. Told him I would leave him if he did anything to put me and the children in any kind of jeopardy.'

Charlotte must have been screaming blue murder if she'd actually convinced Peter to back down from a business deal. Pamela felt an incredible sense of relief that her sister had persuaded him not to get involved with a nasty, scheming man with unsavoury connections like Charles Bedaux. But who else was Peter talking to?

'Anyway, how are things now that you're back and Francis is away?'

Pamela was surprised. Charlotte never asked her anything about herself. She even looked concerned.

'I'm bearing up alright.'

'Not going crackers alone, are you? No, you're probably enjoying it. Lucky thing. At this point, I'd leap at the chance to live by myself.'

'The house feels a bit big with just me in it. The servants have all been called up or left to do war work. But I'm alright,' Pamela insisted, forcing herself to sound cheerful.

Alma bustled into the morning room. 'Charlotte, I do hope you haven't spilled any of that hideous nail varnish on my rugs.' Charlotte rolled her eyes. 'Girls, the garden club ladies are coming soon, and I need you to move some furniture for me. Chop chop!'

As little desire as she had to move in with her parents and sister, spending time with them made Pamela realise that she'd been feeling lonely since she'd come back from Paris. London life had taken on a different tone — as if everyone was bracing for the worst. She was missing both Francis and, despite her best efforts to repress those feelings, Sid. The limbo in which Pamela found herself as she continued to wait for news from Macaulay certainly wasn't helping matters; she was unable to do anything but bide her time.

VI

Nearly two weeks later, Captain Macaulay finally made contact with Pamela and asked her to meet him in Hyde Park for a debrief. She brought Patricia with her for a walk (she'd learned in the past that her dog was a rather good cover for clandestine park meetings). It was strange and unsettling to see the metal railings gone, removed for scrap metal for the war effort, and barrage balloons dotted around the green spaces. Macaulay apologised for the delay in communication and explained that things had got 'a bit hairy' since war was declared, especially with the issue of the Windsors — where to put them and what to do with them.

Pamela told him about her illness at La Croë, her suspicion that her room had been searched and her and Noël's theory about Hale.

'And you think the butler did it, so to speak?'

Pamela couldn't help but feel how absurd it now sounded in retrospect. She wasn't Virginia Dalkeith. It wasn't a murder mystery.

'Well, Bedaux seems to be the one most likely to have ties to Italy or Germany and to sabotage any attempt by the British government to gather intelligence on the Windsors.'

'But he wasn't there that weekend?'

'No. But if he recommended Hale to the Windsors, it's possible that Hale could be a plant.'

'Do you have any proof?'

Thinking of Hale in his pantry doing his stretches, Pamela sighed and shook her head.

'I would tell you to go back and find it but unless we can come up with a new cover, it might be the end of the innings for you. The Board of Trade is too busy negotiating new regulations and blockades with Parliament to be sending delegates to France.'

Pamela was bitterly disappointed, even more than she had expected. She tried to imagine herself doing volunteer work with Flossie and feeling useless, far removed from the action. Rattling around the house on her own, resisting her mother's demands to go to the country. Wondering how Francis was doing. Thinking about Sid, who was probably somewhere covering the front. But worst of all, those little stabs of panic had become more frequent. Pamela couldn't help but feel she'd be able to stave them off if she was doing something. If she were closer to the action. The Soviet Union had just invaded Poland and there she was, twiddling her thumbs at home. The last thing she wanted was to sit around and wait for the Germans to invade and for the Right Club to become the British arm of the Gestapo. She wanted to return to her mission. Or any mission. Wherever it took her.

Pamela had one last tactic. As they reached the entrance to the park across from the barracks for the Household Cavalry, she put her hand on Macaulay's arm.

'Captain, I've heard something else that might be useful.'
'Oh, yes?'

Pamela repeated what Charlotte had told her about Bedaux and how he had tried to get Peter to agree to sell weapons to the Italians with him, even if Mussolini entered the war on Germany's side.

Macaulay looked worried. 'This is exactly the kind of information we needed on him. When the Windsors return to France, we need to keep him and his wife away from them. He's even more unscrupulous than we'd imagined. And if that's only Bedaux, who knows what else the other Windsor hangers-on are hiding? Excellent work, Lady Pamela.'

Pamela felt pleased with herself. Maybe now she could reasonably hope that Macaulay might try to get her back into the field.

October 1939

I

Pamela waited and waited to hear from Macaulay, growing more and more restless as the days passed. After a week, she was beginning to feel as if she wasn't going to hear from him at all, and she feared she would be stuck in London, trying to find some sort of volunteer war work to keep her occupied.

One morning, while flipping through a copy of the latest issue of *Vogue*, Pamela had an idea. What if she volunteered to go to Paris to cover the collections and liaise with their French counterpart? Brogue didn't have anyone based in Paris anymore — everyone had fled as soon as war had been declared. The autumn shows had been postponed but knowing the tenacity of French houses, they would likely soon be resumed. And as far as the fashion world was concerned, to be cut off from Paris was to be cut off from civilisation. Why hadn't she thought of this sooner?

Pamela contacted Macaulay to tell him she'd had an idea. They met again in Hyde Park, this time by the Serpentine. He'd even brought a bag of breadcrumbs to throw to the ducks while they talked, occasionally feeding some to Patricia (who was looking at both the food and the ducks with interest). Although she had been prepared to be rebuffed, he was more enthusiastic than she had anticipated.

'Splendid idea, Lady Pamela. It would be immensely helpful to have someone besides Fruity keeping an eye out for Bedaux — who's now been banned from the Windsor household, thanks to you — but also for others like him, who could be operating with treasonous intentions. Of course, the only journalists travelling to the continent are war correspondents. Bit of a problem there — no one's especially keen on the ladies doing that kind of thing.' He paused and tossed some crumbs to a large, aggressive-looking swan who was busy chasing the ducks and pigeons away.

Pamela felt dejected. And irritated. If she were a man, there wouldn't have been a problem.

Macaulay watched the swan for a moment and then his face lit up. 'Aha! I've got it. We can say you've been assigned to the new Bureau of Propaganda they're starting up in Paris. We've got that playwright running it ... Coward.'

'Noël Coward?'

'The Foreign Office wants a team of writers, journalists and so on to establish a relationship with their opposite numbers in the French Ministry of Information, attempt some joined-up thinking with our allies in the propaganda war with Jerry. And to be perfectly honest, it was useful for us to have a reason to send Coward to Paris. To have another person to keep an eye on things.'

He threw some more crumbs to the mallard who'd appeared as soon as the swan waddled off. Pamela leaned down to pet Patricia, who was looking as if she might decide to go hunting.

'In that case, it makes perfect sense for me to be working alongside Mr Coward, doesn't it?'

'Precisely. We'll tell your people at *Vogue* that your country needs you.'

'To spread propaganda about fashion?'

'Something like that. I'm sure you'll have an idea or two.'

Two days later, they found themselves back in Elizabeth Penrose's office. Only this time the formidable *Vogue* editor-in-chief was seated across the table from them. With ramrod-straight posture and a steady gaze, the thirty-nine-year-old American was an intimidating presence — known for picking on editors and writers in meetings and wielding a considerable amount of influence at Condé Nast. The captain seemed more subdued than usual, and on what Pamela assumed was his best behaviour. They needed her to sign off on this idea if Pamela was going to be sent to Paris to liaise with the Bureau of Propaganda — or at least appear as if she were.

'I want to make sure I understand the situation. Lady More will continue to work for *Vogue*, returning to Paris to cover the upcoming spring collections. And she will be liaising between the London and Paris offices and the Bureau of Propaganda … ?'

'That's the general idea. After all, this is the most influential women's magazine in the country with the largest readership.' Pamela was amused to hear Macaulay echoing what she herself had said the year before. 'Who better to persuade women to do their patriotic duty? Where *Vogue* leads, the hearts and minds of British women follow! And by liaising with the Bureau, we can make sure that what Lady More writes aligns with War Office messaging. After all, the propaganda war must be fought on all conceivable fronts if the Germans are to be kept from controlling the general narrative.'

Penrose was silent, her face impassive. Pamela recognised that unconvinced look from meetings and started to worry that she wouldn't see the merit of the idea.

Macaulay continued. 'Ministers in every department are going to want to find ways of reaching women. With their husbands away at the front, they'll be the ones in charge of the purse strings. And we must encourage them not to keep those purses shut unduly.'

'After years of ignoring them, the government has finally decided women are worth their attention,' the editor retorted sharply, tapping the nib of her pencil on the table.

Macaulay looked caught off guard. There was an awkward pause.

Pamela smoothed her skirt and cleared her throat. 'The spring collections that were meant to be shown earlier this month were interrupted by the war. If Britain is cut off from the new collections when some of the houses push through — which, I think, they will — it will have a knock-on effect on the British fashion and textile industry. What we can export to earn foreign currency. And the national economy. Besides, collaborating with *Vogue* Paris is an act of solidarity with our ally. A reinforcement of our nations' relationship.' Pamela was aware that she was making all of this up as she went along, free-associating from idea to idea. 'And perhaps British women can take inspiration from their French sisters ... to be well dressed is to be patriotic, that sort of thing. And to be perfectly frank, I quite agree. Our government *has* taken us for granted. But this is a moment for a show of strength. And we — British and French women — can show Hitler just how strong we can be.'

Penrose looked at Pamela intently, pursing her lips and twirling the pencil between her fingers. She said nothing.

'Of course, there's the question of the Americans,' added Macaulay.

'We need to send the message that Britain and France are still doing business. The Germans have been trying to persuade them that we're the ones forcing Germany to smash up Europe. And that we're weak. That there's no point in giving us aid. Anything we can do to influence American *Vogue* would help the war effort.'

The editor's face softened. She looked almost moved. Pamela had to admit that it was a clever ploy on Macaulay's part, considering that Penrose was American herself and might want to see her native country come to the aid of her adopted one.

She nodded. 'Rest assured that *Vogue* will make any effort we can to help win the war. Condé Nast feels it's important to bring the war to our readers. And I quite agree. I've asked the other editors to keep abreast of the news and put anything on my desk they think is important.' She paused. Pamela held her breath. 'Yes, this seems like a good idea. The British and French fashion industries are still doing business, come what may.'

II

The war had thrown things into disarray for MI6. While it had been all well and good for the agency to operate like a gentleman's club before the Germans invaded Poland, the war had exponentially increased the pressure on them and exposed their lack of organisation and professionalism. They were more in need of agents than ever before. Most of the ones they did have were being called up to their regiments and those they managed to recruit badly needed training. As opposed to only a few months before, when they sent agents like Pamela into the field with a few words of wisdom and a pat on the back, MI6 had decided training was important, now that there was a war on.

As a result, two days after she and Macaulay met Penrose, Pamela was sent on a course at a big house in the furthest reaches of North London to receive some proper preparation in the kinds of things with which she'd need to be equipped in wartime — like a finishing school for special agents. She realised that she would have to pick up an assortment of skills fairly quickly.

'Can you ski?'

'Yes.'

'Ride?'

'Yes.'

'Shoot?'

'Tolerably.'

'Sail?'

'No. Should I?'

'Climb?'

'Climb what?'

'Mountains.'

'Will I need to … ?'

'It's a good idea never to rule anything out. Ride a bicycle?'

'If I must.'

'Run?'

'Only under duress.'

Although relieved to finally be receiving some kind of education in espionage, Pamela tried not to show the alarm she was beginning to feel at how much they expected her to learn and how quickly she was supposed to learn it. Over the next two weeks, she was taught tradecraft and tactics by a variety of different people, none of whom she would have associated with a secret intelligence agency.

Pamela learned how to wear a recording device and how to hide one inside an object. How to maintain one's cover and how to avoid blowing the cover of another Joe. How to tail someone. How to lose a tail. When crossing a street, use it as an opportunity to check if you're being followed. Though she had learned a bit from Charlie and a little more from Macaulay, she refined her abilities to speak and write in code. 'Coat-trailing' was a tactic used to lure other spies out into the open by dropping hints that you yourself are a spy. 'Chickenfeed' referred to true but harmless information that could be fed to the enemy. It was useful to find out what your target was allergic to so that you could poison them with it in an emergency. They taught her how to pick a lock and crack a safe by a smartly dressed man called Alfred, who had been a housebreaker in a previous life. He cheerfully imparted that he had once been known in the criminal underworld as 'Alfie the Dandy'.

Next, Pamela learned from a Major Godfrey hand-to-hand combat and how to fight someone off using everyday objects.

'That's right, More! Use the edge of your hand! It can be lethal if used correctly on someone's windpipe!'

The alarmingly tall, strapping major from Yorkshire had been in the Royal Marines — and barked orders as if he still was. He drilled in the tactics over and over, until she was sweaty and out of breath.

As she lay winded on the floor, Godfrey towered over her. 'Need to get into better shape, More!' He grabbed her hand and examined it. 'And keep those fingernails long and sharp so you can gouge the enemy's eyes out!' (Pamela had always appreciated a man with an attention to detail.)

Godfrey also taught her how to assemble, dismantle and clean a revolver, and he supervised while she practised her shooting. When he expressed surprise that she was a good shot, Pamela explained that her father used to make her and her sister go pheasant hunting with him as girls.

Dr Hirsch, a short, rotund psychology professor with a heavy German accent and a surprising sense of humour, gave Pamela and some other recruits a lecture on human behaviour.

'Make eye contact when lying. Maintain composure. Keep the face blank.' He looked at his audience thoughtfully and smiled. 'Such a thing should be easy for English people — you are notoriously difficult for foreigners to read.'

She learned how to recruit informants and the reasons why people would choose to spy and inform: for ego, money, ideology or because they themselves have been compromised. 'People will do anything if they think they're doing it for love.'

And why they might reveal certain things. 'Information reveals as much about those who impart it as it teaches those who hear it.'

Dr Hirsch explained the psychology of blackmail, honey traps and double agents. 'As for that mysterious creature, they do not think they are doing anything wrong at all. No double agent thinks he is a traitor.'

Pamela thought of Charlie and how manipulated she had been by her MI5 handler, who had probably seen her as an unwitting asset. She thought ruefully that she might not have fallen prey to his charms if she'd heard Dr Hirsch's lecture three years ago.

Learning how to create disguises was her favourite part. Pamela was assigned to a woman called Edna Bishop who had been a hair and makeup artist for various film studios, and before that, a wardrobe assistant in the West End. She was a tiny woman in her sixties with platinum blond hair, an East End accent and a cigarette perpetually hanging out of her mouth.

'Want to throw a shadow off your tail? A quick change in a loo or an alleyway can work wonders.'

Edna showed her how many ways a scarf could change her appearance. How to make her hair appear shorter or longer than it really was. How to use wads of cotton in her cheeks to make her face look fuller.

Having spent so much time in theatres and on film sets, Edna was able to teach her a variety of different ways to move, how to change her gait, walk with a limp, alter her posture, make one shoulder appear higher than the other.

'When I worked with Boris Karloff on *The Ghoul*, he did this bit where he rounded his shoulders, jutted out his chin and hunched.' Edna did an impression for Pamela. 'You're a very pretty girl with nice, finishing-school posture — and that's what people will remember about you. So, if you pull a Karloff, you'll be unrecognisable.'

Pamela even received an alternative identity in case of an emergency. She was given an Irish passport under the name Kathleen Burke, as it might be useful to travel under the identity of a neutral country. When they asked her if she could do an Irish accent, Pamela nodded, feeling as if it was probably too late to say no to anything.

The one thing everyone kept reiterating was: follow your tradecraft and you won't be caught.

At the end of the two weeks, Pamela was taken to an airfield in Hertfordshire and given a crash course (quite literally) in parachuting by a former stunt pilot called Freddy. One would have thought a stunt pilot would be a dashing prospect, but this one was a bit past his prime, gone to seed and seemed to be hungover.

Freddy wiped his Errol Flynn-style moustache, tried to focus on her with his bloodshot eyes and shouted, 'All you have to do is jump, pull the cord, Bob's your uncle.'

Pamela could hardly hear him over the roar of the plane's engines, but she had become too petrified to take in anything he was saying, anyway. She had already been sick once and was trying not to be sick again. Her stomach leapt and lurched, her heart pounded and her mind raced with all the worst possible scenarios, like breaking a leg upon landing or her parachute failing to open. Freddy checked all her straps, hooks, belts and buckles. Then he wrenched open the plane door and they were hit with a blast of bracing wind. They were flying just below the cloud cover and she could see the patchwork of the fields below. Which would have been a beautiful sight, if she hadn't been struck by a profound sense of terror.

'Ready?' Freddy shouted into Pamela's face as he put a hand on her shoulder.

Pamela shook her head.

'There's a brave girl, off you go!' he cried cheerfully as he gave her a push.

By the end of her training, Pamela was physically exhausted and felt as if her head were full to bursting with information. And while she was grateful for the training, she doubted she would actually use much of it, trailing around after the Windsors in Paris.

November 1939

I

At the end of October, Pamela packed her things, closed up her house, took Patricia to her parents' house in Gloucestershire and said goodbye to her family. By early November, Pamela was back in Paris, which was cold and grey, as if under a permanent shadow. She was pleased to find that both Madame Garrote and Tulipe had warmed to her in her absence and seemed almost happy to see her. No one seemed to think it was odd, that *Vogue* was standing on its head. Like London, the city was now half empty and preoccupied with war preparations. The grass in the parks had been left to grow; buildings and monuments had been sandbagged. Great works of art had been spirited out of the Louvre and stained-glass windows removed from churches. The absence of children was haunting.

When Pamela arrived at Lettice's flat in Montparnasse the day after her return, Lettice threw her arms around her in relief. She had continually refused to return to England, despite Pamela's protestations. She didn't want to leave Mikhail, who, having had his citizenship revoked by the Soviets when he fled Russia during the Civil War, was technically stateless and had a Nansen passport. That, in addition to being Jewish, meant that getting an entry visa for Britain had proven impossible.

'And even if the Home Office allows him into the country, there's a danger he could be interned as an enemy alien,' Lettice said anxiously as she made them a pot of tea in her kitchen.

'But he's lived in France for so many years. Why doesn't he have French papers?'

'He didn't bother to apply for naturalisation until this summer. You know what he's like — he doesn't care about anything apart from his work. And he only did it because I forced him to.' Lettice gripped the edge of the kitchen counter, her mouth a tight, angry line.

'And now ... ?'

'And now, we don't know when he's going to get his papers. They say there's a backlog. I just wish he'd done it sooner.'

'Letty,' she said softly as she put a hand on Lettice's shoulder, 'what if the Germans decide to bomb Paris?'

Lettice gave her a Gallic shrug. 'We'll go to my house in Normandy.' She forced a smile and poured the tea. 'Please don't worry about me, darling. We're going to Bricktop's tonight, probably for the last time. Did you know it's closing at the end of the week? Bricktop is going to New York.'

'I'd imagine most of the Americans are leaving, if they haven't already.'

Lettice absent-mindedly ran a tea towel over the kitchen table. 'So many of the clubs are closing. Everyone's being called up — there's hardly anyone left to serve drinks or play in the band.'

Pamela felt a sudden heaviness; it seemed like the end of an era — of a gayer, more joyful Paris. She looked out of Lettice's kitchen window and towards the Montparnasse Cemetery, worrying what else the war was going to be the end of.

Pamela wanted to catch Bricktop once more before she sailed, to see what she could glean from her regarding the Windsors — if she had seen them and if Wallis was still carrying on with Ambassador Bullitt. However, she couldn't deny that her heart leapt when Lettice told her that Sid was going to be there. She had resisted the temptation to write to him while she was in London, worrying that after the kiss in the station she wouldn't be able to keep her emotions at bay. She tried to remind herself that she needed to remain focused but the moment she saw him, all her best intentions went out the window. She'd thought her silence would have acted as a deterrent but he was as warm as ever.

'Propaganda this time, eh?' He smiled. 'Giving old Goebbels a run for his money. Terrible timing, Lady Right Honourable. I'm leaving in a few days for the Belgian border to see what's happening on the Western Front.'

Pamela tried not to let her disappointment show.

'You can't leave! Pamela's only just returned to Paris,' protested Lettice. 'How long are you going to be away then?'

'I don't know. We might go on to Bucharest after that.'

Rather than letting her emotions get the better of her, Pamela sternly reminded herself that she was there to speak to Bricktop before she sailed for New York and decided to go find her.

'The next time you see our friend Wallis, make sure you thank her for me,' Bricktop told her. 'She's the one who encouraged me to go back home. She booked me passage on the SS *Washington* — and she had to pull some of those strings of hers to do it. Every man and his Uncle Harry are trying to get on that ship. They're saying it's the last one.'

'She did?'

'I told her, I can't go back … I've been here too long now. And I'm forty-five years old. It's too late for me to start over. I told Wallis I wanted to go to Marseille, but she told me that if the Germans occupy France, I'd have to be prepared to face an internment camp.'

A German occupation of France. Did Wallis know something no one else did?

Unnerved, Pamela protested, 'I don't believe anyone who says it will all be over before we know it, but I do think the French and British armies are waiting for the right moment to move in on the Germans. And they'd never be able to occupy Paris. It's impossible.'

Bricktop looked thoughtful and then replied, 'Come with me … I've got something I think you could use …'

She led Pamela down a corridor to a tiny office at the back of the club, crammed with filing cabinets and papers, an overflowing ashtray on the desk and signed pictures of jazz singers and musicians on the walls. She took one of the pictures off the wall to reveal a safe, opened it and took something out. The light from the desk lamp reflected off the metal of what Pamela recognised from her training as a Colt .38.

'We all know what can happen to women in wartime with soldiers running around. You gotta be prepared for anything. I want you to keep yourself safe, ok?'

Pamela couldn't tell her that she already had a gun stashed behind a toilet cistern in a safe house in Pigalle.

'May I ask why you have a pistol in your safe … ?'

'French gangsters.' Bricktop sighed wearily. 'And speaking of gangsters, if you ever find yourself in Marseille, Hecky Smith is a crook if there ever was one, but he's got a little place down there. It's called

Le Jazz Bleu.' She paused and looked at Pamela meaningfully. 'He's not a bad guy to know if you're in a jam.'

Bricktop handed Pamela the small Colt, along with a box of bullets. Pamela was unexpectedly moved that a woman she barely knew had thought of her safety and wellbeing.

'Thank you.'

'You don't have to thank me, just take care of yourself.'

Later that evening, having outstayed everyone else until closing, Sid and Pamela perched on the edge of the fountain outside the club in Place Pigalle. Though it normally lent a Second Empire grandeur to the square, with the water turned off, it looked like a memorial to a bygone age.

'You want to walk up to the Sacré-Cœur?' asked Sid as he lit Pamela's cigarette. 'It's still beautiful up there, even in the dark.'

'Only if you're planning on carrying me, because I'm not climbing up all those steps in these heels, in the pitch black,' Pamela replied playfully.

They sat close to one another. The tips of their cigarettes glowing in the dark of the blackout. Sid turned to Pamela, examined her face and then briefly stroked her cheek with his hand. He leaned in to kiss her. She felt that electricity again in her body. He put his hand on her thigh, feeling the top of her stocking. Pamela pulled him in tighter. Their kissing intensified. For a moment, nothing else mattered; nothing else existed. Like they were simply picking up where they left off at the Gare du Nord.

But then suddenly, Sid pulled away. 'Sorry — I shouldn't have done that. You've just got back to Paris and I'm leaving soon.'

Pamela felt her body cry out, as if she had been starving for weeks and someone wafted a platter of food under her nose.

'It's alright. I don't—'

'We should probably get home … there's a curfew these days.' Sid nervously smoothed his hair. 'Look, I don't want to …'

Pamela adjusted her dress self-consciously and stood.

'You don't want to what?'

'I don't think we should, you know … start anything. Not now.'

'If that's what you want,' she replied curtly.

'It's not what I *want*, it's just … we've hardly been in the same place at the same time since we met. I didn't even know if you were coming back to Paris. And besides,' — Sid looked down at his hat — 'you're married.'

She wanted to say, *I've never felt so desired in my life — not with my husband or anyone. And I didn't know I needed to feel it so badly until now. Come back with me to my flat and make love to me all night and never leave me.*

A taxi drove down the Boulevard de Clichy and Sid flagged it down.

'You should take this. Most of the taxis have been requisitioned to take troops to the front. We might not see another one for hours.'

Pamela's entire body felt numb.

He opened the taxi door for her. 'Look, you know how much I care about you, Pam. But I don't know if I'm going to see you before I leave for Finland.'

She pulled her fur tightly around her. 'As you said, there's no point in us carrying on. Eminently sensible. Perhaps we shouldn't see each other again.'

Before Sid could reply, Pamela climbed into the taxi and shut the door. She was angry with herself, as if she'd fallen into a trap. As if someone had lured her into thinking she was loved and wanted, only to rescind the offer. She should have known better than to give in to her emotions and desires, to have shown weakness. And what was she doing feeling sorry for herself anyway? She was a married woman. Her marriage might not be perfect, but whose was? After all, she didn't know any woman who was married and contented and deeply in love.

Despite all these mental gymnastics, Pamela sobbed the entire way back to the Left Bank and then continued to cry, curled up on her sofa. Once she finally stopped, she lit a fire and poured herself a brandy. Her little flat which had seemed so romantic just weeks before now seemed shabby and sad.

What the hell had she done? To go to France on an MI6 lark during peacetime was one thing. To do it again when all the world was at war was something else entirely. Did she really return to continue nannying the Windsors? With Wallis knitting socks and Edward stalking up and down the Western Front, they seemed far less of a liability than before the war. They were toeing the line and doing patriotic things, like every other person on either side of the English Channel. Perhaps they simply wanted to feel important and now they could pretend they were. Bedaux had been banned from the house and there was no guarantee that Pamela would unearth any more intelligence about anyone else while she was there.

She hadn't come to Paris just to be close to Sid, had she? He was an American journalist who talked about baseball and chewed gum. She was married to a Peer and had been presented at court. Besides, she should have known that he would be leaving again, to cover a new front and a new story. Who knew how long he'd be gone? She might never even see him again. *You're married, you're married, you're married*, her brain hummed.

Besides, Sid was unreliable. A confirmed bachelor and typical journalist — running around the world, using his profession as an excuse to avoid settling down. (Look at Ernest Hemingway — he'd worked his way through two wives and was rumoured to be well on his way to a third.) If Sid wanted romance, he probably could have found it with any number of women he'd met on his travels. And maybe he did have girls stashed away in every port. Maybe what she had built up in her mind was just a fantasy based on her own imaginings.

It was for the best if they stopped seeing each other. Sid was becoming an unnecessary complication in her life. She wasn't in Paris to moon about after Americans — she was here to do a job. When she got back into bed, she felt enveloped by the darkness created by the blackout curtains. Not that she would have seen anything out her window anyway; as in London, all the lights had gone out in the City of Light.

II

The next morning, Pamela awoke to Madame Garrote calling up to her from the courtyard. She was surprised to look down and see her standing next to Sid, who was being barked at ferociously by Tulipe. When she opened her door to him, Sid stood there awkwardly, his hat in his hands. Pamela pulled her robe around her and silently gestured for him to come in and closed the door behind her.

'I'm so sorry, Pam. I was a heel. I wouldn't blame you if you never spoke to me again,' he said as he struggled to meet her gaze.

She raised an eyebrow. 'Perhaps I should send you back downstairs so Tulipe can bark at you some more.'

Sid smiled and absent-mindedly scratched the back of his head. 'I'd deserve it, that's for sure.'

With his bleary eyes, messy hair and unshaven face, he looked like he'd hardly slept and if he had, it had been in his clothes. It made Pamela feel better to see that what he'd put her through the night before had kept him awake too. Besides, she dreaded to think how she herself looked in that moment, having been up half the night crying and the other half drinking brandy. At least she'd managed to put on her nightdress before falling asleep and wasn't still wearing her clothes from the night before. Irritatingly, Sid still looked handsome, even in that state (open jacket, no tie, shirttails untucked). Possibly even more so than usual.

The sensible thing to do would be to leave him in her sitting room while she went into her bedroom to put on some clothes. The sensible thing to do would be to graciously accept his apology and then send him on his way. To shoo him out the door, take a bath and get on with all the things she needed to be focusing on. *There was a war on, for heaven's sake.*

'I don't want to lose you. You're too important to me. Last night … I was just trying not to mess things up.'

'What, you mean by flirting with me, kissing me and then taking it all back … ?'

Sid looked embarrassed. 'Do you know how hard it's been for me to control myself around you for the last year?' he muttered.

'Well, it hasn't exactly been easy for me either!' Pamela blurted out.

Sid looked up. 'No?'

'Of course not.'

'Really?' he asked softly as he took a step closer.

This isn't the sensible thing, Pamela, whispered the voice in her head.

But it was too late. They kissed. And everything else melted away. Her worries, how upset she had been. All of a sudden, they were

174

taking each other's clothes off. Pamela felt her body light up again as it had done the night before, but it was like someone had turned up the wattage.

Pamela had only been to bed with three men until now.

Bunny Russell-Jones, her first boyfriend and ex-fiancé. She'd found Bunny quite exciting at the time but perhaps what she'd actually found thrilling was doing something so illicit rather than the physical act. He was overeager and sloppy — like having one's face licked by a Labrador. And he never lasted for very long.

Francis. Gentle, kind, deferential. But she was always the one who wanted to try new things, while Francis was reluctant and set in his ways. He seemed to enjoy the act but found it so excruciating to talk about that Pamela eventually stopped trying. Maybe he'd been focused on the procreative aspect of sex for so long and she'd been busy hiding her infertility that it had taken the fun out of it for both of them.

Charlie. An echo of Bunny in its forbidden, thrilling nature but far better technically. A man who'd looked like a handsome, mild-mannered librarian, but highly sexually competent. Of course, now that she'd learned from MI6 what a 'honey trap' was, she didn't like to think how many women he'd seduced in service to Joseph Stalin.

If she'd been an Olympic judge, she would have given them three, five and eight, respectively. But the gold medal would have gone to Sid. Ten for style, technique and execution. It seemed as if he could read the cues she didn't even know her body was giving him, anticipating her every desire. In the best possible way, it almost felt as if she were making love — or being made love to — for the first time. She felt not only desired but seen for who she was — her whole self. She hadn't known that sex could be such a mutual act until now. Pamela had always been self-conscious in bed, worried about how her body looked from different angles, what sorts of faces she was making. But in that moment, how she appeared was the furthest thing from her mind. She didn't have to pretend to be anything or anyone.

As they lay curled up together in her bed, Pamela asked, 'Will you be alright in Finland?'

'I can't imagine it'll be any worse than Spain,' he replied as he stroked her hair.

'That's not reassuring.'

'I'm pretty unlikely to be right in the line of fire. Journalists tend to do things like go to restaurants and stay in hotels and head for cover when the shooting starts.'

She wished she were the kind of woman who didn't feel the need to ask but she wasn't.

'Do you know when you'll be back in Paris?'

'Maybe Christmas. Depends on the direction the war takes.'

Pamela also wished she were the kind of woman who could be nonchalant about such a reply. But it frustrated her, how Sid acted as if his life was at the mercy of the winds of fate, as if he had no control over anything. She reached for her lighter and cigarette case on her side table, disentangling herself from Sid's embrace. She sat up to light a cigarette.

She inhaled deeply and exhaled. 'Why aren't you married?'

'Maybe I never met the right girl. And this gig doesn't exactly lend itself to settling down.'

It could be that this was exactly the life that suited him — constant travelling, the rush to meet deadlines, never having to become too involved in others' lives. Coming and going as he pleased, accountable to no one.

Once Sid had left, Pamela took the revolver and bullets out of her handbag. She pulled up a loose floorboard and hid them underneath. Bricktop was right — it couldn't hurt to have a spare handgun at her disposal.

Her life was so much more complicated when Sid was around. She didn't know what to think about what she — what *they* — had done. As with Charlie, it had been startlingly easy to compartmentalise things, to rationalise. She was in Paris, there was a war. Francis was thousands of miles away and who knew when they would see each other?

Maybe it was for the best Sid was going away again. Or at least that's what she tried to tell herself.

III

Despite the fact that it was only two in the afternoon, Noël offered Pamela and Captain Macaulay a brandy in his flat the next day.

'The coffee here is undrinkable and the tea is even worse,' he grumbled. 'I'm sorry it's so terribly cold in here.'

Pamela felt responsible for Noël's living situation. Having mentioned Schiaparelli's spy ring to Macaulay, MI6 decided to move him from his room at the Ritz across the Place Vendôme to a threadbare flat in the building next to the House of Schiaparelli. It had a Steinway but little heating and no hot water.

'I don't know why on earth they thought *I* should be in charge of political propaganda. The theatre is a house of strange enchantment, a temple of illusion.' Noël spread his hands across an imaginary marquee. 'Not a factory churning out polemics. Clearly none of them have seen my plays. I'm hardly George Bernard Shaw.

That pacifist moron is still plumping for a peace negotiation. But one does what one can for one's country.' He stood, crossed the room, sat at the piano and began to play. 'I sit in an office all day and try to come up with ideas with a French playwright who's a bit of a fascist and a novelist who seems to be on the verge of a nervous breakdown. We're meant to be writing inspiring things to put on pamphlets to airdrop onto unsuspecting citizens of the Third Reich. It feels very high-minded and useless. Do you know, I'm going to be forty in December. *This* isn't what I imagined doing at forty.'

He then began to sing 'Any Little Fish'.

'*Any little fish can swim, any little bird can fly … Any little dog and any little cat can do a bit of this and just a bit of that …*'

Macaulay cleared his throat. 'Let's discuss the issue at hand, shall we? Show Boat, you and Vortex are going to keep each other informed as to the movements of the Windsors. Vortex is going to give dinners for various society people — journalists, artists, that sort of thing. Establish himself in Paris as someone to know.'

'Induce people to come to mine, eat and drink too much and run their mouths. What material for a writer!'

Macaulay looked at Noël sternly.

'I was only joking,' he protested.

'Under the guise of liaising with you at the Bureau of Propaganda, Show Boat will carry on with her previous mission. Now that the Duke is at the front with the French Army, we have a man in place, reporting back to us on what he's saying. Of course, we're monitoring the Windsors' correspondence. There's been nothing of concern so far and both of them seem to be maintaining a reasonably patriotic attitude. Which is all the more reason to get the Duchess to confide in you. See if there's anything the Duke might be telling her that we don't know about.

'We have several issues to deal with. One: Charles Bedaux. It's more difficult than we anticipated to keep the Windsors from seeing the Bedauxs. Black Sheep thinks the Duke has managed to stay in contact with him. I want you both to find out what the situation is.'

'I never liked the man,' grumbled Noël.

'Bedaux?' Pamela asked.

'Our former king. Dreadful manners. Impeccably dressed, though,' Noël said as he picked a piece of lint from his mauve dressing gown.

Captain Macaulay adjusted the tie on his regimental uniform and cleared his throat.

'Two: there might be a saboteur in the Windsor household, who doesn't want us to be watching too closely. Show Boat reported suspicious activity in August. I want you to follow up on this.'

Without getting herself poisoned, ideally.

'Our third problem is the Duchess's relationship with the American Ambassador — if she's still carrying on with him and what she might be saying to the Americans at such a critical time. Especially if Bullitt is already predisposed to an anti-British stance. Being positioned where he is' — Macaulay gestured next door, to the House of Schiaparelli — 'Vortex can keep an eye out and see if the Duchess and the Ambassador are continuing their liaisons. Covering both stumps, as it were. And I'd like you both to look into this little spy ring of Madame Schiaparelli's. What are her political allegiances, this designer?'

'She's Italian but against Mussolini,' said Pamela. 'I'd heard she can't go back to Italy because of the things she's said about him.'

'Her shop is all done up in the tricolore. Patriotism is good for business in wartime,' added Noël.

'I'll try to find out what I can when I go to her show tomorrow.'

'And suss out what Madame Schiaparelli does with her information, if she's reporting to someone. And see if Ambassador Bullitt is there. You'll be in the short leg position, as it were.' Pamela and Noël looked at Macaulay blankly. 'The short leg is the player who stands close to the batsman in order to catch the balls he doesn't hit, so that they don't strike the wicket.'

'Doesn't that mean the short leg person is in danger of getting hit with the bat?' Pamela asked.

'Oh, it's just an analogy.' Macaulay waved a hand dismissively.

Pamela was beginning to find the captain's cricket analogies troubling.

IV

Most fashion houses had postponed their September shows until further notice and others had shut down altogether. Coco Chanel had dramatically announced it was the end of an era and that 'no one would ever make dresses again', putting hundreds of people out of work. As her commercial rival and social adversary, Schiaparelli had then declared French fashion essential wartime propaganda and had pushed on with her spring/summer collection. Which, to Pamela, seemed as if it had attracted everyone who was anyone in the Paris fashion world: the chairman of la Chambre Syndicale de la Couture, Lucien Lelong; Michel de Brunhoff; designers like Mesdames Agnès, Grès and Vionnet; Cristóbal Balenciaga; Edward Molyneux and Nina Ricci.

The atmosphere of the *défilé de haute couture* was one of defiance: the world could go to hell and French fashion would still be standing. It had survived two hundred years and would survive two hundred more. Schiaparelli's 'Cash and Carry' collection was a turn away from fantastical surrealism towards utilitarianism. It featured oversized pockets, military-inspired designs and colours ('aeroplane grey', 'Maginot Line blue'), waterproof tweeds and even her own version of a siren suit.

'The spirit of the Frenchwoman,' explained de Brunhoff with his pipe clenched between his teeth, 'is symbolised by the care she continues to take with her makeup, her coiffure, her figure, how she dresses. She remains a coquette. The soldier on leave wants to find his wife or mistress as beautiful as she was when he left her. When he goes back, he carries with him an image not just of beauty, but of courage and hope.'

'And if she doesn't, French fashion will collapse. Foreigners will no longer turn to us for inspiration and half of Paris will be out of work,' added Lelong gloomily.

Lelong had been mobilised at the end of August and then demobilised just days later. As head of the Chambre Syndicale, he had been instructed by the French government to figure out how to keep thousands of designers, seamstresses, cutters, models, illustrators and assistants employed.

'British *Vogue* — and my government — see promoting the fashion industry as an economic imperative. To dress well, to buy beautiful clothes is patriotic,' Pamela asserted.

What she didn't add was that both the Bureau of Propaganda and Brogue wanted to emphasise the idea of the patriotic and pragmatic women of Britain who would pitch in for the war effort, even if that meant casting aside a dress and heels for a uniform, dungarees or a boilersuit. Not exactly the coquette waiting at home with full hair and makeup for her soldier to come home on leave.

Lelong looked sceptical. 'But we do not know when this godforsaken war is going to end. How long will we have access to fabrics — and fabrics of quality, at that? And even if we do, who will be able to afford it? I remember the last war. The shortages of material. The endless parade of widows in their black dresses.'

'I suppose we'll have to make the best of it,' Pamela replied carefully.

De Brunhoff sighed. 'How like an Englishwoman.'

Pamela couldn't tell if this was meant as a compliment or not.

'Besides, the German U-boats are already affecting trade. How long will we have access to markets abroad? Losing the American department stores would be a disaster,' Lelong replied with a furrowed brow.

'Well, I think what Madame Schiaparelli has managed to do — utilitarian chic — is ingenious. The quality, the tailoring and the fabrics are couture but she's responding to the changing needs of women in wartime. Perhaps it's a kind of template for future collections.'

'Merci, Lady Pamela.'

Pamela turned around to face the Italian designer. Schiaparelli was petite and slim, with dark hair and full eyebrows that framed large, dark eyes. She wore a simple black dress with a white collar of her own design.

'Schiap wants to equip the women of France to face the war in comfort, but also in style. French women can look the beautiful coquette while staying warm, no? Especially if she is riding a bicycle! French couture is eternal. And to buy clothes is patriotism, *n'est-ce pas?*'

How long had Schiaparelli been standing there, listening to their conversation, Pamela mused. Her confidence was surprising. If the chairman of the Chambre Syndicale foresaw a difficult future for fashion, what made Schiaparelli see a brighter one? Was it her famous bravado? Or did it stem from another source? Although she seemed as patriotic as anyone else, perhaps her conviction was rooted in the information she might have about all her wealthy and important clientele. Pamela looked around the room at the aristocrats, celebrities, women married to diplomats and politicians — those who hadn't yet left Paris. She spotted Wallis across the room. If Schiaparelli's staff were eavesdropping on them, she would likely have far more delicate information at her disposal than just the Duchess's affair with Bullitt.

'Pamela!' Wallis cried as she embraced her. 'I was so pleased to hear you'd be returning to Paris. Of course, we came right back as soon as we were allowed. From the very beginning, the question uppermost in David's mind was how he might serve his country. He's always had a gift for dealing with troops — it's his common touch and understanding.'

Pamela doubted how common French foot soldiers actually found the former King of England, who travelled with a driver in a private car filled with luggage.

'And he is *so* popular with the French Army. He's started wearing his old uniform from the last war and they just love it. But the problem is that if he does his job too well, he's upstaging his brother, the King. Does it too badly and he's letting everyone down. The Palace doesn't want him to be too visible. They're still carrying on their own little war with us and I can tell you they are giving no quarter. And David's reports on weaknesses in the Maginot Line are being ignored in London. He says the defence lines are inadequate and unfinished, with these big gaps. And the French Army is totally unprepared — their soldiers sound practically untrained.'

Was this true? Weaknesses in the Maginot Line? An unprepared French Army? Was the Duke just exaggerating for effect, to look like he still had a critical military eye, twenty years after his own service had ended? Or was Wallis exaggerating to heighten the drama of the situation and make the Duke sound more important than he actually was? But then Pamela remembered what Francis had said, about the squabbling in the British government and a desperation to get the Americans involved. What if the Maginot Line was more vulnerable than the French were willing to admit? What if their army was unprepared? Pamela thought about what Bricktop had said and tried not to let her mind race.

Two women approached Wallis and started talking to her about the collection. Wallis turned to Pamela and said, 'Pamela, this is Renée Grégoire, my lawyer's wife. He also represents Madame Schiaparelli.'

Pamela remembered what Fruity had said about Armand Grégoire — a 'nasty little chap' with Nazi clients. She wondered if he dropped those clients when the war began or not.

'You remember Fern, don't you?'

The tall, slender woman with the long nose standing next to Madame Grégoire was indeed Fern Bedaux. They had banned Charles from the Windsors' properties but clearly, they couldn't stop Wallis from socialising with his wife. What could Wallis be telling her? What could she be telling her lawyer's wife? What kind of information could Schiaparelli have on all of them? Was it possible that one of these women was the saboteur?

Pamela looked at the three expensively dressed, middle-aged women, their tiny handbags dangling from their hands. They were married to wealthy, powerful men and led lives of unfettered leisure and luxury. How many of them were even aware of what their husbands really thought and did? If so, how inclined would any of them be to help their husbands pursue political ends for a foreign power?

Wallis looked at her watch. 'I'm sorry but I'm late for an appointment. You'll have to excuse me.'

After Wallis left the room, Pamela walked to the large windows of the fashion house that looked out onto the Place Vendôme. She waited a moment and then saw Wallis appear on the street below. A man stepped out of a waiting car, kissed her on the cheek and opened the door for her. As he turned his face, Pamela could see that it was the American Ambassador.

December 1939

I

By the time December arrived, Pamela had been staking out Boulevard Suchet, the House of Schiaparelli, and other haunts of Wallis's — an increasingly daunting proposition now that winter had taken hold of the city and daylight hours were dwindling. Pamela tried to figure out if there were other members of the Windsor set who might be engaging in suspicious or even treasonous activities, but with the Duke at the front, their social life had been largely curtailed. Macaulay was bothered that Wallis was still seeing Ambassador Bullitt and chatting with Fern Bedaux at Schiaparelli's, but he hadn't been as concerned as Pamela had expected about the Duke reporting weaknesses in the Maginot Line to her.

'His brother gave orders that the Duke was to be banned from visiting British troops, because he doesn't want them getting confused about who the real king is. The Duke is probably still cross about that. He wants to feel like someone of consequence, reporting on important matters. And no man wants to appear insignificant in the eyes of his own wife.'

Then, one day in the week before Christmas, Fruity reported that despite being banned from seeing Charles Bedaux by the head of the British Military Mission in France, the Windsors had recently dined with Fern and Charles, who had passed a note to the Duke during dinner.

When they met early in the morning on the Canal St Martin, Macaulay told Pamela, 'We must discover what could be so important that Bedaux would need to slip the Duke a note under the table at dinner. Fruity has been trying to search for it but with the Duke at the front, he has few excuses to be at Boulevard Suchet.'

'And the Duchess doesn't trust Fruity, so presumably, is even less likely to tolerate having him around if the Duke isn't there,' Pamela replied, remembering her conversation with Noël in the garden at La Croë.

Macaulay nodded. 'Which is why we need you to find out where it is and photograph it for us.'

Pamela had a feeling this was coming.

'We assume the note is somewhere in the house, so you'll need to find an excuse to search for it.'

'Do you know what it looks like?'

'From what I understand, it's just a nondescript piece of white paper.' Macaulay sighed and looked at Pamela apologetically.

Scour Boulevard Suchet for a single, nondescript but crucial piece of paper without anyone knowing. Pamela racked her brains to think of a way to be in the house for a prolonged period without being noticed.

'I suppose breaking in while they're away is out of the question? Thanks to your people, I'm a trained housebreaker now.'

Macaulay smiled ruefully. 'That would be ideal but it's impossible with servants coming in and out at all times.'

Pamela watched as a barge floated by them, down the canal. The wind picked up and she pulled the collar of her coat around her neck. Then she had a thought.

'The Windsors' Christmas party is in two days. It will give me an opportunity to search for the note while everyone else is distracted and the servants are busy.'

II

The Duchess had made sure that Boulevard Suchet was decorated to the hilt, intent on providing her guests with the perfect party. Although most people had settled for more subdued Christmas gatherings in deference to the war, Wallis had secured an enormous tree for the entryway, complete with decorations and presents. She had spent the first hour of the evening buzzing around and haranguing the servants with her grumble book. The Duke subjected everyone to a rendition of 'Scotland the Brave' on his bagpipes. Miss Blythewood clapped enthusiastically after every song.

'I was just thinking the other day that what we need in the world is more amateur bagpipers,' Noël muttered as he fixed a cigarette into a holder.

Pamela had never spent Christmas away from her family or Francis before and was feeling a bit sorry for herself. And for the first time in her life, she found herself longing for her parents' home: her mother shouting at her father from the kitchen, even Charlotte and Peter rattling on about Italian wine. Her correspondence with Francis had become more difficult and sporadic, as it was more difficult to get post since the war began (let alone letters from across the Atlantic), so she didn't even know how he was spending the holidays. And she couldn't help thinking about Sid, who was now in Finland, covering the battle between the Finns and the Soviets. If he was warm enough. If he was safe.

They retreated to a corner of the drawing room with Fruity and surveyed the scene. The Windsors had invited British and French officers and a few of their friends, including the Bedauxs. Major-General Howard-Vyse, who had ordered the Duke not to see them again, was clearly irate at their presence.

Fruity was already drunk.

'He won't listen. Neither of them listens to anyone, let alone me. He *used to* listen to me, before he met *her*. But she can't stand me.'

What must it be like, to have been tied to such a man as Edward Windsor, through his various titles and positions within the Royal Family, all one's adult life? Pamela had heard about Fruity covering up Edward's affairs, when he travelled around Europe and Africa as the Prince, when he was sleeping with the wives of local dignitaries. And then after all that, to be snubbed for a position in the palace, without explanation, must have been galling. If Noël was right and they had indeed been lovers, years before, the betrayal must have felt even more painful than a mere social slight. Combined with an unfaithful wife with a penchant for fascist party leaders, it was no wonder Fruity had agreed to become an informant for Secret Intelligence Services. Pamela could well imagine Tommy Lascelles doing the same, given the chance. If Noël knew about Fruity and the Duke's history, who else knew too? As she learned in her training, such things left people vulnerable to blackmail.

'Charles Bedaux is never in the same place for more than six hours at a time. I can't make him out. He knows too much — about every country in Europe *and* our colonies. I'm sick of trying to warn the

HRH about him. And I'm sick of trying to tell him to stop banging on about peace treaties with Germany. I'm damn well fed up with Paris and this war.'

Fruity's voice was starting to rise. Noël caught Pamela's eye. Pamela laid a pacifying hand on Fruity's arm.

'Do you have any idea where this note is?'

'Damned if I know,' he grumbled. 'But if I had to guess, it's probably in the desk in his bedroom.'

'I'll play the piano while Lady Pamela exits stage left to rummage around in His Majesty's drawers — so to speak. Double act, remember? Useful fool,' — Noël pointed to himself — 'slinky, slinky.' He pointed to Pamela. 'You'll slip off to the powder room and no one will even notice you're gone.'

'I'm sure they'll notice once I've been away for more than ten minutes.'

'Then try not to take too long. I'll do as many encores as I can and draw it out with silly little interludes about celebrities.'

Pamela waited until after dinner to slip away, once everyone had had a good deal to drink and Noël had made himself at home at the piano.

Armed with her tiny camera disguised as a pack of cigarettes, Pamela crept up to the Duke's bedroom and closed the door behind her. Unlike its usually tidy appearance, there were piles of papers everywhere. Trying to find a small, innocuous note she might not even recognise even if she did stumble across it was worse than looking for a needle in a haystack. Pamela searched and searched, through stacks of correspondence, fan mail, bills, lists, notes to himself and notes from Miss Blythewood. She dug through the drawers of the desk but found nothing. Just as she was about to give up, Pamela heard footsteps in the corridor. She froze. The footsteps stopped outside the bedroom door. Fortunately, Pamela had only turned on one small lamp; she quickly put it out and hid herself in the wardrobe.

The door creaked open. With a jolt, Pamela realised that she'd left the camera on the bureau. Her heart pounded in her chest and she began to feel flushed. A drop of sweat trickled down the side of her face. She sat in the pitch black of the wardrobe, listening to the person walking around the room, as if they were looking for something. Or someone. She prayed silently that they wouldn't think to open the wardrobe and look inside. And that they would think the camera was just a pack of cigarettes. After a moment, she heard the door shut and the footsteps retreat.

Who would that have been? It was unlikely to have been the Duke, as he was downstairs, playing host and commanding Noël to sing all his favourite songs. It couldn't have been the Duchess or any of the other women because Pamela had heard the softer tread of a man's shoe, rather than the click-clack of heels. And it seemed unlikely to have been Hale or any of the other servants, because they were busy serving guests and going back and forth between the drawing room and the kitchen. Could it have been Bedaux? But he was downstairs as well, unless he'd sneaked upstairs without anyone noticing, like she had.

Pamela opened the wardrobe door and climbed out. She quickly rearranged her dress and hair and grabbed the camera from the top of the desk. As she was coming back downstairs, she passed the morning room and noticed Wallis standing at the window alone, looking out onto the boulevard.

'I think we should probably draw the curtains if we don't want to get fined by the warden,' Pamela said lightly.

When Wallis turned around, it was clear that she had been crying. Pamela had never seen Wallis cry and it was deeply unsettling.

'Wallis, are you alright?'

'Oh, Pamela … I'm so unhappy.'

This was the problem with Americans. You asked how they were and they gave you an honest reply.

As unnatural as it felt, Pamela put her arm around Wallis's shoulders.

'What's wrong?'

'Pamela, I never wanted to marry him. I never doubted that he loved me, but …'

'But … ?' Pamela echoed.

'He's like a child,' she hissed. 'No one understands.'

How ironic, Pamela thought, *everyone did know that.*

'But if I had refused to marry him, I would have been the villainess of all time. Tempting the King of England away from the throne, only to drop him.' Wallis dabbed at her eyes with a handkerchief. 'And those months between the Abdication and the wedding were hell, Pamela. I didn't know what was going happen. David just assumes everything will take care of itself because everyone's always taken care of everything for him. And now *I* have to be the one to take care of everything,' she spat.

'Yes, I'd find that very difficult too,' Pamela carefully replied, which she realised, might have been the first honest thing she'd ever said to Wallis.

'It's awful. I can't even trust him with money. Last Christmas, I gave him five thousand francs to pay the band at our party. But when it came time to pay them, he had no idea where he'd put it, so I had to scramble and find *another* five thousand francs somewhere — in front of all our guests. And once everything was taken care of, he had the nerve to say, "I knew it would all work out for the best."'

Wallis put a hand on her breastbone, closed her eyes and sighed. The light glinted off her diamond bracelet.

'I can only imagine the position you're in,' Pamela intoned. 'I don't blame you at all for how you're feeling. Any woman might feel the same way.'

Wallis squeezed her hand. 'You're so sympathetic, Pamela. I knew I could confide in you.'

Pamela suddenly saw the opening she'd been waiting for over the last year. She reached behind Wallis to draw the curtains.

'Is there anyone else?' she asked, thinking of Bullitt. 'Someone who might provide an escape from all this pressure ... ?'

Wallis didn't say anything at first and simply gazed blankly into the middle distance. She then looked down at the diamond bracelet the Duke had given her during their affair. Pamela worried she'd pushed her luck, assuming more intimacy and candour than Wallis did.

'Well,' whispered the Duchess, looking at Pamela, 'there *is* someone ... He's a very kind and generous man. And he understands the situation. He's been a great comfort to me.'

Pamela inwardly breathed a sigh of relief. Having Wallis confess her affair felt like one step closer to being able to subtly talk her out of pursuing it. But then Wallis got a wild look in her eye. Like a trapped animal.

'Do you know David said that he would kill himself if I ever left?' she hissed. 'I can never divorce him.'

Pamela couldn't help it; her first response to this revelation was that it might simplify a number of things if the Duke of Windsor topped himself. They wouldn't have to worry about him being a liability to foreign nationals or going on about a peace deal with the Nazis. King

George wouldn't have a potential rival nipping at his heels. People like Bedaux wouldn't have a conduit to the highest echelons of British society. And they would be able to get rid of Wallis — pension her off and send her back to the Americans. The file on the Windsors could be closed.

But when Pamela reported back to Macaulay the next day on what Wallis had confessed, his face went ashen.

'The British public are already having to face conscription and rationing, not to mention sending their children away. There's no telling how they'd respond to the news of the death of their former king.'

'Yes, of course,' she murmured in reply, feeling slightly ashamed. She had spent so much time exposed to the more obnoxious side of the Duke's personality that she'd forgotten there were millions of people who still admired and loved him.

'It would be one thing if he died at the front — a death with honour, so to speak. But quite another if the press got word that he'd taken his own life because the so-called Queen of Hearts threw him over. It would be an unspeakable scandal and a disaster for morale. And, if it transpires that she's left him for Ambassador Bullitt, it could be terrible for any goodwill our people might have for the Americans.'

'It doesn't seem as if she's on the brink of leaving him for Bullitt. She's rather resigned, to be honest.' Pamela paused. 'On the contrary, perhaps the affair is what the Duchess needs to stay content enough to remain in the marriage …'

'Capital idea, Lady Pamela,' replied Macaulay, stamping his walking stick on the ground for emphasis.

'Really … ?'

'Whatever keeps her content. Or, at the very least, compliant. But of course, we must make sure it stays hidden from the Duke. Heaven knows how he would react if he found out.'

Nearly three years ago, Pamela had been tasked with encouraging Wallis and Edward's relationship. Now, she was being asked to ensure Wallis's happiness, or at the very least, the suppression of her misery.

She didn't know which undertaking would end up being more difficult.

January 1940

I

When Pamela convinced Macaulay and Elizabeth Penrose that supporting French fashion was patriotic, she had no idea that the sentiment would induce an entire ship full of Americans to brave a U-boat-infested Atlantic crossing in midwinter. When Penrose told the American *Vogue* editor Edna Woolman Chase about this editorial slant, she then persuaded Condé Nast that she absolutely had to get to Paris to see what all the brave, ingenious French designers were up to. And before they knew it, word had got around and all the other editors, designers, journalists and buyers had decided that they had to go too, to make sure that *Vogue* wouldn't be the only one with the scoop on French trends. They disembarked at Genoa and then caught what Woolman Chase had described as the 'train from hell' that took twenty-four hours to get to Paris, crammed with soldiers, and without lighting, heat, food or anywhere to sleep.

Pamela found it unsettling that the Americans were carrying on as if everything was business as usual. Woolman Chase and her *Harper's*

Bazaar counterpart Carmel Snow couldn't stop talking about how happy they were to be back in Paris. One would have thought that rather than the Wehrmacht lurking on the other side of the Siegfried Line, the true crisis of 1940 was the possibility of American women having to wear American designs. Lois Long from *The New Yorker* complained about the blackouts, the buyer from Saks complained about having to take the Métro and someone from *Women's Wear Daily* complained about the food rationing.

De Brunhoff grumbled to Pamela about having to entertain ungrateful Americans. 'But why are they here? Do they not know there is a war on? Could they not have placed their orders for the spring collections from New York?'

The one upside of the flurry of fashion world activity in the city was that Pamela had something with which to distract Wallis while her husband was in England. They sat in the front row of the House of Lelong show, waiting for it to begin.

'It's shocking, Pamela. I told David not to expect anything from those people. I said, they take you for granted. And of course, no one listens to him *still*, even though he's been to the front. Even though he's spoken to all those French soldiers himself. I said, David, what did you expect? *Of course* they're not going to listen to reason,' muttered Wallis.

Pamela knew that the Windsors had started losing interest in the war effort and displays of patriotism, finding it more of an inconvenience than anything else. They even had pulled strings to have their chef demobbed and returned to their kitchen. However, the reasons for the Duke's visit to England had been shrouded in mystery.

'Oh, really … ?'

'David *knows* that if Chamberlain were to sit down with the Hitler government, they could work something out and call an end to all of this. This war is tearing him apart. He simply can't bear it.'

Pamela pictured the Duke of Windsor attempting to shoot himself in the head outside Parliament, à la Unity Mitford. He had been banging on about a peace treaty since the war started, saying it was all an unfortunate misunderstanding — as if Britain, France and Poland had accused Germany of cheating at cards.

'And Monckton had the nerve to suggest that if we wanted to move back to England, we would have to pay British income tax. Can you imagine?'

'Well, that's awfully unfair,' murmured Pamela soothingly

Pamela had to admire Walter Monckton, who, having been the Duke's advisor during the Abdication crisis, knew him well and understood the most effective mode of deterrence: hitting the Duke in his wallet.

'It's a terrible waste. Especially since Beaverbrook told David that if we were to return to Britain and campaign for peace, his papers would support it. At least *someone* has some common sense.'

Lord Beaverbrook was still pushing his appeasement agenda, nearly five months into the war. Could it be that it was he who had attempted to poison Pamela at La Croë? Or perhaps instructed his footman to do it? Was it possible that he would go to such lengths? Moreover, could it be that he was in talks with the Germans, even now?

Or was she clutching at straws?

II

The winter was bitterly cold, and especially so with fuel rationing. The wind had been biting all month, and it had snowed several times, making January feel never-ending. Pamela found herself having to sacrifice style for comfort and warmth. She had taken to wearing wool stockings and had even bought a pair of trousers. She had hoped they would make her look like Katherine Hepburn but she felt she lacked the American rakishness.

She wrote to Captain Macaulay about what Wallis said about Beaverbrook, but he didn't think it was likely. Beaverbrook owned the *Daily Express*, a paper with the largest circulation in the world. Because he was such a high-profile figure and notorious for engaging in this kind of politicking and power play, his fascist sympathies were widely known. MI6 felt he was an unlikely candidate as an undercover Abwehr agent.

Noël agreed. 'If there is a viper nesting in the bosom of the Windsor household, he won't *look* like a viper. One may smile and smile and be a villain …'

Pamela wondered if her original theory was correct: that the viper was Bedaux. But his fascist sympathies seemed to have been eclipsed by his deal with the French government to streamline and increase their armament production. Perhaps he was more like the Duke than she first suspected — another conceited man intent on proving to everyone how important he was. And, like Peter, someone who was more concerned with making money than with influencing politics. All the better if making money could masquerade as a patriotic endeavour.

In an attempt to stave off the malaise of the bitter winter, Noël held a small dinner party for some friends towards the end of January. His flat was bitterly cold and even though he had a fire going, everyone kept their coats on. One of his members of staff at the Bureau of Propaganda had been accused of homosexuality; Noël had threatened to bring the whole operation to a grinding halt if the man was dismissed. Fortunately, having just toured the Maginot Line with Maurice Chevalier to entertain the troops, his fame was proving a bulwark against challenges to his authority.

'I said I didn't give a damn if Peter liked Chinese mice, provided he didn't bring them into the office. I won't have him sent away on flimsy evidence of something that's nobody's affair but his and doesn't make a jot of difference to how he does his job. I wish there wasn't so much innocence in the world,' he lamented as he refilled everyone's wine glasses.

Sitting next to Pamela, Lettice said, 'I used to be quite innocent myself about such things. I think everyone should be allowed to love whomever they like.' She looked at Pamela. 'Do you miss him?'

'Miss who?'

'Come, on, Pam.'

Lettice knew Pamela better than most people, even her mother and sister. Possibly even better than Francis. When they were eighteen, Pamela had fallen pregnant. She didn't know why she was throwing up every morning until Lettice broke the news to her. Bunny had recoiled in horror from the news and backed out of their engagement, spinning her a story that it was all a misunderstanding, and they hadn't *really* been engaged. That none of this was serious. Lettice had an older cousin who had experienced the same misfortune and was able to recommend a Harley Street doctor with a sideline in making society girls' pregnancies disappear. Pamela had pawned a bracelet that her parents had given her and Lettice held her hand through the whole frightening procedure.

What Lettice and Pamela didn't know was that Dr Merriweather was an alcoholic whose hands shook; he had botched the operation, leaving Pamela unable to become pregnant again. She told her parents that she had been the one to break off the engagement with Bunny. Alma was furious and said that it wouldn't do for her to look so flighty, that she was getting a reputation as a bolter. However, she agreed to let Pamela return to Paris and wait it out until the whispering campaign had subsided. Refusing to leave her friend's side, Lettice joined her and the two of them went to live with a Barreau family friend.

For a time, Pamela thought she could simply stay in Paris. Become a writer like Djuna Barnes or Colette. Take lovers, live independently. After all, if she had 'ruined herself' and as a woman who couldn't have children, knew that she was no good to any man of her class, who would inevitably want an heir. Pamela sat in cafés and wrote and met interesting people and went to art galleries and enjoyed the nightlife of *les Années folles*, until Alma and Duncan cut off her allowance and ordered her to return home.

Pamela nodded to Lettice as she played with the diamond earrings Francis had given her. 'Of course, I do …'

Sid was still in the frozen tundra of Finland, where the Finns were, surprisingly, managing to beat back the far more powerful Red Army. His amusing postcards had turned to long, serious letters about the war, the other journalists, people he encountered, the plight of the Jews, of his family and himself.

'Are you in love with him?'

'I don't know.'

'How can you not know?'

'Letty, it's not that straightforward. I'm *married*,' Pamela protested, slightly irked.

'We're modern women. We don't have to be stuck in the marriages our mothers were.'

'Francis is a good man. He's kind and stable and—'

'Yes, yes.' Lettice waved her excuses away. 'Do you love him?'

Pamela paused momentarily. 'Yes, of course I do.'

'But are you *in love* with him?'

Pamela looked away, unable to answer. Across the table, she could hear Noël talking about the soldiers he'd encountered at the front.

'You should have seen their barracks, the little dears. With their pin-ups of film stars and girly magazines under their beds!'

Pamela looked down at her plate and pushed the remnants of dinner around with her fork. 'I don't know. I don't know anything anymore. I care for Sid, but you know what he's like, Letty. Am I supposed to leave my husband for some fly-by-night American journalist?'

As she said it, she realised that she didn't really know the depth of Sid's feelings for her. Or if there was any depth at all. She had, at least, grown to know him well enough to understand that he was the kind of man whose attentions were easily redirected, always willing to leap into a car, train carriage or plane to chase a story. What was to stop him from behaving the same way about women?

'I'd never imagined someone like Mikhail would be the love of my life. My father would be tearing his hair out if he knew I'd ended up with an artist. With a wandering Jew.' The candlelight flickered across Lettice's pale face. 'And no one's perfect, you know. Mikhail has his own history and his own entanglements. But we love each other. I wish I hadn't wasted so much time being married to Ashley. Life is short.' Lettice took Pamela's hand. 'We mustn't waste it.'

Pamela knew she couldn't argue with her friend. Lettice of all people knew the consequences of staying in the wrong marriage. But Francis wasn't Ashley Wakefield. He was a kind man. And he did love her.

'A toast!' interjected Noël from across the table. 'To happiness! Grab every scrap of it while you can!'

April 1940

I

The winter had passed relatively uneventfully. As the frozen ground turned to mud, the Western Front remained strangely quiet and what the British were calling 'the Bore War' and the French *la drôle de guerre* continued. People had stopped carrying around their gas masks and had fallen back into a kind of routine. Ever since the war began, it felt to most people as if they were waiting for something to happen, but now they began to wonder if this was it — if the French and British forces would ultimately fight Germany up and down the Western Front for as long as it took to grind Hitler's army into submission. Of course, it was terrible how Russia seemed to be rampaging across Eastern Europe, annexing one country after another, but the Eastern Front was a thousand miles away and there was little Britain and France could do about it.

The Duke had slowly lost interest in his duties as British liaison to the French Army, but Wallis had joined a group of female volunteers driving ambulances for the Red Cross. Pamela thought it might be her excuse to be away from the house, just as the Duke was going to be increasingly at home.

Percy seemed to be making the most of what sounded like a newly liberated wartime London but complained about how *The Times* was pushing a patriotic agenda in every section of the paper. 'How am I supposed to make rationing sound exciting?' he'd complained in his latest letter.

Alma had found her calling working for the Women's Institute, organising seed distribution and teaching people how to grow victory gardens. Duncan was enjoying teaching their evacuees how to ride on the neighbour's pony.

Charlotte and Peter had found a house in the Cotswolds but Peter was spending most of his time in London. With the children away at school, she had become so bored that she began going into London herself and meeting up with old friends.

Francis wrote to Pamela from Washington but his letters took weeks to arrive. As his cover was a diplomatic posting, he wrote about meetings with politicians and various foreign dignitaries. Francis found the Americans largely sympathetic but unwilling to even contemplate the possibility of getting involved in another European war. Pamela wrote about life in wartime Paris and her work for *Vogue*. Because there was so little the two could actually write about, their correspondence took on a somewhat formal tone. Which, combined with the thousands of miles between them, only compounded Pamela's feeling of creeping alienation from Francis.

The complacency in Paris began to shift towards unease when Germany invaded Denmark (violating a non-aggression pact) and began attacking Norway (an ostensibly neutral country) on 9 April. Noël was ordered by Duff Cooper, who had become the Minister of Information, to tour America for two months to speak to people and join the British charm offensive. He gathered his friends and colleagues together on a Friday evening at the famed Café de la Paix across from the Paris Opéra for a small farewell party. Pamela was sorry to see him go, even if only for a short time. She had enjoyed his company, support and sense of humour. Noël, on the other hand, seemed somewhat relieved to be temporarily released from his post as head of the Propaganda Bureau.

'I've never worked so goddamned hard in my life and everything I do seems to be a bit of a failure. Our last scheme was to send carrier pigeons with messages attached to them into Germany, but the Germans just sent them back with rude replies! I'm used to hard work. I'm just not used to failure,' he told her despondently.

Sid was returning that day from the front for two weeks before heading back; in her excitement to see him, she invited him to join her at the Café de la Paix. He entered when she was in the middle of a conversation with Noël and put a hand on her shoulder. She felt the familiar sensation of her entire body lighting up as soon as she laid eyes on him. He was looking as scruffy as ever, with his beaten-up old hat and two day' stubble. It was ridiculous and irrational, but the moment they made eye contact, she felt that all was right with the world. When Pamela turned to Noël to introduce them, she could see he was appraising Sid.

Later, he said to her, 'You have quite a one-man fan club there ...'

'He's just a friend,' Pamela protested.

'Yes, we all have such "friends" ... Just remember — *l'amour* always causes far more trouble than it's worth. Keep it waiting off stage until you're good and ready for it. And even then, treat it with the suspicious disdain that it deserves.'

Ignoring Noël's advice, Pamela saw Sid every night that he was in Paris, the two of them meeting each other at the end of an evening in some dark bar or at her flat. Pamela had been forced to come clean about Sid months ago, telling Madame Garotte that she had a gentleman who would be visiting her on occasion. Being French, she made no comment. (Pamela imagined how her British counterpart would have reacted.)

It filled her with a light and joy she hadn't known until now. Even just lying in her bed with him, talking quietly in each other's arms felt like a revelation. Pamela felt she had to cherish every moment together because she didn't know how long he would be gone the next time. And, of course, all was not right with the world. Things were only getting worse.

They talked about his experiences covering the front. The battles in Finland, dogfights, the bombings. He described the villages where he and the other war correspondents stayed. The constant, manic energy of people staying up all night, waiting for a free phone line so they could file their reports. And the thousands upon thousands of refugees. The war was only producing more and more of them, displacing desperate people from their homes, ripping apart families and hurling them into an uncertain and frightening future. Sid railed against the blatant injustice of it all. He'd seen a Jewish couple turned back at the Dutch border because they didn't have their tickets for the ship that would take them to South America. They protested that the tickets were waiting for them at the booking office in Le Havre but the border guard was unmoved.

'Those people could have been my parents. I felt so guilty, being able to go right through, with my American passport and my press pass. There was nothing I could do for them.'

II

As the weeks went by, Pamela began to feel a strange sensation, that someone was following her. A man followed her from one Métro line to another and got off at her stop. A couple who paid their bill just as she was paying hers followed her out of a café. She wondered if there was something to it or if she was being paranoid. But as Macaulay once told her, if there's a question, there's no question. He taught her to listen to her instincts and take extra caution if she had the slightest doubt about a situation. So, Pamela dutifully changed her routes on a regular basis, sometimes getting off a stop early or a stop late, taking a detour through a park or a department store.

She asked Madame Garrote to tell her if she saw any suspicious-looking people hanging around outside the building. And one day, as Pamela was walking through the courtyard of the building, the concierge came out to meet her, Tulipe at her heels.

'For the last three evenings, I've seen someone loitering nearby. They were trying to be subtle, of course. Changing positions every time.'

'Was it a man or a woman? Can you describe them?'

'Difficult to say. They always stayed in the shadows and my eyesight isn't what it used to be. A man, I think. An average physique, perhaps a bit slimmer. About your height. With a hat pulled down tight over the head and the collar of his coat pulled over his face. Never stayed long. At first, it seemed like they were waiting for someone but then they came back the next night.'

Pamela told Macaulay, and he asked her to keep an eye out. And for Madame Garrote to do the same. She spent the next three evenings surveilling the premises and the concierge did the same. But nothing. They never saw anyone again.

May 1940

I

To paraphrase Ernest Hemingway's depiction of a character's bankruptcy in *The Sun Also Rises*: the German invasion of Western Europe unfolded in two ways — gradually, and then suddenly. The strange limbo of *la drôle de guerre* was broken when the Wehrmacht invaded the Netherlands, Luxembourg, Belgium and France, one after another, starting on 10 May. The Maginot Line was meant to be impregnable and act as insurance against the very thing that was, in fact, happening. Reports of Germany's panzer divisions and bombing campaigns were beginning to strike a kind of fear into the heart of France not felt since the previous war.

The roads, already filled with Belgian and Dutch refugees, became even more crowded with French civilians and military units moving south and west. 'L'Exode' had begun. However, most people still assumed that it was inconceivable that Paris would be allowed to fall to Hitler. It was too large and important; the army would defend the city at all costs. It would take a good deal of time and effort for the Wehrmacht to break through the city's defences and even if they succeeded, they would be forced to fight street by street.

When Pamela spoke to Macaulay after news of the first invasion, he said grimly, 'Reports aren't looking too cheerful. We need to be prepared for any eventuality.'

Pamela had hardly heard from Sid, who was still at the front. She knew that the increased pressure on the military and the complications posed by refugees fleeing west ahead of the German army had slowed the postal service down considerably. Besides, he was resourceful and hardly the only war correspondent in eastern France. If a retreat was necessary, he would be with a number of other journalists, all heading in the same direction. He would be alright. Besides, if she started worrying about him now, she'd never stop.

While the French government seemed to be in a state of semi-paralysis, the British were busy getting rid of their Prime Minister. After Labour refused to continue serving under the coalition Chamberlain was desperately trying to form, the First Lord of the Admiralty, Winston Churchill, replaced him. The new government then promptly sacked anyone they found to be an apologist, sympathiser, defeatist or fifth columnist. As soon as the French government started making preparations to move to Bordeaux and the British Embassy began evacuating its staff, Churchill ordered the Windsors to return home.

When Pamela arrived at Boulevard Suchet the following week, the tension in the air was palpable. The remaining servants were scurrying around, covering the furniture with dust sheets and packing boxes and suitcases. It was clear that the Windsors had got on Fruity's last nerve. The previous week, the Duke had dispatched him to La Croë, to take the Cairn Terriers to safety.

'When I resigned from my regiment to serve the Prince of Wales, it wasn't to be a valet to his goddamned dogs!' he hissed in Pamela's ear as he showed her in.

Wallis oversaw the packing while the Duke paced up and down the drawing room, drink in hand. Sober for once, Fruity watched him intently, barely able to mask his irritation. Pamela missed Noël and desperately wished he were there to distract everyone.

'I don't see how we can possibly return home when my brother refuses to grant us a royal residence. Has he been told that we would settle for Fort Belvedere?'

'Yes, your Grace.'

'And?'

'As I said, it isn't possible.'

'Not possible!' He threw his arms up in the air. 'Not possible, to house the former King of England and his wife! Order us home and not offer us shelter! Where on earth are we meant to go?'

Although the Duke was careless and selfish in his dealings with everyone apart from his wife, the nature of his frustration with Fruity belied a depth and intimacy Pamela didn't see him express with many people. When they were younger, she could well imagine how they had developed an affinity for one another. They had shared a certain untroubled, playboy attitude, rejecting the formality and stuffiness of their fathers' generation. Edward lent the young Irish army officer from a humble background a sense of importance and Fruity gave the Prince someone in whom he could confide. She felt sorry for Fruity, to have had to endure this kind of treatment from someone who had not only been a close friend but also, perhaps, a lover.

'And I'm very upset that my family persists in denying Wallis the HRH.'

'David let's not go through all that again. You know what your family is like,' replied Wallis irritably. 'Miss Blythewood! Miss Blythewood!'

The Windsors' secretary appeared.

'See that everything is packed *efficiently*. I want to make sure we fit as many suitcases as possible into the cars.'

Fruity sat up straight. 'Cars?'

'Yes, they're preparing the cars,' replied the Duke.

'But Monckton is coming in a plane tomorrow.'

'Flying is impossible. You know the Duchess is afraid of flying. It's why we wouldn't fly last time we had to endure this rigmarole.'

'And we'll be able to fit far more luggage if we drive,' Wallis explained impatiently, as if she were going on holiday rather than fleeing the country ahead of an invading army.

'Your Grace ... *Churchill himself* has ordered the plane,' Fruity explained through gritted teeth.

'I hate aeroplanes,' she snapped. 'They're dangerous. I refuse to die crossing the English Channel.'

Pamela knew she had to say something. What she wanted to do was ask Wallis if she preferred to die in a German invasion. Instead, she put a hand on her arm said gently, 'Wallis, the advantage of flying is that you'll be back in England much more quickly. You won't have to sit for days on dusty, blocked roads on the drive to the coast.'

'Have *you* ever been in an aeroplane?'

The only time Pamela had been in a plane was when she was pushed out of one while flying over an English field.

'I quite enjoy flying,' she lied. 'The miracle of modern travel.'

'We drove to the port last time. I don't see why we can't do it again,' Wallis huffed.

'The situation as it stands is somewhat different from last year,' replied Pamela slowly.

'Yes, last year, the Germans were well behind the Siegfried Line and not actually *in* France,' muttered Fruity.

The Duke began to pack one of his pipes with tobacco. 'Winston must be mad not to see Britain is doomed. The thing he doesn't understand about the Germans is their dogged spirit. They can show endurance in the face of anything, you see. If he knew what was in the country's best interest, he would invite Germany to the negotiating table,' he said matter-of-factly as he lit the bowl of his pipe.

Fruity and Pamela looked at each other. Though they had both heard his pro-German ramblings before, that had been before the war. That was the starkest statement they had heard from him yet, possibly even a treasonous one.

Wallis called out, 'Miss Blythewood! We need to go to the bank first thing in the morning so I can get my jewels from the vault.'

The next day, Walter Monckton came in the plane sent by Churchill. Fruity continued to argue with the Duke while Pamela tried to persuade Wallis. But even Monckton couldn't convince them to fly. They insisted on driving.

'I'm sorry, but I must return to London,' he told Fruity and Pamela. 'Since they won't see reason, one of you will have to escort them by car to Le Havre, where a destroyer will be waiting.'

Pamela had been hoping for a moment when she could take Monckton aside; what the Duke had said about Churchill negotiating with Germany was worrying her and she knew she would feel better, that she'd done her due diligence if she was able to tell him. Monckton looked utterly exhausted and everything was rushed. Churchill had just appointed him Director General of the Ministry of Information and he had to hurry back to London. Pamela could well imagine that he had a number of things to do more important than play nanny to the Windsors. Like helping Prime Minister Reynaud save his country.

II

The next day, Pamela and Lettice watched as Mikhail and his dealer, Georges, supervised the moving men carrying Mikhail's sculptures into the cellar of Georges's Left Bank gallery, where they would be hidden for the duration of the war. Georges also insisted that Lettice and Mikhail come with him to his family home in Provence, now that going to Lettice's family home in Normandy was looking impossible.

When Pamela first saw Mikhail's work at an opening the previous year, she'd found it incomprehensible and unsettling. Now, in the gloom of his dealer's cellar, the artist's sculptures made a kind of sense to her. The jagged edges. The twisted limbs. The teeth in strange places. Things that looked both human and inhuman, like products of tragic, disfiguring accidents. One in particular caught her eye: two figures so entangled with one another that she couldn't tell where one ended and the other began. One had a pair of horns and seemed to be devouring the other.

'The Rape of Europa,' Georges explained with a sad smile.

He was a slight man with red hair, a thin moustache and skin that was so pale it almost seemed to glow in the gloom of the cellar. The image of the small, pixie-like man amongst the large, nightmarish sculptures made Pamela think of the fairy tales her nanny used to read to her and Charlotte as children.

Lettice took Pamela's arm and whispered, 'We've heard stories about what the Nazis have been doing to Jews in occupied countries. All his

Sarah Sigal

artist friends have been making arrangements to leave. Some of them are already in America. I don't know how we're going to leave now.'

'What about his French papers?' whispered Pamela.

'They still haven't come. And I can't imagine they will now. I don't know what to do any more, Pam,' admitted Lettice, desperation creeping into her voice.

Pamela felt her stomach lurch; she had seen in the papers that morning that the French government had announced that all stateless people born in Germany were to report to their local *mairie*. She could well imagine that the law could soon be extended to all the people in France who were *sans papiers*, regardless of their country of origin.

'Have you tried contacting your father?'

'I sent a telegram to the British Embassy in Cairo but I've heard nothing.' Lettice struggled not to cry and twisted a ring on her finger round and round. 'The trouble is … I'm pregnant.'

Then the dam burst and Lettice started to cry. Pamela hugged her and stroked her hair. The thought of her best friend trapped in a war-torn country, pregnant, was almost too much to bear. She felt a lump in her own throat and had to swallow it hard so that she wouldn't start blubbing too. Pamela took Lettice by the shoulders.

'Your father is a brigadier in the British Army. Surely *someone* in Egypt should be able to find him. They can't have lost an entire regiment.'

'Yes,' she sobbed, 'and he's an absolute bloody, heartless bastard. What if he won't help me?'

Pamela had never met such a steely, terrifying man in her life. He'd hardly spoken to Lettice since the divorce. Both the brigadier and his daughter were as stubborn as mules and neither would make the first move to reconcile. But Pamela couldn't imagine he would

214

be so indifferent as to do nothing while his only daughter risked ending up in a German internment camp.

'Think of it this way … it's time to channel your father's bloody-minded English side.' Pamela wiped away Lettice's tears. 'Chin up, duckie. Keep trying the old man until you get through to him. I won't leave this country without you. We'll just have to be resourceful.'

Lettice hugged her tightly. 'Thank you. Thank you, Pam.'

When Pamela turned to Mikhail and Georges, the movers had gone and the two men were standing very close to each other, whispering. Georges was gently holding the tips of Mikhail's fingers. She looked back at Lettice, but her friend was turned around, busy fixing her ruined makeup with her compact and a handkerchief.

III

Fruity and Pamela met at Boulevard Suchet for the final time, to help with the travel preparations and make sure everything was going to plan for the Windsors' departure on the destroyer the next day. When they discovered there would only be room for one of them to accompany the couple, Pamela told Fruity that he should go with them.

'Lady Pamela,' he said as he looked at her in surprise, 'you must leave France as soon as possible. The way things are, it's only going to become more and more difficult to return to Britain.'

'I have a friend I care about very much. I have to make sure she and her' — she paused for a moment — 'husband are able to get out of France. She has a British passport but he doesn't. It's rather a difficult situation.'

'Difficult situation rather sums up the whole blasted thing, doesn't it?' Fruity sighed.

Pamela and Fruity arranged for her to help see everyone off, and he was to escort the Windsors to Le Havre. But when she returned to Boulevard Suchet the next morning to meet them, she found only Fruity, who was utterly enraged. The Windsors had absconded at the crack of dawn, abandoning him.

Quite literally, a French leave.

'He deserted his job in 1936 and he's deserted his job now, at a time when every office boy and cripple is trying to do what he can for his country,' he fumed as they stood outside the house. 'What utterly selfish cowards.'

'But I don't understand. Where have they gone?'

'La Croë, I reckon. The Duke was banging on about his family's silver and those damned Carins. They must have known Monckton would never have allowed it and I would have stopped them. What absolutely useless, stupid, selfish people. And what a fool I've been.' Fruity looked at Pamela. 'I'm leaving. I'm getting the hell out of this bloody country. And you should too.'

And with that, he got on his bicycle and rode off.

Pamela made her way home on the Métro in a daze. She had thought that as long as she could ensure the Windsors went back to England, then she could figure out the rest. It was the first time she had felt a genuine sense of panic, as if everything were falling apart. She had no idea what to do. There hadn't been a contingency plan for what to do if they disappeared without warning.

The next morning, she read that the British and American ambassadors and their staff had attended a service at Notre Dame, in honour of France. While the former English King and his American wife played truant in order to fetch their dogs from the South of France, diplomatic officials were praying for the salvation of the Third Republic.

IV

Pamela attempted to make contact with Macaulay again immediately after the Windsors left and again and again after that as the month dragged on but had heard nothing. He had to know about the Windsors' escape and Fruity returning to England alone. Did he think Pamela had gone with him? Surely, he knew she had remained in Paris, awaiting orders. Meanwhile, even though Reynaud's government had not announced an evacuation order, more and more people were leaving the city — first government officials, then foreign diplomats, then wealthy Parisians. The conversations she overheard amongst ordinary people throughout the city consisted of: if there was any real danger, the government would have told us. But the metallic sound of iron shutters clanging shut over windows became more and more frequent as shopkeepers closed up their businesses.

Pamela tried to control the mounting dread that greeted her each morning that she failed to receive a reply. Macaulay was probably busy. Or communications were slow. Certainly, he would find a way of reaching her soon. But then Paris started to hear news from the front. The Germans were outflanking and beating back British, French and Belgian troops and had them all surrounded on the coast at Dunkirk. Their tanks had found a way around the Maginot Line with their Panzer corps, through the Ardennes Forest and then over the River Meuse. Churchill had ordered an evacuation: the British were leaving France.

At Georges's urging, Lettice and Mikhail decided to drive with him to his family home in Provence. Lettice would continue to attempt to contact her father from the south, through the British Embassy in Marseille. Lettice begged Pamela to come with them, but Pamela didn't want to leave without making contact with Macaulay first. She needed to know what to do and where to go, but even more importantly, if Lettice couldn't get a hold of her father, Pamela prayed that the captain could help get her friends out of France.

To make matters worse, Pamela hadn't heard anything from Sid, who was back at the front, in weeks. She asked Lettice and Mikhail what they'd heard, but they knew as little as she did.

'He's with all those other war correspondents. He'll be alright, darling,' Lettice said.

Pamela said that she wanted to stay behind just a few more days to see if she could reach Sid. And lied, saying that she had plans to head south with a group of people from the British Embassy. Lettice gave her Georges's mother's address in Provence and Pamela said she would join them as soon as she could.

But as soon as they left, Pamela regretted not having left Paris with them. Damn Captain Macaulay, damn Sid and damn the Windsors. She had put everyone else's needs before her own and look where it had got her: alone in Paris, with the German army on the horizon.

June 1940

I

Pamela was having a final glass of wine with Madame Garrote on an uncomfortably warm summer evening before she and Tulipe left the city to stay with a brother in the Dordogne. A native Parisian, she was reluctant to leave, but knew that it was too dangerous to risk an encounter with the Germans, especially if they found out that she had been aiding British intelligence.

'It wasn't so terrible here in the last war. The bombardments didn't get really bad until the end. It was worse in the countryside, poor things. All those villages destroyed.

'And the government took control of everything — where we went, when we slept, what we ate. I was a *munitionette*, making arms in a factory. It was unbearable in some ways, yes — for instance, they banned brioche! Boulangeries could only make a certain type of bread. *Pain national!* But now, there is nothing. No word from the president, from Monsieur the Mayor …'

Pamela petted Tulipe, who was sitting at her feet. 'Do you think the defences of the city will hold?'

'What defences?'

Pamela shifted uncomfortably in her seat. 'Surely, the government isn't going to leave Paris totally undefended … ?'

The concierge looked at Pamela pityingly. 'Do you hear any guns, cheri? Do you see any soldiers guarding the Porte de Charenton? Or Passy? Or Saint-Ouen?'

Madame Garrote was right. Pamela had neither seen nor heard any military defences. She had known it on a subconscious level but hadn't allowed herself to believe it. One of the most significant capital cities in the world, literally left to its own defences.

Suddenly, they heard a screech of tyres outside, then honking and yelling. They got up to see what was happening in the street and saw two stationary cars. A suitcase had fallen off the roof of one of the cars into the road, blocking the car behind it, which had a mattress tied to the roof. A man and a woman, the two drivers, were shouting at each other, while the man's wife struggled to get the suitcase out of the road. Her husband then turned and shouted at her, for having insisted on bringing so many bags.

While the city's wealthy residents had been fleeing Paris via car, their worse off neighbours were either crowding into the train stations to beg, borrow or steal a seat on a train going south or using every available vehicle to navigate the crowded roads. Pamela had seen people using horses and carts, riding bicycles and driving all kinds of vans: from bakeries, moving companies, laundries — even ice-cream vans. Everywhere Pamela looked, she saw suitcases, boxes, furniture, as the city emptied out. The final straw had been when she witnessed a woman tearfully shoot her dog in the middle of the street.

Sick of waiting for word from the captain, Pamela there and then decided to leave Paris before it was too late. When she went upstairs to her flat to pack, she opened the door and to her astonishment found Macaulay sitting at her kitchen table, walking stick hooked over the back of his chair.

'Where have you been? I've been waiting for weeks! Would a message of some sort — a signal — have been too much to ask? Even a carrier pigeon would have been something!' she snapped as she slammed her handbag down on the table.

Pamela got her cigarette case and lighter and lit a cigarette with a shaking hand. She then went to the countertop and opened a bottle of wine. She realised that Macaulay himself looked tired and miserable, so she softened, offering him a glass.

'When the Windsors absconded, I was tasked with tracking them down and finding someone to tail them. But I lost them. And of course, everything has slowed considerably because of ...' The captain waved his hand towards the window. 'It's impossible to get anywhere right now or to get any messages through. The whole country's gone to hell. We're not even batting for a draw at this point.'

Usually so reserved and tactful, Pamela had never seen Macaulay like this.

He looked at her sharply and said, 'I'm surprised you're still here.'

Pamela quickly drained her glass and then refilled it. 'Just because Fruity turned tail, doesn't mean I did. I was waiting for my orders,' she replied pointedly.

Macaulay nodded and loosened his tie. The summer heat was building in the city and becoming oppressive.

Pamela crossed the room and opened a window. 'What's happened to the Duke and Duchess?'

The captain blotted his forehead with a handkerchief. 'I suspect they're heading to La Croë. Hopefully, they'll make contact with the consulate in Nice. We'll have to try again to get them on a boat at Cannes or Marseille, where there are still passenger ships heading to England.'

Pamela leaned out of the window, trying to catch a breeze. She took a drag on her cigarette and looked down into the courtyard, guessing how old the cobblestones below were, how many upheavals they'd seen already. How was it that a city that had survived countless wars and revolutions was now coming apart at the seams?

'Churchill was in Paris a few days ago to negotiate the Dunkirk evacuations with Reynaud. Days before that, he had to fight off Halifax, who wanted to broker a peace treaty. It's outrageous that on top of all of that, he needs to worry about a member of the Royal Family putting himself and his wife in danger,' Macaulay said darkly.

Churchill had been in Paris? And Halifax wanted to negotiate a peace treaty? Things seemed like they were moving so quickly and yet Pamela felt like she hardly knew anything at all because it was being kept so secret. She poured Macaulay another glass of wine and sat down, her elbows resting on the table.

'We still need someone to try to persuade the Duchess to board a ship home.' Macaulay looked at Pamela over the top of his wine glass. '*Churchill* needs someone to persuade her.'

They both knew that it was Wallis who was likely pulling the strings at this point and that Edward would do whatever she wanted. She realised that although Macaulay was surprised she was still in Paris, he hadn't yet offered to help her get out of France. At least not without the Windsors. If Noël were there, he would say that was her cue.

'What if I went to the south, persuaded Wallis to sail for England

and escorted them on their ship? It might be easier to persuade her now that Fruity's gone.'

Macaulay sighed, visibly relieved. 'Yes, capital plan. Very good.'

Pamela topped up his wine glass. 'Captain, I have a friend … She has a British passport. But her— the father of her unborn child does not. I need to help them get to England.'

'French?'

'Russian. He's lived in France for many years but they never sent him his papers. He only has a Nansen passport, unfortunately.' She hesitated. 'And he's Jewish.'

'Christ,' Macaulay muttered. 'Does this friend of yours have any strings she can pull?'

'Her father is a brigadier commanding a regiment in Egypt. She's trying to reach him. But in the meantime, her only other string might be me.'

Macaulay was quiet for a moment, thinking as he looked out the window. Then he sighed. 'Very well. I'll see what I can manage when I reach the consulate in Marseille.'

They agreed that tomorrow, Pamela would take the Windsors' third car, left at Boulevard Suchet, and drive to Marseille, where she would meet the captain.

'By that point, hopefully we'll have figured out where the Windsors are.'

For the first time, Pamela was starting to doubt the captain's wisdom. What the Duke had said about negotiating a peace with Germany had been weighing on her mind for weeks.

'Captain?'

He looked at her. 'Yes?'

'There was something the Duke said to Fruity and me, before they left.'

Macaulay looked apprehensive but waved his hand in a circular motion. 'Go on …'

'He said Churchill was underestimating how determined the Germans are. And that he should initiate negotiations with them.'

Macaulay looked horrified.

'Lady Pamela, please be so kind as to keep that information under your hat for the time being.' He closed his eyes and wiped his brow. 'We're going to have to operate a policy of containment. I needn't tell you how disastrous the consequences could be if a piece of information like that got out. We simply have to get them home before they cause any trouble.'

II

Every day for the last week, Pamela had been going to the *Herald Tribune* offices, just off the Champs-Élysées, asking if anyone had heard from Sid. All his editor could tell her was that he knew Sid was on his way back to Paris, but didn't know when he was meant to arrive. So, the day after meeting Macaulay, after she packed her things, Pamela made one last attempt to see if anyone had heard from him.

As soon as she stepped into the office, she heard: 'Hey! Lady Right Honourable!'

Pamela turned and saw Sid standing next to a desk, looking as if he hadn't washed or shaved in days, still dusty and sweaty from travelling. He took her by the hand, led her into an empty office and closed the door. They embraced and he kissed her fervently.

'Where have you been?' Pamela held Sid's face in her hands.

'Didn't you get my letters?'

'What letters?'

'Nothing else is working — I don't know why the French mail service would be.' Sid rubbed his eyes tiredly and then looked at her. 'What are you still doing here?'

Pamela explained Lettice and Mikhail's predicament and said she hadn't wanted to leave Paris until she could make contact with someone at the British Embassy who could help them. And that she was heading to Marseille later that afternoon.

'Well, if you're driving to Marseille, I'm coming with you. It's pretty hairy out there.'

Pamela hadn't expected to see Sid at all before she left and she certainly hadn't expected him to offer to join her. She had assumed that he would have already made plans to travel onwards with other journalists. She knew it was a risk, to drive with him, and that she wasn't sure how she was going to properly maintain her cover with him there the whole time. But she was just going to have to figure things out along the way. The idea of having someone with her while she navigated the busy roads was comforting and Sid's press pass and American passport might come in handy. But mostly, if she was being truly honest with herself, now that she'd found him again, she didn't want to give him up, especially as everything seemed to be falling apart.

'And then where will you go?' she asked.

'Good question ...' He shrugged. 'Guess I'll check in with the Associated Press or the US Embassy or something when we get there.'

Pamela couldn't decide whether his American breeziness was reassuring or unnerving. They agreed to get their things and meet at Boulevard Suchet later that afternoon, where they would pick up the Windsors' car and start making their way south, with the rest of the population of France.

III

Pamela realised she should have gone to the safe house to retrieve the gun from behind the toilet cistern days ago. Now, it would take too long to get across the city to Pigalle and then over to the 16th.

Follow your tradecraft and you won't be caught.

This was not good tradecraft. She started to curse this oversight, berating herself for being overwhelmed with anxiety and letting it cloud her judgement. But how was she meant to follow her training of preparedness, guardedness and suspicion when her targets had escaped under her nose, her handler had left her to her own devices for weeks and she was only two steps ahead of an invading army? Then she remembered the .38 and the cartridges Bricktop had given her. She unearthed them from beneath her floorboards, clutched them to her breast in relief for a moment and stowed them in her handbag.

Pamela paid a small fortune to what seemed like the last taxi driver in the city to take her from her flat in the Latin Quarter to the Windsors' house on the edge of the Bois de Boulogne. When she asked him why he hadn't left Paris yet, he said he was making more money shuttling people across the city than he had in the last year and besides, where else would he go? He wished her *bonne chance* as he dropped her off in front of the house in the utterly deserted 16th arrondissement. Pamela took her suitcases and went straight to the garage, where the Ford station wagon was still parked. She knew the Windsors' chauffeur left the keys underneath the sun visor on the driver's side. But when she looked, they weren't there. Trying not to panic, Pamela searched the car, and then the garage. But they were nowhere to be found.

She went back around to the front of the house. They must have been left inside somewhere. And if none of the Windsor servants were still hanging around, she would simply have to break in. Pamela breathed a sigh of relief when she saw that the lights were on. If one of the servants asked why she wanted the car, she would tell them that she was driving it down to La Croë for the Duke and Duchess. She wiped her sweaty brow and rang the bell. To her surprise, Miss Blythewood answered.

'Lady Pamela!' she cried, looking anxious and distressed. 'I can't tell you how relieved I am to see you!'

'Miss Blythewood, what are you doing here? I thought you would have gone back to England by now.'

Blythewood started to cry. 'They said they would arrange for me to go home but in the rush and confusion ... with the plane and then taking the cars ...'

'But they left one of the cars behind. Surely, you could have taken it.'

'I can't drive. And besides, there's no petrol in it. They siphoned it off for the other cars.'

'No petrol?' Pamela's heart started to pound again. What were they going to do without petrol? Why on earth hadn't she thought of that herself? What was she going to do now?

'And then, when I tried to get a ticket for one of the trains, the stations were just overrun with people. It was terrifying.'

Margaret Blythewood always struck Pamela as an obsequious and somewhat hapless person: eager to please her employers and capable in her job but otherwise a little naïve and at sea in the world. She could well imagine Wallis and Edward leaving their faithful English secretary behind while they worried about their silver. Pamela was furious at the Windsors for turning their carelessness and selfishness into a crisis for someone else. She felt quite sorry for her and knew there was nothing for it — she would have to join them on the drive to Marseille. Pamela couldn't very well abandon her in Paris. And once they reached the south, hopefully she would become someone else's problem.

Pamela took her by the shoulders. 'Miss Blythewood. Please do try to pull yourself together. The Duchess has cabled and asked me to drive the Ford to La Croë for her. I'm going to drive down with a friend and you can join us. From there, we'll be within reach of the British Consulate in Marseille, where I'm sure they'll be able to arrange something for you.'

Blythewood took Pamela's hands and squeezed them. 'Thank you! I can't thank you enough, Lady Pamela.'

Looking at her watch, Pamela realised that Sid was due to meet her at Boulevard Suchet any moment. 'Do you have the keys to the Ford?'

'Yes, let me get them. I'll just collect my things. I won't be a moment!' trilled Blythewood as she hurried up the stairs.

But what was Pamela going to do about the petrol? She had been too busy worrying about everything else to have thought about it. She took a deep breath. She would go to the nearest petrol station and see if she could buy some. If that was impossible, they would have to get a lift with someone. Maybe Sid knew another reporter who was also leaving Paris.

It was strange, not having Hale or any of the other servants around, and even stranger seeing the house so empty, the furniture covered in dust sheets. The mirrors, the caryatids, the marble pillars — it seemed more like a mausoleum than a home.

The more she thought about it, the stranger Miss Blythewood's predicament seemed to Pamela. It was true, Paris had been chaotic and the train stations had been full to bursting. But why didn't she think to go to the British Embassy? She listened to the secretary's footsteps cross the corridor above her head; unlike most other women, she didn't make a clicking sound when she walked. Her sensible brogues had a softer tread, like a man's.

Suddenly, something clicked in Pamela's mind.

When she had been hiding in the Duke's bedroom at the Christmas party, she thought it was a man who had come in to look for her. Because she thought she heard a man's footsteps walking down the corridor.

Madame Garrote had said the person waiting outside the building had looked like a slim man, around Pamela's height. Miss Blythewood was Pamela's height.

When she had been ill at La Croë, it was the secretary who seemed most concerned with Pamela's health.

'Would you mind giving me a hand? I'm afraid my case is very heavy,' said Blythewood apologetically as she descended the stairs with a suitcase and a handbag, the car keys gripped in one hand.

Pamela looked at the Englishwoman with her high neckline and long hemline, her spectacles and mousy blond hair threaded through with grey. She looked more like a maiden aunt than an enemy agent. And she had always put so much faith in the Windsors — maybe she thought they would send someone for her later. Was Pamela just stressed? Delirious, even? Was she losing her grip on reality?

Pamela leaned down to take the suitcase and heard a click. When she looked up, Blythewood was standing over her and holding a Luger — the kind of semi-automatic pistol used by the Wehrmacht.

The two women locked eyes. Blythewood looked at Pamela unsmilingly; it was as if her face had completely transformed.

If there's a question, there's no question.

'Hands above your head please, Lady Pamela,' Blythewood ordered.

Pamela did as she was told and muttered angrily, 'Left behind by the Windsors, my foot.'

She wanted to kick herself. How stupid she had been. This was the woman who had tried to poison her and had likely poisoned her predecessor when they too became a problem. She had even lurked in the corridor at La Croë to see if she'd been able to finish Pamela off, just before searching her room. And now, she was going to shoot her.

'We needn't have ended up in this unfortunate situation. You should have left with Fruity and gone back to England when you had the chance. You've only made things more complicated and difficult for yourself.'

It was infuriating, being outsmarted and then being told what to do in that bossy, officious tone. She sounded like Pamela's mother.

'You have two choices. You can remain here, in Paris, and wait for the Abwehr to interrogate you as a British spy.'

Pamela already knew what the second choice was. Her heart was beating so hard and so fast she could hear the blood pumping. But before Blythewood could finish her ultimatum, the doorbell rang. They froze. It felt like time was standing still.

'Don't answer it,' hissed Blythewood, the Luger still trained on Pamela.

The bell rang again.

'Pamela?' Sid's voice came through from the other side of the door.

'He'll go away,' said Blythewood confidently.

But she didn't know American reporters and she certainly didn't know Sidney White. He rang the bell again and tried the handle.

Blythewood's gaze flicked to the door and, in the blink of an eye, Pamela lunged at her with the full force of her body. They scrambled and Pamela ended up on top of her. She slammed Blythewood's hand onto the marble floor, trying to get her to release her grip on the gun. Once. Twice. On the third slam, she cried out and dropped it. But just as Pamela reached for the pistol, Blythewood managed to knock her off balance and kick the Luger away, far across the grand entrance. Pamela's handbag was in the corner of her eye. If she could reach it, she could get her hands on Bricktop's pistol. The two women struggled, Blythewood landing blow after blow on Pamela's body. Pamela tried not to be distracted by the pain.

Able to hear the struggling going on inside, Sid began pounding on the door. 'Pam, are you in there?'

Pamela suddenly remembered her hand-to-hand combat training and struck Blythewood's windpipe with the edge of her hand, knocking the wind out of her. While she struggled to breathe, Pamela then hit her solar plexus with her elbow. With Blythewood doubled over, she made a grab for the .38. She cocked it and aimed at her. Was she really going to shoot this woman? Had it come to this?

Blythewood lunged for the gun, and Pamela pulled the trigger. The German agent made another grab for Pamela as she went down, grabbing a fistful of Pamela's dress, trying to drag her to the ground. Pamela braced herself against her weight. She put the barrel of the gun to Blythewood's forehead and shot her again. Her body crumpled to the floor. There was blood everywhere. Pamela felt frozen to the spot. Her mind went completely blank, as if trying to disassociate from the moment altogether.

'Pamela?' The anxiety came through in Sid's voice. 'I heard gunshots! Are you ok?'

Pamela knew she had only another minute or two. As quickly as she could, she started with Blythewood's handbag, where she found her papers — identifying her as British subject Margaret Blythewood. But she knew there must be other identification somewhere. She had to find out who the hell this woman really was.

'Ok, Pam! I'm going to break down the door!' Sid shouted.

Pamela didn't put it past Sid to break down the Windsors' substantial front door, so she hurriedly tore through the contents of Blythewood's suitcase but became increasingly frustrated as she found nothing. But then she remembered something they had told her during training: hide anything valuable or compromising in the suitcase lining. Pamela felt around in the lining of the case but couldn't find anything.

All of a sudden, she heard a thud from the other side of the door. Sid was being true to his word. Pamela couldn't exactly tell him that she needed to find the Nazi identity papers of the woman who had been posing as the Windsors' secretary. She had to hurry.

Damn and blast. Where on earth was it?

But then Pamela spotted Blythewood's coat, which she'd dropped at the bottom of the stairs. Pamela quickly went through the coat pockets. Her heart leapt as she felt something in the lining. Sitting on the cold marble of the Windsors' entryway, she inspected the dead woman's jacket. She was ready to rip it open when she realised that there were three small hook-and-eye closures tucked into the seam where the tweed met the silk lining, too subtle and small to be noticed if you didn't know what you were looking for. Pamela unhooked them and withdrew a small grey booklet with a Nazi insignia that read *Wehrpass*. Inside was the true identity of Margaret Blythewood — or rather, Johanna Hoffman.

Outside, Sid continued to throw his body against the front door, so along with Blythewood's British identity papers, Pamela quickly hid the booklet in the secret compartment at the bottom of her handbag, where she kept the recording device. Pamela turned around to look at the mess in the entryway — Blythewood's body in the middle, a pool of blood spreading around her. What was she going to tell Sid? Certainly not the truth. She had to think of a cover. Or, as Noël would say, perform a bit of theatre. As calmly as she could, Pamela put the gun down, turned around and opened the door for Sid.

'Thank God you're alright. I heard gunshots. Are you hurt?'

Pamela shook her head and stood aside to reveal the bloody scene behind her.

Sid looked ashen. 'Jesus Christ. What the hell happened?'

'It's the Windsors' secretary. They left her behind and …' Pamela took a deep breath. This had to be believable. 'It all happened so quickly. I told her we were going to drive to Marseille and we could take her with us, but she was absolutely distraught. She had been trying to find a way out of Paris. The embassy shutting down and the chaos at the train stations — it was too much for her. She said we'd never make it. She was terrified of being captured by the Germans.'

Sid looked at the body in horror. 'She shot herself?'

Pamela tried to muster up some crocodile tears for Miss Blythewood but found it difficult even to pretend to cry over a Nazi agent who only moments before had been trying to kill her. Then she thought about what Edna Bishop had told her about play-acting and disguises — turning yourself into a different person. Pamela turned away from him, pinched herself a couple of times, started breathing deeply, then began gasping for air. (She remembered watching Charlotte pretending to cry in front of their parents as children.) She turned back around, starting to choke up.

'I tried to stop her. There was a struggle. But there was nothing I could do. I didn't know she had a gun until it was too late.'

Mixing truth with lies.

Sid looked at the body and then back at Pamela, who realised belatedly that she had blood on her skirt. For one perilous moment, she wasn't certain he would believe her. But then he threw his arms around her.

'That must have been awful. I'm so sorry, Pam,' he murmured in her ear. 'God, what do we do with the body?'

'I don't think there's anything we can do,' Pamela replied, trying to feign a kind of sympathetic resignation. 'It's horrible, just leaving her here but …'

Hopefully, the Germans will be the first to find their Johanna Hoffman and be left to clean up the mess, Pamela thought bitterly to herself. She picked up the keys to the Ford that were lying on the floor and took her suitcases. The afternoon sun beat down on both of them as they left the house. Pamela felt a drop of sweat run down the side of her neck.

'Where's the car?' Sid asked wearily.

Pamela looked at the keys in her hand. 'It's just in the garage but we have a problem. There's no petrol.'

Sid's jacket was lying on top of what Pamela thought was another suitcase. With a flourish, he revealed two full jerrycans.

'I've been driving all over France for weeks. I'd be surprised if we found a single gas station between here and the south coast that wasn't overrun or tapped out. It's like every single person in the country has hit the road.' He looked at her again, thinking. 'That woman had a gun, didn't she?'

Pamela pulled out Blythewood's Luger that she had taken off her.

'I thought we might need it.'

Sid looked surprised. She briefly considered telling him about the .38 but decided against it. Pamela worried how long she was going to be able to keep this up, what else might cross their path and what other acts she would have to perform.

IV

Every major road heading to the south or west of France was completely filled with a never-ending river of people. As they inched out of the city, the smell of petrol became suffocating. It was like a portrait of humanity at its most frightened and desperate. Pamela had never seen such chaos in her life. Traffic moved at a crawl. People honked incessantly. Cars broke down in the middle of the road and were shoved into ditches. Suitcases, hatboxes, children's toys, pieces of furniture, clocks, mirrors — it was heartbreaking to watch the entirety of whole families' treasured possessions abandoned. As in the city, people drove cars and vans and horse-drawn carts, rode bicycles, walked. Pamela even saw an old man pushing his wife in a wheelbarrow. Despite the oppressive heat, people wore layers and layers of clothing — jackets on top of jackets, skirts over trousers. Pamela realised that it was mostly women, children and the elderly — as most men between the ages of twenty and fifty were either working in munitions factories or away with their regiments, probably in retreat.

'It's like the end of the world,' said Pamela softly.

'You should have seen Dunkirk. They cornered them with everything they had — tanks, bombs, everything. Germany's a machine now. I don't think anyone's seen anything like this since Napoleon.'

The car in front of them had a mattress tied to the roof, like the one Pamela and Madame Garrote had seen outside their building in Paris.

'Why do they tie mattresses to their cars?' she asked.

'Because they think it will protect them from the bombs.'

Suddenly, they heard the sound of planes in the distance. And then, screaming.

Pamela grabbed Sid's arm with the hand that wasn't on the steering wheel. 'What is that? What's happening?'

The screaming and the planes got closer. And then the rat-a-tat-tat of machine-gun fire.

'Messerschmitts. They're strafing the roads.' Sid's eyes widened as he watched the Luftwaffe formation fly towards them. 'We have to get out of the car!'

Pamela put the car in park and opened the door. Sid grabbed her hand and they ran for a nearby ditch. Along with other frightened drivers and pedestrians, they threw themselves to the ground. Pamela and Sid held each other as the German planes machine-gunned the road. Everyone around them was screaming. A horse that was pulling an old wagon reared and bolted, taking the wagon with it. Everyone had abandoned their cars and bicycles and had thrown themselves into the ditch too. Children and babies were crying. The planes screamed overhead and she could hear gunfire all around her. Pamela had never been a woman of faith, but if there was ever a time to pray, she knew it was then and there. Was that how it was going to end? In a ditch in the French countryside?

As the Luftwaffe passed and the noise died down, Pamela realised that Sid was singing softly to himself.

'*Summertime and the living is easy … Fish are jumpin' and the cotton is high …*' And he carried on singing as they got up and pulled themselves out of the ditch. '*Your daddy's rich … and your mama's good looking …*' He looked at Pamela. 'I sing when I get scared. A soldier in Spain taught me that. Regulates your breathing, gets your heart rate down. Gives you something else to think about.'

When they got back to the road, they could see the damage that the Messerschmitts had done. The bodies of people who weren't able to run for cover lay bleeding in the setting sun. Two small children sat on the side of the road, next to the bodies of a woman and a man.

'Oh my god,' Pamela gasped.

She stopped dead, rooted to the spot. The older girl couldn't have been more than four and the boy could have been as young as two. The boy was wailing helplessly and the girl looked stunned.

'What do we do? We have to do something.'

'This is what happens in a war. Someone will come along and take care of them.'

Pamela turned to face him, suddenly feeling furious — at the war, at the whole situation, at the entire world. *To murder the innocent parents of two such small children, to orphan that little girl and boy. And for what? Why?*

'Someone will take care of them? Who? And what are they meant to do in the meantime? Just sit there, next to the dead bodies of their parents?' she replied angrily.

'I'm sorry. There's nothing we can do.' Sid turned back to the car.

Pamela had never seen this side of Sid before — the hardened war correspondent. She knew he was right, but still felt her heart lurch as she looked back at the children, knowing she wasn't going to do anything to help them.

'Aw shit,' he muttered. Pamela turned to see that one of the tyres was flat; it had been hit by a bullet. 'We're going to have to change this.'

While Sid was doing just that, the car behind them started honking. Pamela watched nervously as cars and wagons behind that car formed an impatient line. More cars started honking. A man leaned out of his car window to shout at them to move.

'Give us a minute, for God's sake!' Sid shouted back at them.

Two men got out of their cars and started arguing with Sid and Pamela. Pamela tried to explain that it would only take a few more minutes while Sid laboured in the heat. One of the men said, 'If you won't get off the road, we'll make you!' And then they both went to the back and started to push the car towards the ditch.

'Hey! What the hell do you bastards think you're doing?' Sid shouted.

Pamela glanced at her handbag in the car. The Luger was in the glovebox, but Bricktop's revolver was in her bag.

'Hey! Come on!' Sid was red faced. He went over and shoved one of the men who was pushing the car. The man shoved him back. His friend grabbed Sid's arms and pinned them behind his back. Before things could get any worse, Pamela quickly opened the car door and pulled the Colt .38 out of her handbag. She fired into the air. The two men — who looked as if they were going to beat Sid bloody — stopped and looked up. Pamela aimed at them.

'If you don't leave this instant, one of you is going to get shot! Get back in your cars, both of you!'

Everyone around them had heard the gunshot and were staring at Pamela. Looking at her in horror, the two men hurriedly backed away. Sid was wide-eyed but took advantage of the brief calm to finish changing the tyre. Everyone was quiet and watched Pamela and Sid. They both got back in and Pamela started driving.

They were quiet for a moment, exhausted. Then Sid looked at the .38 sticking out of her handbag.

'This isn't the Luger the secretary had …'

Without taking her eyes off the road, Pamela calmly replied, 'No, it was Bricktop's. She gave it to me before she left France. She said if I was going to stay here, I needed something to protect myself with.'

Sid nodded and gave a half-smile. 'She did run a nightclub, so I guess she knew what she was talking about.'

Pamela continued to drive in silence, hoping desperately that he wouldn't ask any more questions. She'd signed the Official Secrets Act. She couldn't tell anyone anything. But she couldn't help it if someone had walked in on her shooting an Abwehr agent. No one had told her what to do in this scenario. So, she changed the subject.

'Did you know that Lettice is pregnant?'

'Oh God.' Sid sighed.

'Why didn't that stupid boyfriend of hers get his French papers in order years ago?'

'Mikhail is single-minded. All he cares about is his art. Most of those guys are like that. Soutine, Chagall, Kisling. When they dragged themselves out of the Russian shtetls, they all made a beeline for Paris. The beacon of art. The last bastion of civilisation, supposedly.'

'If only he'd done it sooner, well before the war started.'

'He would have had to have done it a long time ago. The French government has been making it difficult for Jews for a while now. They just don't want any more taking refuge in la belle France.'

'But … he's been living in France for so long.'

'Remember what I said about Jews getting beaten up? The conservative press has been publishing stuff about "the Jewish question" and the "cultural pollution" of Jews for years.' Sid looked out the window at the husk of a burned-out ambulance. 'I just hope he has a backup plan for getting out of here.'

They drove past an abandoned tank. The defiant message on its side, scrawled in chalk, was heartbreaking: 'Vendu pas vaincu.'

Betrayed, not beaten.

'Unless Lettice can reach her father, it's me,' said Pamela. 'I'm the backup plan.'

V

The drive from Paris to Provence would normally have taken a day or two at most. But instead, it took Pamela and Sid nearly a week. It would have taken even longer, but they were able to veer off onto the roads reserved for the military, using Sid's press pass.

They'd picked up a pair of French infantry officers whose car had broken down and gave them a lift to a base outside Vichy. They had been with a regiment at the front and were — like most of the French military forces — in retreat. Morale and faith in France's leadership had been in freefall since Dunkirk and it had become impossible to stem desertion. Pamela found the conversation unbelievably depressing. Sid thought he'd managed to get a story out of it, but when he tried to file it over the phone from a hotel that evening, his editor told him that the *International Herald Tribune* was having to close its operations. The Germans were rumoured to be days away from Paris and the editors refused to operate under 'the Boche'.

When Pamela and Sid woke up the next morning, they discovered that Italy had declared war on France and Britain. Although reporters had been predicting such a declaration for weeks, it still filled her with a deepening sense of dread.

They arrived at Georges's family farmhouse to pick up Lettice and Mikhail. Mikhail wanted Georges to come with them but he couldn't leave his mother and sister, whose husband was in the navy and had three children to take care of. Sid and Pamela packed up the Ford while Lettice was saying goodbye to Georges' family. Georges and Mikhail were standing off to the side, under an olive tree. They made a strange pair — the slight, pale, ginger-haired Frenchman and the stocky, ruddy-cheeked, dark-haired Russian. Mikhail took a step towards Georges, looked around and then kissed him. They kissed briefly, like two old lovers.

Perhaps Pamela should have been outraged on behalf of her friend, who was, after all, pregnant with this man's child. Who could have gone back to England long ago but had endangered herself by staying in France with him. Instead, she felt a heavy sadness descend on her; she thought about all the people whose lives were being shattered by this war, who might not see each other again. Whose future was so uncertain. Did Lettice know? But why would she be fighting to stay with him if she did? Pamela considered telling her but knew it would hardly do any good. Lettice was pregnant and unless they could find an abortionist in the middle of all this, she was going to have Mikhail's baby. It was clear they loved each other, but it seemed perhaps that Mikhail also loved someone else. It didn't make sense. But then again, very little made sense anymore.

VI

They arrived the following day in Marseille, a seaside city of crumbling buildings packed together, winding streets, narrow staircases and an old harbour. It was full of people from across Europe, desperately trying to leave, rubbing along with the local population who, in contrast, largely felt they were still far enough away from the action not to start having to worry.

Lettice went to the British Consulate to see if she could reach her father in Egypt. Pamela's heart sank when she saw the long queue outside, realising that she'd underestimated just how many people would be clambering to get passage out of the country. It seemed anyone with a British passport or even the faintest hope of getting a visa was waiting at the gates. Inside, it was crowded with people begging consulate officials, showing them marriage and birth certificates and letters from relatives.

When they were finally seen, after four hours, Lettice discovered that there was a telegram waiting from the brigadier:

> *Will arrange for your return on next boat. Sorry nothing to be done for your friend.*

Standing there, holding the letter, Lettice looked shell-shocked. She looked around, breathing heavily, in distress. Suddenly, she collapsed. Mikhail and Sid ran to her. A consulate secretary was sent for water and another helped her to a divan in the next room.

'She's pregnant,' Pamela whispered to the secretary.

The woman nodded and then said loudly, 'Everyone please stand back and give the poor woman some air. She doesn't need you hovering over her.' To Pamela, she muttered, 'I was a nurse in the last war. Men are useless in a crisis.'

'Are you alright, darling?' asked Pamela calmly, as Lettice's eyelids started to flutter.

'Have I made a spectacle of myself?' she asked, smiling faintly.

'It's the heat, I reckon,' said the secretary as she gave Pamela a knowing look.

'You've had a bit of a shock,' Pamela said.

Lettice sat up, looked at the telegram again and closed her eyes. 'I knew he wouldn't help me.'

Mikhail lit a cigarette and paced back and forth across the room.

'You'll just have to write back to him. Ask again,' insisted Pamela.

To the secretary, Lettice explained, 'My father won't help get a visa for my …' — she covered up the hand that would have sported a wedding ring — 'my husband.'

The secretary glanced at Pamela and then nodded. 'Does he know you're pregnant, dear?'

Lettice shook her head.

'It's a complicated situation,' Pamela interjected.

'Yes, lots of those about these days. Everyone and his Uncle Harry is trying to get an exit visa from the French, an entry visa from us or both.'

Pamela took her aside and said, 'My name is Pamela More. I'm meant to be meeting someone here. Someone with …' She paused, looked around and then lowered her voice. 'The Foreign Office. Have there been any messages for me?'

The secretary raised an eyebrow. Pamela couldn't tell whether she was surprised or simply didn't believe her. There must have been any number of people outside the embassy gates, claiming to have business with someone important in the British government.

'I'll go ask. Won't be a moment.'

Pamela turned back to Lettice and sat next to her. 'Letty, maybe you should go. Let your father make the arrangements for you. Sid and I can try to figure out how to get Mikhail out of France.'

'No! I won't do it. I won't leave without him.' Lettice had steel in her voice and gripped Pamela's hand. 'If I leave now, there's no guarantee he'll be able to join me.'

Pamela wanted to say there was no guarantee she'd be able to get out of the country at all if she didn't leave now. But instead, she whispered, 'Are you sure? About Mikhail?'

Lettice dropped Pamela's hand. 'What do you mean?'

'When we were packing up the car, I saw—' Pamela paused, unsure of how to phrase it. 'I saw Mikhail and Georges … I saw them kiss.'

Lettice looked away, avoiding Pamela's gaze. She already knew.

Pamela was reminded of what Bricktop had said to her: if you live long enough, you play all the parts.

'It's hard to explain. He and Georges … They've known each other for years, long before I met him. Georges has been very supportive of Mikhail's work. He cares about him very much. They care for each other.'

'But you're pregnant with his child. You're risking your life for him.'

'I know it's all very modern. And maybe it's just something people do in Paris. You'd be surprised how many couples have an arrangement like ours. Mikhail loves me. But he loves Georges as well. You can love more than one person at once, you know.' Lettice glanced over at Sid and then looked back at Pamela, meeting her gaze.

Pamela wanted to protest and tell her that it wasn't the same. But she didn't have the courage of her convictions. Even though Pamela hadn't told her the full extent of her relationship with Sid, she knew Lettice could tell what was playing out between them. Besides, she understood the nature of Pamela's marriage to Francis, having known so many marriages like it in their circle — couples who had been introduced for reasons of social compatibility and acceptability alone. One could pretend that life was simple, but that didn't make it so. No one could ever really know what went on inside someone else's relationship.

The secretary returned.

'There are no messages for you, I'm afraid.'

'There's nothing? Are you sure?'

'Perhaps try again tomorrow.' She paused. 'In the meantime, 'I've seen a number of couples — even married ones — become separated. But it might help if your two friends made their marriage *official*,' she intoned. 'At the local *mairie*.'

Whatever Pamela's reservations about Mikhail and his relationship with Georges, she was going to have to swallow them in the name of pragmatism. And pray that the last vestiges of French bureaucracy could bind Lettice and her true love together before the Third Republic was overtaken.

VII

When they finally found a hotel that had a vacancy (for an exorbitant, grossly inflated price), everyone was hot, dirty, tired and irritable. Once they were alone in their room, Pamela watched Sid unpacking his suitcase and realised she hadn't a clue what he was planning on doing now that they had reached Marseille, especially now that the *Herald Tribune* had closed all its offices and operations.

'Where will you go next, once we leave France? What are you going to do?' She traced the flowers on the wallpaper with her finger, feeling suddenly anxious about what he might say.

'I don't know. I guess I'll go to Spain or Portugal and cover the news from Madrid or Lisbon.' He paused, a shirt in his hand, looking almost paralysed. 'But most of the other journalists I know are leaving Europe completely. Or going to Britain. Everyone knows we're running out of road.'

'Perhaps you should leave too.' Pamela stood up from the bed. 'I think you should get on the next boat or plane leaving France.'

Sid tensed up and his face darkened. 'You think I'm just going to abandon you? I'm not leaving you here.'

Pamela turned to look out the window of the hotel that faced a bleak little alleyway. How was she going to explain to him that he might have to? She never would have imagined herself in a situation like this when she first agreed to Macaulay's offer back in London: stuck on the edge of the Mediterranean, trying to stay one step ahead of the Wehrmacht and another behind the Windsors, worrying about a stubborn American journalist she seemed to be falling for.

'I'll be alright,' she replied in what she hoped was an even, neutral tone. Pamela went to the mirror to fix her hair. Sid followed her.

'You don't know that. You're worried about me but you're the one with a British passport and if you get trapped here …'

She could see Sid's worried face behind her in the mirror. Their eyes met. She dearly wished she could tell him the whole truth, of why she was in France in the first place, why she was stuck in Marseille and why she couldn't leave with her fellow countrymen and women. She felt guilty, for not being able to tell him, knowing that it was adding to the seemingly unbridgeable gulf between them.

'You needn't worry about me,' she replied as she re-pinned one of her curls. 'I have connections in government. I can look after myself.'

Sid put a hand on her shoulder. Pamela turned around.

'And what if your government can't help you?' Sid replied, voicing exactly what Pamela herself had been worrying about.

She couldn't let the conversation go any further because she didn't want to have to dodge any more questions. She needed to put a stop to his worrying somehow.

'I'm not your responsibility,' she replied sharply.

Pamela tried to move away but Sid caught her arm.

'I know that. I could have left by now. We aren't talking about "responsibility".'

'Then what are we talking about?' Pamela jerked her arm away.

'Look. I love you.' Sid paused. '*That.* That is what we're talking about.'

Pamela stared at him. She had to admit to herself that she'd fantasised about him declaring his love for her. She had, at times, been worried that she wouldn't see him again, that he would be relocated to another city or country, that he'd return to America, that he'd be wounded at the front — or worse. Or that he'd simply lose interest in her. Pamela had wanted him to love her. But now that he'd said what she never thought he would, she didn't know what to do. She felt herself reverting to type: the well-bred, well-mannered, finishing-school debutante.

'This isn't an appropriate time to say something like that,' she replied softly, avoiding his gaze.

'Sitting around the Last Chance Saloon, waiting for the German army isn't an "appropriate" time to tell you I love you? Tell me — when *would* the appropriate time be?'

Did she love him? The thought of losing him frightened her. And before this, the thought of being the one to declare her love for Sid first and be rebuffed frightened her too. And now, the thought of replying in kind, that she loved him too, frightened her even more. Where would it lead? Pamela had been so efficient at compartmentalising her emotions and the competing realities of an absent husband and a present lover. She had become comfortable with living in a never-never land of uncertainty and ambiguity; finding herself in the middle of a crisis and being confronted with a declaration of love overwhelmed her.

Pamela didn't know what to say, so she said nothing.

Later, sitting outside a local café with a bottle of wine, no one was any happier than they had been earlier in the day. Mikhail and Lettice looked morose. Sid and Pamela were avoiding one another's gaze. The setting didn't help either; they were close enough to the harbour that the smell of fish and other, unmentionable things wafted in their direction and Pamela was sure she'd seen at least one rat earlier.

'I know someone who might be able to help with the visa,' Pamela began. Lettice looked up hopefully. 'He should be in Marseille any day now. However, in the meantime, the advice from the embassy is that you two should get married. It might improve your chances of being able to remain together.'

'I don't believe in marriage.' Mikhail crossed his arms defiantly. 'I left the old world behind in Russia. I won't have my life dictated by the state. Or some foolish idea of God.'

'I don't want to get married either,' Lettice sniffed. 'It didn't agree with me the first time, did it?'

'That's because your first husband was a blighter and you should never have agreed to marry him in the first place,' Pamela snapped at her.

'So, it was my fault, was it?'

'I'm not saying it was your fault. I'm saying that this situation is different. And there's a degree of urgency here,' replied Pamela through gritted teeth.

'Well, I'm not going to marry someone who won't even ask me,' retorted Lettice, glaring at Mikhail.

'Why should I ask if you don't want to marry?'

'You haven't asked me! How do I know if you'd even want to marry me?'

'I love you, but I don't want to marry anyone!'

Pamela was tempted to ask him if that was because he was in love with someone else. But she knew she had to put a stop to this.

'Both of you are being utterly and entirely ridiculous. You can have it annulled once you get to England, for all I care. But I think you should bloody well take good advice when it's given to you.'

Mikhail stood and glared at Pamela, furious. 'As if you have a right to say such things to me. When it is *your* country that is abandoning the French people to the Nazis. How are they supposed to defend themselves when you take your ships and your soldiers and go back across the water to your safe little English houses? You were so frightened to offend Hitler and now you run away. Leaving all these people' — he gestured to the city behind him — 'to rot! Leaving the Yids to go to hell. Is that what you English say? Go to hell?'

Sid flinched upon hearing Mikhail utter the slur. Mikhail muttered angrily to himself in Yiddish. Sid then offered Mikhail a cigarette and took him aside.

Suddenly, Pamela was aware that it had gone quiet inside the café. The bartender had turned up the radio. They strained to hear the broadcast, then got up and went inside. The bartender came out from behind the bar. There were tears in his eyes.

'The government has declared Paris an open city. And the Germans have reached the city gates. The German army is in Paris.'

A woman in the café cried out and began to sob. Everyone else began murmuring to each other in anxious tones.

Pamela felt a sinking feeling in the pit of her stomach. She turned to Sid. 'An open city? There were never any edicts or orders. Why didn't they say anything?'

'They didn't want people to panic. And now they're rolling the dice. If they don't put up a fight, maybe Hitler won't blow Paris to smithereens.'

VIII

The next day, the Hôtel de Ville was almost as chaotic as the British Embassy had been. People were begging for their papers — identity cards and birth and marriage certificates. There were even some people, like Lettice and Mikhail, trying to get married at the last minute. They finally were able to speak to a harried-looking, balding, middle-aged city official, but he shook his head.

He gestured to the people around them. 'Can't you see that such a thing is entirely impossible right now.' He then eyed Mikhail and Sid up and smirked. 'Perhaps you can try the synagogue instead.'

Mikhail looked murderous, as if he might take the official by the neck and throttle him. But Sid stepped in and whispered something in the Frenchman's ear. The official looked at him suspiciously for a moment and then whispered something back.

Sid then turned to Pamela and murmured, 'He might be a son of a bitch, but he's a corrupt son of a bitch. You got something you can bribe him with?'

She rifled through her purse, but she knew whatever she had, it wouldn't be enough. She looked down at her hand. Her engagement ring. It had been Francis's grandmother's and was worth a good deal of money. The idea of parting with it was painful but she didn't see any other option. This was a crisis. Pamela handed the ring to Sid.

'Offer him this.'

Sid looked shocked. 'Are you sure?'

Pamela nodded and closed Sid's fingers over it.

'Pam, you can't,' replied Lettice in horror as she put a hand on Pamela's arm to stay her.

Pamela shook her head. 'It's alright. Just give it to him.'

'No, wait. Give him mine.' Lettice pulled a thin gold chain out from underneath her dress. On it was her own engagement ring from her previous marriage — a beautiful, square-cut diamond in a platinum setting. 'It only brought me bad luck anyway.' She sighed as she took it off the chain and handed it to the official, who held the diamond up to the light, appraising it like a goblin in a fairy tale.

Pamela had always enjoyed weddings, but this was a miserable affair. Pamela and Sid acted as the witnesses, and it was all over in ten minutes. Afterwards, Lettice was feeling unwell, so she, Mikhail and Sid went back to their ancient, shabby hotel. Pamela decided to return to the embassy.

She asked again if there were any messages but there was nothing. She was starting to get nervous. What if something had happened to Captain Macaulay? How would she even know? Would anyone get a message to her? Should she give up now and try to make her own arrangements to leave France? But how? What other cards did she have to play? No one even knew where she was. Not Francis, not her friends in London, not her family.

What had she done?

Feeling unnerved and unmoored, Pamela wandered around the city, trying to clear her head. She would simply go back to the embassy again tomorrow.

No, tomorrow was Saturday and the embassy would be closed.

She cursed under her breath. She would just have to spend the weekend keeping herself from losing the plot until it reopened on Monday. Macaulay was bound to turn up at some point.

As the sun set, people emerged from their escape from the afternoon heat to go to restaurants, bars and nightclubs. The country might be under siege, but the denizens of Marseille were still going to enjoy all that they could on a Friday night. Pamela heard jazz drifting out of one of the clubs. Feeling sentimental and nostalgic for Bricktop's, she followed the music. It led her up one of the winding streets to a club called Le Jazz Bleu. That was the club Bricktop had mentioned, which was owned by her friend Hecky Smith. The guy to know if you're in a jam. She didn't think he'd be able to help her somehow find British visas, but maybe he could help her friends celebrate their wedding — however unromantic and unhappy it had been thus far.

When Pamela returned to the hotel to drag the others out of their melancholy, she found that Sid had gone out.

'He went to talk to God,' Mikhail told her disdainfully as he tied his tie.

'I beg your pardon?'

'He wanted to find a shul, for Shabbos. To *pray*.'

'Mikhail, there's nothing wrong with having faith,' Lettice replied as she fixed her hair in front of a mirror.

'*Dos land brent un di bobe tsvogt zikh*. The country is on fire and grandma is washing her hair.'

'If he wants to find God, I think now is an awfully good time to do it,' Lettice retorted sharply.

Mikhail looked at her pityingly. 'He can try. But God is dead.'

IX

'Excuse me, do you have any champagne?' Pamela asked the woman behind the bar.

She was desperately trying to salvage the evening and do something — anything — to lift everyone's spirits.

The young, dark-haired bartender with an olive complexion looked at her sceptically.

'We're out,' she replied, as if that were obvious.

It seemed cruelly ironic that Lettice's first marriage, to a man she didn't love, was a beautiful, elaborate, society wedding covered in *Tatler* and *The Times*, while her second, to a man she did — a man she loved deeply enough to risk her life for him — was a bleak, threadbare affair without any joy or pomp whatsoever. But then Pamela thought of something.

'Is Hecky here? Hecky Smith?'

Clearly surprised, the woman raised an eyebrow, turned and went into the back. Pamela looked around at the club. It felt a little like Bricktop's, only shabbier. But the music was good and the patrons looked surprisingly cheerful. The bartender returned with a tall, handsome, broad-shouldered Black man in his forties, wearing a sharp suit and sporting brilliantined hair. He leaned on the bar.

'Who's asking for me?' he said in an American accent.

Pamela reached her hand across the bar. 'Pamela More. I'm a friend of Bricktop's. She said if I was ever in Marseille, I should look you up.'

Hecky Smith's face changed as soon as she said the name. He looked Pamela up and down, reevaluating her, and smiled. 'What can I do for a beautiful woman like yourself?'

'My friends were married today. And I was hoping I could order a bottle of champagne so we could celebrate.'

'Some time to get married …'

'The circumstances weren't ideal. You might even say it was under duress.'

'That gal pregnant?' asked Hecky with a knowing look.

Pamela blushed. She hadn't meant to give so much away.

'Yes, but he also needs a visa. And she's British. They do love each other,' she added hurriedly, not wanting to cheapen her friends' marriage further.

'No time like war for a romance. Guess they're not going on a honeymoon!' he chuckled. 'Hey Rania! A bottle of champagne for this pretty lady and her friends. Our finest.'

The bartender went into the back and returned with a bottle of Veuve Clicquot.

'Any friend of Brick's,' he said with a tip of his head. 'Drink it and think of her. I'm glad she got out of Paris. I was worried she was going to be her pig-headed self and try to stick it out.'

No, that's just me, Pamela thought ruefully. She returned to the table to find that Sid had arrived. When they left the hotel, they had given a note to the concierge — a grim-faced elderly woman — letting Sid know where they would be. He was quiet and looked pensive.

'You went to a synagogue?' Pamela asked him. 'I didn't know you were religious.'

'I'm not. Apart from weddings and some holidays, I've hardly set foot inside a synagogue since my little sister's bat mitzvah. I don't know. It was just something I needed to do. I used to go to Friday night services with my pop.' Sid paused. 'It was a beautiful place — like a cathedral inside. I talked to the rabbi. He's been helping German Jews try to get out of the country. And now everyone else is trying to flee — French Jews, Belgians, Dutch, Ostjuden. Everyone is terrified of what will happen if France capitulates.'

The news that day had been that Reynaud's cabinet was meeting in Bordeaux to discuss Churchill's offer of a Franco-British union in order to continue resisting the Germans.

Sid drained his glass and refilled it. 'I don't know where the hell everyone's going to go. The Evian Conference sealed their fate. Imagine … bringing all those countries together, going to all that trouble, just to agree that no one would take in Jews. That they could go screw.'

Pamela felt sick to her stomach, considering the implications of this. She was afraid even to imagine it. At least Sid's family was safe and sound in Chicago, but Pamela realised she knew nothing about Mikhail's family in Russia. What would happen to them? Where would they go? A trumpet in the band wailed a solo as people danced slowly to the music. Sid turned to watch.

Pamela pushed a lock of hair from his forehead and took his hand. 'I'm sorry.'

Sid looked confused. 'For what?'

'I don't know. It's all so bloody wretched.'

Sid took Pamela's hand. They sat quietly together while Lettice and Mikhail danced.

As they were getting ready to leave, Rania, the bartender, approached Pamela and told her Hecky wanted a word. Rania led her to a dark corner of the bar, where the owner was sitting and smoking a cigar with a squat, dark-haired, brooding man in shirtsleeves and braces, who looked as if he'd had his nose broken more than once. He had a large tattoo of a snake running down his forearm.

'Miss Pamela, this is my friend Salvadore. He's looking for someone to do him a favour.'

Salvadore looked at her unsmilingly.

'What sort of favour … ?'

'You're trying to find a visa for your friend, right, Miss Pamela?' (Every time Hecky said her name, she found it vaguely menacing.) 'If you do a favour for my friend Salvadore here, we might be able to fix your problem.'

Pamela stiffened, suddenly reminded that Bricktop had mentioned Hecky Smith in the same breath as French gangsters.

Hecky inhaled his cigar and then exhaled slowly. 'See, he needs a respectable-looking lady to wear a necklace for him. Someone like yourself, maybe.'

'Wear a necklace?'

'On a train. To Lisbon. And then hand it off to someone when you get there. And if anyone asks, it's your necklace. That's all. You say, I'm Miss Pamela and yes, of course this is my necklace.'

Salvadore continued to stare at her, saying nothing. Pamela's hand instinctively went to her throat.

'So, I would be …' — she had to stop herself from saying "smuggling" — 'carrying a necklace. Which I assume is rather valuable.'

'You would assume right.' Hecky took another puff on his cigar, looking patient. 'After all, if Salvadore here goes around wearing a necklace, folks might think it looks kind of suspicious. But who would suspect a beautiful, classy gal like you?'

They were all quiet, watching each other as the band played on in the background. Pamela looked at the snake on Salvadore's arm. Every time he moved, the snake appeared to be slithering.

'Give me some time to think about it.'

A few months ago, Pamela would never have imagined that she would be considering aiding in an illegal smuggling operation for two gangsters. But there was no guarantee Macaulay was going to turn up any time soon and her options were dwindling.

She left the bar and met Sid outside, where he was smoking a cigarette and squinting up at the neon sign.

'Say, how did you find this place? The old lady at the front desk really turned up her nose when she gave me your note. Said this place is a Corsican mob joint.'

X

An anxious weekend waiting for the British Consulate to open on Monday morning was made worse by the news that Reynaud's cabinet rejected Churchill's offer of an alliance and voted instead to sign a peace treaty with Hitler. Reynaud stepped down. And the hero of Verdun, the elderly Marshal Philippe Pétain, conferred upon himself absolute powers as France's 'Chief of State'. And that was how the Third Republic disappeared — not with a bang, but a whimper.

That day, a CBS radio correspondent declared with a tremor in his voice: 'No American after tonight will be broadcasting directly to America, unless it is under the supervision of men other than the French.'

Pamela got to the consulate gates two hours before they opened, to make sure she would be among the first to be seen. And when she gave her name at the reception, she was told to wait in the corridor. She sat nervously on a hard wooden chair in a row of other distressed-looking people. A stern-looking portrait of George VI watched over them from the opposite wall. Pamela considered how he felt about being the king of a country that was now attempting to defend Europe single-handedly. A young, reedy, fair-haired man approached her and led her out onto the consulate balcony, where Captain Macaulay was looking across at the view of the port.

'I'm very relieved that you made it safely to Marseille. And I'm sorry I haven't been able to make contact. We went to La Croë to try to head the Windsors off at the pass, but we missed them. It seems they only spent an evening there and then ended up in Biarritz. It looks very much like they're going to attempt to cross the Spanish frontier.'

Macaulay leaned on his walking stick, shifting his weight uncomfortably. He had seemed so robust even just a few months ago — a hale and hearty cricketer. Now, he looked older, tired, almost fragile.

'We have reason to believe that the Windsors stopped at Chateau de Candé, outside Tours, on their way to the south. To see Charles Bedaux. We've been able to intercept cables to Berlin, which indicate that Bedaux has been in contact with Nazi leadership for some time. Possibly years. The Nazis confiscated his factories in Germany when they came to power, and we think he had to eat humble pie in order to get them back. Agree to spy for them.'

'And he saw an opportunity with the Duke,' replied Pamela angrily.

'Precisely.'

'Someone with a grievance and no tact. Careless. Who feels no compunction to keep his mouth shut and no obligation whatsoever to his country. No wonder he and Fern were so eager to become friends with the Windsors. Host their wedding. Bring them to Germany.' Pamela knew she was ranting but couldn't stop herself. 'And when the Duke was inspecting defence lines, it was the perfect opportunity to ply him for information. Or just wait for him to open his big mouth. Especially when he started banging on about peace treaties with Germany. It was Bedaux's perfect opportunity to convince him that he could be instrumental in backdoor negotiations. That he could be a hero. What a despicable man.'

Pamela took a deep breath, trying to rein in her fury. She fumbled in her handbag for a cigarette. A breeze picked up across the port. It was a glorious summer's day, with blue skies and even bluer water. In any other circumstance, the perfect weather and setting for a holiday. Macaulay was looking across the port at the basilica that sat high on the hill.

'What on earth do they think they're playing at?' asked Pamela as she watched her cigarette smoke drift in the breeze.

'It may just be a foolish bid to get to safety.' Macaulay leaned against the balcony railing. 'Regardless, Churchill — and the King — are very anxious to ascertain the Windsors' whereabouts. The King's private secretary sent a memo to all the consulates still operating in France. I needn't tell you how urgent it is. The embassy in Madrid is now on high alert.' He paused. 'To make matters more complicated, we have reason to believe that the German High Command has designs on the Duke and Duchess.'

'Designs … ?'

'They may be trying to kidnap them. Now that Reynaud has resigned and French defeat is all but certain, it would be enormously useful for Hitler to have the former King of England and his wife under his control, as a bargaining chip.' The captain paused. 'But also, to use as puppet monarchs, in the event of an invasion.'

Despite the Mediterranean sun beating down, Pamela felt a cold chill creep over her. She had spent the last two and a half months witnessing Germany roll their tanks across Western Europe and still, she hadn't yet fully countenanced the prospect of the same thing happening to Britain. Messerschmitts strafing the roads to London and Manchester. Long lines of refugees heading towards Liverpool.

'There's a good chance we'll be able to track them down. But once we do, we must convince them to get on a ship and return to Britain as soon as possible. Before the Germans get to them.'

At the mention of the Germans, Pamela decided it was time to confess to Macaulay about what had happened with Miss Blythewood.

'Captain, when I went to Boulevard Suchet to pick up the Ford, there was a bit of a problem.'

'What kind of "problem"?'

'I know who the Abwehr agent is. It was Margaret Blythewood, the Windsors' secretary.'

Pamela retrieved her identification papers from the hidden compartment in her handbag. Macaulay inspected the *Wehrpass*.

'She was waiting for me at the house with some story about being left behind by the Duke and Duchess, with no way of getting back to England. But she rather gave the game away when she attempted to hold me hostage so she could hand me over to the Abwehr. I didn't want to do it, you see. I never wanted to hurt her. But she had a gun.'

Macaulay looked at Pamela intently. 'Is she dead?'

'Yes.'

'Who knows about this?'

'Only one of my friends. He came to meet me at Boulevard Suchet so we could leave Paris together. But I told him she'd shot herself.'

Macaulay frowned. 'Do you think he suspects anything?'

'I don't think so.'

Macaulay nodded. 'One less German to worry about then. Well done, Lady Pamela. Excellent work.' He shook her hand. 'Were you able to get any information out of her? Who was she working for? What her mission was?'

'She was pointing a gun at my head, Captain.'

He gave her a look that seemed to indicate that he didn't think that was a sufficient excuse. 'On another note, the Duchess has cabled the American Consulate in Nice, asking them to fetch something from La Croë.' He pursed his lips. 'A green swimming costume.'

'A what?'

'A *swimming costume*. Apparently, she neglected to pack it and is missing it greatly.' Even the usually diplomatic Macaulay was unable to hide his disgust.

Pamela wondered if Wallis had found a way of contacting Ambassador Bullitt. And how he might feel about his lover bothering him about a swimming costume while he was navigating the collapse of the French government.

'We considered arranging for one of her servants to retrieve it, but the ones left are either travelling with the Windsors or have fled to God knows where.'

'You're going to honour her request?'

'She is, as you know, a stubborn woman of selfish whims. If a green swimming costume is the bargaining chip we need to persuade her to leave the Continent with the Duke …'

'Of course, if Miss Blythewood were still alive, she would have been more than happy to fetch it for her mistress.' Pamela paused. 'But if someone *posed* as Margaret Blythewood …'

'It's rather good luck that we have her identification papers,' he said brightly. 'And we can, of course, change the photo on them.'

Pamela shouldn't have been surprised that Macaulay was one step ahead of her.

'One of the problems is how we'd get you there. It's almost impossible to go east. The roads are clogged and the trains aren't running in that direction. And, of course, it would be dangerous. We couldn't guarantee your safety. And we would have to deny any knowledge of you, if you were captured.'

Pamela thought about the cyanide capsule she'd been carrying around in a pocket in her handbag for the past year and a half. No one had ever guaranteed her safety. She had been set up to fend for herself, to not rely on anyone, to know that she was taking her fate into her own hands when she agreed to the mission. And if the worst should happen, the best she could do was end her own life before she was forced to pass on intelligence.

'British intelligence has been spotty at best since the invasion; we've been reliant on aerial reconnaissance and sketchy reports from the few contacts we still have to diplomats at neutral embassies. We've been fighting this invasion nearly blind. We would, in essence, have to find someone to smuggle you into La Croë.'

They both went silent for a moment, contemplating the problem. A ship's horn could be heard somewhere in the distance. Then Pamela had a thought.

'If I can get to La Croë and back to Marseille, could you get me to the Windsors — to Biarritz or Spain or wherever they might be?'

'Yes, we can manage that.'

'And if I agree to do this, will you help my friends?'

'The British woman and her stateless companion?'

Pamela thought about Sid. She didn't trust him to make a sensible decision and get himself out of France.

'It's three people now. But the third has an American passport.'

Macaulay sighed. 'Very well.'

Pamela realised that she'd hardly given a thought to Francis until now. At least if she never saw him again, MI6 would tell him the truth of what had happened — or at least some version of it.

'Might you be able to get a letter to my husband?'

'Yes, of course. We can let him know you're safe and sound.'

For now, anyway.

There was a knock on the window.

'Come,' called out Macaulay.

The fair-haired young man who Pamela had met earlier stepped onto the balcony, appearing pale and anxious.

'Sir, it's just been announced … France has surrendered to Jerry.' His voice trembled. 'Pétain is going to sign an armistice.'

Pamela and Macaulay looked at each other.

Britain was on its own.

XI

Pamela steeled herself and returned to Le Jazz Bleu that evening. When she told Macaulay her plan, he seemed strangely untroubled by the prospect of her collaborating with gangsters. She had heard about the scourge of gangs in Marseille, of their brothels, gambling dens, drug dealing and gun running operations; these were people experienced in nefarious, underhanded dealings. But then again, so was MI6. Macaulay suggested that Pamela tell Hecky and Salvadore that she no longer needed a visa, but rather a way to smuggle something out of a grand house in Cap d'Antibes: she had to collect important papers for the British government before they fell into enemy hands. Apparently, despite the Corsicans resenting what they viewed as the French occupation of their island, they hated the Germans even more, and the war had brought out a patriotic streak in even the most criminal of men. And considering the Third Reich's opinion of jazz in general and Black Americans in particular, he hoped Hecky Smith would hopefully feel similarly.

And Macaulay turned out to be right. Both men seemed to heartily approve of the mission; Salvadore made a toast in Corsican that Pamela took to be some sort of condemnation of the Germans and Hecky said the German Army could 'go straight to hell'. Neither man seemed to think travelling 200 kilometres down the coast would pose a problem, but they said it would take longer than usual because they'd have to avoid the main roads. One of Salvadore's foot soldiers would drive Pamela to La Croë. And she should bring cash, in case they needed to bribe French officials. In return, Pamela would bring the necklace to Lisbon for them and deposit it at a designated location. And then once she had discharged her duties to the gangsters, she would bring Wallis her swimming costume.

What Macaulay had dubbed 'Operation Cleopatra Whim' was officially underway.

XII

Days later, the papers declared that Marshal Pétain had signed an armistice with Germany in the same railway carriage in the Compiègne Forest where the Kaiser's government had signed the previous one in 1918 — a spiteful act of reprisal. Later that day, a relatively unknown French general called de Gaulle gave an emotional broadcast from London, establishing a government in exile and appealing to his nation to resist the new, collaborationist regime.

Honour, common sense and the superior interest of the nation
command to all the free French to continue fighting wherever

*they are and however they can … Long live a free and inde-
pendent France!*

It was also the day that Lettice miscarried.

'Mikhail is distraught. But I told him it would be one less thing
to worry about when we arrive,' she said dully, a hollow look on her
face. 'Besides … who would want to bring a child into a world like
this anyway?'

It was another cruel irony: the pregnancy that had seemed so
perilous only days before was now lost, just as the two of them had
secured their passage to England. Pamela knew that Lettice hadn't
planned it and had seemed more resigned to than happy about the
reality of having a child. While she didn't care what people thought
about what she did and who she saw romantically as a divorcée in
France, no woman they knew wanted to have a child out of wedlock.
And while Lettice and Mikhail were now married, they would face
a difficult enough situation, going to England and starting their
lives over.

'I'm so sorry, Letty. I wish that things were different,' Pamela replied
softly, feeling at a loss for words.

The following day, Lettice, Mikhail and Sid prepared to board a
boat to Liverpool. It was a coaling ship which normally had capacity
for 180 but was carrying 1,600 souls, packed tightly together, and
would travel in a naval convoy as protection against German U-boats.
It was filled with diplomats, British businessmen, civil servants and
their wives, journalists, invalided soldiers, military doctors, nurses
and even former French cabinet ministers — those who had voted
against capitulation.

Marseille, which had seemed to have been holding itself together until now, was giving a very good demonstration of what a breakdown of social order looked like. People sobbed openly on the docks and begged officials to let them on board. Couples fought while their babies wailed. Someone was drunkenly singing 'La Marseillaise' over and over. A man pushed his Rolls-Royce into the water, announcing wildly to no one in particular that he'd be damned if Mussolini got his hands on his car.

Pamela had been as vague as possible about the reason why she'd been able to get them all passage to England and a visa for Mikhail, saying that she'd called in a favour from a friend of Francis's in the Foreign Office. She waited until the last possible moment to tell them she wasn't joining them, to try to minimise the protestations she knew would follow.

'What do you mean, you're staying here?' Lettice was incredulous.

'That's ridiculous!' Sid objected.

Pamela was grateful that at least Mikhail expressed no opinion on the subject and only gazed blankly out into the sea.

'I've been asked to go to Portugal, to meet the Windsors.'

'But why?' demanded Lettice.

'Because they urgently need to be escorted back to Britain, out of harm's way.'

'Couldn't they have found someone else to do it?'

'Our government is a bit short on manpower right now. Travelling makes Wallis nervous, and she doesn't trust anyone. But they think she might listen to me.'

Truth and lies.

Then the realisation dawned on Sid's face. 'You agreed to do this in exchange for places on this ship for us.'

Pamela was silent.

'For the Duke and Duchess of Windsor?' groaned Lettice. 'They can fall into the sea for all I care!'

'You needn't worry about me. I'll be coming back to old Blighty in a royal cortege, as it were. And you'll all be rather jealous of me.' Pamela forced a smile.

'You have always been very glamorous, Panda.'

Lettice started to well up and hugged Pamela tightly. When she released her, Pamela saw Mikhail was standing behind her, watching. He took the cigarette out of his mouth and put his hand on Pamela's shoulder.

'*Ven ir hobn keyn brirh, moubaleyz dem geyst fun mut.* When you have no choice, mobilise the spirit of courage.' He kissed her on the cheek three times and then embraced her. '*Shkoyach*, Pamela.'

'Thank you, Mikhail,' she whispered, worrying that she was going to start crying in a moment.

While the couple boarded the gangplank, Pamela stood on the dock with Sid, not knowing what to say. She felt a wrenching in her heart, realising she didn't know when — or even if — she would see him again. His face was grave.

'I'll be perfectly fine. No need to worry.'

Sid nodded but still looked unconvinced.

'Where will you go?' she asked him.

'Seems like I'm going to be in London now, at least for the time being.'

'No plans to return to Chicago?'

'What, in the States? Where it's safe? What the hell would I do there?' He smiled. 'Look me up when you get back, ok?'

As Pamela looked at Sid's face, with his rumpled shirt and five o'clock shadow, she realised she did love him. She thought of a popular song that was often on the radio and sung in bars called '*Vous avez déménagé mon cœur*' — 'you moved my heart'. But it seemed like the worst possible moment to open that can of worms, as he would say. On top of being married, Pamela was about to embark on a mission that was more dangerous than she had allowed herself to admit until now. After all, if she was captured and found to be a British agent, she would be interned. Probably interrogated. Possibly shot. She didn't know whether or not they made exceptions for women — Macaulay hadn't said. And she had been too afraid to ask.

They embraced and then kissed deeply. The moment of separation seemed a thousand times more painful than the one at the Gare du Nord, all those months ago. Sid made his way up the gangplank with his suitcase, then stopped halfway, turned around and tipped his battered hat to Pamela. She waved at him and then turned away, no longer able to stem the flood of tears that began to roll down her cheeks.

In the port, there was a memorial for those who had died at sea. She wondered if one day there would be another one like it, marking the fall of France.

July 1940

I

Once France capitulated and Pétain's Vichy government was established, it seemed as if the world had ground to a halt. Although Pamela already had her Irish passport identifying her as Kathleen Burke, Macaulay still had to arrange for her forged laissez-passer and exit and entry visas for France, Spain and Portugal under that name, as well as a laissez-passer under Miss Blythewood's name in case she was stopped and questioned en route to La Croë. He had managed to track down a reputable forger, but with everyone in the South of France desperate to leave, business was booming, and they had to wait.

In the meantime, the British Consulate closed, the staff was evacuated, and Macaulay had been ordered back to London. On his last day in Marseille, he and Pamela met on the rooftop of a condemned building. He shook her hand and wished her luck. When they parted, Pamela felt a deep sense of unease settle into her body, almost like a child being abandoned by a parent.

Although the Vichy government was officially neutral, it operated as a collaborationist state under a merely illusory independence from the German occupational government. Pétain had declared that *liberté, égalité, fraternité* would be replaced by the good Catholic values of *travail, famille, patrie* — 'labour, family, fatherland'. A return to the countryside. A repudiation of the cosmopolitan, socialist and internationalist ideals that had so corrupted France and brought about her downfall. And above all, absolute obedience to the state.

Pamela maintained a low profile while she waited, changing lodgings frequently and rarely going out in the daytime, for fear of being stopped and questioned. She'd read about foreign nationals being rounded up by the police, people being taken from their houses and from public places. Walking back to her hotel one evening, she saw two Vichy officials stop a man on the street. When he tried to run, they grabbed him, slammed him to the ground and beat him. People around them were clearly horrified but too frightened to say anything. It took an hour and two strong drinks for Pamela's heart to stop pounding.

Looking at herself in the hotel mirror one day, Pamela doubted that anyone who had known her in London or Paris would recognise her now. Much of her wardrobe looked the worse for wear, she hadn't had her hair set or her nails done for months and she had a general look of fatigue under her eyes. Once Pamela retrieved the swimming costume, when she travelled to Lisbon, her cover as Mrs Burke would be that she was meeting her husband, who was doing business in Lisbon. She realised that if she wanted to pass for a successful businessman's wife — and the kind who would have in her possession a valuable necklace — she would have to alter her appearance. Although clothing was now in short supply, the shops still seemed to be selling accessories, so Pamela bought a new pair of sunglasses and a turban. (Her friend Diana Vreeland always said the right turban could turn any woman into a stranger.) She practised a new way of moving — a more languid, sloping walk to take the place of her bright, brisk step. And then a soft Dublin accent; she'd always been a decent mimic and decided to imitate her friend Jo Nolan.

Macaulay had arranged for the forged papers she would need to get to La Croë and Lisbon would be left for her in an imposing Dominican monastery in the middle of the city, whose priests were known to be sympathetic to the Free French cause. Every other day, Pamela went to ask for Brother Antoine and said she wanted to make a confession. If the papers were ready for her, Brother Antoine would hear her confession; if not, she would be told that the priest was unwell. Pamela repeated this ritual for nearly three weeks, growing more and more worried as time wore on. Finally, one day, an elderly, robed priest with a bald head nodded to her and asked her to wait. He disappeared for a moment, then emerged five minutes later and gestured to the confessional. They both went in. Pamela watched through the grille as the priest silently revealed an envelope from beneath the folds of his robe and slipped it under the gap in the partition.

When she opened the envelope later, Pamela was deeply relieved to find that everything was in order:

A *laissez-passer* for both Margaret Blythewood and Kathleen Burke.

Entry and exit visas for France, Spain and Portugal.

A train ticket to Lisbon.

And lastly, in case she was stopped, a letter from the American Consulate and another from Wallis (both forged), explaining that the Windsor secretary was on a mission to collect some things from the house.

II

The next day, Pamela waited outside a café on the outskirts of the city for Salvadore's foot soldier who was going to take her to La Croë. It had been half an hour already and there was still no one to be seen. Sitting in the blisteringly hot afternoon sun, Pamela was starting to get nervous, wondering if this man would ever show up. Or if Salvadore and Hecky had changed their minds. Or if the police were cracking down on Marseille's criminal underworld and the Corsican had been arrested.

A few minutes later, a motorcycle roared down the small, winding street and pulled up to the kerb outside the café and a man dismounted.

'Mademoiselle Pamela?'

Pamela was startled. Was this the man Salvadore had sent for her? On a motorcycle?

'Yes?'

The Corsican kissed her hand in a courtly fashion, smiled and said, 'My name is Lucca. Salvadore's son.'

He shook out his head of thick, black hair and removed his sunglasses to reveal olive-green eyes, heavily fringed with thick eyelashes. The word 'foot soldier' hadn't exactly conjured up the image of a devastatingly handsome man with matinee idol looks; Pamela had been expecting someone who looked like Salvadore — squat, unattractive, battle-scarred. She also hadn't been expecting a motorcycle.

'I thought he was going to send a car.'

Lucca patted the seat of his motorcycle. 'She is better than a car. Faster.'

Pamela had never ridden on a motorcycle. It didn't seem very safe. But then again, it was far too late to quibble, and her safety seemed somewhat by the by at this point anyway. Lucca climbed on and gestured for her to get on the back. Pamela was about to ask about helmets but didn't want to sound like a little old lady. She sighed and climbed on.

There was nothing quite like riding on the back of a gangster's motorcycle into the unknown to make one feel alive. Or conversely, to make one feel as if any moment could be their last. Lucca drove like a maniac and handled the coastal roads with their hairpin turns overlooking the sea with the insouciance with which he seemed to handle everything. Pamela was too busy worrying about crashing into a tree or being driven off a cliff to fret about failing at her mission or being captured by the authorities.

Once they reached La Croë, they waited in a nearby woods for the sun to set. Even if the letters signed by Wallis and the American consulate would provide a cover for police and Vichy officials, there was still the issue of the La Croë caretakers. It had been Macaulay's suggestion to wait until dark and break into the house. ('You had training in lock-picking, didn't you?')

Sitting on a tree stump, smoking a cigarette, unhelpful thoughts crept into Pamela's mind. What if they couldn't break into the house? What if they were caught? Pamela knew that in such an eventuality her government would deny all knowledge of her. And what if they did succeed and she did make it to Lisbon with the swimming costume, but failed to persuade the Windsors to go back to England? What if they were captured by the Germans and used for nefarious ends? The British public would have to be told that not only had their army been forced into shameful retreat, but their former king and his wife had been allowed to fall into the clutches of Adolf Hitler. As Macaulay said, morale and faith in the government would plummet and the Germans would have a valuable bargaining chip at their disposal.

She pinched herself. She couldn't allow her thoughts to run wild like this. She had to focus.

Pamela and Lucca staked out La Croë and its gatehouse where the caretakers lived. They waited as the husband and his son did their rounds of the property and then returned to the gatehouse before making for the back where the house faced the sea. Suddenly, they saw small, flashing lights. Lucca pulled his gun from its holster and gestured for Pamela to get down. Pamela pulled out her own pistol — the one given to her by Bricktop. As they lay in the dewy evening grass, they breathed a sigh of relief when they realised that it was not gunfire they had seen, but fireflies.

Pamela had forgotten how high the fence around the property was and how difficult it would be to climb. Lucca gave her a leg up and helpfully told her not to get caught on the spikes at the top. Pamela landed with an inelegant thud on the other side, but Lucca somehow seemed to have effortlessly leapt over. When they reached the house, to their surprise, they found it unlocked. Lucca stood guard at the bottom of the stairs while Pamela went up to Wallis's bedroom. Strangely, not a thing was out of place; one would hardly have been able to tell that the owners had fled in the middle of an invasion. The peach- and apricot-coloured bedroom exuded a soft luxury and felt leagues away from the chaotic world outside.

Pamela quickly searched for the swimming costume, finding it in the back of a drawer. Holding it in her hands, she realised this palaver wasn't about the green swimming costume at all. It was about Wallis playing Marie Antoinette, testing the limits of her power. Perhaps she was feeling petulant about being turfed out of both her houses, like an angry little girl. Perhaps she was still resentful of her treatment at the hands of her husband's family. Or perhaps she was trying to see how far the British government would go to keep her happy, or at least content enough to stay in a stifling marriage. Pamela felt her face burning with rage. She wanted to light the damned thing on fire. And after that, every stick of antique furniture, every chintz curtain, every monogrammed pillow in the house. She wanted to burn the whole building in all its carefully decorated, aristocratic glory to the ground.

Suddenly, she heard crunching footsteps on the gravel outside. Pamela drew her revolver and went to the window. There was a half-moon shining through the clouds, giving just enough light for her to see the caretaker, having a cigarette, probably making his last round for the night. All of a sudden, she heard a creak on the stairs and turned quickly, pointing the gun in the direction of the noise. But it was only Lucca. In order to maintain her cover story, she then rooted through the desk in the Duke's study and pretended to find the valuable papers she had claimed to be looking for.

As they were walking back to the fence, someone cried out, 'Who's there?'

Lucca and Pamela quickly ducked behind a tree. It was the caretaker's son. He was carrying a lantern and peered into the darkness, in Pamela and Lucca's direction. For one terrible moment, it seemed as if he might have spotted them. Lucca removed his revolver from its holder and pointed it at the boy. He was slight and when the lantern illuminated his face, Pamela realised he was probably only fifteen or sixteen.

The boy cried out again, his voice trembling now, 'This is private property! I'll call the gendarmes!'

Lucca pulled back the hammer on his gun. Pamela couldn't bear the thought of an innocent young boy being killed, all for the sake of the whim of a spoiled, selfish woman. Slowly, gingerly, she put her hand on Lucca's arm and shook her head, silently pleading with him. Lucca looked back at the boy with the gun still trained on him. The boy glanced once more into the darkness and then, not hearing anything further, turned back towards the house. Lucca put the gun back in its holster and Pamela breathed a sigh of relief.

They climbed back over the fence, recovered the motorcycle from the woods and then made their way back to Marseille, guided only by the shrouded light of the half-moon.

III

When Pamela and Lucca returned to Marseille, he took her straight to a dimly lit warehouse at the port for the handoff of the necklace. They were met by a reedy Corsican gangster sporting a gold tooth and a flashy suit, who made it clear to Pamela that if the necklace didn't turn up in Lisbon, there would be consequences. Later, in the privacy of her hotel room, she opened the jewellery case and held the necklace up to the light. It was made of square and rectangular-cut diamonds and emeralds, and it hung just below her collarbone, likely by Cartier or Boucheron. Thinking of Lettice and her engagement ring, Pamela couldn't help but wonder how it had been acquired.

The next morning, before she caught her train to Spain, Pamela burned Margaret Blythewood/Johanna Hoffman's papers and hid her own British passport in the lining of one of her suitcases in order to travel under her new Irish identity. She then threw both the Colt and the Luger into the sea, knowing that if she were caught carrying weapons, it would be a one-way ticket to an interrogation room. Which was still a possibility — as the cyanide capsule nestled in a secret pocket of her handbag continually reminded her.

The beautiful countryside of south-west France was untouched, but the people on the train and at each stop looked miserable and resigned. She was chilled to the bone when she realised that there were Gestapo officials on board, checking papers at random and searching people's bags. Pamela kept a careful eye on her suitcase, which contained the necklace, not daring to close her eyes for a moment. She worried that the fear grinding away in the pit of her stomach would show on her face, until she realised that everyone on the train looked frightened. Even when she tried to trick herself into thinking that she was simply on a train journey, the announcements that were now given in German instead of French reminded her of the grim new reality. At the border crossing, when Spanish immigration officials went through her luggage, Pamela had been so nervous she thought she might be sick. But Hecky's instincts had been right — when they did find the necklace, they hardly gave her or it a second glance.

In contrast to France, Spain had both demoralised people and a decimated landscape. The civil war had ended over a year ago but after three years of vicious fighting, the country was still marked by burned-out villages, barren fields and blasted, nightmarish-looking trees. When Pamela stopped in Madrid, it was jarring to see the grand, elegant capital as battle-scarred as the countryside. Construction had already begun because Franco was determined to cover up any evidence of the war; but there were bullet holes in walls and craters in the ground, pockmarking the once elegant Spanish capital. People were still having to queue for food and most shop windows were empty. Stray dogs and orphaned children roamed the streets. Knowing that there would be Gestapo agents everywhere, when Pamela checked into a hotel that night, she hardly slept a wink.

Crossing the border into Portugal was surreal. Compared to France and Spain, the country seemed completely untouched. There were crops in the fields and produce in the markets. Department stores displayed their usual wares. At first glance, it seemed as if ordinary life was carrying on as normal in Lisbon and there was no war at all. But on closer inspection, it was a city much like Marseille, crowded with refugees from across Europe, leading temporary lives. Hotels and boarding houses were full and the lines outside the embassies dotted around the city were endless. The ports were packed with people waiting for missing family members, hoping against hope that parents, spouses and children separated from them along the way would finally turn up. Macaulay had said that Lisbon was a nest of intrigue like Madrid, with hotels, restaurants and bars staffed with various countries' secret agents and informers. (For instance, the Abwehr ran a bar on the port that doubled as a brothel, intended to extract intelligence from drunk British sailors.)

Eager to rid herself of the necklace, the first thing Pamela did when she arrived was go straight to the pawn shop to drop it off. The small, bald, moustachioed man proprietor asked if he could help her.

As she took out the box and laid it on the counter, she replied exactly as she had been instructed: 'It was a gift from my late husband. I'll expect to return for it within the week.'

He raised an eyebrow and gave her a meaningful look. He then opened the jewellery box, inspected the necklace and nodded.

As Pamela looked around, she realised that the shop was already filled with valuable jewellery, some even more impressive than Salvadore's necklace. Where better to stash a stolen necklace than a pawn shop already full to bursting? People had clearly pawned their most valuable possessions to pay for passage on ships or planes to faraway countries, hotel rooms where they stayed while waiting for visas and, most probably, bribes to slip to government officials.

When Pamela checked into the Aviz, an ornate, exquisitely appointed hotel patronised largely by well-heeled foreigners, she had her first bath in a week, ate dinner in the restaurant and slept for nearly twelve hours. As she came downstairs the next morning, she stopped dead; there in the hotel lobby, seated across from each other, were William Bullitt and Elsa Schiaparelli. The Italian designer looked cheerful and fresh as a daisy, wearing a sharp suit with a striking hat, both of her own creation. The American ambassador, however, looked completely worn out and miserable, sporting day-old stubble, a creased suit and shoes in need of a shine. Pamela had heard that when the Germans invaded, Bullitt had briefly taken on the role of Mayor of Paris, perhaps a last-ditch effort to protect the city he so loved. What was he doing in Lisbon? Had relations between the United States and the new Vichy government broken down already? Or perhaps Roosevelt was replacing Bullitt with an ambassador who would be more amenable to Pétain and his German puppet-masters.

'Lady Pamela!' Schiaparelli cried as she rose to her feet and kissed Pamela on both cheeks. 'What are you doing here in Lisbon?'

Before she could answer, Bullitt looked at her curiously and interjected, 'I'm surprised you're not back in England by now.'

'I'm on my way to London. But I've been asked to accompany the Duke and Duchess of Windsor back to England.'

'Wallis!' exclaimed Schiaparelli. 'You must give my love to her.'

At the mention of Wallis's name, Bullitt pursed his lips. 'Do give my regards to them both,' he said cooly.

How had things been left between Wallis and him? If she had rung the American Consulate about the swimming costume, he would know about the Windsors' flight from France. Pamela could only imagine his reaction when word reached him that his former lover was troubling the embassy with such an absurdly frivolous, selfish request while France was in freefall. And if Wallis had left him as abruptly and suddenly as she had Fruity, she could imagine how much more maddened he would have been.

'Are you travelling together?'

'No,' Bullitt quickly replied. 'We just happened to run into each other.'

'We're on the same Clipper to New York.' Schiaparelli smiled.

American visas and passage on ships leaving Europe were becoming increasingly impossible to obtain; Pamela couldn't imagine what it had taken for her to get a seat on a plane to New York, let alone gain entry to the United States at a time like this. While a renowned couturier, Schiaparelli was still an Italian and, as Mussolini had entered the war on Germany's side the previous month, was now a foreign national of a belligerent country. And it was clear that while she looked pleased as punch to be sitting with a prominent American diplomat, Bullitt was deeply uncomfortable.

Having started her business from nothing, without training in fashion design or even basic sewing, Schiaparelli was known to be an incredibly resourceful, canny woman. Was it possible that she was blackmailing Bullitt over his affair with Wallis? Before the war, their affair might have seemed simply ill-judged; however, with the increasingly complex political situation, tales of an affair between the American ambassador to France and the wife of a former British royal and prominent Nazi sympathiser had the potential to be damaging — both to Bullitt's diplomatic career and to the image of the United States. Pamela could well imagine Schiaparelli playing all the cards she had to escape from France.

IV

Pamela's contact in Lisbon was Walter Monckton, who had been sent to collect the Windsors the first time and was having to tear himself away from his work in war propaganda to try again. When he met her at the Aviz, he looked as if he had just stepped off the plane from Croydon Airport; his fine linen suit looked sweaty, crumpled and much the worse for wear.

Monckton shook Pamela's hand. 'Congratulations for making it this far. Your bravery and resilience have not gone unnoticed.'

Pamela picked up on an undertone of amazement in his voice, surprised that she had made it at all and not been arrested or killed. He knew how dangerous her mission was and what her odds had been.

He gestured to the balcony of his hotel suite.

'There isn't a room in this hotel free from listening devices.' He sighed as he closed the door behind them. 'In fact, there's hardly a single place in Lisbon where you won't be overheard by someone.'

Pamela thought about Schiaparelli and Bullitt and who might have been spying on them.

'Our agents say the Duke golfs and the Duchess plays bridge all day. Either that or they lounge by the pool, drinking cocktails. Oscillating between boredom and hysteria.'

It didn't seem as if their retreat from the authorities had changed them much; they were still the same self-absorbed, superficial people they had always been. They knew that they could play politics, saying whatever they liked to whomever they liked, and no matter what happened to the world around them, there would always be a soft, protected landing.

'And you need me to try to convince Wallis that they have to return to Britain?'

'Change of plan. Churchill has offered the Duke the position of Governor of the Bahamas.'

'The Bahamas? But why?'

'The Windsors won't be allowed back into Britain. While we've been fighting tooth and nail to avoid surrendering to Jerry, he's been wasting everyone's time haggling over money and titles, and whether or not his mother will receive them. For weeks,' said Monckton, with barely concealed anger. 'If, for some reason, they take it into their heads to try to return to England now, the Duke would face a court martial for disobeying direct orders. I imagine convincing them to keep shtum when it comes to their views on the war, Germans, Hitlerism and so on might prove difficult, wherever they're living. But the Bahamas are the only option they have left.'

'No one wants the Windsors back in London, encouraging defeatists and fifth columnists,' Pamela said.

'And to be perfectly honest with you, it couldn't be a worse time to have people like them making a high-profile arrival. To make matters worse, these smoke signals they've been sending out have inspired the Germans to recruit them to their cause. Last week, we intercepted a cable intended for the Duke, from an SS officer called Schellenberg, offering the Duke and Duchess fifty million Swiss francs in a Swiss bank account. In exchange, they would work for the Third Reich to persuade King George to align himself with Hitler.'

Pamela wanted to believe that as venal and self-interested as they were, the Windsors wouldn't stoop to being bought by an enemy power. Surely, they would find such a thing humiliating — a member of the aristocracy and his wife being bribed into a kind of vassalage.

'And if that fails, they intend to try to lure them back into Spain and hold them for ransom, with the aim of forcing Britain to the negotiating table. In the meantime, they've attempted all sorts of daft nonsense — having agents spy on them, sending bouquets of flowers with notes of warning, sabotaging their car … all manner of things one sees in a badly acted, low-budget film. The Nazis are even pressuring Salazar to keep the Windsors in Portugal. And to make matters more complicated, the Duke has become so paranoid, he refuses to listen to anyone. Apart from her, of course.' Monckton turned to face Pamela. 'The Duchess trusts you, Lady Pamela. We're hoping you can be the one to persuade her that it's the best course of action.'

'I'm going to have to be very persuasive indeed, especially if fifty million Swiss francs are on the table.'

'I don't mean to put undue pressure on you, but you might be our last hope.'

If only she'd known where it was all going to lead four years ago when she said yes to spying on Wallis Simpson for Charlie Buchanan. And if Wallis and Edward had been deported to the Bahamas three years ago, it would have saved everyone a lot of trouble. Pamela wouldn't be in the impossible position in which she now found herself: as the last resort in trying to convince two of the world's most spoiled, self-centred people to do as they were told.

She leaned against the railing of the balcony and looked out over the city. How strange to think that while every other capital in Europe was observing a strict blackout, Lisbon was shining brightly.

'I'm going to have to consider how to approach her.'

'I'm sure you'll figure out something. I've heard you're rather … inventive.' Monckton smiled. 'All for a swimming costume, eh?' (Macaulay must have told him about the Corsican gangsters.) He retrieved a cigar from his pocket, snipped off the end and lit it. The tip glowed orange as he inhaled. 'You deserve a medal for managing to put up with that dreadful woman all this time.'

V

The next day, Pamela and Monckton drove to an area outside Lisbon on the Costa do Estoril, called *Boca do Inferno* — which translated as 'Mouth of Hell'. The Windsors were staying at Casa de Santa Maria, a large pink villa owned by a powerful Portuguese banker who was a close personal friend of Prime Minister Salazar and rumoured to be laundering money for the Nazis. Salazar himself had arranged for the Windsors to stay there so they could be monitored, as having the former King of England and his wife let loose in a city known as a hotbed of espionage was inconvenient for a neutral country. Secluded and surrounded by pinewoods, Casa de Santa Maria sat atop rocks overlooking the Atlantic, next to a lighthouse.

As she and Monckton came up the driveway, it was silly, but Pamela couldn't help but think of all the Agatha Christie murders that took place in grand, cliffside houses. Gunshots no one would hear. Stabbings no one would witness. Bodies thrown into the sea in the dead of night.

The Windsors looked as healthy, tanned and well dressed as ever. Wallis wore a neat, light blue linen skirt and matching top with a navy turban. The Duke wore a jaunty yellow bandana as a cravat, paired with an orange polo shirt. They looked more like holidaymakers than refugees. They were both pleased to see Pamela. Wallis gave her a bony embrace, and the Duke shook her hand.

'We are very relieved to know you're safe and were able to get out of France in one piece,' he said earnestly.

'Yes, it's all been so awful, hasn't it?' added Wallis.

Pamela did her best to suppress the rage bubbling up inside of her by imagining what kind of murder Agatha Christie might have written for them.

While Monckton went inside with the Duke, Walls took Pamela for a walk in the gardens overlooking the sea.

'You can't imagine the pressure we're under right now,' she groaned. 'Surveillance at all hours, by the Portuguese, the Germans, the British — everyone. David's been having to answer phone calls and telegrams day and night. Even our car was sabotaged. The last two months have shattered our nerves. We wanted to get here sooner but we had to wait because the Duke of Kent was in Lisbon. Official celebrations of Portuguese independence or something. And of course, we can't be in the same city — or even the same country — as David's brother. Can you believe it?'

Pamela half expected her to complain that, now they were at war with Germany, Ribbentrop wasn't available to make up a four at bridge.

They sat on a bench in the shade, taking refuge from the noontime sun. Pamela revealed the green swimming costume, which she had kept in her handbag. As she reached in to retrieve it, she turned on the recording device.

'I heard that you were missing this terribly, so I arranged for someone to bring it from La Croë.'

Pamela knew Wallis well enough to be able to predict that she wouldn't bother to ask for details as to how someone would have managed to casually come by and picked up an item from her wardrobe while France was being invaded, the government was collapsing, and half the country was in flight. But she was surprised by her complete lack of enthusiasm.

'Oh, yes, thanks,' Wallis replied languidly as she fanned herself. 'Very kind of you.'

This was the swimming costume Wallis had harangued the American Consulate to get their hands on, at all costs, for which Pamela had negotiated with gangsters, ridden on the back of a motorbike for hours, crossed enemy lines and risked her life. Pamela had been right — at the end of the day, it was an exercise in power. A way to make sure the government was at her beck and call.

She tried again. 'You'll certainly make use of it in the Bahamas, won't you?'

'Churchill is dying to get rid of us, one way or another.'

And onward Wallis steamed, like a U-boat. One complaint after another.

All the things they had to leave behind in Paris and Antibes.

Being without their servants.

The difficult time their terriers had on the journey.

Suddenly, she removed her sunglasses. She looked around and then leaned in, her face tense.

'Pamela, I know I can trust you.'

Pamela held herself completely still, breath bated.

'David has been speaking to some very important people on the other side … You see, what the British don't understand is that Churchill is standing in the way of an end to this war. They think David could play a very important role in peace negotiations. That he might even be able to *end* the war. Could you imagine?' Wallis leaned in further, so close Pamela could feel the heat of her breath. 'He would become so indispensable to Britain that he would be invited back.'

'Invited back as what?'

'As King, of course. "Edward the Peacemaker"'.

They knew about the Duke's fantasies about playing chief negotiator, but no one realised that his aim of usurping his brother and taking the throne was in earnest. While fishing her lighter and cigarettes out of her handbag. She lit a cigarette and took a deep drag from it.

'Invited by whom?' she asked, trying to maintain a tone of casual interest.

'No one other than Rudolf Hess,' Wallis replied, looking pleased with herself. 'We met him when we were in Germany. He's a very important man, very close to the Führer.'

Reichsminister Hess was second in line to take over if anything happened to Hitler, after Hermann Göring.

If only Wallis knew she was being recorded.

'And Hess knows David would be prepared to make himself available for negotiations without any personal investment or ambitions at all.'

The Windsors weren't just pawns whose anger and vanity were easily manipulated by cleverer people. While Charles Bedaux may have initially been the conduit to the Nazi High Command, the Duke clearly had his own direct line in place now. It was even possible that Wallis had been using her own connection — her former lover Ribbentrop. When had this arrangement first been broached? When Wallis warned Bricktop about German occupation and internment last autumn, it was entirely possible she had already been speaking to him. What if the Windsors had abandoned Fruity in Paris and turned tail because they knew they had committed treason?

To paraphrase the Gershwin song: how long had this been going on?

Pamela looked down at the green swimming costume lying on the bench. It made sense that if they stayed away as long as they could, if they led the government a merry dance across Europe and sent them on foolish errands, they could bide their time and see which way the winds of war blew. And bargain with the Germans. Why stop at fifty million Swiss francs when you could get one hundred? And if Hitler did manage to force the British to the negotiating table, they could make their great return, bolstered by fascist support. Like British Vichy-style figureheads.

Wallis picked a bit of fluff from her top, sighed and then looked up at the sky. 'David thinks the time is right, because the bombings will have prepared Britain for peace.'

It was so quiet that all Pamela could hear was the wind and the chirping of the cicadas.

The bombings will have prepared Britain for peace.

She was so horrified she was at a loss for words.

'You must know that Germany is getting ready to bomb the country if they don't surrender. No one wants such a thing to happen, least of all David and me,' said Wallis, 'but we must negotiate with them now, while we can. They're clearly the far superior power, much better equipped.'

In a way, Wallis was right. What Germany had done to Poland, Holland, Belgium and France would likely be visited on her own country. Pamela took another drag on her cigarette, inhaling deeply. The French Army had been broken, scattered across the country, taken into detention camps or, if they were lucky enough, retreated with the British Army across the Channel.

'Churchill and King George and that whole cabal are warmongers. They'd come to the negotiating table if they cared about saving lives.'

The smug look on Wallis's face made Pamela want to punch her. If they cared about saving lives. Warmongering. Churchill and King George had stepped in when Chamberlain and her own husband had failed the country. A selfish act of revenge masquerading as a bid for peace. A personal vendetta against a family, government and people that had slighted them.

A ray of sunlight pierced the fronds of the palm tree above their heads and hit the brooch pinned to Wallis's dress. A flamingo encrusted with diamonds, rubies, sapphires and emeralds.

'Do you like it?' she asked. 'David bought it for me in Paris just before the invasion.'

If you were anyone else, you'd just be another woman in a crowded, stinking bomb shelter, holding your children in fear. Or a refugee walking for days, worrying how you were going to find food or if you'd ever see your loved ones again. I don't know how you can live with yourselves. Carrying on with your sheltered, spoiled lives. Betraying your country, while people all over Europe are being shot and bombed and driven into the sea. You two are the most rotten, selfish, morally destitute people I have ever met in my life. No personal investment or ambitions, my foot. The two of you deserve to be arrested, tried and hanged for the traitors you are.

Pamela thought about Noël, a man well practised at holding his tongue around those who angered him, and what he had told her: that what they were doing was theatre.

It was time for her performance.

Pamela stubbed out her cigarette. 'It's very difficult to tell who your true friends are, who is genuinely looking out for your best interests, isn't it?'

'We never know who we can really trust. Sometimes we can hardly eat or sleep, for fear of what may happen next.'

Pamela thought of the Windsors sleeping in clean, luxurious sheets and dining on black market delicacies at the Madrid Ritz.

'Perhaps I shouldn't say anything, but I would regret it for the rest of my life if I didn't speak now. Wallis, I don't want to alarm you,' she said in hushed tones. 'I say this as a *friend*, as someone who is concerned for your wellbeing. For your *safety*. And of course,' Pamela paused ominously, 'there are those who wouldn't want me to say anything at all.'

'Pamela, please. I know we can trust you.'

Pamela closed her eyes dramatically. She sighed deeply, laying a hand on her chest. Then she looked around. 'I know for a fact that you and His Majesty are in the gravest danger. I have it on good authority that …' She trailed off and then lowered her voice. 'If the Germans are unsuccessful in their collaboration with His Majesty … if those possibilities fall through, or they change their minds …'

'Why would they change their minds?' Wallis asked irritably, fanning herself. 'They know that we—' She paused. 'I mean, they know that *David* could be crucial to peace negotiations with Britain.'

Pamela's eye landed on the priceless Cartier brooch. 'It is possible that they don't want peace with Britain at all. That what they want is conquest. And the two of you are just pawns. After all, we've seen how ruthless they are. In which case, they might plan on having you assassinated.'

'But that's impossible,' replied Wallis, startled. 'We're too valuable to them.'

The sun beat down on the two women. Pamela was struggling to convey an air of mystique while sweat ran down the back of her neck.

The gentle breeze previously coming off the Atlantic had disappeared. The air had grown still and hot. She used her blouse to fan herself, only able to circulate the tiniest bit of air around her face. She was always amazed at how perfectly dressed and coiffed Wallis was. Even sitting in the baking, sun-drenched Portuguese garden, she still looked immaculate. Not a drop of sweat, a chipped nail or a hair out of place.

'Of course, I can only speculate about their motivations,' Pamela said carefully, 'but I imagine they would be sending a signal to the British people that they're serious. If they killed you both, I mean. They seem to be quite keen to demonstrate their brute force. I could be wrong — perhaps they would find you useful as figureheads, to pacify the people. But on the other hand, once they'd occupied the country, they wouldn't need you anymore.'

Wallis looked upset, fanning herself nervously. 'We know we can't stay in Portugal forever, but exiling us to the Bahamas of all places … it might as well be Napoleon imprisoned on St Helena! I said to David, "What on earth would we do *there*?" They just want us out of the way, so they can forget about us.'

Then Pamela had an idea.

'You'll both be safe there. Far removed from the war and the bombings. But … I'm not sure if I should tell you this.'

'Tell me what?'

'I don't want to worry you even more …'

'What is it?'

'If you refuse to go,' said Pamela as she leaned in, a note of concern in her voice, 'Churchill is planning on having you both shot.'

A look of horror crept over Wallis's face. She clutched her fan, white-knuckled. It was clear that she was more frightened of Churchill than of Hitler.

291

'I wasn't sure whether to worry you with this but ...' Pamela paused. 'I was supposed to help Miss Blythewood get out of Paris. But when I went to fetch her from Boulevard Suchet ... oh, it's too awful. I can't say it.' She turned away, as if overcome with emotion.

Wallis dropped her fan and grabbed Pamela's wrists. 'PAMELA — what happened?'

Having managed a few crocodile tears, she turned back to Wallis and said, 'She was dead. Someone had shot her. It was such chaos in the exodus to leave the city — maybe it was a thief, trying to take advantage of the empty house. But I can't help but think ... maybe it was a warning.'

Pamela could only imagine what Macaulay and Monckton would say if they knew she was using a woman *she* had killed to terrify Wallis and reinforce Churchill's position as a would-be assassin.

Wallis's eyes were wide. A hand on her chest, she caught her breath and slowly picked up her fan from the ground.

Pamela gently put a hand on her shoulder. 'Just think, if you go to the Bahamas, you can get far, far away from people who might want to hurt you. And from this ugly war. And when it's all over, you and the Duke will have been seen to have done your patriotic duty. Besides, you must stay alive for your friends, for your people. After all, there are still so many who love and admire you both. Myself included, of course.'

Wallis put her hand on top of Pamela's. 'Pamela, thank you for your honesty. You have always been such a good friend to us.' She then straightened up into her usual, rigid posture. 'All I can say is that they had better arrange to have our things sent to the Bahamas. We cannot do without our linens and silver.'

At least it would be its own punishment, being trapped on an island, thousands of miles away, with a man she didn't love. Who expected her to tell him exactly what to do each and every day. Who she could never leave.

But with any luck, their ship might be sunk by a U-boat while crossing the Atlantic.

VI

Later that afternoon, parked some way from Casa de Santa Maria, Monckton told Pamela that the Windsors had acquiesced and would be on their way to the Bahamas within forty-eight hours.

'I don't know what you said to the Duchess, but she was quite successful in convincing the Duke to accept the post. Apparently, she told him she would feel safer, away from Europe,' Monckton said as he leaned against the black sedan.

'I told the Duchess that if the Germans didn't pick them off, someone else might. And I may have insinuated that rather than having them running around Europe, Churchill might prefer to have them permanently silenced.'

'Did you, indeed?' Monckton peered at her through his thick, round spectacles, surprised.

'I realised that making up a ridiculous-sounding plot might be the only way the Duchess would agree to leave.'

'I would say "plot" is probably the wrong word. "Last resort" is more accurate.'

'Pardon?'

'Oh, it's perfectly true.'

The Prime Minister *did* have a plan to assassinate the King's brother and his wife? When she proposed such a thing herself, she thought it was so preposterous that she felt relieved when Wallis believed her.

'The Duchess took that seriously, did she?'

'I told her that I found a body at Boulevard Suchet. And suggested that it might be a warning. To her and the Duke.'

Monckton's mouth curled into a smile. 'I heard about your encounter with the Abwehr agent. Two birds with one stone, as it were.'

He took a silver hip flask out of his pocket and offered it to Pamela. She took a swig of what turned out to be whisky. They were silent for a moment, watching the ocean. All that could be heard was the seagulls and the crash of the waves on the rocks. Pamela wondered if the blue and white lighthouse marked the furthest westerly point in Europe.

'Excellent work, Lady Pamela.' Monckton raised the flask to her. 'You should be very proud of what you've done for your country.'

So far, she had shot a woman, made an illicit deal with known criminals and lied to the wife of the former King of England, in order to intimidate her into leaving Europe. Though at least the last one had turned out not to have been a lie. And to be honest, if Churchill had ordered her to kill the Windsors herself, she would have obliged him.

But the knowledge Pamela had gleaned from Wallis weighed on her mind.

'Sir, there's something you should know.'

'Yes?'

'The Duchess told me that the Duke has been communicating directly with Rudolf Hess. I know we thought the conduit was Bedaux, that he was passing on information, but the Duke was — and is still — in contact with him.'

Monckton screwed the cap of his flask back on and put it back in his pocket. He looked at her intently. 'Go on …'

'She said they'd established the relationship when they visited Germany three years ago, which means they might have been speaking this whole time. And the Duke wanted him to know he was available to facilitate peace negotiations between Britain and Germany. Which, to be frank, is what he said to Fruity and me when we were in Paris together.'

'Did he?'

Pamela nodded. 'I had initially thought they were just pawns, but now I know they were acting of their own volition. So that they can return to the throne. Once the Germans have won, that is. I suspect they left us behind in Paris because they didn't want to return to England, because they didn't know who knew about what they'd done. Because, of course, that would be treason. But if they held out until the Germans had bombed us all to hell, their return would be a very different one.'

Though Monckton was trying to control his emotions, Pamela could tell he was alarmed. He looked away a moment, towards the sea.

'Sir ... ?'

'Yes, thank you for your report, Lady Pamela,' he replied curtly.

Why wasn't he asking her any questions? Why wasn't he asking for more details?

'I found it very troubling. I assumed you'd want to know right away.'

'Yes, thank you. I'll make sure the information goes through the appropriate channels.'

Pamela could tell he was as troubled as she was, but he didn't want to show it.

'I appreciate your thoroughness. You've done an excellent job all round.' Monckton looked back at the Casa de Santa Maria.

For a moment, Pamela considered offering him the recording of the conversation, but her instincts told her to wait until she had a clearer picture of what was going on when she eventually debriefed with Macaulay back in London. Maybe she was being petty, but she had imagined more of a reaction from Monckton, especially after all she'd done. More outrage. But then again, men like him didn't seem to get outraged. Was it that he didn't want to know? Maybe it was enough that the Windsors were going to be shipped off to the Bahamas and if he knew the extent of their treasonous behaviour, it would mean changing course, more complications, more paperwork. And he'd already wasted enough time on them as it was. It was possible that Monckton simply wanted to be finished with the miserable couple so that he could return his attentions to the war.

August 1940

I

After the Windsors were well on their way across the Atlantic, Pamela flew back with Monckton to England. London was even darker and quieter than she'd remembered it when she was there last autumn, and with far more men and women in uniform. It was hot and the city felt airless — a perennial fug of pipe and cigarette smoke, exhaust from cars and buses and the smell of horse droppings. (Petrol rationing had obliged tradespeople and delivery services to revert to horse and cart.) People gave off an air of grim determination; it felt as if everyone was waiting for something to happen, trapped in an anxious holding pattern with nothing to do in the meantime but go about their business. Like flightless birds, flapping their wings in a murky grey fog. It was just as well that they were all completely unaware of the fact that the former King Edward VIII had been plotting to sell out the whole country in order to retake the throne.

Pamela had been turning the exchange with Monckton over in her mind again and again. While it was possible he hadn't wanted a reason to be forced to prosecute the Windsors and complicate an already-complicated situation further, there was only one other possible explanation for his reaction: he already knew. Monckton knew the Duke was in direct contact with Hess and wanted to keep the whole thing quiet.

But one question remained: who else knew? Surely, if Churchill did, the Windsors would be brought home to be tried for treason. On the other hand, as Monckton kept saying, such a thing would be a disaster for the morale of the British public. And while she understood the argument intellectually, it didn't mean she agreed with it. Why should two people be above the law of the land just because of who they were and what they symbolised?

Then there was the tape on which Pamela had recorded Wallis's confession. She now felt that it was right, not to have given it to Monckton. She had a debrief with Macaulay in two days. She would simply have to wait until then to turn it over.

II

Pamela's excuse to her family and friends for not having evacuated France sooner was that she had been working to use her connections to get Lettice and her new husband out of the country. (Which was partially true.) She was as vague as possible about why she'd flown back with Monckton more than a month later, saying it had something to do with her work for the Propaganda Bureau that she couldn't disclose. (Which wasn't entirely false.) Most people had become used to the atmosphere of wartime secrecy and classified information and had refrained from asking anything further, much to her relief.

However, Pamela was feeling more isolated than ever. She longed for someone to confide in. About the Windsors, what the Exodus had been like, what it was like to survive being strafed by Messerschmitts and what had happened to those who hadn't. Seeing children whose parents had been killed abandoned on the side of the road and people stepping over bodies as they trudged through the heat. The ways in which France had become disfigured under the Vichy regime and the pervasive fear that had spread so quickly. Travelling through fascist Spain with its decimated landscape and hungry people. What it felt like to shoot a woman. But there was no one to tell.

It was strange and lonely to return to an empty house and find herself rambling around in it by herself. She found a letter from Francis, whose relief that she'd returned safely to London was palpable. As was how much he missed her. He mentioned little of what he was doing in Washington but said the weather was unbearably hot and humid, as the American capital had been built on a swamp. He was tired of nightly dinner and cocktail parties, though he had met a congressman who was going to take him foxhunting in Virginia in the autumn — or 'fall', as the Americans called it — which he thought might be good fun.

But he ended on a note that left Pamela puzzled:

I have high hopes that we might see each other again before too long.

It could mean that he was going to be sent home on a kind of leave at some point, maybe for Christmas. Though she had been under the impression that he would be away for quite some time.

She also had a letter waiting for her from Noël, who had been sent back to America on another propaganda mission. And from what he'd written, it didn't sound like the charm offensive to lure the USA onto Britain's side was going particularly well. He told her how he'd tried to get back to Paris but by the time he landed in Lisbon, the Nazis were days away from the city. Worried sick about his staff, he was determined to go anyway but was convinced by Britain's ambassador to Portugal that he would be putting himself in danger. Instead, he ended up catching the last commercial flight out of France from Bordeaux.

To think, that only days before I'd been sitting on the end of President Roosevelt's bed, listening to him tell me to advise Churchill not to surrender the British fleet! I replied that seemed a bit far-fetched but then he reminded me of Chamberlain's idiocy. The nerve of the man to tell us THAT while his country does nothing! Churchill, of course, was annoyed.

Pamela wasn't sure how much he'd been told about her mission, but he did say he was deeply relieved to hear she was back in England and amused to hear that the Windsors had adopted the latest trend of 'refugeeing'.

It is so like the Duke and Duchess to flee to a place where they can work on their suntans while the rest of the world is fighting a war.

Unable to stand being alone in the house in the evenings, she rang Percy up the next day to see if he wanted to get a drink. Not one to get emotional unless he was drunk, Percy was uncharacteristically overwhelmed when he saw her.

'Darling! Thank God you're alright. I've been very worried about you, you know. I would have expected our government to take better care of its employees and keep you out of harm's way! Was it just terrible getting out?'

Pamela was vague and gave a somewhat uninteresting story about queuing and paperwork to dissuade him from asking too many questions. She was relieved when he turned the conversation to the convenience of the blackouts for certain nocturnal activities.

'The police have finally found better things to do than go around arresting men for enjoying themselves. And the downstairs bar at the Ritz has become *so* notorious that the Brigade of Guards have banned their officers from going there.'

At the weekend, she went for tea at the house in Hampstead where Lettice and Mikhail were living. Both of them were greatly relieved to see her. Even the stoic Russian artist embraced her tightly. The two of them looked significantly better than they had when she last saw them on the docks of Marseille, but Pamela could tell that Mikhail's mind was elsewhere. He'd turned the shed in the garden into a studio but was struggling to find the will to begin sculpting or painting again.

'I was frightened that Mikhail would be interned with other enemy aliens, but we didn't have any problems whatsoever,' said Lettice. (Pamela silently thanked Macaulay for whatever arrangements he'd made.) 'We're very grateful, you know, Pam. For what you did for us. I've heard they hung a swastika flag from the Arc de Triomphe. Can you imagine?' She paused to pour them tea. 'I wonder if we'll ever see France again.'

The next day, the two women went to the cinema to see the new Vivien Leigh picture that had come out earlier that year to try to take their minds off things. After two hours into *Gone with the Wind*, Pamela decided that watching a film about war in a time of war was a bit redundant. And speculated whether she, too, would one day have to resort to making gowns out of the dining room drapery. But it was the newsreel that had come on beforehand and flickered with footage of German and Russian armies marching across occupied lands that had unsettled Pamela. (Lettice could barely bring herself to watch it.) Pamela looked around the cinema at the illuminated faces of the other people, transfixed by the pictures rolling across the screen. Did they have any real idea what might happen to them if Germany managed to invade Britain, of the decimation that would surely follow?

III

It was the first time Pamela had seen Sid since she'd arrived in London the week before. Lettice had given her the telephone number of the flat he was sharing with another American journalist; Pamela felt a sense of anticipation and simultaneous apprehension at the thought of phoning him. She had been thinking of Sid continually since she saw him off at the docks, but part of her was also hoping that if she saw him outside the romantic setting of Paris, the spell would be broken. That she didn't love him after all. That it had only been an infatuation and had passed, like a fever.

But seeing Sid's face again when they met at an intimate Italian restaurant in Soho made Pamela realise this was no passing fever. She had that old feeling of everything around her fading into the background as, once again, she felt inexorably drawn to him. They fell back into the easy intimacy they'd shared in Paris, telling stories and making each other laugh; only now, after having survived so much together, their bond felt deeper, stronger, more significant.

After dinner, he took her to a small club nearby that another journalist had told him about. It was seedy but lively, filled with a mix of men and women in uniform and what Pamela had come to know as the night creatures that haunted Soho — people wearing flashy suits, feathers, sequins and liberally applied makeup. One of whom turned out to be Percy.

'Hello, Panda!' he cried, clearly several cocktails into the evening. 'What's a nice girl like you doing in a low joint like this? And who, may I ask, are *you*?'

Even Sid, normally impervious to social interrogation, looked somewhat overpowered by the force of Percy's personality. 'Sid White. Pamela and I knew each other in Paris.'

'You *did*, did you?' Percy gave Pamela a look that could only be described as impish. The two people with him in the club — or rather, one man and one person of indeterminate gender who was dressed like a woman — looked Sid up and down. 'And is that an American accent I hear? Pray tell, what brings you to our fair isle … ?'

'I'm a war correspondent. I'm working for the Associated Press.'

'Oh! How exciting! Pamela and I used to work together at *The Times*. That is, until she got herself sacked,' he said, looking at Pamela with an arched eyebrow. 'Lots of journalists there, but none quite as dishy as you, Mr White.'

The evening reminded Pamela of the difficult reality of the situation: even if she hadn't seen Francis in nearly a year, she was still married. It made her realise what a removed and temporary life she had been living in France. She had put off facing her reality and now here it was, bearing down on her.

Later that night, lying next to each other in bed, Pamela tried to imagine what a life with Sid would look like. He'd taken a room in a friend's flat and had been spending the last month travelling around the country, covering stories about artillery units and air bases.

'How long are you going to stay in London?'

'I was thinking of going to Romania in a couple weeks, to see which way their government's leaning.'

'I meant in the long term.'

Sid grew momentarily quiet. 'Does anyone know what's happening in the long term? I don't think we even know what's happening next week.'

Pamela had forgotten about this side of him — the fly-by-night, noncommittal side. She sat up in bed. 'Yes, but surely you have some sort of idea of what *country* you might be living in for the next … year? Is that too much to ask?'

'Are you sore at me or something?'

Pamela turned on the light.

'I don't know what we're doing. Or where this is going. And of course, when we were in France and everything had gone to hell, that didn't matter quite so much. But this is my life. Here, in London.'

'Pam, I love you. You know I love you.'

'But that's not enough, is it? What am I supposed to do with that? With a man who's in one place one day and another the next?'

Sid got up and started pacing back and forth across Pamela's bedroom.

'What do you want? Do you want me to stay here in London for you?' he demanded. 'Because if that's what you want, I will. I'll do it.

But it's no picnic for me either. My newspaper shuts down because of a Nazi invasion, I have to flee the country, I wash up somewhere else and have to make the best of it. And I'm in love with a married woman who might not even be in love with me.'

Pamela reached over to her cigarette case on her side table and lit a cigarette.

'I never said I didn't love you,' she replied tersely.

'You never said you did either.'

'Yes, of course I love you, you idiot,' she blurted out. 'Sorry. I'm sorry. I hadn't intended to say it that way.'

Sid came around to the other side of the bed and sat down next to her. He took her cigarette out of her hand and kissed her. The kissing, for a start. That was why. The most sublime kissing she'd ever experienced.

'If you want me to stay, I will,' he said softly.

Pamela was surprised; she had never imagined Sid would make her an offer like that.

'I wouldn't say I ever aspired to be the other man. I don't know what's going on between you and your husband, but I can't be kept in limbo forever either.'

Pamela didn't know what to say. She didn't want the kind of situation Lettice, Mikhail and Georges found themselves in, living in a continual liminal state of shared affections and turning a blind eye. At least with Francis, she could be honest with him about her intelligence work and what had really happened in France. Sid only knew the version of the truth Pamela had told him. Then again, Francis had rarely — if ever — been able to express his feelings for her. Besides, it seemed impossible to make such a life-altering decision in the middle of a war, with the barbarians at the gates.

IV

Pamela was debriefed by two men she'd never met, senior to Macaulay at MI6. It was a formal process, with no room for discussion or debate. More or less a confirmation of what they had already heard from Monckton. A handshake for a job well done. A similarly evasive attitude about her intelligence about the Duke and Hess.

'Yes, Lady Pamela — Sir Walter has already passed on that information to us,' one of them had told her blankly.

It confirmed her suspicions that Monckton already knew and revealed that it seemed the rest of MI6 did too. Again, she decided to keep mum that she had a recording of Wallis confessing to the collusion until she saw Macaulay. Pamela had been surprised that he hadn't been present at her debrief and wondered when she'd see him again. Or *if* she would see him again. She had hoped that once the Windsors were safely across the Atlantic and the whole business was finished, she would no longer have trouble sleeping at night. She'd heard that Nancy Mitford turned Diana in to the authorities, saying her loyalty to Hitler posed a risk to the nation. And if Nancy had the nerve to inform on her own sister, what on earth was she doing, helping the Duke and Duchess of Windsor — whose treachery was even more profound — get away? But what could she do? And what was she to do with the recording? MI6 seemed singularly disinterested in her intelligence, perhaps trying to bury it.

A few days later, Pamela found an anonymous note slipped under her door, asking her to go to Highgate Cemetery the next day and be at the grave of William Lillywhite at 2 p.m.

The day was appropriately overcast and gloomy for the setting. When she reached the groundskeeper's lodge, she told him which grave she was looking for.

'North corner of the west cemetery,' he replied. 'You a cricket fan, then?'

'Pardon?'

'Lillywhite. The cricketer.'

When Pamela got to the long-dead sportsman's tomb, she found Macaulay leaning against it. They walked up and down the long avenues of graves, some well-kept and orderly, others choked with weeds and long forgotten, past family crypts and Gothic angels.

'I know you've only just returned to London, but I wanted to broach the subject of your next mission. We would like to ask if you would be interested in going to Washington, D.C. To meet your husband.'

Pamela stopped in her tracks.

'I don't understand.'

'As you know, Lord Francis is a member of an informal diplomatic delegation, tasked with—'

'Convincing Roosevelt to join the war.'

'And of course, gathering intelligence on the Americans' state of mind and any parties that might be influencing their decision to remain neutral.'

Francis's remark about seeing her soon made sense now. He was hoping that she would accept the offer to meet him in Washington. Maybe it had even been his idea. Maybe he missed her. Pamela suddenly felt touched.

'Did Francis ask you to send for me?'

Evading the question, the captain instead said, 'There's another reason why we'd like you to be on the other side of the Atlantic … I understand the Duchess took you into her confidences.'

'She told me about the Duke's traitorous little exchanges with

Rudolf Hess. Which Monckton didn't seem to want to discuss.' Pamela was barely able to keep the anger out of her voice.

Suddenly, the decision to meet in the middle of Highgate Cemetery made sense. No chance of being overheard or having anything they said repeated.

Macaulay looked down as he stamped his stick into the ground. 'Sir Walter already knows.'

'And Churchill … ?'

Macaulay avoided her gaze.

'Churchill has known for some time. It's why he was so anxious to get them in hand.'

Some time. Perhaps Chamberlain had known too. The entire British government had been carefully covering up the Duke's acts of treason for who knew how long. And in the meantime, also giving Bedaux leeway to pass along important pieces of intelligence about the British government, the British and French armies and the weaknesses in the Maginot Line. And Pamela had played an unwitting part in all of it. She felt her face flush with shame and fury.

'What if the Duke was responsible for the downfall of France? He could be responsible for the downfall of our own country,' she replied angrily.

'Indeed, Lady Pamela. Indeed.' Though his voice was calm, she could tell by the dark look in his eyes how he really felt about the whole dishonourable situation. 'Nevertheless, we *must* keep it quiet at all costs. We cannot afford a blow to British morale at a time like this. Please remember that you signed the Official Secrets Act willingly and under no duress or coercion.'

Pamela couldn't argue. For information such as this to reach the British public would be disastrous. And yet, she had risked her life.

To retrieve a swimming costume. In order to spirit the Windsors out of Europe, before they could fall into the enemy's embrace. And it turned out that they'd already been in contact with that enemy for months. Had it all been for nothing?

Worse, could a government that had gone to such lengths to cover up the scheming of a member of the Royal Family endangering the country really be trusted? After all, wasn't that what had led to the downfall of France and the betrayal of the French people? Lies, incompetence and corruption. If the British government was capable of something like this, what else were they capable of?

'We intercepted a message from Ribbentrop to the Duke, just before he sailed for the Bahamas. Ribbentrop is appealing to him to agree to resume their peace negotiations at a later date. In theory, at some point, the Duke will receive a code word, which will be a signal to return to Europe immediately.' He paused. 'The day the Windsors left Portugal, Hitler issued a directive ordering a full-scale attack on Britain.'

To think that Wallis was happily communicating with the Reichsminister of Foreign Affairs, the man who had advised Hitler to invade Poland. Pamela felt furious. Churchill should have assassinated them both when he had the chance.

'The Duke has a dossier he keeps in a locked dispatch case, to which only he has a key,' the captain continued. 'It contains correspondence between him and Samuel Hoare, our ambassador to Spain.'

'I don't think I follow.'

'Hoare was one of the architects of the Hoare-Laval Pact, which gave away most of Abyssinia to Mussolini. He began in Chamberlain's War Cabinet, but Churchill dismissed him and offered him the embassy in Madrid. Although Hoare initially turned it down, he changed his mind when Hitler invaded France.'

'He was involved with Beaverbrook and Halifax, wasn't he? The pro-appeasement set.'

Macaulay nodded.

Beaverbrook, who had invited the Duke back to Britain to campaign for peace, offering the support of his newspapers. And Halifax, who wanted to negotiate a peace treaty with France and Germany just days before the Dunkirk evacuations.

'Hoare is also the first former MI5 officer to become a cabinet minister. He suspended all British intelligence activity for the duration of the Windsors' stay in Spain.'

'My God.' Pamela put a hand to her chest, as if trying to calm her pounding heart. 'Do you think he's actively collaborating with Germany?'

'We don't know. This is why we need to get our hands on the dossier. And keep an eye on what the Windsors might be saying and doing when they visit the United States, which they most certainly will. We can't allow them to undermine our campaign for America's support.'

'Captain, when I was in Lisbon, I ran into Elsa Schiaparelli and Ambassador Bullitt. They were waiting for a plane to take them to New York. I have reason to believe she may have used her knowledge of his affair with the Duchess in exchange for an American entry visa. And we can't be certain what else she knows, what she's overheard the Duchess say. Or what Bullitt might be saying in Washington about the Windsors.'

Macaulay retrieved a handkerchief from his pocket and blotted his brow. 'A sticky wicket, certainly. All the more reason to have all the help we can get over there.' He squinted into the distance, down the avenue of graves. 'I won't press you for an answer today, of course. But it would be good of you to let us know soon. In the next few weeks, please.'

Washington. A reunion with Francis. A new start in an unfamiliar country. She thought about how much closer she felt to him when they had a shared goal, something to work towards together, like they had briefly in Paris. But it would mean leaving England again, not knowing when she would return. And having to continue to ingratiate herself with the Windsors. Would she be able to keep her fury to herself, continuing to pretend to be a friend and ally, especially now that she knew of Churchill's willingness to shield them at all costs? But if she agreed to go, Pamela wouldn't have to face the yawning chasm that opened up in front of her when she was feeling useless and without direction, as she had after her mission for MI5 three years ago and after she'd first returned from Paris last year.

But if Pamela went, that would put an end to her relationship with Sid. There would be no guarantee they'd ever see each other again. And if they did, that their feelings would remain the same. Or that he would wait for her. If she told him that she was crossing the ocean to do war work alongside her husband, without any idea of when she was returning, she wouldn't have blamed him if he ended things completely. And if they did see each other again, someday, he probably would have moved on and met someone else by then.

Pamela remembered the tape in her handbag and how she had originally planned on handing it over to Macaulay. But what would happen if she did? Probably nothing. He seemed to be more troubled by the Windsors' treachery than Monckton, but it seemed unlikely he would use it to take action. The Windsors wouldn't face a tribunal. They would carry on living their sheltered lives in the sunny Caribbean, untouched by the war. And the recording would end up locked in a vault, never to see the light of day. Or perhaps even destroyed.

She had signed the Official Secrets Act. It was her duty to hand it over. But there was something about having it in her possession, about having the proof of the Windsors' treason, that made her feel a little bit better. A little bit less like a pawn herself.

Macaulay knew that she had always been thorough about keeping recordings of anything important. Right there and then, she decided that if he asked her if she had a recording of the conversation, she would give it to him.

The cemetery was uncannily quiet. All that could be heard was the sound of a lone crow, cawing from a nearby tree.

But Macaulay didn't ask for the recording. He didn't even ask her if she'd recorded the conversation at all.

So, she didn't offer it up.

And that wasn't a lie, only an omission. Just like Monckton had omitted the fact that he already knew about the Windsors' treason.

And omissions weren't the same as lies.

V

A week later, Pamela and Charlotte were having dinner at Hatchett's on Piccadilly, which had become enormously popular since the threat of bombings had increased, as it benefited from having three levels, all underground.

'I cannot bring myself to go to another morose cocktail party where people talk about which hotels have the deepest bomb shelters and play "Who Would Be the First to Collaborate".' Charlotte sighed.

'Who on earth plays "Who Would Be the First to Collaborate"?'

'Oh, absolutely *everyone*.'

Pamela assumed this to be the case in Charlotte and Peter's circles because there were probably a good number of people who would indeed collaborate in the event of an invasion. Like Percy, her sister seemed to be making the most of the way in which the war had turned ordinary life upside down. She was a far cry from the frazzled, dishevelled woman Pamela had last seen at their parents' house and seemed to be back to her old, carefully groomed self: her hair was a platinum blond, and she was wearing what looked to be a smart new Hardy Amies cocktail dress. But Charlotte seemed changed in other ways too. For one thing, she was unusually cheerful. A friend from school had asked if she'd help out with a fundraising committee for refugees. It was keeping her busy, made her feel useful and gave her an excuse to go into London regularly.

'You're awfully quiet tonight,' mused Charlotte.

'Am I?'

'Yes, and you're never quiet.' Charlotte peered over her Sidecar at Pamela. 'What happened over there in France? Mother thinks you upended your life and your marriage for nothing.'

'I can't say I much care what Mother thinks.'

'Well, nor do I. Living with her was bloody miserable.'

'But you've always been her favourite.'

'*Me*? You're joking. It was always *you* she preferred. I couldn't keep up with you.'

'She thinks I'm a failure. No children. Won't settle down. Ran off to Paris and left my husband behind.'

'Yes, but you were always the cleverer one. She used to gas to her friends about how her daughter worked for *The Times*. How impressive you were.'

'Well, she never said anything to me. She just made me feel like everything I did was a disappointment.'

'I suppose it's comforting to know we've both disappointed her.' Charlotte finished her drink and stared into her glass. 'Neither of us was ever able to make up for William, were we?'

Looking at her sister, Pamela pondered what their relationship would have been like if they'd had a conversation like this years ago. Or perhaps if the war had come sooner. It seemed to be causing people to let their defences down.

'She thinks I should come stay with her if London becomes too dangerous.'

'I'd sooner brave German bombs than that. I quite like London life. It's been good fun.'

Pamela looked towards the door and froze. There was Peter, entering with a woman on his arm, who looked a little like Charlotte, only younger.

'Shall we get the bill?' Pamela asked hurriedly.

'Already? I was going to have another drink.'

'Why don't we get the bill and then we can have a nightcap somewhere else?'

Pamela started waving to their waiter, hoping to be able to get out of the dining room before Charlotte spotted Peter and the woman. But it was too late. Her face fell.

'Christ, it's Peter ...'

To Pamela's surprise, Charlotte ducked her head to the side, as if trying not to be seen. Peter suddenly recognised the two of them and his eyes widened. It looked like the maître d' was about to lead them to a nearby table, but Peter put a hand on his arm, whispered something in his ear and then walked out with the young woman.

'Thank God for that.' Charlotte sighed. 'Can you imagine how embarrassing it would have been if he'd come over here? Having to listen while he made up some nonsense about how she's a friend or someone from work.' Seeing the look of surprise on Pamela's face, she added, 'I've known about it for a while now. He has his life, and I have mine. After all, I have my own "friends".'

Apparently, it wasn't only Percy who was taking advantage of wartime London's new libertinism. In a way, it made her feel better about her own predicament — that she wasn't the only one whose life was shifting like sand under her feet.

September 1940

I

Betty Penrose had gone to visit her parents in America in the spring and had got stuck on the other side of the Atlantic, caught out short by how the direction of the war had suddenly changed. Brogue's Managing Director had been forced to make the difficult decision of replacing her with Managing Editor Audrey Withers. Pamela had been back in the office working for three weeks when Withers had called Pamela in to ask if she would be willing to take the post of Brogue's Society Editor, which had fallen vacant.

It felt surreal to return to the *Vogue* building and Penrose's office where Pamela had first discussed her mission with Macaulay. Her life had been profoundly changed in the last two years and now she felt completely at sea. Was she going to join Francis in Washington or stay in London? Did she have any desire to recreate her old life, writing about British aristocrats and celebrities?

The two women sat there, politely having a cup of tea, each one trying to take the measure of the other. Though Pamela had attended meetings with Withers and spoken to her on one or two occasions, she didn't know her well. Pamela and Withers were about the same age, but she seemed older than Pamela. It wasn't just the streaks of grey in her hair pulled into a tidy bun or the set of pearls she wore with her modest grey suit, but her air of seriousness and authority. Not intimidating or bullying as her predecessor had been, just calm and assured, if a little tired.

'I know Society Editor might not be the most scintillating post, especially after having been in France at such a crucial time. But you'd be doing me a great favour.'

A great favour. Betty Penrose never said things like that. She made sure everyone who worked for Brogue knew that it was the magazine that was doing them the favour for simply deigning to entertain their ideas — even if those ideas didn't make it to print.

'We've been having difficulty filling Condé Nast's requests for portraits and features,' she continued. 'As I'm sure you know, London society has scattered across the country, all the debs have gone into the WRNS or the ATS. And everyone's wary of posing publicly in anything that looks glamorous or expensive, for fear of being labelled frivolous. To make matters more complicated, the Ministry of Information tried to shut us down because of paper rationing but we convinced them to let us stay open, as long as we do our bit to persuade "the gentler sex" to take part in the war effort. And become a monthly publication. Which at least will be less stressful than having to produce an issue every fortnight.'

Pamela looked at the articles and photos spread across the table, being considered for the next issue. The usual pieces on fashion, cosmetics and housekeeping were interspersed with ones on making do with rationing and dressing for air raids. What a different world they found themselves in.

'I understand that you were in Paris, just before it fell,' Withers said gently. 'I can't imagine what that must have been like. I've heard some terrible stories.'

Pamela usually gave a cursory explanation of the circumstances under which she'd left France, without having to go into much detail or attach too much feeling to it. But there was something about the way Withers asked her, something about her sensitivity and understanding, that incited a rush of emotion in Pamela. That made her think of driving past elderly people who had collapsed on the side of the road, of watching couples who were desperate and screaming at each other, of all the refugees she saw who haunted the hotels, train stations and harbours. All the people she had been powerless to help. And the woman Pamela herself had shot and left for dead. A lump rose in her throat and before she knew it, she felt her eyes welling up.

'It was pretty dreadful, actually,' Pamela finished in a tone just above a whisper as tears slid down her cheeks.

Withers reached across the table and squeezed her hand. She then reached into her pocket and handed her a handkerchief. The two women sat for a minute together in silence.

'I don't suppose you have anything stronger than tea?' Pamela asked.

Withers got up, went to the cabinet behind her desk and brought out a decanter and glasses. 'Sherry alright?'

Pamela nodded, and Withers poured two glasses.

'Have you had any news? About what's happened to Frogue?' asked Pamela worriedly, as she wiped her eyes.

'Mr de Brunhoff told Nast that there was no honourable way of publishing a magazine under the Germans, so he decided to cease operations until further notice. It was horrible, knowing there was nothing they could do from New York or that we could do from London.'

'Is he alright?'

'As far as I know, he's with his family, in the Vichy zone. In the south, I think. Have you heard about what's happened to the Chambre Syndicale? The Germans issued an ultimatum to Lucien Lelong. The entire couture industry would be transferred to Berlin.'

'What on earth did they mean, the entire industry? You can't simply upend 300 years of French fashion production and *move* the whole thing to Berlin. What about supply chains? What about lace made in Chantilly? Silk made in Lyon? And all the workers in Paris! The petites mains, the tailors and seamstresses? How on earth will they find people with those skills in Germany?'

'Well, that's exactly what Lelong said. Somehow, he convinced them to abandon the idea. So, the Syndicale will soldier on. Under Nazi restrictions and rationing.'

'While having to sell dresses to their wives, I presume. A high price to pay.'

'I don't think he had much of a choice. If he had refused, all the houses in the Syndicale could have closed. Many more people would be out of work and the Nazis would probably have requisitioned them anyway.'

'I wonder what will happen to Jewish designers,' Pamela said sadly as she ran a finger around the lip of her sherry glass.

Withers shook her head. 'I don't know. And it's becoming more and more impossible to know what's happening in Paris at all now. It's as if anywhere the Germans are occupying is sealed off.' She paused. 'Might you be interested in writing a piece about Paris? About how you were there, at the end. Our relationship with Frogue. With the Chambre Syndicale. Something written in solidarity, perhaps.'

'I'd be very happy to. Though I'll have to take some time to think about the Society Editor post.'

'We will need your answer soon though. So that if you decide not to take it, we still have time to find someone else before the next edition. In the next week, ideally.'

The next week. Another decision to make.

'Have you heard that Harry Yoxall is threatening to form a British couture syndicate?' Withers asked. 'He's trying to cajole Hartnell, Stiebel and Champcommunal into it. And Molyneux, but apparently, he loathes the idea. None of them can agree on anything. Like cats fighting in a sack.'

'I suppose if they find themselves with the Wehrmacht breathing down their necks, threatening to uproot their houses and take them to Berlin, then they'll have to come to an agreement,' Pamela replied darkly.

Withers nodded. 'Indeed.' She then got up, went to her desk and took an envelope out of one of the drawers. 'I nearly forgot. You received a letter from New York.'

As Pamela rode down in the lift, she opened the envelope. To her surprise, it was from Elsa Schiaparelli.

How wonderful it was to see you in Lisbon. Schiap so enjoys seeing good friends in times like these. She hopes the Duchess is well and safe. Have you any news of her and the Duke? She would so like to know how they are. Are they happy on their island? How surprising that they are not at home, in Windsor Castle! But maybe they will be soon. And if you find yourself in New York, you must look Schiap up! It would be nice to meet again, especially with such an important person as yourself.

Once she reached the ground floor, she sat down on a chair in the building's reception and read the peculiar letter again. At first glance, it was a series of pleasantries from a woman who was having to start her life over in a new country, trying to maintain the connections she had outside France. But upon closer inspection, the letter was unsettling. If Schiaparelli had used the information about Bullitt and Wallis's affair to get a visa and hitch a ride with him on a plane to New York, might she be fishing for more intelligence about the Windsors? A savvy businesswoman like her would have been unlikely to have fled France, leaving behind her atelier, newest collection and fabric stock without some sort of plan in place to ensure the House of Schiaparelli's future. If Lelong and other designers were faced with negotiating with the Nazis in order to save their houses, Schiaparelli was undoubtedly looking for something with which she herself could bargain.

Then there was her comment about hoping the Windsors would be back in Windsor Castle soon. Was this an indication that she knew about Hitler's plan to lure them on to his side and install them as puppet monarchs? Was Schiaparelli inviting Pamela to make contact with her because she thought she might know something? Because she might be sympathetic? And as far as the Italian was concerned, Pamela was a close friend of the Windsors. Possibly close enough to be a covert supporter of their return to the throne. Perhaps even another Nazi sympathiser.

Pamela knew that Schiaparelli and her staff could sell anything to anyone. They convinced conservative society matrons that a Surrealist hat inspired by Dalí was just the thing they needed; mothers that their daughters were far better off in a bold Schiaparelli gown than a demure Molyneux or a Vionnet; husbands that their wives *did* need a new wardrobe for the season. Although from a venerable Roman family, the designer had left her monied life behind to escape an arranged marriage; she had moved to America, had a child with a man who turned out to be a charlatan and ended up penniless — a single mother taking on odd jobs to support herself and a sickly daughter.

Such a woman would be clever and resourceful enough to know how to leverage her knowledge and connections. Had she arranged a deal with the Nazis? Or with the Americans? Perhaps it wasn't just the affair with Wallis that convinced Bullitt to let her board that plane; what if she had information on the Windsors to sell to the US government? Or maybe, like Wallis, she was hedging her bets and waiting to see which country would be the most useful in terms of an alliance.

Pamela realised she had to go to Washington. She knew too much about the Windsors and the treacherous people connected to them to step back from the fray now. As much as she would have enjoyed working under Withers, she couldn't imagine herself staying in London to write about charity fundraisers and whose daughter was marrying which promising young naval officer. She might be angry with Macaulay and Monckton and their policy of 'containment', as they called it, but it didn't change the fact that the Windsors were still at large. They might be on a Caribbean island, but they were also close to the United States — perhaps close enough to drip poison in the ears of Americans who would otherwise have been sympathetic to the British cause.

II

It was going to be a full moon (a 'bombers' moon') and a high tide — the last chance at a landing before the equinoctial gales began. The ports on the other side of the Channel were swarming with German soldiers and sailors as their commanding officers prepared the troop-carrying barges. People were calling it 'Invasion Weekend', as if it were a social fixture like Ascot or Wimbledon, rather than the Wehrmacht's invasion. The tongue-in-cheek attitude seemed to be the prevailing tone with which everyone faced the war, as well as the bombings that had recently begun.

Sid had gone down to the cliffs of Dover with some other journalists to witness the dogfights taking place over the Channel, as well as the possible invasion. It was hard to believe that just three months ago the port of Dover had been receiving troops from small boats during the Dunkirk evacuation and now it was bracing for an attack. The idea of watching German planes and U-boats land on English soil as if it were a spectator sport struck Pamela as macabre. But when Sid invited her to join him, she went nonetheless.

It was a ghastly sight. The beaches were protected by a wire barricade, and there was a scattering of deterrents on the cliffside to keep the Luftwaffe from landing. Anti-tank barriers made from steel girders littered the neighbouring farmland to make the terrain more difficult. Gun batteries had been built along the cliffs to attack German ships. Anti-aircraft guns were pointed towards the sky. A fort housed a team of commandos who had orders to sabotage the port if it fell into enemy hands. The road signs had been twisted in the wrong direction to confuse the Germans if they did manage to land. Despite having been bombed the day before, everyone they encountered in the village seemed strangely unphased, assured that the invasion couldn't happen. 'I'd like to see those bloody Germans try it!' said a local farmer.

Sid had to show his press pass to get through the coastal areas that had been cordoned off by the military. But once they were inside, there was nothing to do but wait, so they sat in the car on the cliffs. Pamela thought she had made up her mind, but now, looking at Sid, she found herself wavering. She realised that she enjoyed his company no matter where they were or what they were doing. It didn't matter if they were in a jazz bar in Paris, on a dusty road in the French countryside or on an English cliff, waiting for an invasion. She was never bored. He always had a story and wanted to know what she had to say. Being with him felt right, both in her mind and in her body. It was as if the two of them generated a warmth when they were together.

But then again, Sid was never in the same place for long. Even though he said he would stay in London, he would be off to another country soon enough to cover some military operation or political development. Pamela knew how much he enjoyed the excitement of covering stories, meeting deadlines, travelling from one place to the next — even facing danger. It was clear that he thrived on it. Pamela couldn't picture Sid settling down to a normal life anywhere. She worried it would kill his spirit. And she didn't think she could bear not hearing from him for weeks, constantly worrying about his safety.

'Joe Kennedy says democracy's over. I bet he'd be the first in line to shake Hitler's hand. Nazi bastard.'

Pamela was jolted out of her rumination. She suddenly had a clear image in her mind of Ambassador Kennedy greeting Hitler at the door of the American Embassy in Mayfair.

'If the worst were to happen, do you think the US would make a deal with Germany?'

'I have no doubt. The war is a faraway thought for most Americans. Something happening somewhere else. Not our problem. We have enough troubles of our own, etcetera. All our politicians care about is getting re-elected. And voting to send people off to fight a foreign war is not a ticket to re-election.'

Pamela felt sick to her stomach. She'd never heard it put so starkly. She looked at Sid, who was resting his arm on the open car window. She did love him. With her whole heart. And it was the first time she'd ever really been in love. But Pamela would never be able to live with herself if she stayed in London and failed to do everything she could for her country. Even if this was her one and only chance at love. Even if no one ever looked at her or held her or kissed her like Sid did ever again. The realisation left her breathless.

'Are you ok?' Sid was looking at her with concern.

'I love you.'

Sid smiled and took her hand. 'I love you too.'

In the distance, she could hear the roar of a plane engine. She wondered if it was British or German.

'But …'

'But …?'

'I've been asked to join Francis in Washington. On a kind of diplomatic mission. To convince your president to come to our rescue.'

Sid's face fell. 'And you're going to go?'

'I don't think I have much choice.'

'What about you and me? It's just over? We call it quits?'

'I don't know what the alternative would be.'

'I could come with you. I could get a job working for the *Washington Post* or something.'

'Sid, I'm going to have to act like a married woman while I'm there. It's part of the deal.'

'But life is short. Don't you think that if you love someone, you should be with them?'

Frustrated, Pamela opened the door and got out of the car. She leaned against the side, her arms across her chest and her hands tucked tightly into her armpits. Sid got out too and came around to her side.

He reached over to touch her shoulder. 'None of us knows how much time we have left.'

'And there might be even less time left if your country lets Hitler do to mine what he did to Czechoslovakia and Poland and Denmark—'

'Yes, sure, but try telling them that—'

'—and the Netherlands and Belgium and France. And once the British and French fleets fall into the hands of the Germans, it might be some clifftop on the eastern seaboard you and your friends will be reporting from, watching the Luftwaffe dogfighting with the US Air Force.'

'Pam, look—'

'I don't want to end up like France, with the Wehrmacht policing our borders. With the Gestapo rounding people up.'

'Pamela, I know! I'm a Jew! You think I don't know what could happen? You don't think there aren't plenty of American Nazis who'd happily cheer on Hitler?'

'I'm sorry,' she whispered.

They stood there in silence for a minute, listening to the waves breaking in the distance.

He sighed. 'Give me a cigarette, will you?'

She felt in her pockets, but they were empty. 'I don't have any on me.'

'Are you kidding me? You smoke like a goddamn chimney! The one time I need a cigarette, and you don't have one ...'

Pamela put her arms around Sid. They stood for a long time, just holding each other. In the distance, she watched a squadron of Spitfires crossing over the beach.

THE END

Acknowledgements

This book is the continuation of a story inspired by one told to me by my grandmother, who keenly followed the Wallis/Edward saga from her home in New Jersey, and suspected Wallis to be an FBI/MI6 plot to derail fascist King Edward VIII. And before it became *The Socialite Spy*, the story took the form of the play *Agent of Influence*, but only with the help of the creativity and hard work of Jessica Beck, Katharina Reinthaller, Phil Hewitt and, the original Pamela, Rebecca Dunn.

The Socialite Spy was my stepping stone into the world of fiction, carefully nurtured by my tireless champion and agent Gaia Banks at Sheil Land. I wouldn't have developed the confidence to finish that book or carry on with this one without her support and advice.

Thank you to the wonderful team at Lume and Joffe, who have been faithfully supporting Pamela's journey since 2022.

Also, a big thank you to my fantastic friends who have been loyal readers and cheerleaders throughout this whole process: Linda Campbell, Katharine Fry, Kate Mulley, Sarah Beck, Louise Stephens, Stephanie Ellis, Erin Hunter, David Djemal, Susanna Fiore, Jason Eddy, Ewelina Kolaczek, Maggie Kate Coleman, Cara Beahm, Beth Levi, Ren Renken and Nora Quinn, just to name a few amongst many others.

Finally, to my mom, who's never stopped having faith in me.

The Lume & Joffe Books Story

Lume Books was founded by Matthew Lynn, one of the true pioneers of independent publishing. In 2023 Lume Books was acquired by Joffe Books and now its story continues as part of the Joffe Books family of companies.

Joffe Books began in 2014 when Jasper agreed to publish his mum's much-rejected romance novel and it became a bestseller.

Since then we've grown into the largest independent publisher in the UK. We're extremely proud to publish some of the very best writers in the world, including Joy Ellis, Faith Martin, Caro Ramsay, Helen Forrester, Simon Brett and Robert Goddard. Everyone at Joffe Books loves reading and we never forget that it all begins with the magic of an author telling a story.

We are proud to publish talented first-time authors, as well as established writers whose books we love introducing to a new generation of readers.

We won Trade Publisher of the Year at the Independent Publishing Awards in 2023. We have been shortlisted for Independent Publisher of the Year at the British Book Awards for the last four years, and were shortlisted for the Diversity and Inclusivity Award at the 2022 Independent Publishing Awards. In 2023 we were shortlisted for Publisher of the Year at the RNA Industry Awards.

We built this company with your help, and we love to hear from you, so please email us about absolutely anything bookish at feedback@joffebooks.com

If you want to receive free books every Friday and hear about all our new releases, join our mailing list: www.joffebooks.com/freebooks

And when you tell your friends about us, just remember: it's pronounced Joffe as in coffee or toffee!